The Lizard

Ula Gudel

The Girl with No Name. Part one

*To those who believe
that one stubborn heart
can change the world
UG*

August 2023

The Lizard

Copyright © 2023 by Ula Gudel

Contact info:

www.ulagudel.com

Cover Design: Racim Bey Benyahia

Translator: Katarzyna Preiskorn

Author Photo: v4good

Illustrations: Racim Bey Benyahia

ISBN: 978-83-67901-00-0 (paperback), 978-83-67901-03-1 (e-book)

First Edition: August 2023

10 9 8 7 6 5 4 3 2 1

The Lizard

Ula Gudel

The Girl with No Name. Part one

To my Dad
Thank you

Prologue

THE TEMPLE OF ANCESTORS WAS SILENT, except for the crackling of fragrant twigs in the ritual burner. Built on a circular plan, the place was deserted at night. Only Sig, the High Priestess of the Stone Nest, came here to meditate when her thoughts troubled her and she could not sleep. Lately this had been happening more and more often. Strange visions haunted her day and night, causing her great anxiety. At such times, she would seek answers from those who had gone to the Fields of Glory. She fervently believed that they had not ceased to watch over her people, even from the other world.

After tossing the ceremonial herbal mixture into the fire, Sig sat back and breathed deeply, letting the vapours penetrate her to the core. Soon she felt a familiar, pleasant tingling in her fingertips that spread to her arms, torso and then her entire body. The real world slowly receded and she came into contact with the spiritual. She felt light, calm and secure. Like a child coming home.

She brushed her long, raven-black hair from her forehead and turned her face towards the fire, trying to absorb the smoke with all her might.

'O noble ancestors!' she called in exultation. 'Grant me your favour once more, answer my cry!'

She opened her eyes and looked down. Her blue robes now seemed to ripple and spill like a lake spreading across the floor of the temple where she was kneeling. Her fingers extended like the claws of a predator and her skin became translucent. She could see all the knuckles of her hands, surrounded by an intricate network of throbbing veins. For a moment she admired them, fascinated, until she realised that she was no longer alone. She lifted her eyes. The huge black statues of long-dead Ha'ami rulers that surrounded her came to life and turned towards her.

'Be praised, the eternal ones!' she exclaimed gratefully. The statues gave a nod. 'Here I stand before you, asking for advice and support. I am consumed with anxiety about the future of our people. Help me to see the danger ahead!'

She stood up, then began to sway as she turned around, bowing in all directions. The stinging smoke made it difficult for her to make out the figures of the Ancestors, but it seemed to her that their hands were pointing at something. She looked in that direction. The entrance to the crypt was shimmering with a green-golden glow. She swallowed hard.

'Should I go there?' she asked aloud, but no one answered. The silent statues continued to raise their hands in a commanding gesture.

Wobbling slightly from the herbal haze, she slowly made her way to the opening in the floor and then, supported firmly by the cold wall, descended the stairs. Her senses were heightened by the effects of the hallucinogenic incense. Familiar smell of dust and lamp oil assaulted her nostrils. The strange, blinding light forced her to cover her eyes with the wide sleeve of her dress. When she finally dared to look towards its source, she froze in horror.

The dragon's skull, the centrepiece of the trophies gathered in the crypt, looked as if it had come to life and the spirit of a long-dead monster had entered it. Its eyes looked straight at her. Cold sweat covered her entire body and every hair on her neck stood up. The reptile's gaze penetrated her. A premonition of impending danger.

Sig felt the Temple of the Ancestors shake in its foundations.

She ran for the exit. Stumbling over her own feet, she managed to reach the gate of the temple, pushed it hard and ran out. Her legs buckled under her and she fell to her knees. Gasping for the night air like a fish thrown out of the water she tried to scream, but her voice cracked.

She stayed like that for a long moment, until the world stopped spinning and slowly returned to its normal shapes and colours. Only then she looked around the square. The city was fast asleep, nothing disturbing the deep silence.

Sig struggled to her feet and limped to the gates of the building. Cautiously, she looked inside. The fire still smouldered in the hearth and the smell of incense hung in the air. The hall was dimly lit, only by the glow of the olive lamps hanging on long chains from the vaulted ceiling. The strange green sheen from the crypt disappeared.

Sig walked slowly inside and knelt before the statues of the ancestors. Their silent faces looked at her sternly.

'Something is approaching,' she thought. 'Danger. We must be on our guard.'

Spark chuckled silently. The look on the priestess' face when she descended into the crypt and saw his bones awaken was priceless. It was the best prank he had played on her yet, albeit unintentionally this time. His regular pastime was to send visions to the Temple

Keeper during her herb sessions. He knew his antics on the haunted poor woman were childish, but he was thoroughly bored in the crypt where his spirit had been trapped for years, ever since that disturbed boy had taken his life and brought his severed head into town as proof of his triumph over the terrible beast.

Humans do not understand dragons. They worship and attack them for one reason. Out of fear. The size and power of these creatures strike terror into the hearts of many beings, even the seemingly intelligent. The ancient reptiles have existed for thousands of years. Born of the elements, they draw their power from Mother Earth. As such, they function in conjunction with all living things. They hear the footsteps of an ant carrying a leaf. The whisper of flowers falling from trees as they bloom. The croak of a baby kingfisher in the branches. The hoot of a tawny owl at night. The roar of an angry bear when a salmon has escaped. This bond lasts as long as there is a physical form into which the dragon's mighty soul has been moulded, and the only thing that can free the chained element is death and the return of its mortal remains to nature. Spark's slayer who dragged his severed head to the fortress did not know that in doing so he had immobilised the dragon's immortal soul and linked it to the city beneath which it rested. Despite being cut off from the power of real magic after being stripped of its physical body, the dragon was still connected to all that was alive. He knew the thoughts and actions of every creature in the Stone Nest, from the smallest worm digging through the oats gathered for the winter, to the lord of the fortress, bleak as the winter sky.

And suddenly, that very day, Spark felt her coming.

The Girl with No Name.

The Girl with No Memory.

The Foundling, as the elves called her.

The dragon was one of the few creatures that knew who she was. His rotting bones responded to the echo of her power. But he was not allowed to reveal this secret. Thousands of years ago, primeval, immortal beings had united and chained his race with powerful spells, fearing that its good magic would shatter the established order of things. These ancient spells commanded Spark and his kind to stay away from the daily vicissitudes of the world.

The fate of the Girl with No Name was difficult for even the wisest to predict. No one knew where it would lead, so she was bound by a powerful curse. It must have seemed a very clever solution to the rulers of the world, as if taking away her memory was tantamount to condemning her to oblivion.

If he had a paw, Spark would have slapped himself on the forehead for such astonishing naivety. Anyone who thinks that destiny looks like an intricately woven web of regular geometric patterns is pathetic indeed. It may resemble a web, but a web spun by a spider drugged with the same herbs the mad Ha'ami priestess was so fond of inhaling.

He was curious to see what would happen when the Girl with No Memory finally broke the curse... but he was unable to help her. The magic of the spell was too powerful, especially for his current strength.

Still...

It was no coincidence that destiny had brought her to these parts across the drugged spider's web.

Even without access to her full powers, her influence on the fate of the world could be immense. In the Stone Nest, only Spark was aware of this, and now he wondered what to do about it. After all, he was thoroughly bored.

Chapter I
How a Lizard embarrassed a Tiger

A FAINT GLOW PENETRATED HER half-closed eyelids. She tried to blink. It was so bright. So very bright. After a moment she caught sight of a canvas canopy high above. The ornate patterns fanned out, then fused into one before falling apart again. She closed her eyes, then opened them once more. The image froze.

Where am I?

The events of the previous evening flashed through her mind. The desperate chase across the dark hills. The enemy circling them. The violent ambush. The fog.

Now, she woke up here, wherever it was. The place was neither friendly nor hospitable, that's for sure.

She tried to move her head and found it difficult. When she finally managed to turn her neck to the side, she saw a heavy wooden door. The exit. She tried to move her arms to see if she could bend them. First the right one, then the left. Then she slowly lifted herself up on her elbows. It felt as if someone had put a sack of stones on her chest. Overcoming the resistance, she managed to sit up.

'It is the first punch that starts the fight,' she muttered one of her favourite sayings. 'Now the legs.'

Her shoes had been removed, but she spotted them right under the wall. She carefully slid her calves over the edge of the bed, then pushed off, trying to get up... and collapsed face down on the floor with a thump. As she lay there, like a frog run over by an ox, she heard the door open. Lifting her head, she saw two pairs of black overshoes.

'The bed we have made for you seems to be uncomfortable,' said a mocking voice. She remembered it well, though she had not seen the face of the speaker when they were captured. He spoke in Common with a heavy accent. Angry at her weakness, she tried to brace herself on her stiffened hands. There was the sound of footsteps and someone's hands embraced her surprisingly gently, lifted her up and placed her on the cushions as if she were a rag doll. Leather gloves felt cool and damp through her clothes. She looked at the face of the man who had helped her. He had shoulder-length straight black hair, dark eyebrows, intense blue pupils and burn scars all over his left cheek. She remembered that gaze.

Out there in the square, in the middle of the night, surrounded by a crowd of armed warriors, a strange premonition made her turn to that man, who was standing slightly to the rear. She usually trusted her instincts. Now that she saw him up close, without his helmet, he looked familiar. But why? It occurred to her that he was watching her with the same question in his clear eyes. He stepped away from the bed, walked around it and stood against the wall, his unadorned military fatigues blending into the half-light of the chamber.

With a rumble, the other Ha'ami pulled up a chair and placed it just beside her. The glow from the hearth illuminated his features. His hair was the same length and colour, and he had the same blue eyes as the first newcomer. And... he was truly fine-looking. In her short life she had seen much beauty: delicate, fleeting, full of harmony and balance. This man was different. Cold as a statue. His smooth skin had not a single blemish, not a single wrinkle, although his eyes betrayed that he was of a similar age to his companion. The proportions of his face and body seemed to have been drawn by an artist obsessed with a vision of the ideal human figure. This was not what she had expected of the notorious, bloodthirsty Ha'ami warriors. In her mind, she had a picture of shaggy, uncouth savages. This one looked more like a demigod. He seemed to regard her as if she were an inferior creature. His mouth, pouting with sarcasm, was the only imperfection in this flawless image.

Beautiful Demon, she named him in her mind. Unlike the other man, he wore richly decorated clothing. His cloak covered an embroidered tunic in shades of blue and his ears were studded with gold earrings.

'You should stay in bed for at least a few hours,' he said, looking at her intently. 'Until the effects of the stupor have worn off. As it is, your muscles are not fully functional.'

His words travelled through her consciousness in slow motion. He noticed her uncertain gaze and paused.

'Do you understand what I've just told you?'

She nodded.

'Do you know where you are?'

'Nowhere I intended to be,' she replied in a less than friendly tone. It did not seem to discourage him. Quite the contrary. He laughed, exposing his even teeth.

'In truth, we weren't expecting visitors either,' he said lightly.

'You have strange customs of hospitality,' she snapped back. 'Usually it involves free will.'

He grew serious, though his gaze still measured her with a cool irony.

'You entered the Ha'ami Lands without invitation or permission. It could hardly be called a courtesy visit.'

The coldness of his voice did not frighten her, although that was probably his intention.

'What have you done with my companion?'

'I see our courtesy has given the wrong impression,' he continued in the same icy tone. 'I'm the one asking the questions here and you're the one answering politely.'

She held back her anger. With difficulty.

'Let's start with something simple. Your name.'

The stranger leaned back in his chair. Thirst burned her throat. She wanted water so badly... but she wasn't going to ask for anything.

'Where is he?'

'You are not particularly smart, are you?'

He continued to size her up with perverse mockery in his eyes.

'I need to know if he is safe,' she croaked, trying to maintain the same impassive tone.

He was silent for a moment. Without changing his position, he tutted slightly in exasperation.

'Both of you have broken the law and will stand trial.'

'I don't remember committing any crime,' she replied calmly. 'Unless riding a horse is considered an abomination in Ha'ami lands.'

'That's right. That is exactly the case,' he confirmed with evident satisfaction.

'I don't understand.'

Despite her surprise, she managed to maintain an impassive expression. Or so she hoped.

'According to our law, women are not allowed to ride horses except in special circumstances. As for your companion, non-humans are forbidden to enter our lands without prior permission. As far as I know, no glyph was found on him to guarantee his passage.'

The man seemed to be carefully observing her reaction to those statements.

'What have you done to him?'

With each question, she became more determined not to reveal the purpose of their journey.

'Your name,' he replied slowly, accenting each word.

'The Horsewoman,' she answered just as coolly, withstanding his glare.

The other voice cut him off. It was deep and soft, speaking in the Ha'ami language. She understood little of it; only a few words reached her. Her interrogator replied, also in Ha'ami and then spoke to her in Common.

'You should reconsider your situation. I hope we can have a more fruitful conversation when we return.'

He got up and both men headed for the door.

'Sooner your sword gets rusty!' she muttered a familiar curse in the Ha'ami language. They turned, clearly surprised.

'What did you just say?' the Beautiful Demon asked in his own language.

'You know what you heard,' she replied in the same dialect.

The men exchanged a quick look and left. Two warriors appeared in their place, dressed in black and masked by leather helmets. As the door closed, they stood guard. Inside the chamber.

Yeah, hospitality... like at the goblins' harvest festival, she muttered to herself.

Dragon and Tiger. That's what they called them. They were almost always together. Once rivals, then brothers in arms, now the closest of friends. When Ha'akon was elected ruler of the Stone Nest, he had no doubt who he should appoint as his Guardian of Defence. He and Ha'teng had been on many a campaign together, saving each other's lives in the field more than once. They had not always seen eye to eye, differing in their methods. Since he had taken over the leadership, Ha'akon had become more cautious and much more level-headed, often having to restrain his comrade's more violent impulses. However, he valued his political acumen and knowledge of human nature. Ha'teng was a great strategist, always ready with an unconventional solution to any situation. And he was effective. He rarely failed.

However, when it came to new captives, the lord of the fortress preferred to have a closer look at the situation himself. The case seemed complicated so he decided to monitor the first questioning of the prisoner.

The previous evening, the two detainees had been led to the Upper Castle just as he was finishing his nightly rounds. The foreigners were reluctant to obey the sentries' orders, but eventually dismounted without resistance. Trouble started later.

The masked man, his head wrapped in a shawl, remained silent while the girl spoke in a common speech with a singsong lilt. Ha'akon could not identify it, though he had travelled many lands in his life. For some reason, she was addressing him directly, even though the ruler, as was his custom, wore the uniform of a guard and kept to himself, and it was Ha'teng who gave orders to the guards who reported directly to him.

The green-eyed stranger was a head shorter than any of them, with a petite figure to match. She looked like a child among giants. But that did not seem to bother her. She stood in the middle of the square, next to her magnificent mount which looked as if it had been created out of mist and light. She raised her head proudly, tossing back a tempest of brown curls and in a resonant voice she gave a speech explaining that they were lost travellers who came in peace and asking to be set free to continue on their way.

Ha'teng sharply ordered her to reveal their names and origins, but she refused to comply until her freedom was guaranteed. This only enraged him, so he threatened her with the dungeon and ordered the man to show his face. When the stranger remained silent, the commander gestured for the order to be carried out.

From then on, events poured out like water from an open sluice. Three guardsmen grabbed the prisoner from behind, and one approached the girl, but she somehow eluded him and was instantly at Ha'akon's side. She grabbed his hand. In the darkness, he could only see her glowing green eyes.

'Please don't hurt him,' she whispered, squeezing his fingers.

A cry of surprise echoed across the square. The ruler looked up. One of Ha'ami's warriors had pulled down the cloth that covered the man's head. Even from the distance, Ha'akon could see it clearly. The porcelain skin of the stranger's beautiful face shone like polished marble. A non-human.

The guards threw him to the ground at once. The woman turned with a scream that froze in her mouth as Ha'teng grabbed her from behind and placed a cloth soaked in a sleep mixture over her nose. She immediately collapsed into the commander's arms. The same treatment was applied to her companion, who also fell lifeless.

At this point the square went into chaos.

The girl's steed reared up and began to bite and kick like mad. The non-human's mount quickly followed suit. Then Ha'ami's horses took off, scattering in all directions.

The air seemed to fill with neighing, trampling hooves, cries of pain and curses from the wounded warriors.

Ha'akon's quick orders, given in a firm voice, brought his men to their senses and into action. Ha'teng handed the lifeless girl to one of his footmen and sprang into action as well. The guards on duty on the walls and all the stablemen rushed to their aid, but it was a long time before the agitated animals were brought under control.

Eventually they managed to get the impetuous stallion, which now resembled a wild beast with foam on its mouth and madness in its eyes, into the farthest stall in the stable. As they locked him in, the other horses calmed down.

'I was on the verge of ordering him slaughtered,' Ha'teng breathed out, pulling off his gloves covered in slush. Everyone in the square looked as if they had just stepped off a battlefield.

'What a demon!'

'Not a demon, a trained battle steed,' Ha'akon corrected him calmly, removing his helmet as mud began to trickle down his face. 'He was defending his lady,' he said admiringly.

'Maybe not a demon, but raised by demons,' laughed his companion. 'We will soon find out anyway. A few days in the dungeons and these vagabonds will tell us everything.'

'Not the girl,' the ruler corrected.

'What?' Ha'teng was confused. 'Why?'

'Look at her left hand,' he replied.

The commander did not even turn around.

'The bracelet,' he shrugged. 'I noticed it.'

'Someone with that much gold doesn't usually have to sneak around,' Ha'akon said.

'Or maybe that's exactly why they have to do it,' his companion replied.

The lord of the castle pondered. The battle-trained steed, the expensive jewellery, the stranger's whole appearance and behaviour suggested that she was no ordinary traveller.

'Put her in a chamber under guard. When she wakes up tomorrow, we will talk to her and decide what to do next,' he finally ordered. Ha'teng opened his mouth but quickly changed his mind and nodded. He marched off and began to give orders to his men.

Ha'akon recalled these events as he returned from the interrogation with his friend. Since the night before he had tried to remember where he had seen the girl earlier. In vain. He was sure, however, that the green gaze was not entirely unfamiliar.

'Her pronunciation is quite good,' he remarked to start the conversation as they marched back to their wing of the castle.

After the incident in the square, he didn't expect to get much on the first try. But the questioning itself amused him. He didn't want to show it in front of his friend, who was clearly irritated.

'That doesn't make it any easier,' Ha'teng muttered in reply. 'She might be a fugitive from one of our fortresses.'

The governor tilted his head thoughtfully.

'That would explain a lot.'

Especially why this girl seemed so familiar to him.

'Send messengers to the fortresses along the southern border,' he ordered.

'That'll take days,' Ha'teng remarked.

'I know. In the meantime, continue the questioning. No violence. We don't know what she's worth.'

He preferred to stress this again. When talking to detainees, his friend often preferred speed to cooperation. It didn't always make sense, it wasn't always necessary. Like in this case.

They walked on in silence.

She did not know what time of day or night it was, for the window was tightly covered with heavy drapes. The only light in the room came from the fire crackling merrily in the hearth. The room was large compared to what she was used to, and lavishly furnished. A heavy bed with ornate columns and canopy, two chairs with curved backs, a table with carved animal paw feet, and hunting trophies that looked rather gruesome in the red glow of the fire.

Her head kept spinning. She closed her eyes and concentrated. From the depths of her memory, she tried to pull out scraps of knowledge about the land of Ha'ami. Everyone had discouraged her from taking this route, but she had persisted because it was the shortest way. Her idea was not to stop here, but to sneak towards the Dragon Mountains under the cover of darkness. Tallen had followed her, trying to talk her out of this mad idea. And now she didn't even know what had happened to him. Yes, it was a real shame that they had stumbled upon a patrol... but they had gotten into this situation because of her own stupidity. She cursed herself silently now.

Little was known about the Ha'ami, for they were not a people open to relations with their neighbours. On the contrary, they had a bad reputation for raiding and seizing land, extorting tribute and kidnapping the population to serve as slaves. They were notorious for their ruthlessness, their iron discipline, their obsession with the superiority of their tribe and their merciless treatment of the weak, even their own kinsmen. It was rumoured that they murdered old people and cripples, or exiled them. But few foreigners were allowed into the Ha'ami lands, and even fewer returned, so it was difficult to tell what was true and what was a tale to frighten children. The behaviour of the boisterous stranger was in keeping with the Ha'ami's reputation for being proud and harsh in their manners. On the other hand, she awoke in a soft bed, in a warm chamber. Guarded by sentries armed to the teeth. And yet... she was treated, as the stranger himself called it, with courtesy. Why, she did not know. One question that plagued her was whether Tallen had been so fortunate, too. It was said that this tribe had a particular hatred for non-humans. Their reaction yesterday only confirmed it.

Concern for her friend's fate dominated her thoughts until sleep took her in its dark embrace.

In his long life, he had never smelled a stench like the one in the dungeon he awoke in. The odour of musty, decaying human remains, rat droppings and mould blended into a cacophony of odours that was hard to identify.

He was alone. Without his cloak, shoes or any warm clothing. All he had left were trousers and a thin shirt.

He concentrated, taking in the surroundings with his mind. There were two guards outside, playing a simple game of stones. He could sense no presence of a thinking being in the adjoining cells. Simronil was not far away. The steed burned with rage. A creature like him is not easy to tame.

His little Foundling was not around.

His power ended there. He could reach no further. He could only hope that they had treated her better.

Something else nagged at him. An echo of powerful, ancient magic that he had felt as soon as they entered the Ha'ami fortress. He could not identify its source. He had never encountered anything like it before. The power throbbed beneath the surface of the city like a heart woven from the elements.

From what he had heard of the warrior tribe, they only practised herbalism and kept away from anything they perceived to be against the 'natural' order of things.

Thus, what did he sense? Did the inhabitants know about it?

Vain musings, he thought. He wouldn't find any answers now. Perhaps the time will come for that. The most important thing is to get them out of here.

He assumed a meditative posture: clasped his hands on his chest and tapped into his inner energy source, which warmed his body and surrounded it with a protective barrier.

He waited.

When she opened her eyes again, her strength seemed to return. Blood circulated better in her limbs, which were no longer so stiff. The girl managed to sit up without too much difficulty. Having learned from her previous experience, she placed her feet carefully on the floor this time. *One, two, three,* she counted in her head and tried to stand. She stayed on her feet, even though she must have looked like a newborn foal, wobbling as it learned to walk with its delicate fetlocks. Supporting herself on the edge of the bed, the girl stepped around it, then pushed off slightly and managed to take a few steps with her momentum, covering the distance to the window. She grabbed hold of the heavy curtain.

Taking a deep breath, she moved the curtains to reveal the view outside. A stream of bright daylight immediately enveloped her. She waited a moment for her pupils to adjust. When she was able to open her eyes freely, she looked outside with curiosity.

She could see the snow-covered rooftops, and further away the Dragon Mountains; so near and yet so distant. As far as she could make out, she was in a fortress of black stone, though the outlines of lighter buildings seemed to be hidden beyond the walls. Unfortunately, the window was too low for her to see more. The chamber she was being held in seemed to be on the second or third floor. Too high to jump out without breaking a leg. Down below was a small square that looked a bit like a spectacle space, as benches had been placed in the surrounding cloisters, possibly for the onlookers. At the moment, however, nothing was happening. A few people were milling about, but otherwise it was rather empty. She pulled on the window handle and turned it without much resistance. A gust of fresh, frosty air came in. She took a deep breath.

'I see your strength is returning,' she heard a familiar voice.

It spoke in the Ha'ami language. She turned around. In the doorway, next to the silent guards, stood the same smooth-faced impertinent she had seen the previous day... or night. The Beautiful Demon. This time he was clad in full leather armour, girded by an ornate belt with a long sword. The absence of her own weapons made her feel almost naked. She wondered if they had found the blades hidden in her boots.

She said nothing. He walked over to the table by the fire, where a tray of food had been placed, and sat down, pointing to a seat across from him. She approached it in silence and sat down gingerly.

'Ha'ami or common?' he asked.

'Common.'

She felt uncomfortable with their language. The words were coming to her with difficulty. She knew it would improve with time, though she preferred not to stay here long enough for it to be necessary.

'I hope you have rested and your mind has cleared,' he said with the same irritating grin he had displayed during their previous meeting. 'The guards reported that you slept through the night.'

'So they can talk,' she replied gruffly.

'When they have something to say. Are you hungry?' he asked, pointing to the table. Bread and a bowl of what looked like a white-grey ooze were laid out on a tray. There was also a pitcher of water and a cup.

Her stomach twisted violently. But she didn't want to show any weakness. Slowly, sparing her movements, she poured herself some water and took a careful sip.

'Good girl,' he said, and her jaw clenched in anger. 'Let's try again then. Your name.'

'The Centauress,' she replied, looking at the bottom of the cup.

'You really aren't too smart.' Blue eyes scowled at her. 'You probably have no idea why you're still alive?' He paused. She didn't answer. 'Or why did you wake up not in chains, not in a slimy dungeon, but in a warm, soft bed, and why are your hosts treating you to breakfast, as if you were an expected guest and not an intruder who has trespassed on their lands? How does your wee mind explain this?'

His impertinent behaviour was beginning to throw her off balance. She grabbed the bowl and bread in one unhurried motion and threw them into the fire.

'As for your hospitality, you can shove it up yours,' she said, trying to restrain herself. 'I want to know what happened to my companion.'

'Just as I thought. We can't expect much from you. Let me do you one last favour and explain things fully. The Ha'ami live by three values. Brotherhood. Honour. Strength.' He counted them off on his fingers. 'What keeps you alive is our respect for our fellow brothers and the treaties we have with neighbouring rulers. As long as we do not know whether or not your sudden and violent death will offend any of our allies, we will keep you safe.'

The girl knew he had deliberately placed emphasis on the words *sudden and violent death*. It did not impress her.

She fell into silence as he waited for her reaction.

'I won't tell you anything until I see him,' she repeated stubbornly.

He rose from his seat, drew his sword from its sheath, pressed the tip of the blade against her chin, and forced her to raise her head.

'As I said, this was my last concession. I give you one day to think about it. Tomorrow my courtesy will end.'

'Well, well, it has not yet rusted,' she replied looking at him unafraid.

He did not respond – just sheathed his weapon, turned and left. She was left alone again, if not counting the silent guards.

'Does anyone really fall for these threats?' she said in their direction. 'I guess I envy you that you don't have to speak. You are spared the dubious pleasure of talking to this moron.'

She poured herself some more water and went to the window, but nothing was happening in the square. Then she casually picked up her shoes and, putting them on, checked the inside. Unfortunately, someone had removed her hidden daggers. They were thorough.

Bastards.

She slowly tried to stretch her muscles by walking around the chamber. There was no point in brooding over everything she had heard. She now knew that the less she revealed about herself, the better for both of them. Nothing in her story would improve their situation. She could do only one thing: prepare for the worst.

Ha'teng left the chamber in a huff. He knew from the start that it was a waste of time trying to talk to this snot. If it had been up to him, she would have been left to rot behind bars without light, food or water. He would have made her talk soon enough. But Ha'akon insisted on treating her with respect due to the highborn. His friend was often too cautious. The Guardian of Defence himself valued efficiency above all else.

Besides, he was sure this girl didn't have much valuable information. She's just a spoiled brat who probably got herself into this situation by accident. The other prisoner was the one he was really interested in. Besides, Ha'teng didn't have to fuss over him like over a newly hatched chicken. Perhaps the day would be more fruitful after a visit to the dungeons.

The pale winter sun rose and began to set, and she felt more secure in her body, even though she was getting hungry. She sustained herself with water until she had drained the entire jug. Then she turned to the guards.

'I need to go outside to relieve myself,' she announced. At first, she thought they hadn't heard her, or that they expected her to find a solution to her bladder-burning problem on her own. They stood still, as before. Finally, the one on the right turned, opened the door and walked out, waiting for her outside. She followed him out and the other guard walked behind her.

'Such an excessive escort? You overestimate me,' she remarked. As usual, they remained silent. The corridor was wide and surprisingly warm, despite the winter outside. Their walk was short, and she had no chance to see anything but a dark corridor of black rock and the castle's privy. They passed several half-naked men wearing nothing but baggy blue trousers. The bottoms of their faces were covered by cloth masks of the same colour. They were carrying trays of food, and as she looked back, she noticed small but distinct tattoos on their bodies. They all had the same pattern, the head of a dragon.

Servants, she thought. *Or rather, slaves.*

When they returned to the chamber, dusk was falling. She went up to watch the sunset. To her surprise, this time the square was filled with young men, apparently training for battle. Dressed only in light canvas breeches and heavy winter boots, they were practising spear fighting. At least that's what she deduced from their movements, as they were only wielding blunt sticks. There were perhaps three dozen of them, and they looked young, younger than her. Their heads were shaved on the sides, with a comb of spiky dark hair running down the middle. She watched them with curiosity, as she had never learned this style of fighting herself. She found that while the Ha'ami handled their weapons with great skill, their movements lacked finesse and speed. She carefully studied the tactics they were learning.

Their instructor was an elderly warrior with long, dark hair, tousled and streaked with grey. He had the powerful build and decisive movements of an experienced commander. His arm was adorned with a large tattoo of a wolf about to pounce, its predatory jaws open towards the man's collarbone. The warrior strolled among the novices, giving instructions and correcting mistakes. At one point he noticed some of his charges looking up. Following their gaze, he turned towards her. For a moment their eyes crossed, but he quickly lowered his gaze and continued to drill the young men.

The sun had set for good, and only torches illuminated the battlefield. In their glow you could see plumes of steam rising from the heated bodies. They made the fighting youth look almost like phantoms emerging from the clouds.

After some time, the sound of a horn was heard. The novice warriors laid down their weapons and marched in unison towards the building.

'The show is over,' she sighed to herself.

She also felt the need for some exercise, so she began to slowly stretch as much as the limited space of the chamber would allow. Her muscles and joints seemed to be working perfectly, except for the stiffness and weakness of hunger. As soon as she thought about eating, there was a soft knock on the door, as if on cue. The guards opened it to let in a maid with a tray.

Similarly to the slaves she had met earlier in the corridor, the girl was clad only in blue loose trousers and a cloth mask covering the bottom of her face. She was quite plump, very pale, and her mouse-coloured hair was tightly braided.

The captive tried to talk to the maid.

'Good evening,' she said, but the girl did not even look at her. Her eyes downcast, she placed the food on the table and left the room quietly, like a mouse sneaking under the claws of a predatory cat.

'Really? Not a word?'

Her question went unanswered. The door slammed shut.

The plate was filled with hot meat and vegetables. The smell of the food, wafting through the chamber, made her nauseous. She tried to exercise, but found it difficult to control her disgust, so she opened the window again, letting the night air in. Without thinking, she grabbed the bowl in her hand and sent it flying outside. For a moment it twirled through the air like a child's toy at a fair, only to fall and crash on the pavement. She looked out of the window to check, but regrettably she had not hit anything or anyone.

'What a shame!' she sighed in disappointment. 'Don't forget to report this to your royal buffoon,' she said to the guards. 'Thank you, a hundred times, for your hospitality, but I would like to continue my journey.'

They stood motionless like dark statues.

She went to bed.

'Good night, Right Guard, good night, Left Guard.'

She drew the curtains that hung from the canopy. For some time she tried to meditate as Tallen had taught her. Without his guidance, however, she could not muster a single ounce of energy. Frustrated, she covered herself up to her ears with the blanket. She decided to sleep off her hunger.

Once Ha'teng had carefully wiped the blood from his arms and torso, the guard handed him his caftan and cloak. The commander ran a comb through his hair, sighed exasperatedly and wrinkled his nose in disgust. He needed to take a bath right away. The musty stench of the dungeon will not dissipate so easily. And he would have to remember his brass knuckles next time. The non-human's mouth did not deserve a personal touch.

'The Dragon has sent for you,' the guard told him.

He nodded briefly as he pulled on his robes and buckled his sword belt.

'Put that thing back in the cell,' he ordered as he walked away. 'No grub. Maybe if he starves a bit, he'll be more willing to talk.'

The guards nodded and Ha'teng headed for the exit.

He marched briskly to Ha'akon's chambers. His friend was waiting for him in his study, accompanied by Ha'sani, the Guardian of the Keys, who oversaw the fortress' supplies and treasury. He was the least experienced member of the Council of First Brothers, having recently been appointed to replace a predecessor who had fallen in battle. His hair, which warriors were only allowed to grow after initiation, did not even reach his shoulders. He was full of new, revolutionary ideas, always thinking of changing things. He followed the lord of the castle like a faithful puppy, trying to convince him of yet another improvement in the organisation of the corn supply, or the way the armour was cleaned... everything could be done better.

Ha'teng didn't always understand his friend's decisions, especially when it came to Council appointments. But he respected him too much to question them.

'*Koru,*' the ruler greeted him. 'It is good that you are here. I wanted to get your opinion on a certain matter.'

'Do you have any wine?' He took a seat across from Ha'akon. He was in a foul mood and he did not expect this conversation, whatever it was about, to change that. 'I've just come from an interrogation, I've been famished all day.'

Instead of answering, Ha'sani handed him the cup he was holding. The Tiger gulped it down.

'You look like the one being interrogated,' the young warrior joked. The Guardian of Defence shrugged his shoulders. There was no reason to explain himself to this novice.

'I heard that the girl was probably a *Ta'uma,*' the cheeky little snot continued unperturbed.

'That's one of the theories,' Ha'teng replied briefly.

'If this is confirmed, have you thought about who will get her?' Ha'sani asked.

'It is too early for such matters,' the Governor interrupted.

'Of course. I'm just curious.' The young advisor spread his hands and laughed. 'You know well enough that I myself have a taste for more mature women. But as far as I understand, this girl is not unsightly, so there will probably be a queue of interested men.'

Ha'teng poured himself some wine.

'I didn't know that as part of your quartermaster's duties you were also involved in pandering,' he explained blandly. 'As soon as I've finished with her, you can take her to the market and negotiate the price at will.'

'Just don't damage her too much!' the other man added.

'Was I not clear enough?' Ha'akon interjected surprisingly sharply. 'The girl will remain in the chamber under guard until we find out who she is.'

There was an uncomfortable silence.

'Ha'sani,' the ruler continued after a moment. 'War in the East? The salt supplies? Isn't that what we should be talking about?'

The warrior straightened in his chair and grew serious. The Tiger did not change his position.

Come on, boy, he thought. *Show how much you deserve to be among men.*

Ha'sani had prepared well for this meeting. He always debated with himself at length before presenting his thoughts to the ruler or the Council of First Brothers. He knew he was the youngest and had to prove his worth in their eyes.

'The situation is the most difficult in years,' he declared emphatically. 'Our treasury is full of gold, but that won't help us. We have no one to buy from. The Azzgoths' rebellion has cut us off from our main supply of salt, and no current trade arrangements can compensate.'

'This must be a problem not only for the Stone Nest, but for all Ha'ami,' Ha'teng interrupted without raising his eyes, much to the young advisor's annoyance. However, he had grown accustomed to being patient with the other First Brothers, accepting their comments with either humour or unwavering calm.

'Not necessarily,' he observed. 'Our lands to the east have a much milder climate. They don't have to plan their supplies for the long winter months as we do. That's why the king is in no hurry to solve the problem.'

'My informants in the capital tell me that a punitive expedition is being prepared for the spring,' added Ha'teng.

'–which could take years. You know well that this stubborn people will not lay down their arms so easily. Despite repeated wars, we have not been able to maintain control for long,' interrupted Ha'sani.

'They don't have a leader to guide them,' continued an undaunted Tiger.

'It doesn't matter. They have long practised the tactics of ambush, not open warfare; they attack travellers along all trade routes and destroy caravans of supplies. For that they don't need a central command,' The Guardian of the Keys commented. There was a moment of silence, which he used eagerly to continue his speech. 'What are we going to feed our troops next winter? Dry bread and raw meat? By the way, do you know that salt is also added to bread? If our supplies rot, we'll be digging up roots.'

'Don't be overdramatic,' Ha'teng replied dismissively.

The young counsellor felt his blood boil, but he controlled himself and turned to Ha'akon with a grave expression on his face.

'I do warn you. We must seek other sources of supply immediately. We have a responsibility to provide for our people. The pride of the Ha'ami will not feed them.'

'Oh, really? Tell me more about my responsibilities,' Ha'teng hissed, playing with the cup in his hand and looking at him sarcastically. Ha'sani was about to open his mouth to cut the Tiger off when the ruler interjected.

'How much time do we have to decide, Ha'sani? By when must we take action?'

'Given the current state of the stockpile, we need to find an alternate source of salt supply by spring, otherwise we may be at risk of starvation next winter,' he declared in the most convincing yet cool tone he could muster.

'We need to know more about the king's plans and the situation with the rebellion in the east.' Ha'akon turned to the Guardian of Defence. 'The Council of First Sisters and Brothers meets in a few days. Will you be able to get some news from the court by then?'

The man nodded grimly. He did not look particularly pleased. The young warrior figured that Ha'teng mostly looked at the world around him as if it did not live up to his exorbitant expectations, so it was hard to tell what was really going on under that mask. Of one thing he was certain. Their commander's words were not a suggestion, but an order.

'You will have a report ready before we go to the City of Sisters,' the Tiger said in a formal tone.

'I'm counting on it,' nodded the lord of the castle. 'Ha'sani, in the meantime, I expect you to come to the next conversation not only with a problem, but also with concrete solutions.'

'Yes sir.'

The Guardian of the Keys endured both his harsh stare and Ha'teng's sarcastic smile, though the blood rushed to his head at those words. He had a plan. A very good plan. But it was a move so bold that he had not yet dared to propose it. Not in this gathering.

The loud sound of a horn woke her up the next morning. Despite the growling of her stomach, she felt full of energy, as if the effects of whatever they had given her when she was captured had worn off.

'Good morning, the Right, good morning, the Left!'

She wondered if they were the same guards. Well, what difference did it make? She rose from the bed, washed her face and combed her tangled hair with wet fingers. After the excesses of the last few days, it had clumped together in an impossible tangle. Resigned, she tied it up in a high bun.

Drinking her water, she watched the morning training in the square. This time, the young warriors were practising their wrestling moves, rolling in the slush. The same man with the wolf tattoo circled among them, shouting instructions. She thought he glanced in her direction several times. Finally, he ordered the troop to fall in. The mud-soaked young men stood in even ranks and ended their training with a thunderous shout of greeting directed at the four burly men standing in the cloister. The commanders looked almost identical. Their faces were clean-shaven, their hair black, their clothes black, their cloaks the same. She recognised the Beautiful Demon and the man with the scar on his face. She had not yet had the dubious pleasure of meeting the other two. As the square emptied, she closed the window.

Missing the exercise, she decided to stretch her legs during her morning walk to the toilet. Afterwards, she began to practise, expecting the promised next interrogation at any moment. No breakfast had been brought to her. 'The message has arrived,' she thought.

The Beautiful Demon came later than the day before. He entered impetuously, without knocking. Proud as a fox who had hunted his first hen, immaculate in his appearance, as if he had stepped out of a portrait. Though his dark robes looked plain from a distance, she could now see the tasteful embroidery in black thread on the collar of the caftan he was wearing.

What a variety of forms evil can take, she thought, meeting the cold gaze of his blue eyes.

'It was brought to my attention that you are not satisfied with our hospitality,' he began without a greeting. An ironic smile played on his lips. He did not sit down, but stood with his bulky body towering over her.

'Thank you for the wonderful days I have spent here, but it is time for me to leave,' she replied calmly, crossing her arms over her chest.

Anger smouldered in his eyes.

'For the last time–' he snarled through his teeth. 'Who are you? What is your name?'

'Probably not for the last time... What have you done to my companion?'

She didn't have time to react when, in a swift movement, he grabbed her by the neck and pushed her against the wall.

'No more jokes, understood?' he hissed, giving her time to defend herself. Taking advantage of the fact that he was holding her with only one hand, she crossed her forearms around it, creating leverage, then with a quick manoeuvre twisted his arm, forcing him to release the fingers clenched around her throat. At the same time, she spun around and ended up behind his back, still holding his right arm with both hands. He was now standing with his back to her, immobilised. He hissed, whether in pain or anger she could not tell.

In a rage, he stepped back and pushed her against the wall, crushing her with the weight of his body. Yet she did not let go of his arm. When his trick didn't work, he turned and bent down, flipping her over so that she landed on her back on the floor. Free of her grip, he swung with a kick. She rolled to the left. He missed. She sprang to her feet and leapt onto the bed. Grabbing the heavy wooden frame that supported the canopy, she spun, gaining momentum, and kicked him hard in the solar plexus. Thrown backwards, he fell into a chair, lost his balance and collapsed to the floor. She landed on both feet and looked at the guards. They were standing still, as always.

She expected it wouldn't end well for her, but it wasn't in her nature to give in. She evened her breath and took up a defensive position, waiting for the Beautiful Demon to rise. He got to his feet, unbuckled his ornate sword belt in slow motion, then took off his cloak and leather gloves, throwing them all at the guards' feet. On his exposed right arm, she saw a huge tattoo of a roaring tiger.

'You're in for it, you little bitch!' he said, lunging at her like a charging predator.

Ha'rim had no idea what to do as he watched the fight unfold before his eyes. His orders were clear: guard the prisoner, make no contact, do not interfere with the interrogations. But his next order was to see to it that she was protected, that no harm came to her, either by her own hand or by the hand of a stranger.

The interrogation had definitely not gone Ha'teng's way. Not only had the girl resisted him, but she was now giving him a good thrashing. Ha'rim would never have believed it had he not seen it with his own eyes. He knew that winning a fight was now a matter of personal pride for the warrior. He exchanged glances with the other guard, Ha'toru, and decided to hold back and wait for the situation to develop. He expected the angry commander to do everything in his power to prove his superiority.

The enraged Tiger attacked, trying to force the girl into a corner. With a rapid series of blows, he tried to hit her in the head or body, but to Ha'rim's amazement, she dodged the blows with almost superhuman speed, never allowing herself to be trapped. She moved with extraordinary agility, like a small lizard, using the chamber's furnishings to defend herself. At the moment, it seemed to be a question of who would tire first. The prisoner had not eaten for several days, so the guard was betting that her strength would soon wear off. He could see her movements slowing a little as time passed. Still, Ha'teng didn't seem any closer to scoring a hit than he had been at the start of the fight. He was also breathing more heavily.

At one point, when he dropped his guard unawares, the girl recoiled in a half-turn with the speed of a whip and kicked the warrior in the face. He stumbled against the wall, a trickle of blood running from his nose. He wiped it away with the palm of his hand in obvious surprise as he looked at the red on his fingers... then burst into a real rage. He grabbed a chair and threw it at her with a vengeance. She turned to avoid the collision. He seized the moment. Like an enraged bull, he caught her in the middle and threw her to the ground. With a quick manoeuvre, he immobilised her with his knee and then used his right fist to deliver a crippling blow to her temple. She fell unconscious.

He did not stop, but showered her with more punches, blinded by his rage. Ha'rim exchanged a quick, knowing glance with Ha'toru. The latter opened the chamber door and rushed out with a report. He, in turn, moved towards the commander, who was kneeling over the unconscious prisoner, continuing his revenge. The guard grabbed him from behind and dragged him away.

'That will do,' he said in a calm but firm tone.

He held Ha'teng for a moment until he heard his breathing even out. Then he let go. The man coughed, spitting blood onto the body on the floor.

'Lousy scumbag!' he snarled, kicked his unconscious captive in the stomach, then turned, picked up his things and left the chamber.

Ha'rim knelt beside the girl and checked if she was breathing. He felt a pulse on her neck and sighed with relief. He would be in serious trouble if the prisoner died on his watch.

Still, he couldn't help but smile as he remembered Ha'teng's surprised face when the little lizard had delivered a kick to his handsome face. The pride of the famous Tiger of the Stone Nest had probably never suffered more damage. And he, Ha'rim, had been lucky enough to witness it.

Chapter II
Where the devil makes a hole, the woman will patch it up

WITA STEPPED CAREFULLY ON THE muddy cobblestones, trying to keep the sedan chair level. All he needed today was to be whipped for the uncomfortable journey of the lady he was carrying. He'd never done the route to the Upper Castle before. Moreover, the winter weather had not been kind this year, and snow still lingered in the narrow streets of the city.

'Run, you miserable lot,' a guardsman growled from his horse.

They were wading up to their ankles in the slippery slush.

Run yourself, you...

Wita, although gentle and patient by nature, searched his mind for a curse.

It wasn't the first time they had treated him like a beast of burden. He didn't mind. He worked hard and did not shirk his duties. He was taller than many a lord, broad in the shoulders and strong for four men. Therefore, it was no surprise that he spent his days lifting, moving and carrying anything that had to be lifted, moved and carried. He just wanted to earn an honest living, so he obediently followed the orders of his masters.

But today even his docile nature was put to the test. Halfway to the Upper Castle he began to lose feeling in his feet, clad only in light sandals. The cold wind lashed his bare back as sharply as Ha'ami's whip. Add to that the constant *Hurry, slackers, move on!* shouts over his head. He could see by the expressions on his companions' faces that they were as eager as he was to throw the weight off their shoulders and tell the scoundrel to let the lady go on her own if she was in such a hurry.

Yet they did not.

No one in the Stone Nest would have dared to defy the masters.

He couldn't believe it when they reached their destination safely. He looked down at his arms and legs, blue with cold. Sweat ran down his neck to his bare back, soaking his trousers. He knew that the wetness would soon freeze and make him even colder.

'Now to the stables, they'll find you a job there!' The heartless guard gave them no respite.

Willy-nilly, they shuffled off to where they were told. At least the stables were warm.

Such was the fate of servants, but what could one do?

'I thought you had at least had a syphilis outbreak in the brothel when you summoned me in such haste, and all I can see here is a beaten child. Quite a sight to see. Even though I know what you lot are capable of,' Temina said as she entered the chamber.

She took off her warm hooded cloak, looked around, and finally decided to throw it on a broken chair. Ha'akon greeted her briefly and waited until his guards had left them alone. They were now standing over the unconscious girl he had moved to the bed earlier.

'Not quite a child. Just look at the results of her duel with Ha'teng,' he replied, pointing to the mayhem around them.

'She fought Ha'teng?' Temina asked with interest, looking at the broken furniture. 'It looks like he fought another tiger, not such a little thing.'

'I could hardly believe it either, but two of my men were standing guard and they saw everything,' Ha'akon replied.

'And it didn't occur to them to interfere?'

He looked at her pointedly.

'Indeed,' she sighed, bending over the wounded girl. 'It would have been dishonourable to interfere with another Ha'ami's duel. But in this case, they could have helped him against such a formidable opponent.'

He made no reply. He had his own opinion about the behaviour of both his friend and the guards, but it would wait for a personal conversation with them. Temina had probably guessed it nevertheless. She knew him better than anyone else. She turned the girl's face gently.

'He couldn't have delivered those blows when she was on her feet.'

'He battered her when she was already unconscious,' Ha'akon admitted with some embarrassment.

She scowled at him. He prepared himself for a cutting remark about the warrior's honour.

'How noble of him,' she just commented.

'I had her given a short-acting infusion to keep her asleep until your arrival.'

'Didn't she just wake up from the last dose you gave her after the arrest?' she raised an eyebrow in clear disapproval. 'I think I'll have to restrict your access to the herbs, since you're so generous with them. It could harm her. More than these injuries, which seem only superficial.'

Ha'akon felt like a scolded child. Temina was the only person who could indulge in such a tone towards him.

'Ha'teng must have been furious,' she remarked, looking closely at the injuries. 'What did he say?'

'I haven't spoken to him yet,' he explained dryly. 'I only know the guards' version. He's licking his own wounds; apparently, he didn't come out of it completely unscathed.'

'Aha,' she just said. Her muttering, as usual, contained at least ten allusions that he could only guess at.

'Temina,' he changed the subject. 'Can you do me a favour? Will you talk to her when she wakes up? We need to find out who she is and what she's doing here.'

'Anything for you, my dear, you know that very well.'

He breathed a sigh of relief.

'But on one condition.'

'What's that?'

'Those pathetic guards who like to watch little girls being abused... keep them outside, please. Perhaps they'll be of more assistance there.'

'Agreed.' He took her hand and kissed it respectfully on the inside. 'Thank you.'

'Don't thank me yet, we'll see what comes of it.'

She glanced at him amusedly. Then she looked back at the injured girl.

'I can't believe that little one gave Ha'teng a thrashing,' she giggled. 'I really want to get to know her.'

She opened her eyes and was surprised to see a new face above her.

'Welcome back, Tiger Slayer!' the strange woman welcomed her cheerfully.

Her straight black hair was cut short, combed to the right and shaved above the ear on the left side of her head. But it was her eyes that stood out the most. Large, dark blue, like all the Ha'ami she had met. Yet completely different. Bright, playful and... friendly?

The girl tried to sit up on the bed, but immediately felt a sharp pain in her chest and hissed.

'Easy now,' the stranger said gently. 'You're a bit banged up.' She paused. 'Why don't you tell me your name so we can continue this conversation smoothly?'

'Everyone asks me that,' she groaned. 'And yet somehow no one has introduced themselves to me.'

'True!' the woman laughed. She had a beautiful laughter, of the infectious kind. 'I am Temina, an herbalist. My brother called me here to look at your wounds and treat them.'

'And your brother is–?'

'Governor Ha'akon, who lovingly rules over us in the Stone Nest and the surrounding lands,' the woman explained, not without a hint of irony.

'I don't think I have any injuries,' said the prisoner, intent on keeping her distance. 'That rag only hit me once, at the end,' she added, looking around the chamber. She noticed with surprise that the guards were gone.

'He whacked you a bit when you lost consciousness,' Temina said, holding a cloth to her forehead. It stung. She hissed in surprise. 'You have a cracked brow and lip, but fortunately the bones are undamaged. The swelling will soon ease and you will once again dazzle the world with your beauty.'

'I can't wait to get back to that,' the girl muttered in reply, reluctantly admitting to herself that it was hard not to feel affection for this cheerful person.

'Can I check your ribs?' Temina asked. She nodded and lifted her sweatshirt. The herbalist carefully felt her side. 'Fine,' she declared. 'Just a bit of swelling... it's hard to believe you survived a confrontation with Ha'teng with only a few bruises.' She laughed wryly again. 'I heard you gave him a good beating yourself. Accept my thanks on behalf of all the Ha'ami women.'

'Ha'teng? Is that the arrogant fop?'

'Yes, the arrogant fop is his second official title, after the Guardian of Defence.'

'And you are Temina, sister of–'

'Ha'akon.'

She took a breath and repeated that in her mind.

'Why are they 'sons' and you have your own name?'

'Ah, you know our language...' The herbalist looked at her with curiosity. 'Do you know what the name of our tribe means? Ha'ami?'

'I know a little... Literally, the word means Sons of Ami.'

'Great. And Ami is...?'

It sounded like questioning a child.

'An extremely fertile woman?'

Temina smiled at her answer.

'Almost. Ami is the mother of us all. The land that gave birth to us. Our one and only goddess. Each of us has been blessed with a piece of the miracle of her fertility, which is why the man who emerges from her womb is named after his mother, in her honour. Ha'akon. The Son of Akona. Ha'teng. The Son of Teng. And so on.'

'I see.' She nodded. It made sense.

'Since that's clear, the only name that remains a mystery is yours.'

The girl lowered her head. She wasn't sure if she should change her mind about not revealing anything about herself.

'My companion...' she stammered out quietly. 'Do you know what happened to him?'

'I was warned you might ask that.' The herbalist blinked knowingly. 'They told me he was taken to a place somewhat less comfortable than your chamber. Probably in one of the many dungeons.... He awaits judgement.'

'I would like to see him.'

She kept her eyes on her hands, not to give away her excitement.

Tallen was alive!

Temina was silent for a moment, perhaps contemplating this bold request. She probably meant to refuse.

'I'll try to organise it. I can't promise anything,' the herbalist finally said. 'Is he your beloved?'

'A friend.' The girl swallowed her emotions. Her knuckles were white from gripping the bedclothes. 'And... my horse. Do you know what happened to my horse?'

She lifted her gaze. Temina's blue eyes widened in mild surprise.

'The horse? I suppose he's in the stables.'

'Do you think I'll be able to see him? He must be very worried.'

'Your horse is worried?' The herbalist repeated her words with obvious amusement.

Indeed, it did sound absurd, although it was the most honest truth.

'Well, this visit shouldn't be a problem as long as you don't jump on its back again.'

'For now, one accusation of this terrible crime is enough for me.'

Temina nodded her head.

'This offence is not unknown to me. I have served more than one sentence for it. But well, it's time for me to go. I recommend rest and wholesome food, though I hear you are not a fan of the latter. I would like to remind you that it is rather essential to life...'

Again, that sounded like scolding a child.

'That's it. Let me tell you one more secret before I go.'

She looked at the woman expectantly. The herbalist snorted loudly through her nose.

'I'm afraid you stink, my dear! And your clothes need a good wash!'

She felt a blush of shame creep across her face. She looked down at her green sweatshirt and noticed the blood stains.

'Is this mine?'

'I don't think so. I think it's the Tiger's.'

'Tiger's?' Her head was spinning from the conversation. She was sure she had misheard, but Temina only nodded in confirmation, clearly amused by her own joke.

'Every Ha'ami man, before he reaches adulthood, goes on a solitary expedition to hunt down the largest beast possible. The beast in question is then tattooed on the arm that dealt the fatal blow. Ha'teng returned with the body of a tiger. This is a rare victory. In the Stone Nest, he is the only one to have done so. Hence the nickname.'

'Yes, I've seen the tattoo,' she said.

'Let me send a servant to escort you to the baths and arrange a change of clothes... although we may have to look for children's garments,' the herbalist laughed, rising from her seat. She was as tall as her brother, her blue shirt cinched with a thick belt and her dark trousers tucked into high boots. Throwing her warm cloak over her shoulders, she picked up the bag she had come with.

'Till next time!'

'Eli.'

'What?'

'That's what they call me. Eli.'

'Pretty. Eli, the Tiger's Bane. See you tomorrow!'

'See you, Temina. And thank you.'

'We are dealing with a typical porcupine here,' Temina explained to everyone present.

Ha'akon waited quietly for her to explain her point. He knew that since he had asked for her help, he could expect a small showdown. The three of them, together with Ha'teng, gathered in the castle lord's chambers, or to be more precise, in a small room reserved for private conversations. He himself sat comfortably in an armchair, his sister paced back and forth, talking about her visit to the girl, while his friend stood at the window, pretending to be very interested in something outside. In reality, he was digesting the bitter pill of defeat. After Ha'teng's most recent performance, Ha'akon had no intention of soothing his commander's bitterness caused by Temina's success in interrogating the mysterious prisoner.

'You have to be slow and patient with a porcupine. Feed it, give it water, pet it until it hides its spikes and reveals its soft belly,' she continued. 'Otherwise, wham! It gets moody and you don't even want to go near it.'

'It's a good thing we have your talented caressing hands to help us,' Ha'teng sneered without turning around.

'How's your nose? Need a bandage?' she snapped back mercilessly. He did not answer the taunt.

'To recap,' Ha'akon interjected. 'Her name is Eli, she doesn't know much about Ha'ami, though she speaks our language, and she claims friendship with the other prisoner. That is progress... though it raises many new questions.'

'That's right,' she confirmed. 'Tomorrow we can continue, and as for the petting, I made her some promises.'

'Here we go,' Ha'teng coughed sarcastically.

'First a bath and a change of clothes. I assume she had some luggage?'

'Those items will remain in my custody,' the warrior protested.

'Keep your toys to yourself. It's just a matter of clean clothes. Can I count on you to see to that?'

'Yes,' Ha'akon assured her. 'Ha'teng will send a servant.'

'Excellent.' She smiled cheekily, knowing that this was actually a punishment for the warrior.

'Second, she asked about her horse. She said the animal was worried about her – proof of how badly you've hurt her head, my handsome.'

'The beast has already smashed down the third stable door.' declared the Guardian of Defence. 'For now, we're keeping it without water and food to teach it humility.'

'I see your tactics are as brilliant in dealing with animals as they are with humans,' she remarked. 'But perhaps we can solve both problems if you allow her to visit the stables.'

'Agreed.' Ha'akon forestalled his friend's objection. 'She can go there under escort.'

'Great,' Temina said happily. 'And one last promise... Eli is very anxious to meet her friend, whom I understand you are keeping in the dungeons.'

'None of that,' Ha'teng replied promptly this time. 'He is a dangerous prisoner, he shows no willingness to cooperate... her visit will not help us in any way, and will only reduce the chance of breaking him and making him talk.'

Finally, he turned towards the herbalist, clasping his hands together on his chest, clearly ready to defend his position.

'Do you know what the problem is with people like you, my handsome?' Temina smiled softly, as if explaining something obvious. 'You see every situation in terms of a win-lose arrangement. It doesn't occur to you that sometimes both sides can benefit by working out a win-win solution. But the likes of you take as much pleasure in your own victory as you do in crushing your opponent... a very sad view of the world.'

'I think Ha'teng is right about this,' the governor interjected before the two were at each other's throats. 'I'm willing to make a concession regarding their meeting, but for now we don't know enough. We need more information.'

She didn't seem to be put off by his refusal.

'As you wish, *koru-to*. You'll know more tomorrow.'

She approached him and held out her hand in farewell. He kissed her palm respectfully.

'Thank you, Temina, see you tomorrow.'

Ha'teng stormed down the corridor to his chambers like an ill-tempered thundercloud. Ha'akon's words had hurt him deeply.

And then there was Temina's sneering grin when he was ordered to prepare a bath for the vagrant. If only he had made some progress with the other prisoner. But no. That one remained silent as if under a spell. Not a word. Not a whimper.

He pushed open the door to his bedroom with all his might.

'Anni!'

The maid, paler than usual, entered the chamber on tiptoe.

'Go to *Ta'uma*, take her to the baths and help her scrub. See that she changes her clothes and bedding too. Have her chamber cleaned. It stinks like a badger's den.'

The girl only bowed her head in agreement.

'When you have finished, come back here and tell me everything you find out. Keep your eyes and ears open, is that clear? Anything, even an insignificant detail, can prove to be important.'

Turning away from the maid, he poured some wine into one of the richly decorated goblets on the table.

'And send your brother here,' he barked before she left.

Once he was alone, he walked over to a mirror in an ornate bronze frame. He looked at his face and gently touched his nose. It would take a few days for the swelling to go down. Everyone would know of his humiliation. Damned, bloody bitch.

The servants had already finished saddling his mount, but Ha'sani deliberately delayed his leaving. His patience was soon rewarded, for Temina, clad in a warm hooded cloak, appeared in the square, exactly as he had predicted. The guardsman accompanying her called the porters.

'Hail, o noble one,' the young advisor smiled a welcome.

'How official!' she responded to the bow. 'Greetings, Ha'sani.'

As usual, she addressed him with slight reserve. This did not discourage him. He believed that in time he would gain her trust.

'I heard you came to the rescue. Apparently, the snack got stuck in the Tiger's throat.'

'As usual, news in the Stone Nest has wings.'

'And the speed of the wind! How's the snack feeling? Not chewed too much?'

'Looks like more than one predator could break their teeth on this one.'

He laughed loudly. Maybe a little too loudly.

'Good thing he didn't choke!'

Temina gave him a sideways glance.

'Well, it's been nice talking, but it's time for me to go.' She turned to the sedan chair that was waiting for her.

'I happen to be on my way to the City of Sisters.' He held out his hand to help her get in.

'How nice. I wasn't expecting such an escort.' She took his hand. 'Pleasure or business?'

'You know I like to combine the two.'

'So I heard.' She sat down on the cushions. 'Anything in particular on your brilliant mind today?'

'If you fancy listening to boring stories about how to feed the populace, I'll be happy to entertain you on the way.' He shrugged, trying not to sound pushy.

'I didn't know we were having food problems,' she teased. To his satisfaction, she didn't pull back the curtain.

'Not right now,' he sighed and climbed into the saddle. 'But still...'

She looked at him sharply and ran a hand through her hair.

'Tell me.'

He touched his horse's flanks and vigorously repeated his earlier speech, hoping it would fall on more favourable ground this time. He may not have had Ha'teng's experience on the battlefield, but unlike him, he valued building a coalition with the City of Sisters far more. After all, they held half the votes in the Council. Underestimating their influence was a mistake made by the senior commanders, and one that Ha'sani was keen to capitalise on.

There was a knock at the door, which opened to reveal the same slave girl who had brought her a meal yesterday. She was dressed again in baggy trousers and a linen mask, her mousy hair braided around her head. She nodded at Eli.

'Shall I come with you? A bath?'

The girl bowed her head. They passed the guards standing outside, who did not move. The long corridor took them in a new, unfamiliar direction this time. Marching behind the maid, Eli noticed a small tattoo of a tiger on her right shoulder blade. Undeterred by the servant's silence, she showered her with questions.

'Where are we going? Who are you? What is your name? Where are you from? Can you speak? How much further?'

All her efforts to start a conversation went unanswered, so she concentrated on watching the route they were taking. Soon they turned into a narrow, winding staircase and descended three floors. Finally, they came to a solid wooden door. With surprising strength, the slave pushed it open. The warm, humid air hit them unexpectedly. They stepped inside.

They were in a small room where the only furnishings were narrow benches lined up along the walls. A pile of white sheets lay in the corner. The grey-haired girl removed her mask. She spoke in a deep, squeaky voice.

'We are in the bathhouse. I'll help you wash, lady. My name is Anni. I serve lord Ha'teng. I come from the North. I can speak. I am not allowed to take off my mask or speak in public. Oh, and I hope it hasn't been too far,' she finished without changing her expression for a moment or looking the captive in the eye.

'No, quite a short walk...' Eli collected her thoughts after all that. 'Wait, wait, I have more questions.'

'You can undress here, my lady.' Anni added in a voice that was almost a whisper.

Eli slowly began to remove her sweat and dirt-caked trousers and blood-stained sweatshirt.

'But will I get new clothes other than yours?'

She hesitated to hand over her belongings, which, though worn, were familiar and her own. A slight look of consternation appeared on Anni's face, but she quickly returned to her learned indifference.

'Yes, lady *Ta'uma*... I have found suitable Ha'ami outfits. There is also a whole trunk full of robes waiting for you in your chamber.'

Eli finally got rid of her underwear and handed Anni her old rags. She folded them on the bench, but the servant was still waiting for something: she looked suggestively at a gold bracelet on the prisoner's wrist.

'Where to now?' Eli just urged her on.

The servant girl gave up and took a white cloth from the pile. Then they walked into the next room, straight into the creamy clouds of steam.

'Where are we?'

'In the servants' bath,' squeaked Anni. 'Nobody's here at this hour. There are no women's baths in the Upper Castle. Forgive me, lady *Ta'uma*. Bathing here must offend your dignity.'

Eli looked around curiously but, surrounded by the vapours, she could see almost nothing except a pool of water right next to her. She dipped her toe in and felt the wonderful warmth.

'Don't worry, Anni, my pride is still intact. Can I jump in here? Ow!' she cried, unexpectedly feeling a splash of ice-cold water on her back.

'Lady *Ta'uma*, you need cleansing before the bath.' The servant, holding a bucket of water in one hand and a bristly brush in the other, gestured to a low stool.

'Interesting customs,' Eli muttered, but sat down as instructed. 'What did you call me? *Ta'uma*? Daughter of the people? What does that mean?'

'*Ta'uma*—' Anni seemed to hesitate for a moment and instead of answering, scrubbed her back with an eagerness worthy of a better cause. '—*Ta'uma* is the daughter of a noble family. The Ha'ami welcome her as a sign of peace and friendship between the tribes.'

Some kind of hostage, Eli thought. *Great. My noble family could rest easy knowing how well I'm being looked after. If it existed.* Out loud, however, she asked a question of great interest to her.

'How did you come to serve here, Anni?'

'Many knock on the gates of Ha'ami asking for work, lady *Ta'uma*. I was lucky. Lord Ha'teng chose me. It is an honour for me. He is a wonderful master.'

'Yes, I've met Ha'teng. You're right, he is charming. So you came here of your own free will?'

The idea that someone would voluntarily agree to parade around half-naked with a tattoo on their back as if they were someone else's property seemed unacceptable to her.

'Yes.'

'Why?' She realised that Anni was only answering factual questions and rephrased hers. 'Where do you come from?'

'From Gertan, a small principality in the north.'

'What's it like there?'

'Life is hard. And poor, lady *Ta'uma*. The noble lords fight among themselves, driving us from place to place. My family and I have fled to the lands of Ha'ami to beg for service. Lady *Ta'uma*, now your legs, please.'

Eli rose from her seat, trying to ignore the fact that a strange girl was scrubbing her buttocks.

'Yes, I've read about the Duchies of the North... Gertan was founded relatively recently, wasn't it? After the great principality of Miran was divided among the sons of the ruler, right?'

'Yes, lady *Ta'uma*, you are very wise.' Anni confirmed. 'Few have heard of this place.'

'I like to read.' She wanted to return to the subject that had interested her so much. 'I thought the servants in the fortress were only people who had been kidnapped. I didn't know that some came here of their own free will.'

'The Ha'ami have not invaded the North for a long time. These are poor lands and they pay tribute anyway. They only fight among themselves. Lady *Ta'uma*, now your hands.'

Eli raised her elbows.

'Then who do all these armed Ha'ami fight with?'

'The last few years only with the Azzgoths in the East, lady *Ta'uma*. They are a bad people. Always rebelling. Bad, bad people.' Anni's face expressed disapproval.

'Scumbags.' The servant nodded. 'Why are they rebelling?'

'They don't want to pay, lady *Ta'uma*. They don't want to serve.'

'None of the Azzgoths have signed up to serve, like you?'

'Not by themselves... but we have many who have been assigned here after the recent wars, lady *Ta'uma*.'

Assigned. Interesting choice of words, Eli muttered to herself. 'And how are they doing here?'

'There's no use for them... They're lazy, they don't listen to orders, they just whisper in corners.' Anni shook her head disapprovingly. 'Lady *Ta'uma*, how are servants treated where you come from?' she asked unexpectedly.

'Where I come from, women rule and men are their slaves.' Since Ha'teng wanted to question her with the help of this girl, she decided to give him some interesting information. 'We keep them in chains and they have to obey our every whim.'

'This must be a very distant country,' Anni muttered.

'Yes, very far away, no one here has heard of it,' she added. She hoped the servant was clever enough to understand that she had no desire to be interrogated. 'You said you came here with your family. Where are they? Ow, careful!' she groaned as the brush reached her bruised ribs.

'Sorry, lady *Ta'uma*,' the maid squeaked even softer.

'It's all right, I'm just a bit sore,' Eli reassured her. 'Tell me more, please, it's very interesting.'

'My parents were too old, lady *Ta'uma*. They were sent away.'

'Do you know how they are now?'

'No, lady *Ta'uma*.' She sounded rather indifferent.

'I'm sorry.'

Anni did not answer.

'Do you have anyone else?'

'A sister and a brother, lady *Ta'uma*.'

'Are they here? What are they doing?'

'They are the kept, lady *Ta'uma*.'

'The kept?'

'They serve the warriors to satisfy their fleshly needs, lady *Ta'uma*.'

'And your siblings have accepted it?'

51

'Yes. Done, lady *Ta'uma*. You may now dip into the spring. Let me wash your hair.'

Eli slipped happily into the warm water. She felt her body melt like a spoonful of honey dropped into a hot brew. What a relief! Anni meanwhile continued to groom her hair. Acting a little more gently this time, she managed to comb out her tangled curls.

'The Stone Nest was built on hot springs, lady *Ta'uma*.'

'How very clever,' concluded Eli. She was silent for a moment while the servant rubbed a fragrant oil into her hair.

'Is that lavender?'

'Yes, lady *Ta'uma*.'

'I will sleep well tonight.'

'I've finished, lady *Ta'uma*, we can go now.'

'So soon?'

'Yes, time for dinner, lady *Ta'uma*.'

'Well...' Eli sighed. She didn't want to get the maid into trouble with the gracious lord Ha'teng, so she decided to follow her instructions and wrapped herself in a linen towel. They walked to the second dressing room where Anni handed her a dark green, plain robe. Eli didn't like to make a fuss about clothes. She was just hoping to find a pair of trousers in the trunk she had been promised. In the meantime, she put on what had been brought to her.

'You look gorgeous, lady *Ta'uma*,' Anni said, still with her eyes fixed on the floor.

Eli smiled at these words, thinking of her swollen face.

'Thank you, that's a lovely garment.'

With quick movements, the servant made her hair into a simple braid, then announced that they may now go and put her mask back on. They returned to her chamber, where Anni left her alone for a moment, only to return with a hot meal.

'Thank you for everything,' Eli said, and the girl just bowed her head slightly and left, stepping so quietly that she almost floated above the floor.

By now the room had been cleaned, the bedclothes changed and the broken furniture replaced.

Like at the wave of a magic wand, she thought. She had never had servants in her life and was used to taking care of her own needs. Having someone around to bring her clothes and even scrub her body felt very strange. *Incapacitated*, she thought. *Yes, that's the right word.*

The plate was once again filled with roast meat and bread, with a bowl of hot vegetable soup next to it. Eli felt that her stomach had shrunk to the size of a peanut, so she nibbled at a piece of bread to see how her body would react to her first meal after such a long fast. She had just finished a sip of wine when a knock sounded and the door opened to reveal the lord of the fortress himself, this time dressed in less formal robes. Though the black trousers and equally black boots still gave him a military look, he carried no weapons, and the loose, sleeveless blue caftan made him appear more casual. A huge dragon was tattooed over his muscular right shoulder.

Eli, who already knew what such a tattoo meant, almost dropped her mug in astonishment. But she recovered quickly and rose to greet him.

Before retiring to bed, Ha'akon decided to see for himself if his commander had completed his task this time. Since Temina had given her word to the prisoner, he wanted to make sure that his sister's promise was kept. At least that was how he explained to himself the reason for his visit.

He found the girl preoccupied with her meal. She seemed surprised to see him.

'Good evening,' he said as the guards closed the door behind him. Hesitantly, she placed her wine cup on the table.

She's alert. A typical porcupine, he thought. Temina's words resounded in his head, and he smiled involuntarily at the memory.

'Good evening!' she replied slowly, looking at him warily. He noted with satisfaction that she had been provided with suitable robes. Her petite figure looked surprisingly alluring in the green gown, which also highlighted the olive colour of her skin. Her brown hair was combed back smoothly, revealing a shapely neck. Seeing her swollen face, he felt a renewed surge of anger at Ha'teng.

'We have not been formally introduced,' he began. 'I'm Ha'akon.'

'I'm called Eli,' she replied with a tentative smile. 'But you probably already know that from your sister.'

'Yes.'

'Temina is an extremely kind person,' she said cordially. The lord was a little surprised by her good manners, given the tone of the conversation he had witnessed two days earlier.

'Yes, and a very capable herbalist. I hope she helped you,' he replied politely. There was an awkward silence.

'Would you like to sit down?' The young woman gestured to a chair. 'It's your castle, so I probably don't need to invite you.'

'Yes, um, thank you.' Ha'akon felt a little absurd. The girl was right, after all, she was officially his prisoner and he was standing there observing the etiquette as if he had come on an official visit. He sat down opposite her, and Eli rested in the other chair.

'I only have one goblet and I've already drunk from it,' she apologised.

'It is Ha'ami custom to share a cup.' The governor held out his hand, feeling that he could actually use a drink. He wasn't sure any more why he got the idea to come here.

'Really?' the girl handed him the wine. 'Why?'

Ha'akon took a healthy sip before answering her.

'To avoid the risk of being poisoned by the other guests.'

Interesting, he thought, *she doesn't know even the most basic Ha'ami traditions.*

'Ah, who would have thought that the rules of brotherhood and honour would not be enough of a guarantee,' said Eli, a spark of mockery flashing in her green eyes. Her words embarrassed him. He quickly changed the subject.

'How are your injuries? Are they painful?'

Ha'akon wondered if he should somehow mention that he disapproved of his subordinate's behaviour, but he didn't know how to put it. He didn't want to sound like he was apologising to her. After all, the girl was a prisoner who refused to cooperate.

'I don't really feel them. You tell me if they look very bad. I don't have a mirror, so I rely on what Temina said.' The girl touched her cheek lightly.

In the light from the fireplace, the bruises on her tawny face were less visible.

Ha'akon gave a slight grunt.

'I'm sure the swelling will go down soon.'

'So it is bad.' Eli laughed slightly when she saw his confusion. 'Well, it doesn't matter so much. Luckily there's always soup, so I don't have to worry about chewing,' she added cheerfully.

'I see. Does our food suit you?'

He looked at the full tray. Hardly anything has been touched.

She shrugged.

'I'm not a fussy eater. But I don't eat meat.'

'Why?' Meat was a staple of Ha'ami's diet. It was the first time he had met a person who did not eat it by choice.

'I don't kill animals.'

It didn't sound like a reproach, to be honest, but he felt uncomfortable. Again, there was an awkward silence. And again, it was Eli who broke it.

'I don't suppose you've come here to talk about my habits,' she asked.

'Yes... indeed.' Ha'akon sipped the drink slowly from the cup. 'I would like you to tell me about your fight with Ha'teng. If... um... if it's not too distressing.'

'Distressing?' The girl seemed genuinely surprised. 'It's not the first time I've been hit on the head.' She got up from her seat. 'I'll try, but I don't know if I'll be able to show you everything in this.' She lifted her skirt slightly.

He hadn't expected her to take his question so seriously. 'We were talking there.' Eli pointed to the wall by the entrance. 'He grabbed me by the throat and pushed me, about here. Then I twisted his arm, like this.'

The governor watched with curiosity. The excitement in her voice grew as she told the story.

'He threw me to the ground and I landed here. I rolled over, then used this beam for momentum and kicked him in the chest. He crumpled up like a flattened mosquito.' She chuckled slightly at the memory, but quickly stopped herself. 'Oops, I'm sorry. Yes, then he came at me with his fists, but I kept dodging and he couldn't hit me.'

The girl demonstrated vigorously.

'This went on for a while... eventually he lost his fortitude and kept exposing himself, so I took the opportunity and kicked him in the face.' Eli lifted her leg slightly in a half turn. 'Then he struck me with a chair, knocked me to the floor and the next thing I remember is your sister.'

She sank back in her seat, her eyes sparkling slightly and a blush appearing on the olive skin of her unbruised cheek. She took the wine from him and took a healthy sip.

'You knew you were going to lose,' he remarked.

Ha'akon was well aware of all the emotions that accompanied her story.

'With a trained warrior and two guards at the door? What chance did I have?' The girl snarled like a cat.

'But you chose to fight.'

She handed him the cup.

'Knowing you're going to lose is not the same as giving up.'

Eli shrugged.

'Do you think it would have been better for me if I had let your commander do whatever he wanted to do after nailing me to the wall? If I'm going to be eaten by a tiger, I want to be the worst meal of his life.'

'Now you sound like a real Ha'ami,' he said, not without a touch of admiration in his voice.

'That's where our similarities end.' She cut off his enthusiasm and looked him fearlessly in the eye. 'I am not like you and do not understand your laws. I am grateful for Temina's help, permission to bathe, a meal... but Ha'ami's hospitality to me is still being hunted in the middle of the night, it's bruises on my face and my friend locked in a dungeon. I don't know what you want from me. If I am to be punished for something I don't understand, then so be it. If you are consumed with questions for which you seek answers, you will not beat them out of me with your fist, nor will you draw them out by trickery, by feigned kindness, or by sending inquisitive servants. Either I am a prisoner, or I am your equal. There is no third way.'

The girl pierced him with her eyes and he felt angry at himself for being lectured like that.

'You're right, you're not Ha'ami,' declared Ha'akon firmly, setting his empty cup down on the table. 'However, you have come to our land of your own free will and there are laws that you must obey like everyone else.'

Her expression did not change, nor did she answer.

The governor got up and left without a word.

Hearing noises from inside the chamber, Anni knew she had to wait by the door. Although she had been instructed by lord Ha'teng to report to him as soon as she had completed her task, she knew him too well to risk interrupting his evening.

Anni's goal in life was to become the perfect servant that her master could not do without. His satisfaction was crucial to her future in the fortress. Her brother and sister were not as sensible as she was. Maybe they worked less now. Maybe they even got nice presents from the warriors now and then. But the attractiveness of the kepts diminished as they grew older, until eventually no one wanted them. Then, if they were lucky, they were assigned to menial tasks that no one else wanted to do. Or worse, they were cast out to fend for themselves.

Anni was never blessed with beauty or charm, which meant she didn't have to worry about their passing. The gifts she received at birth were much more lasting. Anni knew how to listen and was wise enough to recognize when to keep quiet. After being taken into Lord Ha'teng's service, she quickly became one of his spies in the fortress. But that was not enough for her. The maid hoped that one day he would give her the shirt that senior servants were allowed to wear. But all that had to be earned. Determined to achieve her goal, she was prepared to make any sacrifice.

The chamber was silent, so she waited a moment and knocked lightly, as was her custom.

'Come in, Anni,' she heard an order from inside. Lord Ha'teng stood naked by the inlaid fireplace, gazing into the fire and sipping wine from an ornate goblet. She did not need to raise her eyes to know that he looked like an otherworldly statue carved in marble, almost perfectly fitting into the refined interior of the room he was in. His body glistened with sweat and a tiger tattoo curled dramatically around his muscular arm. The beautiful face was still marred by swelling.

The maid tried to ignore her brother, who was clearly intoxicated with wine or mushrooms, sprawled on a wide, elaborately carved bed. His hazy, stunned gaze showed that he was completely unaware of her. He was in another world.

Anni made her report, carefully watching her master's motionless face. During her years of service, she had learned to read its tiniest grimace.

'It's not much, really,' he said coldly when she had finished. 'No tattoos, but the fact that she is not a servant was to be expected. We still don't know where she's from, she doesn't know our ways, but I've noticed that myself. Is that all?'

His tone conveyed discontent. The maid felt a painful sting of disappointment and frantically searched her mind for something else the lord might be interested in.

'She likes to read,' she stammered uncertainly.

'What are you muttering about?' He turned to her with an expression of impatience.

'She likes to read,' she repeated with more determination.

'And that, Anni, is called valuable information.'

Lord Ha'teng took a long sip of wine, his thoughtful gaze clearly analysing something.

A blush of happiness mixed with astonishment flushed the servant's face.

Chapter III
Man is a wolf to non-human

THE RED-EYED RAT WAS IN a foul mood today. Until now, it had been in charge of this dungeon, or so he deemed. That meant it was usually the first to revel in the bowl the guards had left for the prisoner. Today, however, nothing was brought. Again.

Annoyed, the red-eyed rat ambushed other creatures that crawled on the cell floor. Cockroaches and spiders were not his favourite. Finally, just when it had given up all hope of a better meal, a soft scurrying sounded in the corner.

A small, silly mouse got lost and wandered into his territory. The rat lurked quietly, watching from a corner as the mouse tentatively made its way through the dungeon, cautiously examining the floor. When it finally got close enough, the rat pounced on it with a violent leap. In panic, the mouse tried to run away from its attacker, but it was slower and not as familiar with its surroundings as the larger predator. The rat, keen to satisfy its hunger, quickly drove the mouse into a corner from which there was no escape.

Unexpectedly, without any warning in the form of a sound or movement, a slender, pale, almost translucent hand appeared between them. The hunter watched in helpless rage as the fingers closed in on its potential prey, snatching it high into the air.

'Not today, Rat King,' he heard the prisoner whisper.

All it could do was squeal in frustration.

Eli sat on the windowsill, watching the swirling snowflakes. She rested her cheek on the cold glass to ease the soreness in her jaw. She awoke with a sharp, splitting pain in her skull that bored into her eyes, ears and teeth. She wrapped herself in the soft cloak she had found in the trunk Anni had sent the day before. There was also a pair of breeches that fit her well and a loose shirt, all black.

'Just as well,' the girl thought. 'If I upset someone again and they get the urge to beat me up, less blood will be visible.'

She was worried about Tallen. Eli had no idea what the dungeons in this fortress might be like, but they hardly sounded like a pleasant place. It occurred to her that the smooth-skinned bastard might want to take revenge on her friend. Ha'akon's visit did not fill her with hopefulness either. If only she was capable of keeping her mouth shut. But she had to chide the lord of the castle himself. She should concentrate now on coming up with a plan to get them out of there. But how could she when an army of gnomes had opened a mine right in her brain? *You won't find any gold there, let it go.* But the gnomes, stubborn creatures that they were, did not give up their search. They kept digging, right into the centre of her head.

There was a knock at the door. As usual, she expected the guards to open and let the newcomer in, whoever he was. No one here had waited for her invitation; the knock was merely an announcement of entry. Nothing happened, however, and after a while the same noise was heard again. She jumped down from the window and pulled the handle.

On the other side was Temina.

'Good morning, how are you today?' Her voice was as cheerful as the day before. 'You certainly do smell and look better.'

Eli looked around the corridor suspiciously.

'Ha'right and Ha'left are gone?'

'Ha'akon called them away,' the herbalist explained. 'After you scolded him yesterday.'

Eli looked at her in surprise.

'Do you tell each other everything?'

'Almost!' Temina replied cheerfully. 'May I come in?'

'Yes, yes, I'm sorry.' Eli stepped back into the chamber to make way for her.

'This is for you.' The herbalist rummaged through her bag and handed her a heavy object. To her surprise, it was a leather-bound book. 'A gift from my brother in reconciliation, in the hope of a better start.'

'*The History of the Ha'ami People. Written by Selene the Elder,*' Eli read the title of the volume. She knew the books were extremely valuable. 'Is this for me?'

'Ekhm, just a loan, the archivist will rip my head off if I don't return this volume in perfect condition,' Temina explained. 'Normally, they don't let us take anything out of the building. So please, read it with your gloves on.'

'I don't know what to say... thank you,' Eli replied, not hiding her astonishment. 'It will certainly help me to practise your language and understand your customs better.'

Suddenly she felt dizzy. She had to sit down on the bed and hold her head.

'Ouch.' The herbalist looked at her. 'Not feeling well?'

'I've been in a bit of pain since I woke up, but it's probably not a big deal,' she explained evasively.

'It happens in the days after the injury.'

Temina nodded in understanding. 'Sit down, I'll prepare something to help you.' She opened the door to the corridor.

'Hey, you!' She called to a passing servant. 'Bring a kettle of hot water! Be hasty!'

'No need, it'll probably go away on its own,' Eli tried to make lessen of it.

'You want to deprive me of an excuse to visit?' Temina explained with feigned reproach. 'Have you officially declared me a fatmouth and a spy?'

'I just don't want to cause any trouble.'

The girl felt she was blushing at the direct insinuation.

'Listen,' Temina perched herself on the bed next to her. 'I do tell my brother everything. We trust each other implicitly. That is why he sent for me yesterday. He wanted someone competent to look after you, and you won't find such people in this part of the Stone Nest. I will ask you nothing. You'll tell me what you want... or not. Either way, I want to help you get better.'

'Why?' Eli asked suspiciously.

'As I told you yesterday, it's an honour to meet the woman who gave Ha'teng a thrashing. This act qualifies you to be the heroine of the year, perhaps of the last few years, in all of Ha'ami Country.'

There was a knock at the door and a servant entered with a steaming cauldron. Temina motioned for him to place it on the table, then set about stirring the herbs. After a while she returned with a cup of the aromatic brew.

Eli sniffed hesitantly.

'What is it?'

'An elixir that will turn you into a slave, obeying my every command,' the herbalist joked.

'Will I sleep again afterwards?' Eli wouldn't be distracted.

'Oh, true, that's your only experience with Ha'ami herbs so far. Not this time. It's just to ease the pain.' She encouraged her with a look. 'Bottoms up!'

The girl raised the mug to her lips, but at the same moment she felt her breakfast going up her throat. She shot out of bed and, seeing no other option, vomited into the cauldron. When she finished and raised her face, the chamber swirled beneath her feet.

'Temina, I think I need to lie down,' she muttered, then collapsed to the floor as if hit on the head with a frying pan. Everything turned to darkness.

'Concussion,' the sentry reported. 'Your sister had a pallet brought to the room and announced that she would stay by her side until she got better. She also said...' He hesitated.

'Yes?' Ha'akon urged him.

'Well, she asked me to pass on the message that if anyone with a tiger tattoo comes near this part of the castle, she will personally poison every last one of them.'

'Do as she tells you,' he ordered dryly.

The guard left the chamber.

The lord of the castle grimaced and turned back to Ha'sani. The latter refrained from commenting. He grunted slightly leaning over the table on which he had spread the maps he had brought from the Archives.

'As I said, we don't have many options at the moment. The principalities in the north are fragmented, in chaos, and soon we will probably have to build a wall to protect ourselves from the incoming folk. Besides, there's nothing to buy there except basic crops and livestock, and that's what we're already getting in tribute. The lands of the Azzgoths and the Elven Kingdom block access to the Sea to the east and south. As long as the rebellion continues, the land of Ha'ami will be cut off not only from the raw materials that the Azzgoths were supposed to provide in tribute, but also from all ports and waterways. This leaves only one direction. The west. And two options.'

The Guardian of the Keys drew an arc with his hand. Ha'akon said nothing. He listened intently.

The young commander tried his best to contain his excitement before presenting his idea.

'The first one: find a new route to the Kingdom of Patri. That would mean crossing the Dragon Mountains. Not impossible, but–'

'–dangerous and very uncertain,' the ruler finished. Ha'sani just nodded his head. The governor was the only man to have ever returned from those parts alive. The Dragon Mountains were inhabited by hordes of monsters, most of them known merely from legends. Solely convicts and renegades risked such a crossing – those who had nowhere else to go and knew no fear.

'The second solution is also risky, but only politically. A group of dwarves discovered the entrance to long-forgotten, resource-rich mines to the north, in the valley of the Ona River, in the pass between the Dragon Mountains and the Blue Mountains. They established a thriving trading post there and began to trade with both Patri and the principalities we border.'

'Trade with non-humans,' Ha'akon muttered, clearly analysing the proposal in his mind.

'It is not forbidden,' Ha'sani interjected immediately.

'No,' the ruler of the Stone Nest was studying the map intently. 'But it may bring upon us the displeasure of our brothers and the wrath of the king.'

'The Sisters are willing to support this endeavour,' the advisor dropped his main argument. The lord of the castle gave him a questioning look.

'I was in the City yesterday. Both Temina and Teena believe that we should do what is best for the people of our lands.'

'We don't know if the dwarves will trade with us,' his lord remarked. 'Nor on what terms.'

'That is true. That is why I would like to send envoys there to inquire before we make a decision.'

Though eager to proceed, Ha'sani waited patiently. He knew the ruler well enough to know that he needed time to think things through. He stood with his arms folded, but ready to spring into action. The young commander knew it was a good plan. It was time to let go of ancient prejudices.

Ha'teng stroked the surface of his brass knuckles thoughtfully, planning in his mind today's interrogation.

'Bring in the prisoner,' he ordered the guards.

The information from Anni finally confirmed the girl's noble background. But it was not enough for Ha'akon to forgive him for disobeying an order and beating the captive girl. He wanted to prove his usual efficiency as soon as possible and regain the trust of his lord and friend.

The sentries led the non-human into a dimly lit room. He seemed so pale that he was almost translucent. His light, long hair hung in matted strands soaked in sweat and blood. And yet, still, despite all the shabbiness, some intangible beauty emanated from him. Ha'teng had a weakness for anything that brought a touch of finesse, harmony or allure to a bleak reality. He liked to surround himself with ornately crafted objects, drink the best quality liquor and indulge in exquisite delicacies. Therefore, he was not blind to the beauty of the captive who fell into their hands. However, this creature represented everything that every Ha'ami had been taught since childhood to hate to the point of obsessive fear.

The non-humans.

'Pull him up,' he barked out a command.

Temina proved to be not only a considerate carer, but also a consistently cheerful companion. After two days together, Eli admitted that she had never been so pampered or given so much attention during her illness.

The headaches and nausea were getting weaker, but the herbalist did not allow her to get out of bed too often. In return, she entertained the girl with stories of Ha'ami life in the Stone Nest. The tribe's existence seemed to be governed by many complicated rules, and the girl often found herself trying to understand how one could function on a day-to-day basis in the maze of laws and traditions the Ha'ami held sacred.

'Do you know when I can call on my horse?' she asked, hoping the herbalist would reply that they could go right away.

'Not yet... You always talk about it as if you wanted to invite it for tea,' Temina laughed. Eli found she had to figure out how humans usually talked about their mounts. Otherwise, she would always sound strange.

'If you rejuvenate at this rate, I'll be out of here in two or three days, and you can sit in the stables all day if you like.'

A wave of joy washed over her.

'What about a visit to the dungeon?'

'That's a bit of a problem,' the herbalist disclosed. 'They don't really feel like letting you in without knowing who your friend really is.'

'What do you mean?'

'We have never seen such a creature before. We can guess who he is, of course, but... we don't know what he's capable of. Besides, he seems very resistant to Ha'teng's persuasion.'

'I'm not at all surprised,' Eli muttered, and Temina just shook her head. 'If I tell you who he is... do you think they'll let me see him?'

'I'll do my best to convince them. I can promise you that much,' the herbalist assured her. It sounded sincere.

The girl took a deep breath and considered it carefully.

'All right,' she said finally. 'He is an elf. His name is Thairác. I hope that's enough for you to believe in my good faith.' She lowered her eyes with a resignation that was untypical for her. She needed to process this. Temina seemed to understand and gave her a moment to do so. 'I have heard that the Ha'ami have no warm feelings for this race,' Eli added.

69

'To put it mildly,' the herbalist admitted. 'We have no warm feelings towards any non-humans, but elves are earnestly hated by most Ha'ami.'

'Why?'

'Don't you know? We even count the time of our era from the Battle of the Jasmine Field.'

The girl just shook her head.

'You'll find the answer in the book Ha'akon sent you.' Temina took the volume in her hand and leafed through it, finally stopping at the relevant chapter. Here it is. *The Cursed Elven War*. Read it while you drink your herbs, and, in the meantime, I will go and talk to my brother.'

The golden age of Ha'ami continued uninterrupted amid the victories and glory of the indomitable warriors. Until the Year of Disgrace came. It was the hardest test for the brave Tribe, the greatest humiliation.

King Ha'rig, later called the Loser, had planned an expedition against the elves. The non-humans had ruled the Southern Continent long enough. It was time to end their presence and establish the power of the Ha'ami to the shores of the Sea.

He recruited vassals and neighbours, greedy for the famous treasures of the Green Kingdom. Thus was born the greatest army history had ever seen. Ha'rig was confident of the victory.

Yet his hopes were dashed. The foul elves put up a fierce resistance with sword and magic, led by the White Witch, may her name be forgotten forever.

After years of fighting, when the time came for the Final Clash, the honourless, cowardly rulers who had called themselves allies of the

Ha'ami fled in terror, leaving the proud tribe alone in the face of an enemy many times their numbers.

And so, they prepared for battle. The place they chose to challenge the non-humans was called the Jasmine Field. It stretched from the border of the elven kingdom to the Dragon Mountains in the west.

For seven days and seven nights, without sleep or rest, the brave Ha'ami battled the overwhelming forces of the enemy, the ground shaking beneath their sturdy feet. Finally, the scales of victory began to tip in their favour.

The filthy non-humans retreated deeper into the forest. Slowly at first, soon after in panic and fear, they began to flee. The loud horns of the Ha'ami trumpeted victory, a shout of triumph bursting from the thousands of throats of the brave warriors.

At that moment, the White Witch swooped down from the sky on her lizard-like monster. With her arrival came a wind so powerful it could have uprooted many a tree. Her ghostly voice rang out over the heads of the fearless Ha'ami. It carried a terrible curse that would bring them to their doom.

Suddenly, the sea rose from its shores and broke into the land as far as the Jasmine Field. A mighty wave hit the brave warriors with magical fury, sweeping them into its depths. The Ha'ami fought in vain against the water demons. King Ha'rig perished, the commanders perished, thousands of brothers perished... drowned in the depths of the foredoomed abyss.

Thus were born the Swamps of the Dead, where no man or beast dares tread, for they are forever guarded by legions of restless warriors who were denied a proper burial.

The bones of the fallen were not laid to rest in the Temple of the Ancestors, they were not given a place in the Fields of Glory, and their deaths forever shrouded our tribe in shame. Only a few warriors escaped with their lives to tell the tale. And when they had done their duty, they all threw themselves on their swords, unable to bear the disgrace they had suffered.

Only women and children were left in the Ha'ami lands, and the glory of our people had to be built anew.

All because of the curse of the White Witch, may her name be forever forgotten.

Eli put the book down lost in her thoughts. The White Witch.

She knew who this was, even though she had never heard the nickname before. The name was not forgotten.

Meindothel.

The legendary elven queen and the most powerful sorceress who ever walked the world. Even her own people were ambivalent about her. Her might was too great, her powers unsurpassed. And though she dedicated her life to defending and strengthening the Green Kingdom, the tragic events that ended her reign cast an unforgettable shadow over her character. Too many lives were lost forever.

However, the war with the Ha'ami itself held little place in elven history. It was just one of the many skirmishes that took place during the several hundred years of Meindothel's reign.

Eli could not recall a single song about the battle she had just read about. She would have to ask Simronil. Surely he had been there. He must remember.

The dungeon was in a darkness impenetrable to human eyes. But Tallen could see everything clearly. Bizarre creatures crawling around. Bugs, cockroaches, centipedes, spiders, rats... this small stone expanse with a few scattered clumps of straw seemed to be home to everything that shunned light. He was already used to their presence. He was getting to know their ways, their habits. He already knew how the cycle of life unfolded. Who was the prey, who was the predator. He could sense which creatures were excited by the scent of his blood and which were hiding in the nooks and crannies of the rocks at the slightest sound of movement. He felt neither disgust nor fear of the creatures of the dark. He knew that each of them had its place in the endless cycle of life and death.

It had been his world for the past few days. They thought they would crush him with their despicable methods. But elves have something these short-lived creatures cannot understand.

Elves have time. Lots of time.

Meditation allowed him to stave off hunger, pain and thirst, even as his physical body suffered.

Unexpectedly, a key clanked.

For the second time today, he thought. *Looks like someone's in a great hurry.*

He didn't move from his seat. No reason to make their task any easier.

The light of the torch penetrated the dungeon, piercing the darkness. He did not need to blink. His eyes adjusted instantly.

A dark silhouette he knew well by now appeared in the entrance. The torturer came towards him slowly. Tallen did not raise his eyes. This butcher was not worth it.

'Your little friend Eli has come to her senses,' he hissed overdramatically. 'She started talking.'

The figure paused a step away. The elf continued unresponsive, so his tormentor pulled the chain around his neck, forcing him to come closer.

'At least one of you shows some reason... *Thairác*! Perhaps it's time also for you to second your friend in need?'

His head was right in Tallen's face.

Thai rác; "I'm an idiot" in Elvish.

Ah, Eli, you couldn't have said it better... I hope you are holding on, you're in a good mood, he thought.

He measured the torturer's countenance with a loathing glance. Tallen noticed the bruises around his nose and purple circles under his eyes.

My little one... I hope this is a reminder of his encounter with you, elf laughed in his mind. With a movement so quick it was almost imperceptible, he aimed a headbutt at the same wounded spot on his tormentor's face. The powerful blow sent the dark-haired man flying backwards. He lost his balance and crouched for a moment. But not for long.

Ha'ami warrior sprang to his feet and pulled on the chain, knocking Tallen to the ground. He swung for a kick, but the elf was ready, in a defensive position. The torturer stepped back.

'I see you haven't had enough of our conversations.'

The man walked towards the dungeon door. 'Take him out!' he ordered the guards standing outside.

Elf knew what was coming. He was ready. He despised these pathetic creatures. They could not harm him in a way that would really hurt. Their efforts would be in vain. He would remain silent.

A terrible scream shattered her head. It took her a moment to realise it was coming from her own throat. She felt her body shake in a violent spasm. She gulped the air greedily with her mouth to save herself from drowning when she felt someone grab her by the shoulders and pull her out of the abyss.

'Eli!' a voice reached her.

The darkness before her eyes cleared and she saw two faces before her, as if woven from mist. The first was Temina, staring at her anxiously. The second was a masked sentry holding a torch behind the herbalist's back.

'Water...' the girl murmured, still feeling giddy.

'Do you want to drink?'

'Water everywhere...' she repeated, and only then did she realise she was no longer drowning. She was sitting on the bed. In a chamber. In the fortress. 'Y-yes...' she stammered. 'Drink.'

She felt the hands on her shoulders loosen. Temina turned back to the guard.

'It's just a bad dream. You can go,' she said. 'I will take care of her.'

As if through a glass wall, Eli heard a door slam and, after a moment, felt the cold surface of the mug in her hand. It wasn't a nightmare. She was *seeing* again. But this time Tallen wasn't there to help her recover her balance. As if in a delirium, she absorbed the life-giving liquid, pinching her hands to try and regain feeling in her body, to get her senses working again. As usual, whenever this happened, she remained suspended between different realities.

Eli was unable to control what the elves called the Gifts. For her, they were more like a curse. No one could explain where they came from. The Gift of Healing appeared at the least expected moments and not at all when she needed it most. On the other hand, it was only with Tallen's help that she was able to meditate and cut off her own sense of pain. He himself was a master at it and endured injuries with an unparalleled indifference.

The Gift of Seeing came regardless of Eli's will. She did not always understand what was happening. Sometimes she suspected she was seeing the past. Sometimes the future. And sometimes things that were happening in the present, but far away. The problem was that she was not just witnessing, she seemed to be physically transported to another reality. Her body and mind paid the price every time.

A moment ago, the girl was in the middle of the battle. She screamed in terror with the other warriors. Water rushed into her lungs as she was engulfed by the depths of the sea.

And unlike the scribe of the book, whoever they may have been, Eli knew now the truth of what had really happened to the Ha'ami army in the Jasmine Field.

Spark sensed the disturbance of the power, and his mind immediately drifted in that direction.

As he had expected, strong emotions made the Girl with No Name reach into the treasury of her magic. Even if she was unable to control it, the consequences could be far from trivial.

From what he read in her memory, the elves tried to teach her to control what they called the Gifts. However, they were not aware what power she really possesses, so their efforts were always doomed to failure. But this proud tribe was too swollen-headed to even attempt to understand the source of their defeat.

If only she had had a proper teacher... one like him. Someone who would guide her properly.

He felt tempted to try.

Chapter IV
Certain ladies' wine songs

DROPS OF SWEAT TRICKLED DOWN between his shoulder blades as he diligently scrubbed the black stones of the corridor floor. Most servants disliked this job, as it meant spending all day on their knees. Jor didn't mind it. At least he was alone and did not have to endure the presence of both the masters, whom he sincerely hated, and the other servants, whom he resented even more because they reminded him of his own fate. A slave without the right to wear a shirt. Even that had been taken away from him. Jor, lean and bony by nature, knew that without clothes he looked pitiful.

He came from the land of the Azzgoths, once a great realm, rich in minerals and other natural goods that the local people traded. Ships from all over the world arrived at their ports every day. His family had run their own salt pits for generations. It provided an income that allowed them to live a life of plenty, or better – until the Ha'ami raid. The lands of the Azzgoths were completely plundered. The tribute levied on the mines was so heavy that there was little left for the local population to live on. On top of that, every family had to sacrifice their youngest son and send him to serve the Ha'ami. That is how Jor found himself in this cursed place, scrubbing the floors under the boots of his enemies, half-naked and tattooed like an animal. The very first day he was herded here and forced into slave labour, he swore revenge.

Even now, as he scrubbed the floor, he hummed a war song in his own language, promising death and destruction to all enemies of Azzgoths'. Suddenly he heard a voice behind him asking him a question in his native tongue.

'Sorry to disturb you. Do you know the way to the stables?'

Jor turned abruptly. Before him stood a slight girl with a tawny complexion and curly brown hair similar to his own. Though she spoke to him in his language, she looked neither like a servant nor a kept woman. She was dressed in dark green foreign robes that bore no resemblance to Ha'ami clothing. The beautiful floral brooch that fastened her cloak to her neck shone from afar.

'I didn't mean to startle you.'

The girl raised her hand in a reassuring gesture as he sprang to his feet. He was slightly taller than her, but standing there half-naked, with a wet rag in his hand, he felt dwarfed. Jor looked around. They were alone. He took the cloth mask from his face.

'You didn't startle me–' he replied in the indifferent tone he had learnt in this place as the key to survival. '–my lady,' he added.

'That's a relief.' She gave him a smile. 'Do you happen to know how to get to the stables?'

'It's a bit far, my lady,' he replied hesitantly, not meeting her eyes.

'I knew I'd get lost in these corridors. Everything looks the same,' she sighed, more to herself than to him. 'Could you... I'm sorry, I see you're busy, but would you be so kind as to take me there?'

Jor looked around once more, a little confused as to how to respond to this request. For the first time in years someone had spoken to him in a way that didn't sound like an order. He dropped the rag.

'Of course, my lady,' he nodded, feigning indifference, still not looking at her.

'Thank you... What's your name?'

He was genuinely surprised that someone would ask him that.

'Jor,' he choked out in emotion.

'They call me Eli. And I'm no lady.'

He froze at these words. He did not know what to say. She just kept smiling, looking him straight in the eye. Jor put his mask back on and walked forward.

'I've only been here a short time, and it was only today that I was able to leave the chamber by myself for the first time, when Temina went to another meeting. I thought: great, they've finally let me out, at least for a while, so I'll go to the stables. But all the corridors here seem the same. Black. Almost windowless. I don't know how to find my way around. Well, I suppose if I stayed here longer, I would get used to it, but I hope there will be no need for that–'

The girl chattered on all the way, undeterred by his silence. Finally, they reached the door. He opened it and let her through. She hesitated.

'Jor, maybe you can just point me in the right direction, I'll find it somehow.' The girl looked down at his feet, clad only in sandals. 'I wouldn't want you to get cold.'

He waved his hand in the direction of the stables.

'Thanks for your help, Jor.' Eli put a hand on his shoulder. 'See you later!'

She turned and ran ahead.

He stood there confused. Who was this woman? Had she come from his land, since she knew his language? And most importantly, had she heard the words of the hateful song he was singing in the corridor? Would she keep it to herself?

The stablemaster looked at Eli as if she had been drugged with herbs when she told him why she had come. But when he heard that she had permission from Ha'akon himself, he showed her to a stall at the far end of the long shed. She asked him for water and fodder, which he gave her, but he chose not to accompany her. He just watched her from a distance with the utmost curiosity. He was not the only one. She noticed that all those present had stopped what they were doing and started watching her warily.

As she came within earshot of the stable, a warning, familiar snort sounded.

'Easy, horsie, it's only me!' she called cheerfully.

Horsie?! An indignant voice rang in her head.

We have to keep up appearances, the girl replied inwardly.

Eli put down the buckets, pushed open the stable door and hugged his neck, burying her face in his soft mane.

I've missed you so, Simronil!

Me too! As usual, their consciousnesses merged directly, without the need for spoken words. She loved this wonderful feeling of union with a magical being.

I brought you water and food– She ran to get the buckets. *–I'm so sorry they treated you like this. I heard they starved you...*

Before dipping his muzzle into the bucket, he nudged her face with his nose.

Bruises, he remarked.

It's nothing. Eli stroked him in response. *My opponent looks worse.*

He drank for a long time, until the water was gone. Then he turned to the fodder. She waited patiently for her mount to finish eating. Finally, when he was full, she could share her troubled thoughts with him.

I don't know what's happening to Tallen. Apart from the fact that he's in the dungeon...

Yes, he is. In there. Simronil stamped his hoof on the ground.

Really? And you can hear him?

Yes.

And you're only telling me this now?

Hungry.

Well, yeah... She sometimes forgot that even magical creatures could put very ordinary needs first. *What have you learned?*

More water, he just snorted. Knowing there was no point in arguing with him, she hurried to get another bucket. Outside, Eli noticed that all the grooms were still anxiously waiting to see what would happen next.

'Calm down, he hasn't devoured me yet!' she shouted in their direction. She returned as quickly as she could with water. Only when he had finished gulping greedily did he speak again.

Dirty. Stinky. Elf counts rats. Wounded.

I knew this couldn't be good... Now she was really worried. *Can you give him a message? Tell him I'm all right, that I'm going to get us out of here, and that I'll do my best to see him later today.*

Simronil whinnied softly. Eli waited for him to communicate with Tallen. Finally, a voice rang in her head again.

The elf says Eli should run away.

I'm not running anywhere. I'm going to get us out of here. You'll see.

He nudged her with his muzzle again.

Sure thing.

She tried to question Tallen further about their treatment of him, but to no avail. The elf wouldn't reveal anything more. Finally giving up, Eli turned to grooming her mount. As she carefully combed his glossy coat, she recounted the events of the past few days.

Oh, wait. I was going to ask you something. Did you take part in the battle of the Jasmine Field? I don't know what name it bears among the elves... but that's where they clashed with the Ha'ami.

The Meadows of the Drowned, he acknowledged.

Yes... I think that's what they call them today in the Green Kingdom. Have you been there?

No. My Gorgeous was riding Sheen at the time, he replied with slight resentment.

My Gorgeous. That was what Simronil had called Meindothel, the only person he had allowed to ride him before Eli.

Sheen? she asked, puzzled. She didn't know that the elf queen had a second mount.

Yes, Sheen. The Great Lizard.

Are you telling me that a dragoness agreed to serve the sorceress?

Not any dragoness. Sheen, he replied simply. *And it was not service. Sisterhood.*

She smiled under her breath.

Right you are. Sisterhood it is then. She stroked his back for a moment in silence. *Because of this battle, the Ha'ami hate the elves.*

They believe that Meindothel magically lifted the sea from its shores to bring them defeat when she could not win in the field.

Not magic. Great water... he snorted.

Yes, I saw it... I dreamt about it yesterday.

A mountain of fire. The Hundredfold Wave.

She was trying to save them, wasn't she? Meindothel.

Yes, both of them tried. Great Lizard, great magic.

And even that wasn't enough... that underwater volcano must have been powerful...

He whinnied softly in confirmation.

My Gorgeous grieved. Sheen grieved. The great lizard went away. Never came back.

'Any news from the capital?' Ha'akon asked. He recognised the apparent nonchalance with which his friend waited for the sentry to close the door behind him. In reality, the commander was seething inside, but only someone who knew him so well could see it.

'Yes,' he finally confirmed. 'The falcon is back.' He paused, presumably to increase the impact of his words.

'And?'

'The king has decided to send a search and kill force to the Azzgoth lands. He intends to turn the area into another Ha'ami province,' he announced coolly.

Ha'akon raised his eyebrows in surprise. A pacifying expedition. It had been a long time since he had heard that obtuse phrase in their language, which in practice meant the slaughter of all who resisted.

'Who did he put in charge?'

'Ha'gard. That is the fulfilment of that louse's greatest desires.'

'Yes... no doubt he will put his heart into it.'

'The King has also officially confirmed that he will appoint him the Governor of the land if he manages to regain control of it,' Ha'teng ended his report.

'He will manage,' Ha'akon confirmed grimly. 'Even if he has to rule the wastelands.'

'Yes... I don't think Ha'gard will try to negotiate with the Azzgoths. Rather, he will slaughter them all before they can open their mouths,' the commander agreed.

They were silent for a moment, absorbing the news. Ha'gard was their peer. They had been on more than one expedition together. But even the fiercest warriors stayed away from him; they considered him a scoundrel without honour. He had no respect for anyone or anything, including his comrades. For years, the king had restricted his inclinations, knowing that the other commanders resented him. Finally, he decided to unleash the beast. Ha'akon knew that this meant the inevitable massacre of anyone who stood in the way of the demonic chief's feral troops.

'I suppose they will soon order all the fortresses to send support?' The ruler finally said.

Ha'teng confirmed with a nod.

'Probably by the end of winter.'

'It will not solve our supply problem.' The governor rubbed his forehead and changed the subject. He needed time to absorb the news. The land of the Azzgoths will not recover quickly under the boot of that butcher.

'Has our master cook stewed a plan?' asked his friend. As always, Ha'akon ignored the tone of his remarks and focused on the content.

'Yes.' He gestured with his head to the maps spread out on the table. 'He suggests we open negotiations with the dwarves.'

Ha'teng's face took on an expression of infinite contempt.

'A solution worthy of the nitwit he is,' he began, but when he realised that the ruler did not necessarily share his opinion, he turned serious. 'We should avoid this desperate step at all cost. The king will interpret it as treason. Many Ha'ami will see it that way too.'

'We need to keep all our options open. Especially when the spectre of a long war looms on the horizon,' the governor replied after some thought.

'It will not take that long. Ha'gard will want to get his paw on the prize as soon as possible.'

'You remember the lands of the Azzgoths, don't you, *koru*,' Ha'akon replied, shaking his head. 'The impassable hills, the forests, the many rivers, the hidden valleys, the desert... that tribe has already turned into brigands, ready to ambush us in dark corners. It would be better to negotiate with them.'

'To negotiate? You know very well that war is the only option in keeping with Ha'ami's honour,' his friend replied with a frown.

'Yes. War. But no one will meet us there on the open field.'

Ha'akon sighed in his mind. He considered how much of his true thoughts he could share with his friend and advisor. Finally, he decided on a different strategy. 'Let's sit down,' he suggested. 'This requires a longer discussion...'

Ha'teng eagerly accepted.

The ruler knew that they did not always have to agree. But he respected his friend enough to at least listen to him.

86

Eli spent the whole day with Simronil. Finally, late in the afternoon, Temina showed up.

'I was told I could find you here. I see that you have taken to heart my words that you don't have to leave this place if you don't want to. I was worried that you might have fainted again.'

'I feel quite well now. I've just been lost track of time,' Eli explained as she stroked her faithful friend goodbye.

Together with the herbalist they left the stables and walked back the way they had come. Then Temina led her along the walls of the castle. Eli was able to enjoy the fresh air of the quiet day.

'Congratulations,' remarked the governor's sister. 'You have been tentatively recognised as an official *Ta'uma*.'

'Really? That made me feel a head taller.'

'Laugh all you want, but it's a good step forward for your cause. Granted, it still has to be approved by the full Council of Sisters and Brothers, but you can feel a little more at ease now.'

At ease. Eli wasn't at ease at all. She seemed as far from it as when she woke up in the fortress that first night.

'The Council of Sisters and Brothers? How many members does it have? What do they do?' The girl asked hesitantly. She had heard the name many times.

'More specifically, the Council of First Sisters and Brothers. Each governor of a province appoints four warriors to the council, and his mother her four trusted companions. They administer the various spheres of Ha'ami life, and it is up to them, by law and tradition, to make the most important decisions.'

'Aha. I didn't know I was so important that they had to discuss my fate,' Eli remarked with a wince. 'Or are they just bored during winter?'

'But my dear Tiger's Bane!' Temina laughed. 'Of course, you're very important, especially now that you've been accepted as the *Ta'uma*.'

'Tentatively,' the girl corrected.

'Nevertheless, the First Brothers would like to welcome you to the castle in the proper manner and invite you to dine with them this evening.'

'News of the day...' she muttered. 'I'm in for the most enchanting evening of my life.'

'I can see you are elated.' Temina measured her with playful eyes. 'Come, tell me what has got under your skin so much.'

She took Eli's arm.

'I'm worried about my friend in the dungeons. Now that I know how much the Ha'ami hate elves.'

She hesitated. After coming to her senses the night before, she told the herbalist the truth about her Gift of Sight. She also revealed the contents of her nightmare. Now they both knew what had happened that day.

'And yet there is no reason for it.'

The lord's sister did not take up the subject.

'Did... did you tell Ha'akon what I saw yesterday?'

'Yes, Eli, I spoke to him about it just as we agreed.'

'And?' the girl looked at her expectantly. 'Shouldn't all the Ha'ami know? Wouldn't it change their attitudes?'

'My dear...' Temina stopped, turned to her and looked her in the eyes. 'It was only a dream. Surely, we cannot, on this basis, question the story of what happened hundreds of years ago, as has been recorded by the chroniclers of our people. A story known to every child here.'

Eli lowered her head. How naive she was.

'What do you think they will do to him?' she asked cautiously.

'Well, as far as I know, the court meets in ten days and will hear all current cases, including his.' Temina hesitated. 'I wouldn't count on any leniency. Our laws are extremely harsh on servants and non-humans. That's why Ha'akon was so insistent in convincing them to recognise you as of noble birth.'

'Oh, right, I'm facing judgement too...' She waved her hand. 'Never mind that, what about my friend?'

'Hmm... I would prepare myself for the worst. Corporal punishment, years in the dungeon, even death... anything is possible.'

'As for you, as a *Ta'uma*, you won't have to wait for the day of judgement. They'll probably give you some small penance; I was usually the one scrubbing the stables, cleaning the weapons, carrying water–'

Eli didn't listen. She was wondering what she could do to help Tallen. The herbalist seemed aware of her thoughts, or simply thought the girl was afraid of her impending punishment. She fell silent.

The sun was slowly disappearing from the sky, giving it a ruddy glow. They had now descended the steps of the cloister and almost bumped into a man hurrying somewhere. It was the same elderly warrior with a wolf tattoo on his arm Eli had seen in the square giving instructions to the young. His hair, streaked with grey, was dishevelled and his expression was somewhat troubled.

'Ha'min!' Temina greeted him warmly. 'How good to see you.'

They embraced like close friends. 'Eli, allow me to introduce the most distinguished member of the Council of First Brothers, Ha'min, the Guardian of the Young, who is responsible for the training of all warriors in the Stone Nest.'

'Most distinguished... You are having a laugh at me as usual.' Abashed, he looked at her with slight disapproval. 'If your brother could hear you–'

'–he would certainly agree. As would many girls of our city, spoiled by your gifts, I am sure.' She patted him confidentially on the shoulder, embarrassing him even more.

'It is an honour to meet you.' Eli bowed her head slightly, unsure of what an official Ha'ami greeting should look like. Fortunately, that much seemed to be enough in the current situation.

Ha'min returned the gesture by looking carefully into her eyes. He had a clear, honest gaze, and although his face was already ploughed with the furrows of years of experience, there was a strength in it that commanded respect.

'I heard about your, um, duel... He battered you, huh?' His voice was very deep, almost bass.

'Wasn't that bad.' She shrugged.

'Yeah, right... eh, littlun, how old can you be anyway? Fifteen?' He looked her over from head to toe.

She blushed. Everyone always thought she was much younger than she actually was.

'Well over twenty,' she grunted.

'No way! I would never have guessed. You're too short to be over anything! Well, since you're so grown up, it's time to get some sense. I'm in a hurry, but I hope, my littlun, that with the help of this mischief lady here, you'll be able to spruce yourself up soon. Until then.'

He gave them a wave and marched with a brisk stride towards the square, where the young warriors were already gathering.

'The man's a straight arrow,' Temina whispered, although the phrase *quirky but nice* came to Eli's mind instead. 'Look,' the herbalist whispered. 'The evening training is about to begin, would you like to come and have a look, bother them a bit?'

Eli thought it might help to take her mind off all her problems for a while. They sat on the stands surrounding the training ground. Temina called out for the servant to bring them blankets.

'No need to freeze your bottom,' she chuckled merrily. 'We could use some more mulled wine,' she added to the masked servant. He bowed slightly and left, returning immediately with two smoky cups of the aromatic drink.

The courtyard filled with young warriors who had begun training under Ha'min's command.

The conversation about possible directions for potential expeditions absorbed the two friends for a long time and let them take a momentary break from reality.

'Think about it, *koru*,' Ha'teng said enthusiastically. 'Let Ha'gard rule over that wasteland. We should focus on something far greater. Something that will truly make history! I believe the appearance of the elf is a sign. It is time to avenge the past, to wipe out the stain on Ha'ami's honour, to exterminate the non-humans and to gain permanent access to the sea from the south. In this way, we will create an empire that no one can challenge.

'That elf...' Ha'akon said. 'Have you found out what he's doing here?'

'Not yet,' he replied, not hiding his disappointment. 'It's downright impossible. I'm beginning to think it might be magic,' he concluded.

Ha'akon walked over to the window and looked out into the courtyard where the training was taking place. He noticed his sister and *Ta'uma* watching the exercises from a bench in the courtyard.

'So we're back at the same point. Which of the two do we have a better chance of getting information from?' he said finally. 'I have a hunch about this girl–' he started, but his friend cut him off.

'A hunch?' the commander asked in a tone that made the ruler correct his words.

'Well, we shall find out in time. Perhaps dinner tonight will clear things up. We have a lot to think about, *koru*.' A mischievous thought struck Ha'akon. 'What do you say we stretch our bones and teach these *namio* a lesson? Ha'min is far too gentle with them.'

Ha'teng quickly finished his wine.

'This may be the best thing that has happened to me today,' he laughed as they walked out together.

'They are all *namios*, meaning apprentices before initiation. That's why they don't have tattoos,' Temina explained as she emptied her cup. She nodded for the servant to bring her another. 'Be swift, I'm thirsty!' she called.

'At what age do they take the initiation?' Eli inquired as she slowly sipped her drink. She was contemplating the dinner with the First Brothers that awaited her.

'They start at sixteen. If they fail to kill an animal, they must try again the following year. And the year after that. And so on for five years...'

'And then what? If they fail?' She was curious.

Temina just ran her finger down her throat and stuck out her tongue.

'You kill them?!' Eli was outraged.

'Of course, not... they commit honourable suicide themselves. They never come back. Oh, here's my wine. At last. What took you so long?'

The servant just bowed in silence.

'Suicide does sound so much better,' muttered Eli, but the herbalist seemed to ignore her as she focused all her attention on the *namios*.

As Temina emptied more cups of the warming drink, her comments about the young men grew louder and more frivolous, drawing disapproving looks from Ha'min. But nothing could stop her. Soon she was bluntly advising Eli which *namio* she should spend the night with and in which position.

'Temina!' Eli turned crimson. 'They might think you're serious.'

'As serious as I can be!' the herbalist confirmed emphatically. 'Take advantage of being the only girl of high lineage in a castle full of lustful warriors! You can choose whomever you like. Believe me, there will be no shortage of willing men. This one, look how firm his buttocks are!'

'Temina!'

'Oh, my dear, what a lovely blush! Another lesson about Ha'ami. We are open to all kinds of pleasures,' the herbalist said. 'The only thing you need to be aware of is that many warriors value their relationships with their brothers in arms above all else. They see it as the highest form of soul kinship. We call it *koru-koinen*. Bonded brothers. They swear lifelong loyalty to each other.' She nodded again for the servant to pour her more wine.

'Women and men do not have such a bond in your people?' Eli was puzzled. 'What about children?'

'Yes, I know, the couples of other peoples are often mated for life to have offspring, and stay together for a long time, even a lifetime. What a burden! For the Ha'ami, our tribe is our family. We raise our children together and do not commit ourselves to one person forever. And it's up to each of the gals to decide when we want to have children.'

'Hmm, yes, and the boys are named after their mothers...' Eli nodded. 'What if a woman has a second son?'

'After giving birth to her first son, we do not have another.'

'Do you mean women stop... interacting with men?'

Temina smiled playfully.

'Oh, that would be too terrible a solution.' She began to rummage through her bulky bag and after a moment pulled out a vial of purple potion. 'We call it *norush*. It gives us complete control over our fertility. You only need a few drops once a day. All the Ha'ami women who just feel like having fun take it. We also give it to the kept women to prevent unwanted trouble. You know... the purity of the race.' She handed the vial to Eli. 'Just in case you ever need it.'

She winked knowingly at the girl, causing another flush to appear on her face and neck.

'Yeah, um, I doubt it.'

'You never know,' Temina laughed.

Eli grunted slightly and slipped the bottle back into Temina's bag.

'Yeah... that explains everything, but what... what about feelings? I mean, sometimes someone has to... fall in love?' she stammered.

'It happens. Like in the case of Ha'akon and Layla. They were besotted with each other. But well, nothing lasts forever.'

'Ha'akon and Layla?'

She couldn't imagine the serious and strict lord of the castle being head over heels in love.

Temina suddenly frowned. For a moment, they both stared at the young warriors.

'All right,' the herbalist continued in a low voice. 'I will tell you. This story has become a legend. I'm sure you'll hear it more than once, there's no shortage of gossip around here. Most of what they say is complete absurd.'

She fell silent again, sipping the brew from her mug.

'And what is the truth?' Eli pressed her curiously.

'I'll tell you as much as I know.'

'So?' the girl urged her again. It was probably the wine that had made her so keen.

'Layla was our childhood friend, our mothers also were best friends and we were inseparable: me, Layla and Ha'akon, until my brother had to move to the Upper Castle.'

'How old was he then?'

'Ten. As time went on, these two also shared a more romantic bond... they were young, naïve and very much smitten with each other. She was the whole world to Ha'akon.'

'Really?' Eli asked, her face flushing. She loved stories like that.

'Yes, yes.' Temina waved her hand. 'Unfortunately, when they were both seventeen, Layla was kidnapped by mountain bandits who had somehow ventured into our territory. An expedition was sent to find her, but the warriors returned with nothing. Only Ha'akon continued the search on his own. After many months, he returned. Without Layla. But with a dragon's head, which he dragged behind him with ropes made of dragon's entrails. I know, disgusting.' She grimaced.

Eli opened her mouth in astonishment.

'Really?'

'Uh-huh. It took us a long time to get the details out of him, and even now he won't say a word about it. What is known is that the monster killed her and Ha'akon slayed it in retaliation. He also got to the mountain men and slaughtered them all, every last one of them. That's pretty much it, as far as the facts go. Everything else you hear is balderdash.'

Eli listened to the story with bated breath. She couldn't decide which question to start with.

'What a tragic tale! What was she like... Layla?'

Temina's smile was absent, as if she was looking back at a distant memory. She lowered her voice even more.

'Strong. Determined. Independent. Even for a Ha'ami. I miss her very much. Together we broke more than one rule, served more than one punishment and always covered for each other. I have never had a closer friend.' For the first time Temina sounded melancholic. 'The fact that she fell in love with Ha'akon made me extremely happy. They were the two people closest to me. Her passing broke more than one heart...'

'I am so sorry...'

Eli impulsively placed a hand on her companion's shoulder.

'Ha'akon at least had his revenge, I was left here waiting for his return for months. He came back without her, but he gained fame, power, admiration...'

'Do you think he forgot her too easily?'

She wondered where the bitterness in the herbalist's voice was coming from.

Temina shook her head.

'On the contrary. Despite what I told you about Ha'ami, my brother is an exception. He hasn't chosen another woman since, and believe me, there isn't a girl in our lands who wouldn't pine for him.'

'Really?'

'Oh, don't get me wrong, he's no monk, no way,' Temina laughed. 'He's got quite a bunch of kept women. But he's never looked at a woman of his own birth.'

'What a story. It appears the Ha'ami have feelings,' Eli sighed as she watched the heavily breathing *namios*, clearly tired from their training.

'A far-fetched conclusion,' the herbalist laughed. She returned to her cheerful tone. 'I can see that you are moved by such tales.'

'In fact, you could say I am a bit naive,' Eli admitted, deep in thought. She felt that the wine and the stories had made her a little melancholic. 'I always hope that every scoundrel can summon a bit of heart. Even Ha'teng!'

'My dear, that is truly unimaginable! You'd rather ride the Pegasus than see an ounce of human emotion in that rapscallion.'

Suddenly, the door to one of the buildings opened and Ha'akon stepped into the yard with Ha'teng.

'You summoned him!' Temina laughed remarkably loud. The men cast fleeting, slightly surprised glances at them.

The lord's personal guards followed at a steady pace, and the herbalist, once again in the mood for a folly, did not fail to throw a few shameless remarks in their direction. None responded to her shouts.

The young warriors paused to greet the commanders with a group cheer.

'A spectacle is about to begin,' Temina nudged her.

'A spectacle?'

'Wait, you'll see,' she said, summoning the servant once more with her gaze.

'I've had enough.' Eli put down her cup. 'I'd better be less spirited when I go to that dinner.'

'You'd better get numb before you go there.' The herbalist giggled and ordered both cups to be filled.

Meanwhile, events in the courtyard were gathering pace. Ha'akon seemed displeased. He exchanged a few words with Ha'min, then all three First Brothers took off their cloaks and caftans and marched into the practice grounds. Eli could now admire Ha'ami's famous tattoos (and the torsos that bore them) in all their glory.

Ha'min gave the order. The *namios* divided into groups of five. Each of the First Brothers lined up in a defensive position. She didn't know what to focus on. Events were unfolding very quickly. Ha'akon shouted 'Attack!' Like young wolves circling a bear, the young warriors took off.

Eli focused her attention on the Governor. Five *namios* armed with wooden clubs attacked him at once. Ha'akon blocked the first blow using his forearm like a shield, grabbed the attacker's weapon, twisted it, forced the young warrior to bend over and delivered a powerful knee kick to his face. Blood gushed from the boy's shattered nose, staining the snow red. Using the momentum of the blow, the ruler grabbed the club and swung it at the next *namio*. This one managed to dodge so that the wood hit him sideways instead of straight in the chest, but he was instantly impaled with his chin on Ha'akon's left fist. The blow knocked him backwards.

The three remaining opponents attacked the commander from different directions, but they were too slow. One received a blow to the crotch, another a crushing one to the temple. The fifth warrior, although he looked the youngest, resisted the longest. He crossed his weapon fiercely with Ha'akon and shielded himself for a long time from the storm of hardwood blows. He was finally forced to surrender when an unusually swift swipe aimed at his legs knocked him off balance, and the next blow landed on his neck, sending him to the ground.

The Governor threw away the splinters of the stick he had broken on the last opponent. He looked at the next group of *namios*. 'Attack,' he ordered. Eli looked around the square. Ha'teng and Ha'min were also triumphing over their adversaries. The defeated and wounded warriors were retreating from the battlefield. Some lay still. After a while, the carnage was over. Youth had to yield to experience.

The three First Brothers stood alone in the square, the snowflakes swirling in the darkness. Temina began to whistle and shout, but they ignored her.

Eli watched as Ha'teng approached the ruler to exchange remarks about the battle. Ha'akon said something in response and they both laughed out loud. It was the first time she had seen these serious men burst into carefree glee. For a moment it looked like they were *namios* again, teasing each other after a training session. But they quickly turned serious.

'If you want to walk of the square, you can only walk on your own. There will be no help getting up,' Ha'akon's loud voice rang out. 'Penalty night watch for all, and stall cleaning tomorrow,' he announced. One of his guards handed him a caftan, another a cloak.

'Come, let's go and get you ready for the diner with these heroes of the evening.' The herbalist pulled her by the hand.

'You were right, it was a spectacle,' Eli whispered to her once they were in the corridor leading to their chamber. 'I pity those *namios*... what's it all for?'

'I'm sure my brother had his reasons. Probably more than one, knowing him as I do...' Temina giggled and hiccupped loudly.

'Why don't you spend the night in my chamber?' Eli asked, wondering if the herbalist, who was actually leaning on her with all her weight, should travel by sedan chair or rather by a stretcher.

'That was my intention. As I understand it, you will spend the night in a different, more interesting way.' She laughed again.

'What do you mean?'

'Ah, I'm not allowed to say anything, my dear, nothing at all... Just let me pick out a nice dress for you and help you with your hair.'

'How about going to rest instead of helping me? I don't think I need a fancy outfit today.'

Eli became upset again. The company of the cheerful Temina was a temporary respite from the problems that would not go away. Real and pressing, they filled her head. On top of that, she was forced to spend the evening with those who were the cause of all her misfortunes.

Ha'teng looked at the girl as she followed Anni into the living room.

'You were supposed to help her get dressed.' He turned to the maid with displeasure. She shrank back as if he had hit her with a whip.

'It's not her fault,' *Ta'uma* spoke up, raising her chin proudly. 'I can take care of myself.'

'Your appearance is no proof of that.' He glanced at her hair, which, though pinned up, still looked as if a whirlwind had combed through it.

'Well, I didn't know I'd be dealing with such a sophisticated company today,' she replied simply. 'However, I now understand that this will not be a modest evening.' She looked around the chamber ostentatiously.

Ha'teng's quarters were undoubtedly the best equipped in the entire Stone Nest. At least he was convinced of that. There was no shortage of precious furniture, ornate paintings and carvings, all made by the greatest masters, with the finest materials. He had taken part in so many victorious campaigns in his life that he had easily amassed a considerable fortune, which he liked to spend on making his surroundings more pleasing to the eye. He also had no qualms about taking whatever he liked for his collection from the castles and noble houses he entered after victorious battles.

He dismissed Anni with a wave of his hand. There were enough servants for the dinner. In addition, tradition dictated that only men were at the service on such occasions. Immediately one of them appeared with a goblet of wine, which he handed to *Ta'uma*. She accepted it, but did not drink.

'An impressive collection,' she remarked, still looking around at all the objects displayed in the chamber. 'Each of them must have an interesting story.'

Before he had time to reply, Ha'sani came in with Ha'min.

'Here is the famous *Ta'uma*,' the young advisor announced with vigour. 'After you bested this brave warrior, I assumed you were at least two heads taller than him.'

'A stroke of luck in the heat of combat,' she replied in a polite tone that Ha'teng heard for the first time. He was surprised that she did not take the opportunity to mock him in public.

'Hello, littlun.' Ha'min hugged her affectionately. As usual, he played the role of a good uncle brilliantly, the host thought. 'What about that sassy lady, Temina, who entertained us today with a display of her liquor-laced eloquence? Did she make it to bed on her own two feet?'

The girl smiled shyly. She handed him the wine she was still holding, as if hesitating what to do with it.

'Yes, she's sleeping soundly.'

'How else... tell her I'll give her a piece of my mind when I see her.'

'Whose delicate sensibilities has Temina offended this time?' Ha'sani interjected, taking the cup from Ha'min.

'Whoever triggered her tongue, I suppose,' replied Ha'akon, who had just appeared in the doorway. 'Has she managed to climb into her sedan chair?'

'She has retired to the chamber where you placed me,' the girl replied in the same gentle tone.

The conversation bored Ha'teng. Fortunately, Ha'aki arrived just then, and after the final introductions and greetings, they were able to proceed to the dining room.

Eli arrived at the supper with a firm decision not to speak unless spoken to, but she quickly realised that this would be impossible. All attention was focused on her. Temina, in between chuckles, had earlier lectured her on numerous Ha'ami traditions, which she should supposedly know. The girl was sure she had not even memorised half of these instructions, which she struggled to understand from the herbalist's rambling speech.

But lo and behold, she found herself in a room with the five men who held the highest office in the fortress known as the Stone Nest. From a distance, the First Brothers looked like true siblings. All dark-haired, tall, blue-eyed and clean-shaven. As if that weren't enough, they were dressed identically in black trousers and sleeveless blue caftans, revealing the tattoos of once-slaughtered beasts.

Up close, however, she could see the differences.

Ha'teng's robes, although of the same colours as the others, were made of the finest cloth and decorated with beautiful embroidery. Their owner had his hair anointed with oils until it shone in the evening light of the chamber.

Ha'min's hair was dishevelled, as if he had just come from the battlefield. His clothes, too, were worn and did not look fresh.

Ha'sani was easily distinguishable because of his shorter hair. In style, he most resembled Ha'akon. They both dressed simply and neatly, without unnecessary ornamentation. What set them apart was their tattoos. The young counsellor's arm was adorned with the image of a puma.

And finally, Ha'aki, with a crocodile etched on his left shoulder. Eli met him for the first time. He greeted her with a stern look and hard eyes. He was older than the lord of the castle, but younger than Ha'min, spoke little and scanned his surroundings grimly. His clothes seemed to fit him perfectly, but the warrior occasionally corrected invisible creases.

Eli was forced by Temina to wear a sapphire-coloured dress to match the elegant setting. She had no desire to do so, for she did not wish to be part of this world.

They were now seated in low chairs, served by half-naked servants who were enslaved to these people, if not by force, then by poverty. A small table was set for each guest to eat and a bowl of water to wash their hands. As expected, all the food was eaten with the fingers.

Ha'akon made the toast everyone had been waiting for.

'May your time in the Stone Nest be one of peace and friendship, *Ta'uma.*'

'May my presence bring prosperity to your doorstep,' Eli replied in Ha'ami with the formula the herbalist had taught her.

Those gathered nodded in acknowledgement and raised their goblets. Each guest then passed the vessel to the person sitting to the right. By a stroke of luck, she was seated between Ha'min and Ha'teng. She was surprised to find that the goblet she had received was almost full, as if her predecessor had not drunk at all.

'Well, bottoms up!' The older warrior encouraged her.

'How did you enjoy today's exercise?' her host asked her as she obediently emptied the goblet.

'I was surprised you took part,' she replied. 'Is that standard practice?'

'No,' the Guardian of the Young replied. 'First Brothers do not usually duel with those before initiation.'

'They were due for a lesson,' her other companion interjected mockingly. 'Winter began to linger in their guts.'

'I heard you caused a bit of carnage in the yard,' Ha'sani added.

'That was not too difficult,' Ha'teng replied sarcastically with his usual smile.

'The *namios* were just surprised.' Ha'min tried to defend his charges.

'In battle one must think quickly.' Ha'akon cut him off.

'That's right.' Eli interrupted, looking at the bottom of her empty goblet. At last, not knowing what to do with it, she handed it to the right and, seeing this, the host nodded to the servants to start topping up the wine. 'But in battle,' she continued, 'you attack the enemy and you are, so to speak, prepared for the unpredictable. It's another thing to raise your hand against a leader you respect. It's a bit like suddenly being told to fight your own father...' She bit her tongue, realising the comparison wouldn't work with Ha'ami and sighed, feeling that she had gotten herself into a mess. 'I mean... I just wanted to say that I wouldn't judge them so harshly.'

Ha'min looked at her gratefully.

'Words of wisdom, Eli. Down to the bottom!' He handed her his goblet and she emptied it to the last drop, then placed it completely empty in front of Ha'teng.

'Wine!' he ordered again.

'When I came here, I noticed that several *namios* were still kneeling in the square.' Ha'sani changed the subject. 'Some punishment?'

The Guardian of the Young nodded.

'They helped to revive and carry out their comrades.'

'And for that they have to kneel in the cold?'

More to her surprise, another full cup was handed to Eli. She decided to wait for the meal. Her head was already beginning to buzz.

'The order was clear. No help getting up,' Ha'akon replied. She bit her tongue, remembering her earlier decision to keep her temper.

At last, the dinner plates were brought in. The hot dishes filled the room with a spicy aroma. The servants put the trays on small tables among the guests and then began to place the portions on individual plates.

Eli looked worriedly at what she had been served. Temina told her that she should eat everything she was given, otherwise it would be an insult to the host and a suggestion that he was trying to poison a guest. The Ha'ami seemed obsessed with this. She should check the book she had been given to see if they had a history of disposing of inconvenient people in this way.

Not only was her portion huge, but it consisted mostly of all kinds of meat. She noticed that both Ha'akon and Ha'teng were watching her intently.

Sorry, dear animal, but you're dead and I'm trying to save an elf, she thought and slowly took a red chunk between her fingers, gingerly touching the slimy surface dripping with oil. She managed to overcome her disgust, put it in her mouth and slowly started to chew. Despite feeling slightly nauseous, she swallowed and immediately, this time of her own free will, poured the entire cup of wine down her throat.

'Do you like it?' Ha'teng asked, evidently amused.

'Yes, it is delicious,' she said nonchalantly, looking him straight in the eye. Fortunately, the conversation was going on without her at that moment. She did not listen to much, concentrating hard on emptying her plate. She was also beginning to feel the effects of the liquor she had consumed; it was making her so dizzy that she wasn't sure she could stand on her feet if required.

'What an extraordinary trinket,' Ha'min said, pointing to her bracelet.

'Thank you,' she replied, struggling to swallow another piece of meat.

'May I see it?' Ha'teng asked unexpectedly. She set her plate aside, washed her hand, wiped it on the cloth that hung over the back of her chair and held her wrist out to him. He took it very gently and began to turn it over, looking at the bracelet. His fingers were as cool as a mountain stream in winter.

'I would like to examine it more closely. May I?' He tried to pull the piece off.

'You won't be able to do it.' she explained to his evident surprise. 'It's a dwarven handcraft. You'd have to cut off my arm to get it, although–' she tilted her head playfully '–that probably wouldn't be a problem for you.' She reached down to her forearm and removed the bracelet. 'It only listens to its owner.'

'Elven friends, dwarven adornments... well, you're full of surprises, *Ta'uma*,' Ha'teng murmured, turning the ornament in his fingers with the face of a connoisseur. 'These marks on the inside... I can't read them.'

'These are dwarven runes,' she explained, taking a good swig from the goblet Ha'min had handed her. She was feeling more and more out of it.

'Do you know what they mean?'

'They're not that difficult.' She shrugged and read aloud the dwarven language, then returned to the common. 'In free translation: *Beware of straight paths. They make it more likely to fall and bruise your arse. As sure as my name is Zak.*'

She smiled at the memory of an old friend.

'Zak?' Ha'sani interrupted unexpectedly. Only then did she realise that all the attention of those gathered was focused on her. 'As-sure-as-my-name's-Zak? Zak the Forkbeard?'

'Oh, I know, I have told him so many times that he needs a better nickname: Zak the Magnificent or Zak the Noble, but he just laughed me off. He kept repeating that he never paid any attention to such trivialities.' She waved her hand, which had become strangely soft, as if boneless.

'Are you saying you know him?' Ha'sani did not back down.

'Yes,' she replied, as if he had asked the most obvious thing under the sun. Seeing the stares of everyone in the chamber, however, she reminded herself that perhaps she should be a little more careful and certainly cut off the wine.

Ha'teng ran his fingers over the surface of the bracelet. Like a mirror. It was a simple ornament, but of extraordinary quality. The precision and care of the workmanship amazed even his finicky eye.

Reluctantly, he handed it to *Ta'uma*, who put it back on in a mild dismay. All because of Ha'sani. The cursed dilettante. Ha'teng had finally managed to get some interesting information out of her, and that snot must have frightened her with his enthusiasm. He almost wet his pants from excitement at the sound of the dwarf's name. And she shut up immediately. From the beginning, Ha'min went out of his way to get the girl completely drunk, which helped a lot that evening. Ha'teng wasn't sure what was driving his companion's actions until he smelled the warming herbs in her cup. The cunning fox must have been sprinkling them discreetly into her drink, knowing what was in store for her later. Well, it turned out to be very useful. But now it was all for nothing. Silently, she picked up her plate and went back to nibbling at her food.

The fool Ha'sani still hoped to learn something.

'How do you know Zak?'

'An old story...'

'Where did you meet him?'

'Far from here...'

She answered all her questions perfunctorily and without enthusiasm.

Ha'teng made a last attempt to draw her into conversation, though he was sure little would come of it.

'All your friends are non-humans?'

She swallowed another bite of meat with obvious difficulty.

'No. All my friends are honourable and noble beings,' she replied slowly, choosing her words carefully. 'I don't care much about race or origin.'

'Such views mainly serve those from the lowest ranks of society,' Ha'aki interjected.

Ha'teng realised he'd been seething inside for some time. The talk of non-humans and Ha'sani's enthusiasm had clearly annoyed him.

'The Ha'ami represent all that is best in humanity. Therefore, we have a responsibility for the purity of the race and we do not fraternise with those who are unworthy of it.'

He spat out the words meticulously, without looking at anyone.

'I suppose we have different views on who we consider worthy of our esteem,' she said calmly, smiling slightly.

'The Ha'ami live by clear rules. There is no place for personal opinions,' he retorted sharply. 'We have noticed that you have a problem with following our laws. Which brings us back to the offence you have committed–'

Ha'teng knew they were in for a long lecture.

Eli picked tirelessly at her plate as she listened to Ha'aki's oration.

'When you are part of a greater whole, you must conform to the universal laws and know your place,' he instructed her in a cold voice. 'Otherwise, chaos would reign. Moving on–'

Yes, please, let's get to the point, she thought, losing patience. She was sick to death of this evening, of these conceited men, of all their pointless rules and their never-ending judgmental attitude towards her.

'It will take us some time to officially confirm your *Ta'uma* status,' Ha'aki continued. 'However, riding a horse by a woman is a minor transgression, so we have decided to dispense justice without further delay. When the meal is over, you will join the *namio* and kneel with them in the cold and snow for as long as you have the strength. You may, of course, ask for an early end to your punishment, although this would normally be considered a loss of honour. However, we are aware that you do not have the endurance of Ha'ami in you–'

'You said I should go there after supper?' she asked, trying to control her emotions even though her tongue was a little tangled with wine.

'Yes... but you can go to your chamber first and change into something more appropriate,' he explained slowly, with a hint of disdain.

'They're kneeling there in nothing but their breeches, aren't they? So, by *"more appropriate clothing"* you mean you want me to go there in just my knickers?' she asked, seemingly calmly and without changing her serious tone.

'No...' Ha'min interjected, embarrassed. 'We thought you might want to wear a cloak or other, warmer garments–'

'But why delay such a well-deserved penance?' She rose from her seat, trying not to wobble. Her legs were quite limp. 'I will go there at once with your noble permission.'

The men looked at each other. Ha'akon nodded. Ha'min reached up and grabbed her elbow.

'I will walk you out,' he declared.

'How courteous of you,' she answered, though her tongue twisted at such a long word. 'Thank you for your hospitality and a wonderful evening,' she added and walked away gladly into the darkness of the cold night.

Chapter V
Friends in need

HA'KAME FELT HIS SWOLLEN ANKLE pressing against his boot, though the frost had dulled the pain. He had to admit that after the lesson the First Brothers had given them today, it would be a shame to complain about injuries. The truth was that he could have avoided them if he had fought better in his duel with Ha'teng. Not only had he twisted his leg in the confrontation, but the punch to his head had knocked him unconscious. *Namio* was angry with himself, but he was even more angry at Ha'perin for coming to revive him and now receiving punishment for it.

He could see him now, kneeling on the cold stone in the middle of the square, snowflakes falling on his dark hair, while Ha'kame stood on the walls, serving the night watch they all were ordered to do.

Koru-koinen is a unique bond, and he knew his *koru* would lay down his life for him. They pledged lifelong loyalty to each other on and off the battlefield. Ha'perin showed great purity in his feelings and took his commitment very seriously. He probably even enjoyed the punishment he was serving now, proud that he could prove his loyalty to his oath. Always ready to sacrifice, always with a head full of ideals...

Suddenly there was a noise in the northern corner of the square. Ha'kame turned abruptly in that direction and felt a sharp pain in his ankle. He cursed under his breath and shifted his weight back to the good leg. He concentrated on the source of the commotion. Ha'min entered the square, leading by the hand the *Ta'uma* they had seen watching their exercises. A small, petite girl with olive skin and messy hair, she must have been younger than Ha'kame. From the start he had noticed her eyes. Large, green and extremely focused, as if constantly analysing everything she saw around her. She reminded him of a lurking animal, ready to defend or flee at any moment.

She was following the First Brother, staggering slightly. It seemed she was not feeling well, for at one point, reeling, she ran to a water bucket at the edge of the square and vomited into it for a long time. Ha'min stood over her, holding her up so she would not fall. When she had finished, he rubbed snow on her face and led her to the centre of the square, next to Ha'perin. She knelt down. The Wolf stood over her for a moment, saying something, then quickly marched off in the direction they had come from.

'Ow! That's cold!' she exclaimed as Ha'min shoved a handful of snow into her mouth.

'It's not the worst thing that's about to happen to you today. I told you to swallow some earlier, so you wouldn't puke like a dwarf at the opening of a mine!' he scolded her. He was very irritated. All his efforts to give her herbs to numb her for the night and make her body immune to the cold were probably in vain.

'Ha ha ha... Like a dwarf...' she giggled under her breath. 'I must remember it. Who would have thought you were so funny, Wolf.'

'Have you finished?'

'Throwing up that delicious dinner? I think so. Talking? Not necessarily!' she replied teasingly.

'I think we've had enough of the stream of your puke and of your words alike.' He pulled her up so that she was standing upright. 'I hope you have some of it left in your stomach.'

'I doubt it...' she muttered. 'Since I came here, hardly a day has gone by without me feeling sick. Besides, your meat won't do me any good...'

'I didn't mean the meat,' he mumbled.

'What are you growling about, Wolf?'

'Nothing. Now go to the square and kneel beside this valorous warrior, the only one still hanging on.'

'He seems to have frozen. Look at the icicles hanging from his ears.' She reached out a finger, intending to touch the *namio*. Ha'min jerked it back.

'Stop fooling around! You'll be lucky if you don't faint or freeze to death!' He tried to sound harsh, but it seemed nothing could spoil her good spirits.

'It's your opinion! From my point of view, the possibility of falling asleep in the cold for eternity doesn't seem so bad after tonight's enchanting evening with you all. Hey, are you all right?' she asked the kneeling young man.

Ha'min took a closer look at the boy. Both his jaw and his fists were clenched; he did not react to their presence.

'Ha'perin!' the commander called in his direction. 'Have you had enough?'

The *namio* just shook his head.

'As you wish. Well, have a peaceful night, don't you die here tonight, you're too young for that.'

'Peaceful night...' The girl giggled again. 'You and your jests, Wolf. Ah, how I've grown fond of you.'

Ha'min just shrugged and marched off to finish his dinner with the First Brothers, thinking she was right. He would rather freeze his arse here than return to this chamber.

Eli took a deep breath of the cold night air and decided to take Ha'min's advice and put some snow in her mouth. Swallowing quickly, she felt a comforting chill in her stomach. The frost was already starting to get to her limbs. The skirt she was kneeling in was soaking wet. The drink numbed her a little, but she knew it wouldn't last long.

She glanced at the *namio* who was swaying on his knees beside her. His lips and hands were bruised, frost had gathered on his eyebrows and a spiky tuft of hair stretched across the middle of his head. The warrior had a round face and a slightly upturned nose that made him look very young, almost childlike.

'Hey!' she whispered. He didn't answer. 'Hey!' she repeated louder. He lifted his eyes at her. 'They call me Eli. And you?'

His almost blue lips were tight, as if glued together by frost. 'No one is here,' she continued her effort to make conversation. 'You can tell me. Let me guess, it starts with '*Ha'*...'

'Ha'perin.' He spoke softly, chattering his teeth.

'Oh, nice. And they call me Eli. And, as I told you... I was punished for riding a horse. Silly, I know, but such is your law. Not for riding poorly, mind you. Just for riding. They say I can't... I wonder what my horse would say to that? He'll probably laugh. I've heard that you're also here because of a terrible crime... You helped someone, right?'

Ha'perin just nodded.

'I saw it, the First Brothers battered you pretty badly... and you helped your friend to get back on his feet, right?'

'*K-k-k-koru k-ko-ko-inen,*' the young man stuttered with difficulty.

'Ah, yes, your beloved. I understand. It's good that you have someone you care about... it probably doesn't happen very often in this dreary place.'

The warrior staggered slightly. She glanced at the blood drying beneath his knees.

I don't think he'll stay conscious much longer, she mused. *My ears are starting to burn from the cold too...* She pitied him. His punishment made no sense. She knew that it was probably the wine still running through her veins that was giving her preposterous ideas, but nevertheless she decided to try to help him.

'Peri... may I call you Peri? You know, the elves have taught me how to reduce the sensation of pain with something they call meditation. Maybe it will work for the cold too? Well, I don't know, because it's always been spring there... but maybe it's worth a try? Would you like to?'

He didn't answer, kneeling with his head down; she noticed that his eyelids were beginning to droop.

'They taught me that you have to separate yourself and your feelings from what surrounds you. You have to imagine yourself enclosed, as if in a glass box, so that nothing from the outside can touch you. Your body moves into another space, it stops reacting to what is hurting it, as if it were not there... I know it sounds a bit confusing, but it works, I have experienced it myself. In the end, you imagine what you want to feel and focus only on that... peace... joy... warmth...'

Ha'perin did not respond. She took his hand.

'Let's try, Peri!' He did not lift his gaze; she breathed deeply, holding his icy palm. 'Don't give up yet!'

An old memory of the Elven Kingdom appeared before her eyes. The patient gaze of Tallen, explaining with infinite calm how to control her energy. She stood by the murmuring stream again, the gentle rays of the sun caressing her face. Her friend's calmness always gave her strength, helping her to clear her mind of unwanted thoughts, of which she always seemed to have too many. His clear, almost translucent eyes guided her deep into her soul, allowing her to anchor herself and then direct the flow of energy where it was needed.

If only you were here... she sighed in her mind. *I don't know if I can do this myself... And I want so much to help this poor boy...*

So far, Spark has been content with minor interference in the events. The unenlightened usually referred to the voices of beings like him as 'premonitions' or 'intuition'. Little did they know that the whispers they heard in their souls came from those who could toy with fate.

This time, however, he was tempted to intervene more directly.

It was hard to believe that the Girl with No Name, in whom lay dormant layers of power, was having difficulty wringing out something as simple as warmth.

The curse on her was powerful indeed.

Her thoughts drifted to the dragon like a gossamer thread in the breeze. The cold... the pain... the loneliness... all these feelings reached him at once.

For a moment, Spark considered what he could do to remain unnoticed by the masters of destiny, but the temptation was too great. He was too eager for her to succeed.

The dragon sent a whisper to her, frail as a butterfly in the wind.

Shhh... Focus. Look inside yourself for what you think you lack. Trust it. You have all the power within you to make it happen.

She heard him. Though confused, she answered.

I am weak...

Only if you acknowledge yourself as such.

He led her deeper, to the very core of her soul.

Look. It's still there. Your beautiful, powerful energy. Draw it in. Slowly... you know how.

A stream of golden-green light spread out before her. The web of her delicate thoughts trembled in the void, so he blew gently on it, sending it towards the source of power. The fragile strands of her weakened will came into contact with the glowing surface, flickered and grew a little.

Your power is always available here... just a thought away.

Spark fell silent and watched further events in the square silent and focused.

Eli felt a wave of energy grow in her abdomen. It spread with the blood in her veins, filling every part of her body. She felt the snow melt beneath her knees and the darkness of the night dissipate. Her thoughts were clear and simple again. She opened her eyes and focused on the young warrior's clenched, icy hand. Where their bodies met, the colour of his skin began to take on a healthy tone. Slowly, but visibly, his muscles relaxed, and after a while, even the snow on his hair melted and began to drip onto the pavement in thick droplets. The *namio's* lips turned the colour of raspberries. Finally, he opened his eyes and looked at her in surprise.

'This warmth is real!' she explained with a smile. 'Meditation works!'

He looked at her uncertainly. There was something innocent and sincere about him.

He has good eyes, she thought. *I knew it.*

'It does work,' he replied finally in a surprisingly sonorous voice. He covered their clenched palms with his other hand. 'Thank you... Eli.'

They sat like that for a while in silence.

'Will you tell me about him?' The girl asked at last.

'About who?'

'About the one for whom you decided to freeze to death today. What's his name?'

'Ha'kame,' *namio* answered, blushing slightly.

I like it... How did you two meet?' she asked, and he began the story in a low voice. Not only about his *koru-koinen*, but also about *namio's* ways and his own life story. In return, she told him about everything she had experienced since waking up in the fortress, and about her impressions of Ha'ami. He burst out laughing when she described how Ha'teng had somersaulted over a chair after she'd kicked him.

'This is the first time I've had such a good chat with someone other than a *namio*,' he admitted, wiping the moisture from his eyes after another fit of giggling.

'It's the first time I've had such a good chat with a Ha'ami,' she replied, feeling grateful to fate for this encounter. 'At last, I am not being interrogated.'

'How do you know, maybe this is my clever tactic and I am in fact Ha'teng's spy.' He poked her shoulder.

'I don't know if anyone would make such a sacrifice for this snot-nose that they would even freeze an ear,' she laughed heartily. 'They'll be quite surprised when they see us in the morning, all healthy and pink, won't they?'

'*Neru-to–*' He whispered in her direction. She felt herself blush as he called her 'little sister'. '–Just know that I won't tell anyone about your... your glow. You have my word.'

'What do you mean?' She raised her eyebrows. He looked at her, clearly puzzled.

'I have no idea how you did it, or what powers you have–' He combed his unruly hair. '–But you helped me. I feel neither cold nor pain. My wounds of today, nay, even old wounds, seem to have healed. I shall be forever grateful to you... but the Ha'ami do not accept what they do not understand. I don't want you to get into trouble because of me. I won't tell anyone about this. Not even Ha'kame. I swear.'

'Trouble is my middle name.' She shrugged. 'But you're right, I've gotten into too much of it here. Maybe it's better not to talk about it. Thank you for explaining, Peri.'

'If there's anything I can do to help, you can always come to me.' He shook her hand firmly.

Eli read the earnestness in his dark blue eyes.

Ha'kame blinked in amazement. Perhaps he was dreaming. For a moment, it really seemed to him that the girl's body was gently glowing with a soft, golden-green light, which transferred to Ha'perin when she touched him. The light faded in an instant, but the snow around them melted.

I must be delirious with fatigue, he thought and took a few deep breaths. He could see nothing out of the ordinary anymore, just two people in a dark square. They were holding hands, chatting as if they were sitting in comfortable armchairs by a fireplace, and even giggling now and then, like a couple of children.

He watched them with curiosity, looking forward to the morning when he could ask his *koru* about everything.

'Say what you will, but this has been one of the most enjoyable evenings we've had in a while,' said Ha'teng, stretching his legs in front of the fireplace. They were sitting in his private chamber, where they usually retired to after dinner. Just the two of them.

'I noticed you were having a good time,' his friend confirmed.

'It wasn't just me. I could clearly see that you yourself were choking back your laughter,' he replied truthfully. 'Ha'aki's face when he was talking about the dwarves was worth a ton of gold!'

Ha'akon just took a sip from his cup and did not pursue the subject.

'Do you think she will survive the night?' Ha'teng asked.

'Judging by the amount of spiked liquor Ha'min made her drink–' the castle lord replied.

'So you noticed.' Ha'teng smiled confidently. 'Someone really thoughtful placed him on her left, knowing that the old man would try to help her somehow.'

'It is fortunate that we had such an insightful host today.' Ha'akon gave him a slightly amused look.

'Truly, fate in the flesh,' Ha'teng murmured, staring into the flames of the fireplace. 'But back to serious matters. The news of the expedition does not seem to have made much of an impression on the others. What do you think of Ha'aki's offer? He seems eager to lead the troops we will send east in support.'

The ruler looked pensive.

'I would prefer to give the command to Ha'min.'

'Yes? Why is that?'

'He's better in the field. Both in strategy and in command. And the brothers worship him.'

'Don't you think he's too old?'

'No. On the contrary. I think stretching his bones would do him good.'

Ha'teng remained silent.

Ha'min may have been able to wield his sword, but his wits were drowned in the torrent of wine he had drunk over the years. The *namio* were, to say the least, enthusiastic about him, but that was probably because he was overly indulgent to them. The Guardian of Defence, however, was not at all sure that the other warriors would take him seriously as a leader. He also wondered if Ha'min would be up to the task of representing the Stone Nest with dignity when the commander in chief was Ha'gard, known for his disrespect for his fellow warriors. That scum will eat the old man for breakfast.

The Ha'ami regarded all members of the community as equal. Both the king and the governors of the various provinces were elected from among all the brothers in voting. Any of them could be removed from power if they were deemed to have broken the law or the traditions of the tribe. However, Ha'teng felt that the Lord of the Stone Nest relied too much on the opinions of his councillors. The very choice of the First Brothers also aroused mixed feelings in the commander.

His own position was, of course, non-negotiable. Not only because of his competence, but also because of his unwavering loyalty to his friend. But the others...

Ha'aki was, in his opinion, the most unpredictable piece of the puzzle. Ha'teng could not, however, make a clear accusation against him, for the Guardian of Tradition fulfilled his role without fail. Like Ha'min, he had served on the Council under the previous ruler and was one of the contenders for the leadership of the Western Province after the death of the governor on the battlefield. However, Ha'akon, whose bravery during the wars had brought him great fame and recognition among his brothers, won by an overwhelming majority. Tiger was sure that this had bruised the experienced advisor's pride, and while he was surprised when the newly elected Governor decided to offer Ha'aki the old position, he was even more astonished that Ha'aki accepted. Ha'teng trusted the man as much as he would trust a crocodile to guard a herd of cattle. But even if the ruler of Stone Nest had doubts about this one or any other of the First Brothers, he never shared them. Perhaps Ha'akon thought it safer to keep a fierce rival around, which would also explain why he did not want to put him in charge of the upcoming expedition.

Ha'teng respected his *koru* too much to question his judgement. But he had long hoped that this haphazard gathering called the Council was only a temporary solution. Who knew, perhaps the upcoming expedition would help resolve issues with at least some of its members.

The horn sounded its wake-up call long before the winter dawn. Eli and Ha'perin let go of the hands they had clasped all night and waited for further developments. Heavy clouds hung low in the sky, but it was not yet snowing.

The square quickly filled with warriors gathering in even rows. The First Brothers appeared on the steps of the cloister.

'Here comes the Wolf to relieve us of our punishment,' Peri whispered to her. Indeed, Ha'min strode towards them at a brisk pace.

'It is done!' he announced loudly, then turned to the young warrior. 'Do you need to rest or will you join us immediately?'

The *namio* leapt to his feet.

'Ready for practice!' he reported brightly. The First Brother looked at him intently. 'Then get in line. Make sure you get to the stables after breakfast.'

Ha'perin nodded.

'You are finished as well,' Ha'min announced to the girl. The young warrior, Eli's companion in misery, pulled her to her feet. Then he placed her hand on his cheek and brushed his lips lightly against it.

'See you soon, *neru-to.*'

'See you soon, Peri,' she replied; he turned with a boyish grin and marched off with a spring in his step, taking his place in line. 'Until next time, Wolf,' Eli remarked to Ha'min as she passed him on her way to the cloisters.

'Greetings to the First Brothers,' she said with a slight curtsy. 'I hope your night was as pleasant.'

'I see the frost has put you in a good mood,' Ha'teng remarked sourly.

'Not so much the frost as clearing my conscience of the greatest transgressions,' she replied with vigour.

'I am glad that you have survived this night in good health and, moreover, in dry clothes,' Ha'min chimed in. She realised he was standing behind her now.

'I do not know what your customs are, but I do not wet myself at night,' she replied in the same cheeky tone. 'Speaking of which... I would like to take care of my morning ablutions now. Have a nice day!'

She curtsied again, leaving the bewildered First Brothers behind.

Anni knelt by the door again and listened carefully to the conversation coming from the chamber. She was slightly inconvenienced by her heavy belly, which hung between her knees. It was too big and her back was too stiff for her to bend down and put her ear to the crack, no matter how hard she tried. And she did try. Lord Ha'teng had been pleased with her recent efforts, so she was highly motivated to bring him some new, useful information for which he would praise her. She did not want to disappoint him.

'Wake up! Get up, Temina!' *Ta'uma* called.

'Yoicks and away, you damned thing,' the lord's sister snapped back, clearly displeased.

'Come on... get up, let's go to breakfast!'

'Breakfast will come to us by itself!'

'But I want to eat with the others!'

'You can't eat with the others in the Castle. We're not allowed to.'

'What do you mean? Another thing we're not allowed to do?'

'Break the fast together. They eat their meals separately, in the Warriors' Hall. Are you a warrior?'

'Yes!'

'That's what you think. Let it go and send for the servants instead of pestering me.'

'But why can't we eat there?'

'Ha'ami rules. The answer to all your nagging questions.'

Silence.

'Temina...'

'What?'

'I'm still hungry, I've been kneeling in the freezing cold all night.'

'You don't look it. I don't see any frostbite.'

'I had great company, time was flying by.'

'I'll send you flying by right now if you don't let me sleep...'

Silence fell again. Eventually, the grumbling voice of the fortress lord's sister rang out again.

'Call that viper that crawls under our door in the hallway. I'm sure she knows where to scrounge up some grub for you.'

Anni retreated quietly into the shadows, trying to make as little noise as possible.

King Ha'attik awoke before dawn and immediately spotted a familiar old falcon on the windowsill. With a soft whistle, he summoned the trained bird and opened the cage containing water and food for the winged messenger. The bird needed no invitation; it moved to its meal without hesitation.

Ha'attik carefully untied the note attached to its talons, then walked over to the fireplace to read it.

News from the Stone Nest. Fortunately, he still had loyal brothers there he could count on, no matter what Ha'akon was up to.

Many were deceived by the pose of an honourable, loyal leader put on by the famous dragon slayer. But Ha'attik was not fooled. He knew that Ha'akon was his greatest rival, and that one day, when he grew powerful enough, he would speak out against him, challenge his leadership. The king had no intention of letting that happen.

In fact, he trusted none of his commanders completely. He relied on a network of dedicated people to monitor the moves of potential rivals and report back to him on possible risks.

The message was brief, as usual, and dealt with the reaction of Ha'akon and his council to the news of the expedition to the Azzgoth Lands in the spring. It seemed that the king should expect reinforcements from the Stone Nest. Good. He needed every warrior. There was also mention of two prisoners. A foreign girl and an elf. A strange combination. Nothing he should pay more attention to at the moment. His man would surely keep him informed of any further developments.

The king tossed the message into the flames. He saw no need to reply.

Ha'akon arrived at the stables early in the morning, sending the servants into a panic.

'We are not leaving yet,' he snapped in their direction. 'Have you seen *Ta'uma* here?'

They nodded and pointed to the end of the corridor.

When he reached it, he watched her for a moment in silence as she devotedly combed the immaculate hair of her mount, humming an unfamiliar tune. She was wearing her own garments again, the ones she had worn when she was captured. The green-grey, warm cloak that wrapped around her almost made her blend in with her stable surroundings.

It was the horse that sensed his gaze first. He shook his head slightly. She calmed him by whispering something in his ear but did not turn around, nor did she stop what she was doing.

'Good morning, Ha'akon,' she said simply.

'I thought you might need some rest after last night,' he replied.

'Temina is still occupying the bed.' She smiled, more to herself than to him. 'When I'm done, I'll sleep here, on the hay.'

'I can ask the servants to prepare another chamber,' he suggested.

'Don't bother. I don't need much. And I'm comfortable here.' Ha'akon didn't know why she still didn't look at him.

He opened the stable door. The horse panicked at the movement and it took the girl a moment to get him under control.

'Slowly... I have to introduce you,' she said, cuddling up to the snow-white mane. 'Simronil, this is Ha'akon. The lord of this castle. He is not the worst here...'

'Not the worst? That's a description I've never heard before.' He took off his glove and held out his hand.

'What can I say... I'm no poet.' She gestured for him to stop. Then she took his hand in her fingers and gently pressed their joined palms against the horse's neck. 'Don't be afraid,' she whispered into the white horse's ear. 'He won't hurt us for now.'

Ha'akon tried to catch her gaze.

'Are you afraid of me?'

She finally looked at him. He felt a sting at the sadness in her eyes.

'I'd be a fool not to be afraid. You have all the power here. But I'm not afraid for myself, I don't care what happens to me. I am afraid of what you are doing to my friend. And what else you will do to him...'

'The elf refuses to cooperate. He suffers by his own choice. Besides, he will get a fair trial,' he explained dryly.

'By laws he doesn't know. While his only crime is to be who he is...'

Ha'akon did not know what stung him more - the touch of her hand or the accusing flame in her pupils.

'Ha'akon. This elf is the noblest person under the sun. He is worth more than many a Ha'ami who live in this fortress. He has too much honour, you will not be able to make him speak, whatever you do to him will be ineffective. You must see this. You must appreciate it.'

He stepped back. Her opinion of this non-human annoyed him a little, though he didn't know why.

'He broke the law,' Ha'akon repeated calmly.

'That's what every conversation around here boils down to.' She lowered her eyes and began to brush her mount's coat again. That statement hurt him even more.

'I came to tell you that we are going to the City of Sisters tomorrow. You will go with us to be presented to the entire Council. This is necessary to confirm your nobility,' he announced in an official tone.

She remained silent.

'Eli?' He urged her.

'Were you waiting for an answer? I thought that was an order,' she replied coolly. 'When do we leave?'

'After breakfast.'

'Yes, sir Ha'akon.'

Angrily, he turned and walked out. He barely made it a few steps between the stalls, then swore under his breath and turned back.

'As a gesture of goodwill, I will allow a brief visit with the prisoner,' he said through clenched teeth. 'Ha'teng will be present and you may only speak in the common language.'

This clearly caught her off guard. For a moment she was speechless. So, this was possible. Without waiting for an answer, he marched towards the stable door.

Soon he heard the light, swift footsteps behind him. He felt the girl touch his arm. He stopped and turned. This time her eyes were bright with excitement.

'Thank you.'

She took his hand in hers and pressed her forehead against it, making a bow. He had never seen such a gesture in his life, but he understood what it meant.

'I will send for you when Ha'teng is ready. For the elf's sake, try to persuade him to speak,' he said dryly, though he could feel the blood beginning to pulsate in his temples.

She stepped back, nodded, turned on her heel and ran back to the stables.

Eli was relieved to be alone with Simronil again.

Ha'akon stallion, she heard the mount's voice in her mind. She gave him a light slap on the nostrils.

You are a stallion yourself, she replied.

Sure thing!

She was angry with herself for once again failing to act sophisticated or hide her true feelings. But she was more disappointed in Ha'akon than in herself. Despite a semblance of honour and fairness, despite all the praise she had heard about him from Temina, he was as much a moron as the other Ha'ami.

But she was overjoyed that he had allowed her to see Tallen. She looked forward to seeing her friend. Finally!

Drops of moisture fell slowly from the crumpled ceiling to the floor, gathering a small army of vermin at the watering hole formed in the hollow of the uneven stone. He heard the clank of a key in the door. He didn't react when the door opened or when someone entered. Only when he heard footsteps did he raise his head.

'As promised... I am here,' Eli announced, smiling broadly even though he saw worry in her green eyes. He must have looked really bad.

'We can only talk in common,' she warned him before he could speak, pointing lightly at the door with her head. It remained open; his tormentor stood there, leaning against the frame.

She placed a small lamp on the floor and he rose from his seat ringing the chains. They hugged each other tightly. He was relieved to have her close by his side again.

'Are you safe? What have they done to you?' He ran his fingertips over the bruises on her face.

'Nothing... not much, just a few scratches.' Her eyes clouded as she watched him closely. 'You, on the other hand, look...'

'Blooming, I know. And I have a charming chamber.'

'Very funny... I brought you some food.' She handed him a small bundle. 'Just bread, cheese, water and some dried fruit. Whatever I could grab...'

'Thank you.' He held out his left hand.

'What's wrong with your right palm? She hissed at the sight of his fingers bent at the joints. 'Do you need anything?' she asked, swallowing her tears and struggling to hide her emotions.

'Only to know that you are well and safe.'

'I am. And I can only envy your company in this place...'

'It's true, I have excellent company.' He reached into his pocket. 'Look.'

'What is it?'

'My new foundling. I named her Little Eli. Elili.'

The tiny mouse he had rescued from the rat's jaws was sleeping unusually peacefully, considering its surroundings.

'She definitely snores less than you.'

'And she asks fewer questions.'

'That never bothered me. That's your charm,' he laughed.

'Enough of that sweet talk.' A sharp, familiar voice came from the door.

'I'm going to get us out of here.' She looked at him earnestly with those big, naive, childish eyes.

'Don't do anything stupid, little one. Remember, everything passes.'

She nodded, picked up the lamp and walked towards the exit.

He stroked Elili's furry back gently.

'You'd better wake up, my friend, we're going to have to eat these treats right away, because competition is fierce here.'

As if in a trance, she trailed behind Ha'teng up the dungeon stairs. He said something to her, but she only answered in half-words. She had to use all her willpower not to get into another fight with him, to pay him back for what he had done to Tallen... She walked with a stiff step, full of tension, trying to keep an indifferent expression on her face, to suppress the natural impulses of anger that the sight of the injuries on the elf's body had awakened in her.

His beautiful face was bruised and swollen, his hand was broken in such a way that she didn't know if he'd ever be able to use it again, and she noticed burnt skin on his torso.

What kind of monster do you have to be to abuse another being like that, especially one so good, so noble, so unique...

She breathed slowly, trying to control her rising emotions.

Everything passes.

A favourite saying of long-lived elves. She couldn't look at his suffering like that. It happened here and now.

When they stepped outside, all she asked was for someone to show her the way to the stables. Ha'teng ordered one of the guards who escorted her silently to the place.

When she was finally alone with Simronil, she was able to drop her mask of indifference and cried for a long time, burying her face in her friend's soft mane.

Elf is brave. Eli will cope, he only repeated, helpless in the face of her despair. Finally, her eyes dried and the natural reflex to act returned.

I will cope. She repeated with conviction, wiping her face. *In the meantime, let's take a walk. Fresh air always helps.*

Jor had hoped the woman would return to the stables, and now, satisfied that his wish had come true, he watched her surreptitiously from a neighbouring building. The grooms had just gone to supper; she was alone. That is, if you don't count the most beautiful steed he had ever seen in his life. The horse was as white as the snow, which covered the yard like a soft carpet. Its mane and tail seemed woven of mist. In the torchlight, he resembled a ghost as he followed the girl's footsteps. The thread of understanding that bound them together was apparent at first glance. The animal stayed close to her, seeking her gaze, her touch. And she played with him like a child, throwing snowballs at him, then snuggling up against his neck for a moment, whispering in his ear and laughing out loud.

Jor had never seen anything like it. The whole scene seemed almost like a dream or magic. It reassured him that he might be right, that he had met a most exceptional person here, perhaps the one everyone had been looking for, someone whose return his countrymen had been hoping for...

As the woman and her steed made their way towards the buildings, he followed intuitively. He felt he had to see her up close. He wanted to speak to her again, to hear his native tongue from the mouth of someone who was not a slave. He slipped quietly through the shadows of the buildings, not wanting to frighten her away, not wanting to break the spell that someone had cast on this place that seemed to be cursed every other moment.

Reluctantly, they returned to the stables. These were the happiest moments since she awoke in the Stone Nest.

Don't worry, I'll visit you again tomorrow, Simronil, she purred softly and scratched his nostrils. She felt lighter and more at ease, confident that she would find a solution... They would get out of here. All of them.

Unexpectedly, at the entrance to the building, she saw three silhouettes heading towards them. After a moment, they emerged from the shadows. They were Ha'ami warriors, two of them dressed for the road and leading mounts. A third man, dressed in simple black robes, was the only one to greet her. It was Ha'sani.

'Good evening, *Ta'uma*. I see you enjoy tempting fate.'

His voice sounded friendly, but nevertheless, she reacted defensively.

'Is it also forbidden to walk beside a mount?' she replied indignantly.

'That's not what I meant. You let the terror of our grooms out of the stable,' he replied quietly.

'Ah, no, he doesn't endanger anyone when I'm around.' She stroked the neck of Simronil, who stood docilely beside her like innocence incarnate.

'If I hadn't seen the trouble this horse has caused before, I wouldn't have believed it was the same animal... may I?' he asked, holding out his hand.

'Yes, slowly... shhh...' She whispered into the pale mane as he placed his hand on the horse's neck.

Act like a polite stallion, she asked Simronil in her mind.

And Eli like a polite mare, he retorted immediately. She almost burst out laughing, barely managing to remain serious.

'What a majestic creature,' Ha'sani said in awe.

She smiled.

'He has no equal.'

True that, she heard in her head.

'Where did you get it? You must have paid dearly for it!'

'He chose me himself,' she replied hastily. 'He has his own will, he doesn't listen to anyone.'

'You have something in common,' Ha'sani joked.

'An apt observation,' she agreed.

'Ha'sani, it's time for us to go,' one of the riders urged, mounting a grey horse.

The man raised his hand, asking for time.

'Both I and the lord of the castle would be most grateful if no one found out about our meeting today, *Ta'uma*,' he whispered. She felt her jaw drop a little and tried to clench it.

'Oh, yes... of course. I'll be as quiet as if a basilisk looked at me,' she replied, not knowing why she was doing him a favour, but she was alone and there were three of them, the night was dark and this part of the castle seemed deserted... so compliance seemed a reasonable course of action. Besides, she did not care about Ha'ami's affairs.

He nodded approvingly.

'Good night,' he said and walked towards his companions.

'Same to you,' she replied, turning towards the stable door.

A friend? Simronil's question rang in her mind.

I doubt it, she replied.

After dismissing the messengers, Ha'sani moved quickly across the courtyard. If they were surprised at the purpose of their expedition, they did not show it. The orders had come directly from Ha'akon.

The fact that they had to leave in secret was no great surprise either; discretion is the norm among messengers. The dwarven factories were many days away. And time was of the essence for him.

He took a last look at the girl as she walked away with her beautiful mount.

What a beast! Worth a fortune... but beauty is its only asset, such a wayward character knocks the price down by at least half, he thought. *I'd better not meet anyone else today. Especially none of the rats of Ha'teng, of which there are always plenty...'*

He turned and caught a shadow out of the corner of his eye, but did not stop, just looked back in the same direction. He was not wrong. A thin creature was creeping along the wall in the darkness, and then slipped into the stables.

Ha'sani sighed. Whoever the skeletal figure was, he had certainly overheard his conversation with the messengers. And now he was creeping up, following *Ta'uma* for some unknown purpose. Better check it out.

He pretended to walk in the opposite direction, out of sight of the intruder, then turned back to the stables.

Eli brought water and food to Simronil's stall.

Please, remember to be nice. We don't need any more trouble right now.

Eli herself trouble, he answered, throwing back his head.

That's right, she laughed, bidding him goodbye. She was about to head for the exit when the sound of a fight reached her from the corridor. She ran outside. The sight she found there took her completely by surprise.

The Guardian of the Keys, whom she had just met outside the stables, was brutally beating a half-naked poor man who was lying on the ground, shielding his head with his hands from the whip lashes.

'I'll teach you to ambush people at night, you bastard!' she heard the warrior's harsh voice.

'Ha'sani!' Eli said loudly, but he paid no attention to her and went on with the beating. She resolutely grabbed his rising arm as he was about to deliver a blow.

'Ha'sani!' She repeated, trying not to let the tone of her voice provoke him any further. To her surprise, the man's face showed no anger, only determination. He lowered his hand.

'On your knees, dog!' He turned to the scrawny man. Slowly, unsteadily, the man began to rise. Eli bent down, a little to help him and a little to shield him from further blows, just in case. Admittedly, she didn't know if it would help at all. She might as well have earned a whiplash herself.

'What has this servant done?' She turned to the warrior again, her voice calm.

'Step aside,' he replied coolly.

'All right, but stop hitting him.'

The scrawny man knelt with his head bowed.

'What do you want with *Ta'uma*, why are you following her? Speak at once or I'll rip your tongue out!' shouted the Guardian of the Keys.

'Is that what this is all about?' Eli interjected again. 'This poor fellow must have been sent by Ha'teng.'

'I don't serve that bastard,' the man snarled in a foreign language that Eli understood but Ha'sani clearly did not. She had no time to react as he slapped the kneeling man's face hard enough to knock him back to the ground.

'You will speak in human, dog!'

Eli leaned over the man as he lay on the ground. She saw a streak of blood on his mouth from the blow.

'Don't make it worse,' she murmured in a hushed voice, carefully helping him to sit up.

'Do you know his filthy language?' Ha'sani was so surprised that his aggressive urges seemed to subside for a moment.

'Obviously,' she shot back. 'I also know that this is not Ha'teng's man. Look, he has a tattoo of a dragon. I met him earlier in the fortress, he showed me the way to the stables... Jor, right?' She looked the scrawny man intently in the eyes. His pupils dilated at the sound of his name.

'And now he ambushed you when you were left here alone...' Ha'sani added.

'Be reasonable, Ha'sani. He came here barefoot, unarmed. What harm could he do to me?'

'Go back to your chamber, *Ta'uma*. I will deal with him.' The warrior seemed relentless. She stood up, walked over to him, pulled him aside.

'You will deal with him in the next few days. It's late, we're all weary, no time for such nocturnal adventures. This poor fellow was probably just curious. You said yourself that my horse is notorious throughout the fortress for the trouble he caused... I'm sure it's nothing more than curiosity about this steed... Let him go, he's so frightened that I'm sure he won't breathe a word of it to anyone. You always know where to find him. And as far as I'm concerned, I'll forget I saw you both here as soon as I step outside. No one needs this ostentatious commotion...'

He weighed her words in his mind for a long while.

'So be it.' He declared briefly.

'Good night, Ha'sani.' She turned and grabbed the thin man under the elbow, helping him to his feet. 'Come on Jor, show me the way back or I'll get lost again,' she said, pulling him towards the stable door.

'Thank you, my lady...' he muttered quietly, not meeting her eyes as they left the building.

'It wasn't wise, even I can tell, and I've done a lot of stupid things here.' She shook her head. 'You have no need to hide from me. If you want something, just ask. There wouldn't be so much drama.' She handed him a cloth mask. 'You left it in the stable. No more trouble for today, understand? And not a word to anyone about what happened here, if you want to live.'

When they were inside the castle, she took the torch from the wall. 'But you really must show me the way back, I have no idea how to get to my chamber.'

He pulled a piece of wet, mud-soaked cloth over his face and nodded. Then he picked up the torch and led her through the dark corridors without a word.

Chapter VI
Tracking down truth and conspiracies

WHEN THE CASTLE RULER'S SISTER returned to the City, Anni was reassigned to her previous tasks as *Ta'uma's* maid. She brought her meals, attended to her needs and, most importantly, gathered information for her master. Immediately after leaving the breakfast tray in her chamber and offering help with the morning toilet, which her mistress refused, the girl crouched in the corridor in the shadows, waiting for when she could come to collect the empty dishes.

Crouching like this, she was contemplating what other questions she could ask *Ta'uma* to draw new information from her unnoticed, when an unexpected visitor appeared.

A short, slender, even emaciated-looking servant with a small dragon tattoo on his back and mane of frizzy hair approached the chamber door hesitantly and knocked. *Ta'uma* opened it.

'Hello, Jor,' she said and let the man in.

Anni sensed her chance. Maybe this was something she could report to Lord Ha'teng and earn his praise. She tiptoed through the corridor, glancing around to see if anyone was coming. It should be rather empty at this hour. She knelt down and put her ear to the crack in the door near the floor.

They were speaking in an unfamiliar language and she could not understand a word. She went on like this for a while, but finally had to give up in disappointment. She retreated cautiously.

Jor. She didn't know him, but she would ask around. She would find out what his relationship with *Ta'uma* was that he could afford the luxury of seeing her in private.

She almost trembled with excitement, anticipating lord Ha'teng's satisfaction.

He reported to her chamber in the morning, as she had asked him to do the night before. She did not order him. She kindly asked if he would find time to take her back to the stables after breakfast. Jor was beside himself with joy, and although he had to beg a favour from his friends to cover for him in his absence, the meeting was worth risking another beating for.

It certainly exceeded his modest expectations. The noble lady repeated that he should address her by her first name, invited him in, and not only asked him thoughtfully about his injuries from the day before, but also requested that he join her for a meal. He would never have dared such an audacity, so he declined as politely as he could. But he could not refuse when she insisted that he sit down until she had finished eating. Like an equal, he rested on his chair. Like an equal...

To his growing amazement, she asked him about his family, his country, his life before he was taken prisoner. At first, he was frightened by her inquisitiveness, but her direct and friendly manner inspired a confidence he had not felt for a long time. It was clear that she was genuinely curious about his fate. Moreover, she used an unusually beautiful register of speech that he was accustomed to at home. Not the jumbled dialect of the lower classes that he heard every day among servants from every corner of his land.

He dared not ask her any questions. As he finished his story and they began to gather to leave, she put a hand on his shoulder.

'I have not lived long in this world, Jor, but in moments of hardship I find comfort in one thing. Everything passes. Both happiness and sorrow come to an end one day,' she said, and he was speechless with emotion. He swallowed his tears and turned away, putting on a humiliating mask.

After escorting her to the stables, he returned to his work, happy as a lark. He felt light, as if a weight had been lifted from his shoulders and he was almost floating above the ground.

Suddenly he felt a strong, leather-gloved hand on his shoulder.

'Here you are hiding, mutt.' He turned to hear the voice of the lord who had whipped him the day before. 'I've found you. Time we had a talk, isn't it?'

Ha'teng wriggled impatiently in his saddle as Ha'min barked orders to the last *namios* to arrive at the assembly point. A field exercise had been scheduled for today for all warriors, including those still in training. And clearly the latter had not taken the preparations very seriously.

Both the Guardian of Defence and the Guardian of Tradition with their squads had been waiting in formation for some time when Ha'akon rode into the courtyard in full gear with the elite unit that served him. He looked with displeasure at the few *namios* who were still saddling their mounts.

'March off!'' he gave the order in a loud voice. 'Ha'aki, you go in the vanguard, Ha'amin follows, then Ha'teng, I close the formation. All who are not yet on horseback stay to clean the stables. And zero wine allocation for a month.'

The young warriors looked at him mournfully, but no one protested. With lowered heads they withdrew to the buildings.

The Guardian of Tradition quickly led his squad to the gate, while the other First Brethren waited their turn. Out of nowhere, Ha'sani, who was supposed to stay with his men to guard the fortress, appeared in the square. He was leading a scrawny servant who was screaming loudly and writhing in his iron grip. He dragged him to Ha'akon and threw him directly under the hooves of the governor's mount. The man tried to rise, but two guards immediately held him down and forced him to remain on his knees.

Ha'teng rushed over to see what the commotion was about. He saw that Ha'min was also heading that way.

'This is the one I told you about,' said the Guardian of the Keys. 'Speak, why are you hanging around *Ta'uma?*'

He grabbed the scrawny man by the back of his curly hair and pulled. The servant looked at him hatefully. He did not answer.

'Has this man done something to Eli?' asked a clearly surprised Wolf.

Ha'sani let go of the man and turned to the First Brothers.

'Not yet. But he is following her. He was heard talking to her in Azzgoth. I tried to question him, but he won't talk.'

'One must have an innate talent for persuasion,' Ha'teng remarked sarcastically. 'Why didn't you give him to my people? Surely, they would have taken good care of him.'

'I ordered that he be brought to me immediately,' the ruler explained calmly, then turned to the servant. 'You. The lord asked you a question. Answer it.'

The scraggy slave looked directly at the governor, then spat juicily at his mount's feet. Ha'sani immediately struck him in the face. Blood spurted from the servant's shattered nose. He did not fall only because he was supported by the guards.

The ruler measured the frail man with a dispassionate gaze.

'You have a simple choice,' he declared. 'Either you answer now, or the guards will deal with you. One way or the other, we'll find out everything.'

'I will never betray her!' the man panted. 'You can kill me!'

'So much drama over such a triviality!' Ha'teng remarked impatiently. He decided to intervene before they delayed their departure any further. He nodded to the other First Brothers and stepped aside. They followed him.

'This slave is out of his mind. He has delusions about *Ta'uma*. It was reported to me this morning. I intended to arrest him on my return,' he explained in a hushed voice.

'Delusions? Is he stalking her?' Ha'min asked. 'Is she in danger?'

'No, nothing like that,' the Guardian of Defence corrected and sighed. Obviously, he needed to clear this up quickly to avoid further misunderstandings. What a shame Ha'sani had to get involved in this. How did he find out about it?

'This possessed man had deluded himself into thinking that *Ta'uma* was the lost princess of the Azzgoths,' he explained hurriedly. 'He spreads these rumours among the servants.'

'And you did not see fit to tell us about it?' Ha'sani was indignant.

'Shall I report to you all the tales of the slaves?' He replied nonchalantly, but the displeasure on Ha'akon's face made him quickly correct himself. 'I don't believe the rumours, but he is sowing unnecessary ferment among the other Azzgoths, which is why I wanted to throw him in the dungeon.'

'The lost princess?' The eldest warrior interjected. 'You don't mean Berennike, do you?'

'Yes, that's madman's word.' Ha'teng tried to keep his tone dismissive. Nonetheless, the sound of that name caused a visible stir among the First Brothers. A dramatic silence fell. It was broken by the Governor.

'Ha'min, it's your troops' turn. March off,' he barked. The commander wordlessly mounted his horse and rushed towards the assembled *namios.* 'Ha'sani, have this man detained for questioning. I want to be there for it.' He directed a meaningful glance at the Guardian of Defence.

They both nodded briefly in acknowledgement, then each moved off as ordered.

Ha'teng realised he had made another mistake.

When she arrived at the stables, Eli fed Simronil and gave him water, then promptly fell asleep on the hay in the corner. She had spent the whole of the previous night sleepless, alternately trying to come up with a new plan of action and trying to rekindle the magical energy she had managed to channel so successfully during the frosty night. Her efforts had failed on both counts.

She slept like a log and awoke when the sun was high in the sky.

Someone called her name.

Rubbing her eyes, she stepped out into the aisle and bumped into Ha'perin.

'I almost thought you were a dream!' he laughed at the sight of her.

'I'm so glad to see you! What are you doing here?' She hugged him in greeting.

'Punishment again.' He scratched his short hair in embarrassment. 'I fell asleep...'

'Me too! I was exhausted today! You just woke me up! We're real soul mates. Come in, don't be afraid, he won't hurt you.' She pulled him into the stable.

The *namio* watched the horse carefully.

'Simronil, this is Peri, the sincerest person in this crazy stronghold,' she introduced her friend.

'He is so... calm around you,' the young warrior remarked in amazement.

'As I am around him.'

She smiled and buried her face in the light mane. She couldn't explain the bond she had with her mount to anyone. Not even to Tallen.

'As I told you, he is truly remarkable... a unique creature. I doubt he will trust you immediately, but please be patient.'

Ha'perin stood at a loss, clearly not knowing what to do. 'Can you bring the brushes?' she suggested. 'Now–' she instructed as he slowly approached her, still clearly apprehensive, '–give me your hand. Yes, all right. That's a polite horse. Try stroking him, let him feel your touch... See, you survived.'

After a while they stood side by side, stroking the light hair on the horse's back and flanks with long movements.

'He likes you,' Eli said at last.

'How do you know that?' Ha'perin asked.

'I can feel it... besides, he has the right feeling about people.' She smiled. 'Much better than I do. Peri... tomorrow they are taking me to the City of Sisters. I'm to meet the whole Council. I'm not quite sure what that means.'

'You're going to meet my mother,' he said excitedly.

'Really?'

'Yes, she's Akona's adjutant, the Guardian of Health. She's in charge of the healers and herbalists.'

'I'm glad of it...' she said pensively.

'Is something troubling you?'

She nodded.

'Come outside,' he said. 'Too many ears in here,' he added in a whisper.

Ha'perin looked around carefully, then took her hand and led her through a narrow aisle between the stables. When they reached the wall, he moved the sacks of feed standing beside it and exposed loose planks. They pushed them aside and crawled out through the hole. This took them to the back of the building, into the narrow passage that separated it from the fortress wall. Ha'perin showed her how to use the uneven bricks to climb onto the roof.

After a while, they were sitting on a narrow part of the castle wall, behind the roof of the stables, so that they could observe their surroundings while being almost completely hidden from prying eyes. For the first time, she could see more than the courtyard and admire the vastness of the fortress she was in. Thick walls surrounded the buildings with numerous rings, forming several levels of the city. The lowest were filled with spaces that looked like gardens. At other times of the year, they would have brought life to the now gloomy Stone Nest.

'Amazing,' she sighed, admiring the view. 'I hadn't expected anything like this.'

Ha'perin gave her a wistful smile.

'I like coming here. You are the second person after Ha'kame that I have brought here. This has been my place since I was a little boy and I wanted to be alone at least for a while, away from the crowds, the drill and the orders...'

She looked at his profile and the same feeling as the night before came over her.

'How old are you, Peri?' she asked pensively.

'Twenty.' He looked younger. Even the warrior's hairstyle: the shaven head and the spiked hair on top, seemed to contrast with the rest of his innocent, childlike countenance. 'I know, no one believes me...' He winked at her.

She thought they were similar: she too was hardly taken seriously by anyone because of her appearance, her small height and petite figure.

'Same here.' She smiled. 'Especially among the Ha'ami. I feel like a halfling here.'

For a while, they admired the scenery in silence.

'This sight makes me proud of the achievements of my people.' he declared emphatically.

'It is said that the first settlement was established here three hundred years ago. Over time it was expanded to include other circles. Each lord added something of his own. Ha'akon, for example, enlarged and enriched the Temple of the Ancestors.' He pointed to the distinctive large dome a few levels below. 'And his mother, Akona, contributed greatly to the expansion of the gardens.'

'Where is the City of Sisters?'

'Over there.' She followed his hand with her eyes. 'We are in the oldest part of the Stone Nest, also known as the Upper Castle or the Top Nut.'

She looked at him. He was not serious. They both laughed.

'Well, maybe it's just an unofficial name we've given it with the other *namios*... but if you go outside the fortress, you'll see that it reflects the view well.'

When I leave the fortress– she repeated in her mind, *– I doubt I'll be looking back...*

'This is where the First Brothers, their Guard and the *namios* live. The circle below, the City of the Brothers, is, as the name suggests, for those after initiation and their servants.'

'Your place names do not leave much room for interpretation,' she joked.

'Rather not... imagination is not a virtue celebrated by Ha'ami,' he laughed.

'How many warriors live there?'

'About eight thousand. That's my guess.'

'I see they have their own training grounds,' she remarked.

'Yes, there are separate stables, baths, several pleasure houses...' he confirmed.

'All they need to be happy...' She didn't want her voice to sound too mocking, but she couldn't help it. Fortunately, her teasing did not seem to offend Ha'perin. On the contrary, he often added his amusing observations.

'You forgot about good food and drink, which you can only get in the City of Sisters. That's where all the feasts and celebrations take place.' He pointed to another circle of the fortress. 'There's also the Temple of the Ancestors I mentioned earlier, the Healing House, the Archives... you'll see them tomorrow. It is a beautiful place,' he concluded proudly.

'Do you go there often?'

'No... until I become a fully-fledged warrior, I am not allowed to leave the Top Nut, except for the most important ceremonies, when we all gather in the square in front of the temple.'

'Well... What do warriors do all day? Maybe it's a silly question, but most of the time I see the courtyard and corridors empty, except for the morning and evening exercises.' She was relieved to finally find someone she could ask openly about even the simplest details of Ha'ami life that she still didn't understand. 'And all the punishments, of course. Because I'm guessing that takes up a lot of your time on a daily basis too...'

'You're right.' He confirmed with his childish, carefree smile on his face. 'But I suppose the *namio* serve most of the punishments in this city. Warriors are no longer supervised like that, unless they commit some really serious transgression.... But that rarely happens.'

'Ha'ami are too honourable to steal, rape and kill?'

'Not necessarily... but you can always challenge someone to a duel if you want to get something that belongs to them or take revenge on them. And as for rape... well, I suppose there's no need for that with so many options, the Ha'ami girls know how to defend themselves well, while the kept women and maids–'

'– can be raped without it being a crime?' she guessed.

'Exactly,' he replied, looking away. 'The same goes for their murder or mutilation... unless they serve another influential Ha'ami who was attached to them. Then compensation for loss of property could be claimed.'

She frowned, and sighed heavily. She had to change the subject, or she would sink back into the despondency that always came with listening to tales of Ha'ami morality.

'Is see. Tell me, what do warriors do?'

'Oh yeah, right...' He noticed her sadness and eagerly returned to her previous question. 'In spring and summer, if they don't go on expeditions to neighbouring lands, they compete with others. And in winter... they train. Apart from what you've seen, we spend the rest of the day in the field training in various forms of combat, drill, archery, so most of the time the fortress is pretty empty. We are actually only here for breakfast and dinner.'

'It makes sense.' She nodded. 'And what is in the lowest part of the fortress?'

'There?' He waved his hand. 'The buildings where the servants live, the tradesmen, the workers divided into guilds... and everyone else.'

'People with strong legs and good knees for climbing,' she remarked.

'Definitely!'

'It looks impressive. The whole fortress must hold many thousands of people.'

She looked around the area once more. Despite her dislike of the Ha'ami laws, she was truly impressed by what they had managed to build.

'Oh yes!' he confirmed.

'So, when you and Ha'kame pass your initiation this year, you will live together in the City of Brothers?'

'Yes...' He lowered his head and frowned.

'This is your last year to hunt your animal, isn't it?' She still couldn't come to terms with this ritual, which seemed like an unnecessary killing to her. The *namio* nodded. 'Don't worry, Peri. I'm sure you'll be able to catch at least a bear.'

She did not say this with great conviction. Someone's life will be sacrificed this year because of a barbaric custom. On the one hand, you have innocent animals who do not even know why they are being hunted. On the other, the frank and cheerful young man she had come to like so much. There was no just solution here, except to stop this primitive tradition.

'It shall be so,' Ha'perin declared firmly. 'Now tell me, what is troubling you?'

She fell into thought, her eyes sweeping over the extraordinary city that spread out at their feet. A magnificent prison.

'My elf friend. I don't know how to get him out of the dungeon. They treat him very badly. I don't know what else they will do to him and I am helpless.'

She fell silent, feeling the anger sweep over her again.

'Eli... you helped me the other night. Why?' he asked her in reply.

'I hadn't thought about it... But, to tell you the truth, I didn't know if I could. It was a reflex. It could have failed.'

'You see, *neru-to...* these are the kind of deeds you wouldn't expect from Ha'ami.' He smiled warmly. 'First, you reached out to a stranger in need. You showed mercy. And secondly, you have just admitted your own weakness.'

He took her hand, pressed it to his cheek and kissed it.

'What... what does this gesture mean? She blushed at the tenderness he showed her. 'I have seen Ha'akon say goodbye to Temina in this way.'

'It is the way a Ha'ami warrior respects her sister and recognises her as an equal.'

She felt her cheeks grow red.

'I thought Ha'ami women and men were equal.' She lowered her eyes, hoping the joke would mask her confusion.

'Not every warrior thinks like that... otherwise they wouldn't have invented the gesture, don't you think?' He looked at her with amusement. 'You are an extraordinary person, Eli. Unfortunately, I'm afraid few Ha'ami will understand that. If you want them to respect you, you must speak to them in their own language. If there is something you really want that Ha'akon or Ha'teng are not prepared to offer, you won't get it by pleading. They will show no mercy. The only thing that will make the Ha'ami negotiate is power.'

She thought deeply about what he had said. It made sense. Only when she showed them her worth did they make concessions. Like the fight with Ha'teng.

'You must have something they care about,' Ha'perin continued. 'Otherwise, they wouldn't have called you *Ta'uma*, they wouldn't have wanted you to talk to the Sisters, they wouldn't have helped you after you were injured in the fight... My advice: don't sell it cheaply or break it up into small bits and give it away piece by piece. Make them a single, irrevocable offer they cannot refuse.'

'You speak like a merchant now, not a warrior.' She smiled sadly.

'My mother always told me that a career as a Guardian of   Keys is waiting for me... who knows! Do you understand what I mean?'

'Yes, Peri... you've given me a lot to think about. You are very wise.'

'Who would have thought that after all the blows that have rained down on this skull, I would still be able to extract something with sense.' He tapped his head. 'You are a tough beast, *neru-to*, the Tiger Bane I believe in you!' He winked at her. 'Come on, let's go or I'll earn another punishment when they discover my absence.'

'Shall we meet at dinner?' she asked hopefully. 'I'd like to meet Ha'kame.'

'We can't...' He shook his head. 'I am obliged to dine in the warrior hall, and you– '

'So I've heard... no exceptions for the Tiger's Bane?' she sighed.

'Unfortunately, it's not my decision to make, you'd have to convince most of the Ha'ami living here of your skills in combat.'

'Most Ha'ami... that's a lot of duelling.'

'Or maybe next time you'll just punch Ha'teng's pretty nose in public,' he laughed as they walked down the hill.

Ha'akon watched from the hill as their troops moved in neat battle formation. After a shaky start to the day, things now seemed to have returned to normal. Even the *namios* under Ha'min were keeping up with the others, holding   ranks under the onslaught of the seasoned warriors.

His thoughts drifted back to *Ta'uma.*

Could she be the Berennike both Ha'ami and Azzgoth had been searching for? Was that why she seemed so familiar to him?

The Wild Princess. That's what they called her. She fought like a demon, and her people treated her almost like a goddess, believing in her supernatural powers that allowed her to triumph over her opponents.

He himself had only seen her once, from a distance on the battlefield, on his first journey there. They were both much younger.

After the defeat of the Azzgoths, she led the shattered armies hiding in the forests and hills, continuing to wage a guerrilla war against the Ha'ami forces. As the last surviving member of the royal family, she was the heir to the throne. This is why they were so keen to find her and force her to sign an official vassal declaration to King Ha'attik.

But no one has seen her for years, despite the continued attacks on the Ha'ami armies and the resistance of her rebellious people.

How would she have ended up in the Stone Nest, so far from her homeland? Had she been hiding among the elves all these years? Was that why one of them was with her now?

It would explain a lot.

Ha'akon sighed heavily. This could really complicate things. He hoped it was all just a bizarre coincidence.

You must have something they care about. Ha'perin's words echoed in her ears.

But what?

She kept thinking about it as she walked through the corridors of the fortress.

Jor hadn't come to see her off. He must have been kept busy with his duties.

What did they want from her? What did she know that could be useful? She had so little experience, and everything she had learned in her short life she owed to Tallen.

She stopped in surprise as she recognised the door to her chamber. By some miracle, she had arrived there by herself. Deciding to take this as a good sign, she stepped inside and looked around, trying to control the chaos in her head. She slumped back in her chair in frustration.

What was she thinking about?

And yes, that all her knowledge of the world came from what Tallen had told her. And from books.

She looked down at the table.

The History of the Ha'ami People was still there, gaping in amazement at her stupidity.

Suddenly she slapped her forehead.

'You dumbhead!' she said aloud. 'Why haven't you thought   of this before?'

Tallen examined the injuries carefully with his fingers. He knew he had lost three teeth so far. His left shoulder was dislocated, his right hand crushed and his ribs broken. Of that he was certain. He did not feel the pain because he had learned to cut himself off from it.

All the more reason for him to check every time to see what had been damaged during the torture.

They burned him with irons, hung him upside down, submerged him in water and beat him incessantly. Although the torturer's repertoire was limited and repetitive, he was exceptionally dedicated. Tallen assumed he would start again tomorrow.

Meanwhile, his body was weakening. Malnutrition was inevitably taking its toll. He had conserved his energy and was far from exhausted, but never in over a hundred and fifty years had he felt so weak.

He awaited the inevitable end. The torturer reminded him every day of the coming judgement and the probable death penalty. He was not afraid of that moment. He knew it was only a transition to a new reality. His spirit would remain strong.

Therefore, he didn't want Eli to risk anything for him. His clever but simple-minded foundling... she hadn't met many people in her short life. What a shame that her first contact had to be with this bunch of shameful buggers. Tallen knew he wouldn't be able to convince her to leave him and run away. His brave little foundling... may fate not be too hard on her once he is gone.

Eli had not expected to return to Ha'teng's private quarters so soon. The guard let her through into a small hall furnished only with narrow, sleek, elegant benches set against the wall. Across the hall was a row of windows overlooking the exercise yard, now dark and empty. A large painting hung above the seating area.

The door at the end of the corridor opened and Anni stepped through, as quietly as a praying mantis creeping towards a lizard.

She approached her at arm's length, then removed the cloth mask from her face.

'Good evening, lady *Ta'uma*,' she said in her thin voice as she bowed.

'Good evening, Anni. I've come to see Ha'teng,' she declared firmly.

'The master is not receiving anyone at this time. May I deliver a message, lady *Ta'uma*?' the maid squeaked.

'Yes, you may convey that I will wait here until he sees me. I come on an urgent matter that will be of the utmost interest to him.' Eli's tone indicated that no objection was in order.

To further demonstrate her intention, she sat down on a bench against the wall and stretched out comfortably. Anni did not reply, but simply bowed and tiptoed away from where she had come.

Eli busied herself looking at the canvas that adorned the room. It depicted a battle in which the Ha'ami had triumphed over another nation. The painter had rendered the details of the fighters with extraordinary care, especially the shoulder tattoos of the dark-haired warriors and the fear-stricken faces of the vanquished, trampled by the heavy boots of the victors.

Brotherhood. Honour. Strength, proclaimed the inscription at the top of the painting in bloody letters.

What else could be the subject of their art. She shook her head, contemplating the repulsive, bestial details of the scene.

'The master will receive you, lady *Ta'uma*,' Anni's falsetto reached her. The maid stood at the end of the hall, by the door. When they passed through it, they found themselves in a study, which, however, was empty. It was decorated with equal splendour to the drawing room where Eli had dined the previous day, full of ornate furniture, carvings and paintings. They made their way to the next room. It looked like a place for private visits. There were several soft armchairs, a couple of low tables, and the walls were decorated with beautifully woven kilims. Ha'teng was standing by the fireplace. He was barefoot, wearing only black trousers and a light shirt carelessly thrown over his bare body. The blue bruises around his nose had almost completely faded, and there was no longer any sign of swelling. During her stay among the elves, Eli had become accustomed to admiring their unspoiled, soulful beauty emanating goodness and eternity. Ha'teng's allure was of a different kind, though one could be equally enthralled by it. Cold, menacing, as unfeeling as a boulder.

He measured her with his gaze as he sipped from the chalice he held in his hand. He did not show her a place to sit, offered her no refreshments, did not respond to her greeting.

The only thing that speaks to Ha'ami is power, she repeated in her mind while she waited for Anni to leave.

'I hope it's something urgent, since you decided to disturb my only moment of peace during the day,' he snarled as the door closed.

'It won't take long. And you want to hear this,' Eli replied, walking over to one of the tables. She poured herself some wine, took a sip and then came so close to him that she could smell his body odour.

'Really?' he asked, watching her actions with a spark of curiosity in his eyes. She took the goblet from his hand and offered him hers in return, then sat down in one of the chairs. He seemed amused by her behaviour. The usual ironic smile blossomed on his face, so effectively disrupting the perfect symmetry of his features.

'It's about the elf,' she began. 'You're interrogating him.'

They measured each other for a moment with their eyes.

'That is my predicament.' He finally replied.

'He won't tell you anything.' Said Eli, tasting the drink again.

'I can be persuasive.'

Silence again.

'How many elves have you met in your life, Ha'teng?' He didn't answer. She continued, as she had planned earlier. 'Your methods, however charming, will not be effective in obtaining the information you so desire. You will irretrievably lose an opportunity... perhaps the only one in this century. But there are other ways for you to find out the things that preoccupy your mind.'

'And you've come to tell me about them.' He took a sip, his gaze sweeping over her.

'Indeed.' She rejoiced inwardly. He caught the hook. With a slow step, he walked over to one of the armchairs and sat down.

'I'm all ears.'

'Everything you need is here.' She tapped her head with a finger. 'I have lived among the elves for the past few years. I know the location of their cities. The roads. The fighting techniques. The armaments. The population figures. We can even talk about baking recipes and shoe making, if that's your thing.'

'The last few years? How long would that be?' This was a question she hadn't expected.

'Five, six years... time passes differently there.'

He was thinking. Clearly calculating something.

'And you are going to share this knowledge, motivated by a newfound affection for me, or for the Ha'ami people as a whole?' he remarked with a wince.

She smiled broadly.

'My feelings for you and the Ha'ami people are as strong as ever, Ha'teng. You have enchanted me since the first time we met.'

'What do you want?' He took a long sip from his goblet.

'I want you to leave the elf alone. You will let him go free.'

'Is that all?' He replied sarcastically.

'Only after that condition is met can we begin to speak directly.' She managed to keep a stony face.

'Talk to you. Who could resist such an offer?'

'Indeed, who could?'

'Well, it's a charming proposal.' He rose from his seat. 'It's just that I'm not at all convinced that this little head contains any useful knowledge.'

'I think the exact opposite is true,' she said, rising from her seat as well. She put her goblet down on the table. 'I think you know perfectly well that I am your only chance. You wouldn't be where you are if you didn't have a keen nose for such things... Well, I'll leave you to continue–' she measured him with her eyes, '–your rest. Have a good time!'

She said goodbye and left.

Anni, who was waiting for her in the next chamber, escorted her to the exit.

Eli could feel the blood in her veins pulsing faster now. She was certain that Ha'teng had taken the bait. She just didn't know how long it would take him to make a decision, so it was necessary to carry out the next steps of the plan to spur him on.

Ha'kame moved restlessly in his chair and stared impatiently at the door where Ha'teng had disappeared. He was unsure if he had done the right thing. Although he had come here of his own free will, he felt somehow compelled by Ha'perin's silence. He inquired endlessly about the events of that night, about the glow he had seen, about how he had survived the punishment unharmed. His *koru-koinen* merely dismissed him with a laugh. For the first time in his life Ha'kame felt that he had concealed something from him. And they had known each other for ages. It had to be her. He had seen them whispering with each other in the stables. How they sneaked through the secret passage. THEIR secret passage. What had she done to him? Had she cast a spell?

He needed to consult someone more experienced, someone with more knowledge in these matters. Thus, he came to Ha'teng. He told him what he had seen while standing guard. About the light, about the melting snow, about Ha'perin's healed wounds.

Then their conversation was interrupted. The small, fat, servile rat came with a message. The First Brother had ordered him to wait in the bedroom while he received an unexpected guest in the living room.

That is how he got stuck here, not knowing what to do with himself, counting down the time in his mind.

Finally, the door opened and Ha'teng returned.

'I'm sorry we were interrupted.' Tiger put a hand on his shoulder, stopping him from getting up and pushed a chair right next to Ha'kame.

'You were telling me about the light you saw?'

'I don't know what to make of it.' *Namio* frowned, now quite unsure if he was coming across as a superstitious fool. 'Maybe I imagined it... Ha'perin denied everything... it was late, and I was suffering from a sprained ankle.'

'A duel in the square?' guessed the First Brother.

'I wasn't fast enough for you,' he replied, embarrassed.

'Not many people are.' Ha'teng laughed, showing even, white teeth.

It was hard not to admire him. He had it all. The position, the acclaim, the glory gained in battle... Many thought he was proud, but Ha'kame was convinced that the Guardian of Defence surpassed all those malcontents in skill. Few could match him in battle. Only Ha'akon, perhaps... Perhaps. No one had ever seen them in direct combat.

'Ha'kame.' He was surprised that the First Brother took the trouble to remember his name. '*Koru-koinen* is the most unique bond there is, don't you think?' The commander leaned towards him and looked deep into his eyes. The *namio* felt intimidated by the attention being paid to him.

'Yes,' he replied slowly.

'Nothing and no one should separate two brothers.' Ha'teng went on, emphasising each word. 'They swear allegiance to each other forever.'

'Yes.'

'That's why you feel ... that's why you know Ha'perin is not telling you the truth.'

'I think–' he considered the answer. 'I think he was hiding something when he told me that story.'

'It is understandable that you are disappointed.'

Ha'kame felt that at last someone understood his dilemma.

'Tell me again, in detail, everything you witnessed yesterday and today,' Ha'teng encouraged him in a calm voice and handed him a cup of wine. 'Perhaps together we can find some clues that will allow us to discover what really happened.'

Late in the evening, King Ha'attik returned to his chamber after an interminable meeting with his commanders. The campaign against the Azzgoths had met with resistance, as he had predicted. No one wanted to serve under Ha'gard. It seemed that he would have to send him forward only with the troops directly under his command, and over the next few months make arrangements with the governors of the provinces to send reinforcements.

The plan was clear. Wipe this tribe off the face of the earth. No one was better suited to the task than this scumbag, Ha'gard. The king despised him as much as the other brothers did. But right now, he needed just such a person. Someone who would take on the task of drowning a rebellious country in a sea of blood. He would solve the problem and he would do it faster than anyone else.

Then it would be a matter of finding a way to get rid of him.

The servants had just finished preparing king's bath. They helped him to remove his armour, then he ordered them outside. Ha'attik plunged into the hot water, not stopping his internal debate on the most effective moves for the coming days, when he noticed a new bird perched on a beam near the ceiling.

He whistled.

The falcon swooped down gently on his outstretched arm. He was surprised to see that it was another bird from the Stone Nest.

So soon? Something must have happened.

He dried his other hand on a towel and carefully unwrapped the message.

Berennike.

The cursed bitch makes her presence known again. Why now? Why there, in the far west? Is this some clever plot by Ha'akon against him? It can't be the real Wild Princess... After so many years... But the stupid crowd will buy it if someone handles the rumour properly.

And the elves... What if the Azzgoth form an alliance with their eternal enemies?

Ha'attik angrily threw the parchment into the fire. The falcon shied away and returned to its place under the ceiling.

The king sighed in frustration. He scrubbed his body carefully, then got out of the bath and, marking the floor with wet steps, walked over to his desk. He scribbled a few words.

Death to both prisoners. Stay in the shadows.

He rolled up the scrawl, walked over to the cage, opened the door, tied it to the leg of the previous messenger and whistled the command to return to the nest. The falcon spread its wings, flew out through the parted shutters and sped west through the frosty air.

Chapter VII
The city of intrigues

WITA STOOD WITH HIS HEAD down, awaiting developments. They had been summoned here at dawn with the task of transporting a noble lady in a sedan chair from the Upper Castle to the city. He did not know why this woman was alone among the warriors. He cared little. His task now was to move her from place to place. The problem was that when the young lady saw the litter, she immediately refused to sit in it. The porters were left staring at the cobblestones, not knowing what to do, when the lords on horseback arrived and began to negotiate with the displeased noblewoman.

'Eli, I have already told you. This is the only solution in accordance with the Ha'ami law,' the lord of the castle himself repeated once more. His steed shifted impatiently from hoof to hoof. 'If you do not wish to sit in the sedan chair, you may ride with one of us on horseback. The choice is yours,' he finished in an unusually calm tone that Wita had never heard before.

'If you ride with me, I'll even let you choose the position. From the front or from behind?' The other Ha'ami joined the conversation. The one who was in charge of the guards and the prison. The one everyone feared. He laughed at his own joke. No one else joined in.

Wita looked at the girl. She was flushed up to her ears.

'I'm not injured to be dragged around like a puppet. Go on your own,' she muttered, unclasping her cloak. She folded it into a roll, smaller than one would expect.

'I will run after you.'

Wita felt everyone freeze at those words.

'Eli, that's inappropriate,' another of the men interrupted. The oldest, with slightly greying hair. 'Besides, it's a long way, you won't keep up, you'll get lost...'

Not surprisingly, it was to him that the woman handed her cloak.

'May I ask you to keep it, Wolf?' she asked. 'I don't want it in my way. I'll take it back at the Temple.'

'Eli–' he protested.

'I'd rather crawl there on my own than be carried like a sack of oats.'

She spoke with strength and confidence.

'Your will,' the ruler of the Stone Nest declared after a moment. 'Porters, back to the City of Sisters!' he commanded, then turned his mount towards the mouth of the courtyard. The riders set off at full speed.

It made no difference to Wita. Such a petite lady would not weigh much. With or without her, he had to go the same way. Let the lords fight among themselves, he did not care. Still, he wondered who this impertinent youngster was, whom the lord of the castle himself treated with kid gloves.

Eli waited until they had disappeared around the corner and ran through the stables to the passage Peri had shown her the day before. Yesterday's view of the city panorama had given her an idea of how to get there in a way that would also help her convince Ha'teng that her skills were worth a lot. Even in the grey of the winter morning, she could clearly see the topaz roof of the Temple of the Ancestors.

It took her a moment to work out her route. Admittedly, it was hard to judge all the distances in the half-light, but the buildings seemed to be relatively close together, and most of them had flat roofs.

Dear shoes, don't let me down, she muttered to herself.

Elven footwear was perfect for climbing in the wilderness, she hoped it would work just as well in the city. After all, a rock is a rock.

She trotted along the wall behind the stables, taking a moment to jump onto the roof of the nearest building below. With quick, nimble leaps she moved from one stone building to the next. She was relieved to discover that there was no ice under the thin layer of snow, but she still proceeded cautiously, wary of lurking surprises in the form of a weakened ceiling or treacherous hoar-frost.

The most important thing is to get there, even if I am a bit behind them, she repeated to herself.

Even though she was careful with the ice, she quickly caught up with the riders. Ha'min was closing the column, looking around the whole time, as if searching for something with his eyes.

'I can't see her!' he shouted to the others at one point.

'You're looking in the wrong direction!' Eli laughed from above. Astonished, they stopped and raised their heads.

'What are you doing, crazy?' Ha'teng growled.

'I've decided to be in front of you!' she announced, gathered speed and leapt to the next building with a showy somersault, landed softly and run on.

That was stupid, she scolded herself. *You should only run as fast as the ground can catch you!* It was as if she had heard Tallen when he was teaching her to climb...

Eli didn't know if the riders had sped up, but she didn't look back. She enjoyed the movement and the freedom. They had to get through the winding streets of the city, which were now filling up with people. She had a chance.

The sun shone low over the horizon directly in front of her as she balanced on the edges of roofs. From time-to-time   Eli had to take a risk, dive and roll across the flat surface. Some of the buildings in her path were higher than others, which meant not just jumping, but climbing up a slippery wall.

By the time she reached the City of Sisters, she was drenched in melted snow and sweat, though her elven clothing somehow kept her warm and her boots were fairly dry. As of now, Eli could run faster, as the buildings were newer, lower and seemed to be better constructed. With efficient leaps the girl moved forward until she was on top of the last house in the square that surrounded the temple. She slid down the roof, dangled for a moment and then began to descend, grabbing at windows and ledges. After traversing two floors in this manner, she landed lightly on the pavement, to the astonishment of a servant who stood outside beating the dust from the cushions. Eli laughingly apologised to the frightened girl, then jogged towards her destination, catching her breath in the cold. The sharp air stung her lungs.

Tallen would be proud of me. She thought of the elf imprisoned in the dungeon, and immediately became sombre. *I will convince them,* she repeated forcefully to herself. *My plan will work.*

Eli paused on the threshold of the temple, waiting for the riders, and looked curiously at the building. It was built of grey stone that must have come from the nearby hills. She had never seen such material before. The columns and steps surrounding the entrance were as smooth as water and seemed to have a life of their own, like the depths of a great lake. Enchanted, she touched the surface of the wall and for a moment felt as if her hand would sink into it. But this did not happen. She watched in delight as the black patterns swirled beneath her fingers like schools of fish in the column. The stone seemed to pulsate.

'Amazing,' she sighed.

Suddenly she felt a slight vibration in her fingertips that slowly spread throughout her body. She withdrew her hand abruptly. The temple seemed to be calling her. Something was urging her to move forward and go inside.   A voice speaking directly to her soul. A familiar voice. The same one that had helped her through the night in the cold. Confused she looked around. She was alone.

The First Brothers, escorted by guardsmen, had appeared in the square and were rushing towards her. They jumped from their horses, threw the reins to the servants and quickly climbed the steps to where she was standing.

'In your letter you said that I should expect a visitor in the form of a girl, not a gecko, my son.'

Eli turned abruptly. On the threshold of the temple stood five tall, strong women, dressed in identical blue robes that hugged their upper bodies tightly, only to fall freely in the form of loose trouser legs tucked into winter boots.

'I did mention, however, that there were many talents hidden within this person, did I not, Mother?'

Ha'akon turned to the tallest of them all, the one with the close-cropped hair. He approached her, raised her hand to his cheek and planted a kiss on it.

'Welcome,' she said, looking into his eyes with clear joy. 'We are glad to have you in the City of Sisters' She turned to the other newcomers. They all exchanged greetings. When they had finished, Ha'akon gestured to Eli, who stood aside, watching the scene intently.

'This is *Ta'uma*, whom we have welcomed to our castle.'

'Noble *Ta'uma*, I am Akona.' his mother said in a warm voice. 'I am delighted to receive you in our home.'

It sounded very much like some official formula for a greeting, and Eli had been among the Ha'ami long enough to suspect that there was some universally accepted, appropriate response to it. Which, unfortunately, she did not know.

'It is an honour for me to be here and to meet you.' She replied only as courtly as she could.

Akona nodded her head and pointed to her companions. 'This is Sig, the Guardian of this Temple and keeper of our traditions. Perin, the healer who looks after us in time of need. Keera, who guides our scholars and spreads knowledge to all who seek it. Teena, patroness of craftsmen, merchants and landowners.'

'And Temina, protector of rebels and hooligans.' Eli felt a hand on her shoulder. She turned to see the laughing face of the herbalist. They hugged each other warmly.

'You are soaked to the bone!' her friend exclaimed. 'Your sedan tipped over on the way?'

'Long story,' she mumbled uncertainly in reply.

Ha'min approached her and threw her elven cloak over her shoulders.

'Thank you,' she murmured, wrapping herself in the dry fabric. 'It is an honour to meet you all,' she said, turning to the First Sisters.

She looked at them with as much curiosity as they did. Sig, a woman with an inspired face and straight, waist-length hair. Keera seemed to be her opposite, with a shaved head and ears pierced with multiple earrings; her gaze was clear and penetrating. In Perin's face, Eli recognised her friend's features: the same softness and strength as in the young warrior. Teena broke into conversation with Ha'sani immediately, seeming as specific and direct as he was.

'It is time to honour the ancestors.' Sig announced and they all went into the Temple.

'Council meetings always begin with a visit here,' Temina whispered into girl's ear. 'Sisters and brothers turn to the ancestors for wisdom and support in making the right decisions.'

As Eli approached the door, the tingling she had felt earlier in her body increased. She could feel the building drawing her in with increasing strength; she was sure that someone or something was waiting for her there.

He knew the torturer would not show up today. Simronil told him that they had all left for a place called the City of Sisters. Including Eli.

Tallen had a bad feeling about this. He understood little of the horse's half-words, but he guessed that she was trying to make some kind of deal with the Ha'ami. This did not bode well. He did not believe that negotiating with these people could change anything for the better.

Suddenly he felt a strange presence, even though the cell door remained closed. And he was not the only one touched by it. The fur of the little mouse resting on his hand stood on end, as if ruffled by a cold gust of wind.

But the power that surrounded them was not hostile. He sensed ancient wisdom and good magic in it. More powerful than anything he had ever known.

Who are you? he asked silently.

I am wind and earth, fire and water, joy and sorrow... replied a hissing voice in elven.

And a riddles' enthusiast?

Aren't we all?

What do you want?

To protect the Girl with No Name.

She has a name. Eli.

A low laugh rang in his head.

The name the elves gave her does not reflect her destiny.

Do you know her real name? Do you know who she is?

Yes, I do.

He is not going to tell me, the elf thought.

No, I won't.

Tallen was utterly astonished. The creature had read his mind without permission.

If you don't want to answer my questions, why did you come here?

You are one of the few who can hear me. This place is full of closed minds.

On that, I agree with you.

You have to protect her.

I always do.

You can't do that sitting in a dungeon. She is in danger.

I am not sitting here for my own pleasure.

You sit here because you are a proud, selfish person.

174

How well you know me.

I know you better than you think, Tallen. You think you are noble because you show pity to a little mouse. You feed your proud mind with the appearance of kindness. Instead of helping the Girl with No Name, you wait to cross over to the side of the Spirit – while she is fighting for your freedom.

I urged her to run away.

He didn't know why he was defending himself against the accusatory voice. Did he feel, deep down, that it was right?

I am right. And you know it. Forget elven pride. Help her. You have little time. Danger is coming.

The voice faded as suddenly as it had appeared.

Tallen was left alone with his gloomy thoughts.

The spacious interior of the circular building was made of the same bright grey stone. A shaft of light streamed through an opening in the centre of the dome. All who had arrived headed in the direction indicated by the sun's rays, but Temina pulled Eli aside to show her the statues lined up along the walls.

'They are our ancestors,' she explained in a hushed voice. The statues were at least fifteen feet high, made of stone as black as nothingness. 'This colour symbolises their passage into the other world,' the herbalist added. 'To the Fields of Glory.'

Each of the statues was dressed as they had been in life, in bright blue robes, Ha'ami's favourite colour.

'This is Ha'tis, the founder of the Stone Nest. Legend has it that his mother was a soothsayer who could predict the future.'

'Is that her statue standing next to his?' Eli asked.

'Exactly. She prophesied that one day the Stone Nest would become the capital of Ha'ami, that a king would come from here, and that he would make our people the most powerful in history.'

'Has it come true?'

'So far it has turned out to be just a dream of many ambitious local mothers,' Temina smiled cheekily. 'This is Ha'kate, the second Lord of the Stone Nest.'

'He rode a bear?' The warrior rested on the back of the massive animal. The statue of his mother stood beside him, and a huge eagle perched on his shoulder.

'It is said that Ha'kate was blessed by Ami with the ability to communicate with animals, which he used in battle. The ranks of his army were to be filled with countless predators: wolves, bears, tigers...'

'But not dragons?' She grinned and suddenly felt a sting in her heart. The voice that had called to her had grown stronger. It urged her on.

'No, not dragons,' Temina giggled.

Eli breathed slowly, trying to release the tension she felt in her body.

'Do many Ha'ami have such unusual gifts?' she asked, trying to dispel the strange feeling she was sensing.

'Well, those are just legends. I myself have never met anyone with similar powers, such as clairvoyance. The Ha'ami are a practical people. We trust in the strength of our hands and the knowledge of our minds. Nowadays, such beliefs are treated as superstition.'

'What about... magic?' She had long been afraid to broach the subject, but here it seemed to fit naturally into the conversation.

'There are two schools. One denies its existence, the other is panicked about it, which manifests itself in a good old-fashioned hatred of anything that might bear its traces,' Temina replied in the same light-hearted tone as usual. 'Personally, I only believe in the tangible. There is nothing magical in my potions. Just specific herbs and specific ingredients that I use to cure ailments.'

'What's over there?' Eli decided to change the subject, and pointed to the place where the First Brothers and Sisters had gathered, exactly where the sunlight was streaming in.

'That's where Fing is. The Sword of Ha'tis. The source of our ancestors' strength.'

'Anyone still using it?'

'For fighting, no. Admittedly, the blade has not dulled despite the centuries.' They slowly walked towards the assembled people. 'But it is only used for ceremonies, such as the initiation of young warriors or the ritual anointing of a new lord in the castle.'

A huge, two-handed sword with a straight handle was placed on a platform in the middle of the Temple.

'He must have been a giant,' Eli sighed.

She did not know if any of them would have been able to use the weapon effectively. The First Sisters and Brothers stood around in concentration and silence. Not wanting to interrupt their moment of bonding with their ancestors, Eli also fell silent. Finally, one by one, those gathered began to leave their seats and head for the exit. The persistent voice in girl's head urged her to stay.

Sig watched out of the corner of her eye as Temina showed *Ta'uma* around the Temple of the Ancestors. The priestess didn't particularly like letting strangers into this place; she was convinced that the Temple was only for Ha'ami. But the rules of hospitality demanded it this time, and honour and tradition were Sig's highest values.

She watched intently as the women admired the statues and discussed them in whispers, and regretted that she could not hear them. It made her nervous and she found it hard to concentrate on the ceremony. If the rumours were true, Akona would surely urge everybody to give the girl more privileges. Sig burned with reluctance: it was impossible to consider someone of impure blood as equal to Ha'ami. Rather than rely on the opinions of others on the matter, she decided to assess the situation herself before the vote would take place.

Nor could she forget the warning her ancestors had sent her. It happened on the very night the strangers were captured and taken to the Stone Nest. It could not be a coincidence.

As the Council began to disperse, the priestess decided to make sure *Ta'uma* was properly supervised. She could not count on Temina. Although the herbalist was Akona's daughter, she had always shown an extreme disregard for the rules and laws that governed the community. It would be better for Sig to serve as the guide. It would also be an opportunity to get to know the stranger better.

'Where does this entrance lead?' Eli whispered, pointing to a narrow opening in the floor just behind the sword.

'To the crypt,' Sig spoke, appearing unexpectedly from behind them.

An inexplicable feeling pushed Eli there.

'Would it be possible for me to visit it?'

The Guardian of the Temple agreed, although she did not seem entirely happy about it. She led them to the entrance, and then down a narrow, winding staircase into a room lit only by the diffuse glow of oil lamps suspended from the ceiling on long chains. The grey walls seemed to pulsate even more vividly than upstairs.

The voice urged her on, impatient, the girl could feel that they were getting closer. Step by step, the view of the crypt unfolded before them. The room, as large as the temple, was built entirely of bones.

Human skulls adorned the walls, columns and portals, surrounded by shinbones and other parts of long-dead bodies. As they stood on the last step, Eli noticed that even the floor was littered with remains, with snakes crawling among them.

'They don't attack humans,' Temina said reassuringly. 'Their venom is very useful in healing potions.'

'They are blessed by Ami,' Sig added emphatically.

Both Ha'ami stepped onto the moving surface without hesitation, as if strolling among seashells. Eli took a deep breath and stepped onto the macabre carpet. It creaked under her weight. Step by step she joined her companions who now stood in the middle of the crypt. Questions came to her lips, she didn't know where to begin. Fortunately, Sig spoke first.

'Here rest the remains of our ancestors,' she explained, her eyes shining with exultation. 'They are the source of our tribe's power.'

'Is every Ha'ami ... brought here after death?' Eli asked. She felt something climb up her calf and shook her leg slightly without looking down. The snake fell to the ground with a soft plop. She hoped that what they had told her earlier was true and that she would not be bitten in retaliation.

'Anyone worthy of it,' Sig confirmed. Looking around, Eli noticed bones that did not resemble human ones.

'They are the heads of animals killed during the initiation.' Temina followed her gaze.

The voice inside her grew louder, calling, demanding action. On top of a high pile of the remains of various animals, she saw a huge skull.

'It is the head of the dragon that Ha'akon slew.' The herbalist confirmed her guess.

Eli knew now what was the source of the whispering she had heard from the entrance. It was the dragon that was calling her.

'We have to go back,' announced Sig.

'Not yet...' The words escaped her in response. They both looked at her bewildered. 'I mean, I would like to learn   still more about your traditions.'

Sig smiled understandingly.

'The Temple of the Ancestors is an impressive place. I will gladly answer your questions, *Ta'uma*, but later. Now is the time to begin the gathering.' She pointed to the stairs.

Eli had to give up and reluctantly followed her to the exit, the voice in her head hissing with irritation. Every step seemed hard to take, as if some unknown force was resisting her. By the time they were outside the temple, she was drenched in sweat again.

Temina looked at her carefully.

'Are you all right?'

'Yes... just a bit cold.' She waved her hand, trying to keep her tone cheerful. The herbalist nodded.

'Mother, Ha'akon.' She turned to her relatives standing on the stairs. 'I want to take Eli to my place and give her some dry clothes. It is not right for her to face the Council in this state.'

Akona nodded in understanding.

'There's no need to hurry, we have many important things to discuss, we won't expect you until late afternoon. I will send someone to fetch you,' her brother said, then turned and moved on with the others.

'Let's go,' Temina took her hand. 'I live nearby.'

Akona knew her son better than anyone. Such was the lot of a mother. When you spend the first years of a child's life guessing its every need by gesture or facial expression, without being able to get a clear answer, even the smallest wrinkle on the face becomes readable. She had been able to read everything unerringly from the countenance of her beloved, long-awaited child. When he had been hungry or restless, when he had farted, when he had been hiding something, when he had been happy and when he had simply been content. That's why she knew instantly that he was fond of this petite, rebellious creature. She was not surprised.

There was not a girl among the Ha'ami who did not fancy him. But he did not like easy prey. First, it had to be worthy of desire. Second, the prize should not come so quickly. The road to victory had to be arduous and full of obstacles, so that he could feel the throbbing of victory in his veins. Such was the warrior's nature.

This wild girl had the necessary air of mystery, combined with a hard-to-tame nature that must have piqued his interest. However, Akona would have dismissed this as a meaningless adventure that might provide entertainment during the dull winter, had it not been for the recent news of this *Ta'uma's* origins.

Berennike, the Azzgoth princess, had been pursued by the Ha'ami for years. The sole surviving heir to a royal family, commander-in-chief of an army. Adored by her people, hated and yet respected by her enemies. Disappeared one day without a trace.

If this had been true... if she had been found after all this time... if it had been Ha'akon who had formed an alliance and made peace with the rebellious people... wouldn't it have been clear to everyone that he should be the next Ha'ami king?

Akona had always known that her son was second to none. He was a source of her pride and hope for immortal glory. Unfortunately, he did not share her ambitions. He treated power as a service. Though he enjoyed competing on the battlefield, he did not seek fame for its own sake and detested politics.

She was always aware that she had to be the helmsman on his road to triumph. Setting him on the right path, making sure his worth was widely recognised... that was what happened after his victory over the dragon. Her son would have continued to wallow in despair over his lost beloved if Akona had not roused him from his slumber and pushed him on a series of expeditions that not only provided new goals and a break from old life, but also brought him further fame and respect among the Ha'ami, ultimately leading to his election as the ruler of the Stone Nest.

Today's meeting with *Ta'uma* gave her an opportunity to reframe the situation so that Ha'akon would get the most benefit from it. She wanted to assess the girl and see if she was suitable for her purposes. If so, she was once again going to take the helm into her own hands. So far, her first impression had met her expectations. The wild however naive youngster may not have been easy to tame, but bringing her into the game didn't appear to be a problem, even without her being aware of it. She seemed straightforward enough.

The first thing Akona had to take care of now was to make sure everyone recognised the girl's heritage, and that her son's initial interest would develop into something more.

Temina's house was indeed close to the temple. It was surrounded by a large garden, which was rather gloomy in winter, though it must have been a lovely place at other times of the year. The building was quite light inside, with large windows and tastefully decorated rooms, without the ostentation Eli had seen at Ha'teng's. However, the wealth of the household could not be overlooked. They were now in a spacious dressing room, and the girl was convinced that there were more robes hanging there than there were days in the year. The walls were decorated with beautiful mosaics of small, colourful pebbles depicting scenes from everyday life in the city. There were chests everywhere, no doubt filled with valuables. They were served by six girls of different ages.

'Thank you, I'll dry myself.' Eli turned to the maid who was standing over her with a towel. 'The hot springs reach this far?' she asked, wrapping the white cloth around her.

'No,' her hostess replied. 'We heat water in each house for personal use. But we do have baths connected to the springs from above. I don't know how they work, you'll have to ask Keera,' she added, anticipating more questions. 'Catch!' she called, tossing a pair of trousers and a blue sweatshirt in Eli's direction. 'We still need to do something about your hair.'

'Thanks! What's wrong with it?'

'It's getting awfully frizzy,' Temina winced.

'It's the humidity. It doesn't bother me at all.' Eli shrugged and pulled on baggy trousers. She wondered if she'd have to roll them up.

'Do you want to look dignified or not?'

Eli sighed. *Ah, this untameable hair of mine...*

'Right now I look like a Ha'ami child,' she added with a laugh, pointing at her loose robes. 'I'm not sure if they're still trousers or a skirt.'

'That's just fine. Sit down, I'll sort out that mess on your head.' Temina pointed to a simple chair with a pale wooden back.

Eli obediently sat down and let the herbalist comb her hair.

'What is the most attractive part of a woman's body, Eli?' Temina asked, carefully gathering her curls with a comb.

'To be honest, I've never really given it a thought.'

'Legs, my dear, legs and bottom!' She pulled her hair into a tight bun on top of her head and fastened it with a beautiful silver clasp.

'Aha.'

'That's why the servants wear trousers, though we don't bother with their tops, and why our trouser legs are so loose. An air of mystery, you see...'

'Aha.'

'Good. You're ready. Let's go then!'

'Where to?'

'I want to show you the true source of power in this town.'

'Another old sword or a pile of bones?' Eli remarked with a wince. Temina laughed out loud.

'It'll be a different kind of temple. We're going to the school.'

As usual, the beginning of the meeting was a bit of a warm-up, with relatively trivial matters being discussed. Ha'teng was forced to listen with little interest to a report on the state of the granaries, the new births, the list of deaths, the demand for servants... none of these matters required decisions or even discussion. A waste of time.

Then came the highlight of the day, Ha'sani's salt stories. Much to Ha'teng's surprise, they decided to accept the plan to establish trade relations with the dwarven factories.

The Guardian of Defence watched his friend carefully during the debate, trying to read his intentions. He was reluctant to openly disagree with Ha'akon.

Tiger himself was still unconvinced. He believed that the unrest in the East should be quelled as quickly as possible by the combined forces of the Ha'ami, after which they could turn south to attack the Elven Kingdom. In conversation with him, the ruler had shown some enthusiasm for this expedition, but it had not yet translated into action. In the end, the Governor gave his support to Ha'sani's plan. Only Sig and Ha'aki were against it. Not surprising. It was no secret that the priestess harboured a fierce hatred for all non-humans, and the grumpy commander would rather starve to death than admit that his tribe needed help from the dwarves.

The Guardian of Defence, on the other hand, simply did not want to stand in the king's way. He felt that the Stone Nest was not strong enough. Ha'attik was still very popular among the brothers, and he was overly sensitive to potential rivals. Ha'akon, the Dragon Slayer, had a special place on that list. Why tease the beast...

Tiger still hoped to convince his friend to change his ways. He would talk to him later today, maybe at the feast, maybe it would work. After all, they were brothers in battle, and once, long ago, Ha'teng had hoped they would become something more. Though those hopes had been dashed, there was no denying that they shared a strong bond.

For the sake of them all, he now had to convince Ha'akon that the current course of action carried too much risk.

'Then the Ha'ami boys graduate when they are ten years old?' Eli asked as they made their way through the corridors of the building. They had already visited the children's section, where toddlers of both sexes were reciting facts about the tribe's history and learning the basics of arithmetic, reading and writing.

'Yes,' Temina confirmed. 'After that, they go under the care of the warriors in the Upper Castle and focus mainly on training the skills they will need on the battlefield. The girls, on the other hand, continue their general education and choose what they want to specialise in. Professions we have no shortage of... oh, this should interest you. *The history of Ha'ami.* Come on, let's listen.' With that, she pulled her companion through the door into the room where the lecture was taking place.

The teenage girls, about three dozen of them, sat in a semi-circle on cushions on the floor, and in front of them stood a middle-aged woman with a strong figure and a powerful voice. She was wearing a simple turquoise dress. Temina and Eli crouched on the cushions at the back.

'The last time this occurred was when the current Lord of the Stone Nest, Ha'akon, took over after the death of Ha'ding, which occurred on the battlefield.' The lecturer was clearly finishing a lengthy argument. 'Who knows what happens in such a case?'

Several hands shot up, and the teacher pointed to one. The selected girl spoke in a very matter-of-fact tone.

'All the brothers who have undergone initiation gather to vote for a new leader.'

'Very good, Tig,' the lecturer complimented her. 'And then what?'

'The mother of the new ruler and the ruler himself choose four advisors each and form the Council of First Sisters and Brothers,' the student added.

'That's right. What is the matter, Dona?' The reader turned to another girl who was whispering to her neighbour. The latter was moving uneasily on the cushion.

'Sister, are there any other circumstances, apart from the death of a member of the Council, under which a change of leadership can take place, according to tradition?'

'Good question,' the lecturer replied, clearly pleased with the student's curiosity. 'Firstly, the ruler or his mother can decide to replace members of the Council if they feel they are unable to fulfil their duties. Secondly, the ruler's mother can be replaced by another close relative of his, such as a sister. The most complicated situation is with the change of the leader. According to tradition, this can happen if he breaks the rules of honour or the Ha'ami brotherhood. In such a case, the king can ask the Council to end their obedience. If they do so, the Judgement of the Ancestors takes place. Who knows what it is?' She looked around the chamber. 'Yes, Meera?'

'The First Brothers duel their commander to the death,' one of the girls replied.

'There has not been an instance of this in our part of the Ha'ami lands for over a hundred years, though it has happened in the East.' The teacher paused as another listener raised her hand. 'Yes?'

'What happens to the ruler's mother if he dies as a result of this duel?'

'If a ruler is defeated in the Judgement of the Ancestors, members of his immediate family suffer an honourable death at their own hand,' the lecturer explained.

Eli sighed reflexively.

'So, if something happens to Ha'akon, you and your mother–?' She whispered to Temina.

'Only in the event of an honourable removal from power,' the herbalist reassured her. 'I don't really see that possibility.'

Eli nodded. Indeed. It was hard to imagine.

'Remember also–' the lecturer went on, '–that the consequence of a leader's death in battle is that his mother takes over the regency until a new ruler is elected. Good. That's all for today. Time for the meal.'

The girls began to get up, some of them glancing at Temina and Eli, nudging the others and whispering to each other.

'They'll be here in a moment,' the herbalist laughed. She did not move from her seat. As she had predicted, a small crowd quickly gathered around them, bombarding Eli with questions.

'Are you the *Ta'uma*? Is it true that you speak our language? Where do you come from? Can you fight? How did you defeat Ha'teng?'

Temina raised her hand to break the flood of words.

'Whoa, whoa, girls. Where are your manners? This lovely lady is our guest, which means she must first be fed and then talked to death. Which of you would like to take us to the dining hall?'

Amid whispers and squeaks, they made their way down the corridor, eventually reaching a large hall where round tables, each seating six, had been set up. Temina and Eli took the first available seats.

'The quickest to return here with food can share it with us,' Temina announced. 'But know that our *Ta'uma* does not eat meat, so those who return with sausages will be sent away without mercy.'

The girls scattered. The herbalist leaned back in her chair with contentment.

'Now you can taste the joys of fame for a change, my dear, and not just the burden of it. You wanted to know more about the life of the Ha'ami girls. Rejoice in it!'

Ha'sani was overjoyed. The day was going exactly his way. He knew from the start that the First Sisters would be on his side. After all, their responsibility was to look after the interests of the local populace, not the king in the distant capital. Teena kept her word and convinced the other council members to vote for his plan. They knew from the start that Sig would vote against it.

Ha'teng's decision was a mystery. He usually supported Ha'akon in all official matters, but this time he decided to oppose him. Ha'sani suspected that this was due to a down-to-earth jealousy. In the end, it was young warrior's idea to trade with the dwarves that won the ruler's favour. The Guardian of Defence had nothing to do with the idea, which is probably why he did not want to support it. He was also under pressure from the *Ta'uma* case.

As for the mysterious girl, here too Ha'sani had some hopes. If it turned out to be true that she had such a close relationship with Zak, the founder of the merchant posts they wanted to start trading with, perhaps she would agree to help him. Surely, they could offer her something of value... even if Ha'teng didn't like such a compromise. The Governor's support was crucial.

It was definitely a good day.

'I see, Tig, that you are as quick on your feet as you are with answers. Sit down!'

The girl perched obediently on the edge of the chair, as if unsure if she would be allowed to stay. Despite her young age, she was taller than Eli, though equally slender, and her figure was still somewhat angular. Like all the schoolgirls, she wore a light blue dress and her hair was cut evenly at shoulder height. After a while they were joined by three other equally excited students: Lana, Kori and Greeta. Up close, it was clear that all the girls liked to emphasise their individuality. Some of them had shaved their eyebrows and then drawn lines in different colours: green, purple, red... Their ears, like their noses, were full of earrings and chains.

As soon as the food was laid out on the table – bread, cheese, olives and dried fruit – Temina struck up a conversation.

'My ladies, this is Eli. As you know, she is new to the area. I'm showing her around the City of Sisters today, revealing to her the life of the oppressed part of our community... I thought you might like to share your experiences with her.'

'Oppressed?' Greeta was outraged. She had a round face and turned up nose. 'Without us, this whole fortress would be in chaos faster than a warrior can count to ten... if you can find one who can.'

They all burst out laughing; it was clear that this was a common kind of joke.

'Do you really think so, *Ta'uma?*' asked Tig. She seemed more serious than the other girls. 'Why?'

Eli finished chewing her cheese.

'Oppressed is a big word ... but since I came here, I've experienced a lot of rules and restrictions, and a hoard of men with weapons dictate what I'm supposed to do, what I'm allowed to and what I'm not allowed to do every day.'

Just to make sure they wouldn't ask her anything else for the time being, she stuffed a sizeable piece of bread into her mouth.

'Well... I see it differently,' Tig replied. 'Among the Ha'ami, both men and women are bound by a number of laws and traditions–'

The other girls nodded vigorously.

'True, only warriors use weapons on a daily basis, that's their role: but all trade, handicrafts, agricultural work is managed by us,' added Kori.

'Perhaps it used to be that most of the funds came from war expeditions. Nowadays, it is from our work that we get the most revenue. That makes us the treasurers,' Lana supported her.

Eli's eyes darted from one speaker to the next, trying to keep up with the flow of their arguments. Seeing this, Temina laughed.

'Didn't I tell you that you were in for an interesting day?' She elbowed her in the side. 'What do you think is the purpose for which the Council meets most often? When the warriors need to look into the treasury. And that is administered by the City of Sisters.'

'Oh, the Council is meeting today?' Greeta sighed. 'Will there be a feast? I would so like to be invited...'

'Why?' Eli asked, thinking that this was the last place she wanted to go herself.

'There will be many recognized warriors there,' the girl replied, explaining as if it was obvious. 'Such a chance to meet someone. And, of course the First Brothers will be there, too!'

'Meet?' Kori laughed. 'Just say who you want to sleep with.'

Eli nearly choked on her bread. She sipped some water.

'Well, I need to try as many as I can before I decide if I want to have offspring,' Greeta replied unmoved. 'And it is well known that the First Brothers and their guards are the elite.'

'Wouldn't you prefer someone closer to you in age?' Eli asked.

Greeta sighed dramatically again.

'I've had my fill of those. But it's hard to find someone among the warriors who is brave and not stupid at the same time.'

'And wouldn't you like to make a long-term commitment to someone?' The girls looked at her as if she had spoken in a foreign language.

'Well, if Ha'akon wanted me, I could spend a few months in his bed.' Lana broke the silence, leading to an outbreak of general merriment around the table. They began to tease each other about who would make a better lover for the lord of the castle and why, eventually asking Temina to settle their dispute.

'None of that, you're not going to make me my own brother's pimp,' she laughed in reply.

'*Ta'uma*, you live among the warriors up the hill. Which ones have you already tried?' Greeta asked curiously. 'Can you tell us which ones are worth dealing with? I don't want to waste my time with boring men who can't give me pleasure.'

Eli's ears turned pink at the question. She hated such conversations and sharing of intimacy, even in a group of girls.

'Come on, don't be silly,' Tig interjected. '*Ta'uma* wouldn't   sleep with just anyone. Eventually they will assign her someone who will accept her into their family, as a sign of alliance with the people she comes from. Do you already know who you will be assigned to?'

'Assigned?' Eli blinked and looked at Temina questioningly. 'I have no intention of bonding with anyone or needing anyone's protection... I'm fine on my own.'

'You seem to know how to fight, like warriors. Is that true?' Kori asked.

'Better,' Eli corrected her, causing widespread excitement.

'You heard she gave Ha'teng a beating,' Temina confirmed. 'To this day, he walks around with a battered face.'

'How did you do that? You are so small!' Tig marvelled.

'With a kick.' Eli shrugged.

'Can you show us?' Lana asked.

'Perhaps another time,' Temina saved her. 'Now let's go, we have to stop by the archives before we appear before the Council. Thanks for the food! It's time for you to return to your studies.'

'Are you going to visit us again?' Greeta asked. 'You must tell us about today's feast!'

'Of course, I'll try,' she murmured. Her head was foggy from all the new knowledge. The girls' energy was infectious, though, and a nice change after many days spent among mostly serious and stern warriors. It seemed, however, that they were going somewhere much more peaceful now.

During a break in the session, Akona was busy giving instructions to the servants who were preparing the dinner. Her mind was not idle. So much news in one day, so many pieces of the puzzle! If only everything would go her way...

For one thing, the king's supply problems and the Azzgoth rebellion could only be the beginning. The conquered peoples, seeing Ha'ami in trouble on one of their borders, may be tempted to take risks and try to throw off the yoke themselves. This will create the need to fight on multiple fronts, giving commanders the opportunity to gain even more glory on the battlefield. And Ha'akon was one of the best.

Secondly, if Ha'sani's plan works, it will be they, the Ha'ami of the Stone Nest, and more specifically their ruler, who will come up with a solution to the salt supply problems for the entire land. This could weaken the king's position and at the next gathering the brothers will choose someone new... someone younger, braver and more deserving.

Akona summoned a servant who had been charged with preparing the evening's robes for the feast.

'What robe have you for *Ta'uma*?' she asked. The girl showed her three suggestions from which to choose.

'Hmm... this one will highlight her eyes the best.' She pointed to one. 'Make sure it fits her figure well. Call a seamstress, just in case.'

The servant bowed and left.

Yes... there's also the matter of the girl. Berennike... Akona was the last person to believe in the dreams of desperate slaves. But that didn't mean she wouldn't use them for her own ends. A formal alliance with the Azzgoths might increase Ha'akon's chances of finally being elected to the position he was worthy of. And the Stone Nest, as prophesied, would become the capital of the Ha'ami lands. Yes, this was her time.

She believed it with all her might.

'Temina, may I ask you something?'

'Of course, but I reserve the right not to answer,' the herbalist replied playfully.

'Ha'ami men commit themselves to each other for life as *koru-koinen*–'

'–and we as *neru-koinen*', the woman added.

'Yes. But the girls have made it clear that they do not wish to be with a warrior for any length of time. How does that fit in?'

'Well, it's true, it's rare for such a couple to spend more time together. But there are exceptions... When I was young, my mother spent several years in close intimacy with a man. I doubt they had an exclusive relationship, but they saw each other regularly.'

'What separated them?'

'He died in battle.'

'I'm sorry...'

'Don't be. I didn't like him at all,' she remarked dryly.

Eli didn't know what to say.

'Here is the Archive!' Temina announced.

They stood in front of a bright two-storey building. Stepping inside, they found themselves in a spacious room with a high ceiling. Shelves of books and manuscripts stretched as far as the eye could see.

They were greeted by a woman in a cobalt dress with beautiful, straight, loose, waist-length hair. She looked to be in her forties and gave them a surprised but friendly look of her piercing blue eyes.

'Welcome to our Temple of Knowledge!' she said, measuring Eli with curious eyes. 'I am Anneke. To what do we owe your visit?'

Temina hugged her warmly.

'My dear, I bring you an extraordinary guest today. Meet our *Ta'uma*. She calls herself Eli, but in the City she is better known as the Tiger Bane.' The herbalist introduced the girl, much to her confusion. 'She loves to read and wanted to see this seldom visited place,' she added jokingly.

Anneke replied with a smile.

'I know we are less popular than the Baths, but the benefits of being here are disproportionately greater... it is a pleasure to welcome such an avid reader to our doorstep.'

'Thank you... that's really impressive.' Eli looked around in delight. 'This looks like a wonderful collection.'

'I'd be happy to show you around and then you can tell me what interests you most,' the archivist offered.

They made their way along the vast shelves, Anneke explaining how the books and manuscripts were organised. Eli could not contain her admiration at the number and variety of items collected. There were writings from all parts of the world, in many languages. But she bit her tongue before asking another question about the source of these impressive collections. *Robbery,* she thought. On the one hand, she was relieved that the Ha'ami respected the achievements of other cultures enough not to burn or destroy them. On the other hand, her palm trembled as she reached for the book, wondering what its presence here had cost.

'Now that you know what's on these dusty shelves, would you like to have a look at something in particular?' Temina asked when the archivist had finished showing them around the building.

'Yes...' Eli began shyly. 'I'm very interested in books that describe Ha'ami laws and traditions.'

'That's an unusual request,' Anneke said, clearly intrigued. 'But I suppose it is understandable for someone who has just arrived here.'

She led them further down between the shelves.

'Here you will find a section with all the items on the subject that we have collected in the Archives.'

'Would it be possible for me to... browse through some of them now?'

'We still have some time left,' Temina agreed. 'But I'm afraid we'll have to leave you to it, the laws of Ha'ami are certainly not my fascination. But I would like to drink some warm herbs with this nice woman,' she declared, taking Anneke's hand. 'Let's go, my dear, we'd better leave the little bookworm here with those perverted manuscripts.'

The archivist nodded.

'If you need any help, you'll find us in the chamber near the entrance,' she said, and they both walked away, whispering something between themselves.

Eli eagerly went through the titles of the thick tomes that looked seldom used. Finally, she found the one she wanted. The heavy volume in Ha'ami bore the simple title *"Crimes and Punishments"*. She took it from the shelf, placed it carefully on the table by the window and leafed through it, not knowing where to start. Eventually she decided that she had to read it in its entirety, hoping to find something that would give her an idea of how to help Tallen. She immersed herself in it, forgetting the passage of time, when she suddenly felt someone's hand on her shoulder.

'I'm afraid we have to go back,' Temina whispered in her ear. 'Ha'akon has sent for us.'

Eli sighed in disappointment and put the bound volume back.

'Why am I actually appearing before the Council?' she asked, not wanting to be judged by the ten people she had met earlier.

'You know they're here to decide whether to officially recognise your status as the *Ta'uma*.' The herbalist put her arm around her shoulder and led her to the exit. 'They will probably ask you a number of questions. They've also asked me to be a witness.'

'Will you be there with me?' Eli was pleased. The knowledge that a familiar face would be nearby brought her relief and gave her courage.

'I will! We rebels must stick together, my dear.'

After a quick goodbye to Anneke, they set off after the guard. On the way, Eli repeated in her mind the statement she had decided to make to the Council. Much depended on it. She had to do her best.

The matter of recognising the prisoner as the *Ta'uma* was the last item on the agenda, and it was Ha'teng's turn to lead the discussion. He began with an account of the circumstances of her arrest, the interrogations he had conducted with her and the elf, the decision to give her the punishment for riding her horse, which she eventually served. He did so indifferently, keeping the knowledge Ha'kame had shared with him to himself. He then briefly reviewed the rumours that were circulating about her among the servants.

'And so, we are dealing with another Berennike,' he concluded, not without a hint of irony in his voice. 'The   king should have dragged the body of this witch all over the Azzgoth land for everyone to see her dead... That would have put an end to all this nonsense.'

His words, however, were not met with universal applause. Ha'akon spoke up unexpectedly.

'We must consider every possibility,' he declared, looking directly at the commander.

What game are you playing, my friend? Ha'teng thought.

'You are right,' he corrected himself aloud. 'We must be careful in our judgements. I spoke too hastily.'

He saw the muscles in the leader's face relax. Clearly, the Governor was determined to acknowledge the girl's status.

Temina was invited to give evidence. She recounted the circumstances under which she was summoned to the Upper Castle. She spoke briefly and only told the Council about helping the wounded Eli and the conversations they had during those days. Despite her brief account, Ha'teng noticed the furtive glances that were cast his way. He was sure that rumours of his duel with this brat were quite popular in the City of Sisters.

'To recapitulate,' he interrupted her, irritated, 'despite all the time you spent with her, you were unable to learn of her origins?'

Ha'akon's sister looked at him with a gleam in her eye that he read as mockery.

'No. But everything suggests that–'

'We're not interested in your assumptions, just the facts,' he cut her off again. She did not answer.

'Have you discovered what her relationship is to the elf rotting in our dungeon?' Sig asked with a hint of disgust on her lips.

'You mean, are they lovers?' Temina shot back, looking at the assembled with increasing amusement. 'They are not.'

'What makes you so sure?' Sig was openly offended by her mocking tone.

'Eli is quite innocent in these matters, if I may put it so,' she continued, her sarcasm leaving no doubt in the mind of even the most obtuse listener.

'If all this turns out to be true,' Akona interjected, saving the situation, 'the girl must be cared for, and everything must be done to persuade her to form an alliance. The raison d'etre of the Ha'ami state demands it.'

As usual, both Ha'akon's mother and sister would support his intentions, whatever they might be, Ha'teng thought to himself. He was concerned with one thing: gaining strategic information about the Eternal Enemy that might contribute to an effective invasion plan in the future. If they succeeded... their glory would be everlasting. Adding the story of the slaves into the mix only served to complicate matters, distract the people and divert their attention.

It's time to end this, he thought.

He ordered the girl inside.

The door opened and the guards let *Ta'uma* into the council chamber. She sat down in the chair prepared for her, facing the Council, who were seated in a semicircle. She had managed to change her clothes and was now dressed in the official Ha'ami robes, black trousers and a blue caftan.

A bit theatrical, Temina, even for you, he mused.

Her hair was tied back in a high bun and her face was powdered to hide the bruises he had given her. Even Ha'teng had to admit that there was something endearing about her appearance. Despite her small stature, she exuded a strength that contrasted with the strange, almost childlike innocence that shone from her green eyes. Until now, however, he had been convinced that she was not very bright, but as stubborn as a hungry goat.

'For the sake of formality, can you confirm your name?' he asked dispassionately.

'Eli,' she replied simply, her voice strong and determined.

'Is that your only name?'

'Yes, it is.'

'Where are you from?'

This time she was silent.

'Is there anything you want to tell us about yourself?'

Again, nothing.

'Do you know why you are here?'

She took a deep breath and exhaled slowly.

'I found myself here because I was arrested after crossing the borders of the Ha'ami lands,' she replied. 'With your permission, I would simply like to leave this place in peace, together with my companion.'

'That will not be possible. You have broken the law,' he pointed out coldly.

'Then... I will answer all your questions and, as I promised earlier, I will give you the strategic information about the elves that you so desire,' she began slowly, weighing her words, 'but only after my companion has been released and escorted back to the border of the Green Kingdom. I can stay here as long as you wish.'

'That is a very generous offer,' he replied in a mocking tone. 'But we decline it in its entirety.'

'One moment,' Ha'sani interrupted. 'You haven't mentioned anything to us about an offer to exchange information about the elves, Ha'teng.'

'I didn't mention it because I don't believe in it.' He did not grace him with a glance.

'And yet I think the Council should hear it.' Ha'sani did not give up. 'What do you know of elves, Eli?'

'Everything,' she replied in an even tone. 'I have lived with them for the last few years. That is why I have made you an offer: my cooperation for the freedom of the prisoner you hold.'

Ha'teng read her emotions. She was determined, but calm.

'Why do you care so much for him?' Sig continued to ramble on about the same subject that was obviously still on her mind. She visibly could not accept the thought of a warm relationship with a non-human.

The girl gave her an honest look.

'I owe him a debt of gratitude. He saved my life. Surely the Ha'ami understand this honourable obligation.'

'Elves have no honour,' the Guardian of the Temple hissed.

'On the contrary,' Eli continued with stoic calm, but Ha'teng could still hear her breathing quicken. His watchful eyes traced the pulsating veins in her neck. 'Elves are honourable and noble. Your dislike of them is a great mistake.' He almost burst out laughing when he saw Sig gasp at those words. 'If you knew the truth...'

'We will consider it,' Ha'akon intervened, clearly wanting to avert the impending disaster. 'Is there anything you wish to add to your case?'

She turned to him with the same sad smile.

'I will answer all your questions, but only after my companion has been released and returned to the border of the Green Kingdom. I can stay here as long as you like.'

'Yes,' he replied briefly. 'We've already heard that. You may go.'

She rose slowly from her seat and moved gracefully towards the door. Ha'akon's face was impassive, but Ha'teng knew his friend only too well. His gaze betrayed him as he watched the girl intently. Hm... maybe he wants her for himself and prefers to get to her through kindness. Ha'teng understood. He himself enjoyed the art of hunting and breaking the resistance of the unwilling. Especially in winter, when there was nothing else to do. Submissiveness was boring... He decided to help him a little. He will vote in favour. It remains to be seen what will come of it.

Chapter VIII
More wine and ladies, and a little singing

SPARK DID NOT BELIEVE THAT his attempt to reason with the elf would work. This race is remarkably impervious to suggestion, even from those far wiser than themselves. Still, he was determined to avert the disaster that loomed on the horizon. The Girl with No Name had to live to fulfil her destiny. It was better for the world.

It was time to find her another protector.

'Is the dinner really so grand?' Eli asked as two servants anointed her hair with oils.

'Absolutely,' Temina snapped. 'I'm supposed to make you presentable.' With that she took a healthy sip from her cup. 'Akona's orders. She even sent you a dress. Believe me, you don't want to be in her way.'

That I admit, Eli muttered to herself as the servants finished with the fragrances and energetically set about braiding her hair in a sophisticated way.

She could barely recognise herself in the huge mirror she was facing. The green flowing dress was the same colour as her eyes and contrasted with her tawny complexion. It would have been a simple outfit had it not been for the deep neckline at the back, which almost exposed her bottom, and the split in the skirt, which reached down to her left hip. Her skin was anointed with some sort of lotion that not only hid the bruises, but made her look as if she had been gently bathed in the golden rays of the sun. Black coal liner highlighted her eyes. Her naturally dark eyebrows were left alone by Temina, who said they didn't need any more colour. Eli breathed a sigh of relief. After today, she was afraid her friend would shave them off or dye them blue. Her hair, on the other hand, was apparently in need of levelling and more careful care.

The girl endured it all with mixed feelings. However, she had to admit that if the herbalist's appearance was going to set the standard for the style expected of the guests at the feast, then she had better go all out and get beautified in the local fashion.

Temina was dressed in a tight black gown that accentuated her curves. She instructed the servants as they attended to Eli, while she tried on the richly ornamented jewellery and tried to decide which earrings to wear.

'What should I know so as not to make a blunder?'

'Drink when everyone else is drinking. Applaud during performances and toasts. And if someone asks you to go away with them, it means they want to cuddle with you,' Temina explained.

'What?'

'That's how all Ha'ami feasts usually end,' she laughed. 'One big orgy.'

'Can I leave before that happens?' Eli felt the heat rising in her cheeks.

'You may.' The herbalist adjusted her hair, which the maid was styling. 'Actually, you can leave when the performances are over.'

'What performances?'

'Usually there are several female performers who show off their skills. Singing, dancing, reciting,' she listed indifferently.

'Sounds amusing.' Eli was curious, remembering fondly the evenings in the Elven Forest when she would listen to the beautiful songs that echoed between the trees late into the night.

'To each his own,' Temina muttered. 'Well, now you look like a human,' she complimented the girl as she looked in the mirror.

'You mean, like Ha'ami?'

'I haven't messed you up that much... I hope!' the herbalist giggled.

Ha'akon sipped his wine slowly, reflecting on the day's events. He was pleased with the Council's support for Ha'sani's plan, but the matter of *Ta'uma* weighed heavily on his mind. Unlike trade matters, it took the unanimous support of the Council to acknowledge someone's nobility. Sig's vehement opposition proved to be an insurmountable obstacle. The only thing they agreed on was more time, so that Ha'teng could investigate more thoroughly and provide clear evidence.

'Cheer up,' his mother, sitting to his right, murmured to him. She put a reassuring hand on his shoulder. 'Enjoy this wonderful evening. We have prepared a most interesting programme for you tonight.'

He sighed. Singing and reciting was about the last thing that gave him pleasure. He glanced around the room where a large crowd had gathered. Some of the festively dressed Ha'ami rested on low chairs and chaise lounges arranged in a semicircle in the centre of the room. Others stood along the walls and columns, sipping liquor and engaging in casual conversation. Ha'akon endured with irritation the lingering glances the women sent his way. As always, he was tired of being the centre of their attention. When he was leading warriors into battle, he was in his element. Fending off the persistent advances of the wine-drunk was a very different kind of challenge.

'Look who finally showed up,' his mother whispered in his ear. Temina stood in the doorway, leading a petite figure in an emerald gown. Not for the first time, he was struck by how one person could look so fragile and innocent, while at the same time exuding an unfathomable inner strength, best seen in her bright, unusually sharp eyes. Slowly, his sister and Eli made their way towards the revellers. The girl's shapely leg appeared from a long slit in her skirt as she walked.

He felt a pit in his stomach. Yes, he desperately wanted to take her in his arms and meet the warmth of her filigree body.

'You've groomed her up pretty well, Akona,' a voice came from behind. It was Ha'teng, standing over them. He took a healthy sip from his goblet. 'It's hard to recognise this savage.'

'Wise eyes will always see hidden potential,' his mother replied with a satisfied smile. She rose from her seat. 'If you will excuse me, I would like to introduce our wonderful *Ta'uma* to the other guests.'

Ha'akon just grunted in response. He was well aware that he was staring at the newcomers like a dimwit, but as much as he wanted to, he could not take his eyes off the girl. His friend snapped him out of his trance by placing a firm hand on his shoulder.

'We need to talk, *koru*' he said firmly. 'It seems to me that we are making a big mistake with this whole business of trading with the dwarves. Hear me out.'

The governor came to his senses and looked at him with a sobered expression.

'You know I always value your opinion,' he replied, preparing himself for a long debate that he really didn't feel like having that evening. But he respected his friend too much to refuse him. Especially since he knew that it had definitely not been a successful day for Ha'teng. The lord of the castle hoped he wouldn't cause him any more disappointment with what he had to tell his commander.

Ha'akon had no intention of changing his mind.

And his friend, however unhappy, would have to accept that.

The Assembly Hall, the largest room Eli had seen so far in the Stone Nest, was already filled with guests when they arrived. Beautifully decorated, slender columns in two rows divided the long pavilion into three sections, with low chairs in the centre arranged in a horseshoe, like an auditorium. But the gathered guests were lounging here and there, engaged in more or less noisy conversation.

Although no one wore shoes, everyone looked festive. The tall, stocky men wore loose, dark tunics that came down to their knees. The women, on the other hand, were dressed in exceptionally lavish and defiant gowns in all the colours of the rainbow.

The servants consisted entirely of those who had been given the right to cover their torsos with clothing. They all wore identical black trousers and blue asymmetrical caftans, their shoulders exposed to show the tattoo that identified their master. A short, fawn-haired man led the two women to their seats. Temina made her way to her assigned chair. Eli sat between Ha'min and Teena, who had Ha'sani on her right.

The girl could not take her eyes off the colourful crowd that had gathered for the feast. The sheer abundance of pattern and colour of the extravagant outfits made her dizzy. They all had one thing in common: defiant cut-outs, necklines, transparencies designed to seduce. She felt overwhelmed by the ubiquitous glamour of the place.

Now I understand what the girls were talking about, she said to herself. *It seems they weren't the only ones trying to lure a warrior for the night. Today the men are the game...*

Unexpectedly, at the far end of the room, Eli spotted a figure that seemed to come from a world as different as her own. In a low chair sat an ancient woman with long, snow-white hair, slurping contentedly from a deep bowl of soup handed to her by a servant.

'Who is she?' She turned to Ha'min, who had filled the goblet to the brim and handed it to her with an encouraging gesture. After the experience of the previous dinner when they had met, she only dipped her mouth into the wine and immediately handed the vessel to Teena.

'The Eldest Woman,' he replied in a tone as if it were common knowledge.

'Plain as day,' Eli admonished him. 'But who is she and what is she doing here?'

He laughed easily.

'Right, my littlun, I forgot you don't know much about us,' he said, filling another cup. 'She is the treasure trove of the olden times. Our archivists consult her on various subjects when they need to add to the books. In the old days, all Ha'ami history and tradition was passed from mouth to mouth.'

'This is the first such respectable person I have seen here,' Eli remarked, passing the wine on again. She did not mention that this was, in fact, the first lady of such advanced age she had met in her entire life.

'That's true.' Ha'min nodded. 'As body and mind weaken with the years, every honourable Ha'ami leaves so as not to be a burden to the tribe. Though women remain among us longer than men, they too move on when they are no longer able to care for themselves. A dignified death is the only way out.'

'If you say so,' she murmured. 'She must be very clever. I'd like to talk to her.'

He laughed in embarrassment, then burped unexpectedly loudly.

'I don't think you'd hear anything sensible. Her mind is a bit lost, if I may say so...' He explained with some embarrassment. 'But apparently there is no one to replace her yet, and Sig finds her extremely helpful. They are related somehow, as far as I know.'

'Eli, how good to see you!' She heard a voice above her. She turned and rose from her chair. Akona stood before her, statuesque, her hair neatly combed, wearing a simple white satin gown. Long, richly ornamented earrings dangled from her ears, and countless gold bracelets clanked on her hands.

'I see the robe I have chosen for you fits you well.' She offered her hand and turned her around.

'Yes.' Eli bowed slightly, blushing as the woman treated her like a puppet. 'Thank you very much.'

'Oh, it's really nothing, my dear.' Akona smiled softly. 'Ha'min, will you forgive me if I steal your interlocutor for a moment? I would like to introduce her to the other guests.'

The warrior had no time to reply as they moved on. Fortunately, the servants had begun to distribute the snacks, so he turned his attention in that direction. Meanwhile, Akona led Eli through the crowd, introducing her to countless people. Names flashed in and out of her memory like lightning in a spring storm.

'Our *Ta'uma*', the hostess repeated over and over with the same polite expression. They were inundated with courteous responses and words of welcome.

'You've met these warriors before,' she announced as they reached the place where Ha'akon and Ha'teng sat in deep discussion. The latter was clearly vexed. He measured Eli with an irritated look.

'Have you decided to look for someone who wants to enjoy your meagre charms today?' he asked venomously.

'I'm not looking for anyone because I haven't lost anyone.' she snapped back.

'Great. Then you can sweep the floor with your skirt somewhere else and stop interrupting our conversation,' he replied impatiently. She felt herself blush with anger and was about to open her mouth to reply when she heard Akona.

'I'm glad I can always count on your civility, my dear,' she rebuked him, maintaining her diplomatic tone throughout. 'Fortunately, there are many more amiable guests here... so we can just wish you a pleasant evening.'

That said, she pulled Eli along and left. They passed Ha'akon, who gave her an absent-minded look, as if he had not heard the exchange. He did not say a word, just turned back to the conversation with his friend.

Eli wondered what had been the subject of such an engaging discussion, which clearly frustrated Ha'teng.

Ha'min had emptied at least two jugs of wine by the time Akona finally returned with Eli. Ha'sani and Teena were poor company as they started making eyes at each other almost immediately. As usual.

'Anything good to eat?' the girl asked, taking a seat next to him.

'Not much that would appeal to you,' he muttered. His tongue was beginning to tangle. He tried to concentrate on his plate instead of staring at her lovely muscular leg peeking out of the slit in her dress. Clearly, she had noticed his gaze, for with a sudden movement she pulled the fabric of her skirt down to cover the enticing sight.

He rebuked himself silently. He shouldn't have drunk so much. In such a state, he certainly wouldn't find any company for tonight.

'How about some olives?' He pointed to a bowl on the table.

'Oh, great,' she replied a little too loudly, making it sound rather artificial, and immediately began to devour one after another.

'Wine?' he asked.

'I'd rather have some water. It's hot in here, I'm thirsty,' she explained.

'Yes... of course.' He nodded at the servant, trying to figure out how to change the subject. 'Hey over there, a jug of water, quick!'

The servant trotted off to fetch the vessel.

'Eli...' He turned to the girl to correct his earlier impropriety. 'Have you heard the story of how Ha'akon slaughtered the dragon?'

'Yes, I have,' she said to his disappointment, but immediately added. 'But only vaguely. I'd like to know more.'

'Great.' He beamed. 'It happened a good while ago... maybe ten, maybe fifteen years. By the ancestors, we were all in a great rage when we found out what had happened to that unfortunate girl.'

211

'Did you take part in the search?' She became curious and this time sounded sincere.

'Yes,' he confirmed. 'But we wandered around for days looking for the culprits and got nowhere. Such is life, damn it. After a few months we had to give up.'

'You had to? Why?'

'Winter was coming, we couldn't find a trace... These mountain folk can be cunning. They had hidden in caves somewhere and we couldn't reach them. Everyone gave her up for lost,' he said sadly. A wave of old memories washed over him.

'But not Ha'akon,' she said rather than asked.

'No, not Ha'akon. He is as stubborn as anyone, you see, and even then, when he was so young, he was a warrior no one could match. We urged him to come back, but no way... you would not convince him. He refused and went alone... he was so in love with her. *I would rather die here in a pit than let her rot in captivity,* he told us. It doesn't happen very often, believe me... it doesn't happen.'

'I can believe it.' She nodded and took the jug from the servant.

Ha'min paused for a moment, taking a healthy sip from his goblet. He wiped his eyes, feeling that they were damp.

'And he returned with the dragon's head,' she urged him.

'Yes.' The Wolf confirmed. 'He returned. He was dragging that head like a convict. In truth, he looked like a dead man himself. Nothing got through to him... nothing. Many days passed before a word, a sentence could be coaxed out of him.'

'And then?' He could tell the girl was moved.

'And then? Well... the king announced another expedition, and so we went into battle. Ha'akon fought like a demon. He feared nothing. Neither death nor wounds. He raged like mad. Dragon Fury. That's what they called him.'

'Why do you think he's changed so much, Ha'min?' she asked with a flushed face.

'What can I...' He felt his tongue tangle again. 'You see, littlun, I'm not an expert in such things.' The elderly warrior combed his messy hair. 'I could make love to a different gal every day. There's something interesting about every woman... it's just my nature. I don't know what it's like to be so attached to one...' he mumbled, and she just patted him on the shoulder, understanding.

Then the instruments sounded. Keera, dressed in a beautiful purple dress with a plunging neckline, announced the first performers. Eli and Ha'min stopped talking and turned to the centre of the room where the newly arrived performers were taking their places.

After the exchange with Ha'min, awkward at first and then very engaging, Eli watched with excitement as the girls prepared for the performance. She loved music and singing as a listener; it was an unrequited love, at least according to her elven friends. Despite her best efforts to learn, she was never able to satisfy their sophisticated tastes. Fortunately, she was aware of this and was able to enjoy the performances of others far more talented than herself.

To open the evening, a choir of young girls, clearly suffering from stage fright, sang about the legendary origins of the Ha'ami, born of Mother Nature, hard as rock, with blood as hot as lava and minds as pure as the sky. *Ha'ami the nation of the rulers*, the refrain emphasised over and over again. Surprised by the pathos of the song, Eli felt uneasy and busied herself picking at the bread to keep her eyes down and not laugh.

'A fine performance!' Ha'min exclaimed as they finished, his voice full of emotion. 'Great song!'

The artists changed, but the message and tone of the songs remained the same: brave stories of Ha'ami deeds... Ha'ami the chosen people.... Ha'ami were created to rule all nations.... Ha'ami have no equal...

Fortunately, food was served and she set about filling her stomach.

Once the glorification of the Ha'ami as world leaders was complete, it was time for songs praising the greatest warriors in history. Most of them extolled Ha'akon's legendary victory over the dragon. Eli glanced in the direction of the fortress' ruler. He did not seem to take much pleasure in the acclaim: just sat there with a dull expression on his face, sipping his drink. After five songs, two recitations and a theatrical re-enactment, even Eli's curiosity about the details of the event was satisfied.

She turned to Ha'min, whose eyes were once again glassy with emotion.

'Is this how your art shows usually go?' she asked.

'Worse,' said a hateful voice. 'They usually take much longer...'

Ha'teng slumped into the empty chair left by Teena, who seemed to have disappeared somewhere along with Ha'sani.

'We repeat these stories until even the rats in the dungeons can recite them,' he explained, slurring his words slightly.

'Drunk Ha'teng,' she thought. 'Just what is needed.'

While Ha'min was drifting towards complete confusion, the Tiger seemed to be getting even meaner than usual.

Trouble, a warning sounded in her head.

He was furious. Ha'akon did not take his arguments to heart. He may have pretended to listen seriously, but Ha'teng was no fool. He knew it was only an appearance. His friend's attention was focused on this wench today; he stared at her as if she were at least a unicorn.

The Guardian of Defence didn't usually indulge himself at public events, but he involuntarily began to seek oblivion in the wine. And after a while, some very stimulating ideas came to his mind. Ha'akon wants to acknowledge this girl's nobility? Great. Let's see what the Council would say to a demonstration of her training in the arts... after all, it is well known that all high-born women undergo a thorough training in this regard.

'Eli,' he mumbled, trying to control his somewhat alcohol-soaked thoughts, but without much success. He liked the suggestions his dark side was making. 'Do you have any other talents besides jumping over rooftops? Music? Singing?'

She looked at him sceptically.

'I'm afraid I'm completely useless at those things,' she replied.

'Great,' he rejoiced and rose from his seat before Keera spoke again.

'Dear guests,' he announced loudly, and all eyes turned to him. 'As you know, we have a very special guest at the feast today, *Ta'uma*, who has come from very far away.'

Ha'min tried to stand up to stop him.

'Ha'teng, wha– what are you on about... j– just get d–down,' he muttered, but he did not have the strength to get up and sank heavily back into the chair.

'You may even have heard that *Ta'uma* spent years in elven captivity, from which she managed to escape and find asylum in our lands.' His hazy gaze landed on Ha'akon and his mother. He began to wonder if he had gone too far. But it was too late for such thoughts. Grave silence reigned in the hall. Even the servants had stopped passing the plates and listened with curiosity.

'As a token of gratitude for the generous hospitality we had shown her, she offered to grace the evening with a song she had learned during her time of oppression. This is a wonderful opportunity to educate our community about culture, so... applause!' he finished, pulling her up by the elbow.

Ha'min finally managed to stand up.

'You're–' He burped loudly. '–drunk.' He burped again. 'Come on, let's go back to the castle together...'

Ha'teng sent him back into the chair with a gentle shove. He leaned over the girl.

'Come on,' he said with increasing amusement. 'You promised me everything from knowledge of the art of war to recipes for bread. It's time to show us what you can do. Think of your friend!'

Out of the corner of his eye, he noticed Akona rising from her seat and without waiting, he pushed *Ta'uma* towards the centre of the hall. She looked at him with obvious hatred, which pleased him greatly. Then she turned to the others, bowed with courtly grace and marched towards the musicians.

Ha'akon was seething. He could see that Ha'teng was clearly upset by their discussion when he disagreed with his opinion on strategy towards the non-humans, but he hadn't expected him to pull a stunt like this. He was clearly drunk and quite out of control. It looked as if he had set out to ridicule not only himself but the entire Council. Eli seemed confused by his actions, but whatever he said to her, it forced her to take part in this pathetic spectacle. She played her part. His mother reacted too late. The girl was already tuning her *kithára*, taking her place on a stool among other female performers.

He moved nervously in his chair, not knowing where it was all going.

Eli took a deep breath. She didn't raise her eyes. Didn't want to think about all the people listening to her now. She did not care if she would be ridiculed. All that mattered was proving to Ha'teng that she was not afraid of him. And that her knowledge of elves was enough to be relied upon.

She thought of Tallen. Of all the evenings they had spent learning to play and sing. About all his banter about her   missing pitch. About his voice calming her when she woke up from nightmares. About the melodies that brought her solace in her pain. She could see him now in her mind's eye, sitting on a stool in her bedroom singing to the accompaniment of his lyre, leaning against the wall in the moonlight that gave the whole environment a silvery glow. His velvety voice lulled her to sleep.

She started to play.

Ha'teng enjoyed his joke. Finally, he could have some small satisfaction after his *koru* had completely disregarded him today. He sent *Ta'uma* in the hope that her performance would be ridiculed now and in the future. She began to strum the *kithára* cautiously, barely touching the strings.

He relaxed and took another good drink from his goblet.

'You are a son of a bitch,' Ha'min muttered and leaned towards him. In retaliation, Ha'teng grabbed the leg of his chair and jerked hard, knocking it over. The old warrior fell backwards, hitting the floor hard.

'Lie down, you old dud,' the Tiger growled in his direction, looking around to check if anyone had seen it, but no one was looking at them.

All eyes were on *Ta'uma*.

The melody, faint at first, slowly began to gather strength. As the music flowed, his mind began to turn to strange memories, as if spirited away.

He was a little boy again, chasing birds and dreaming of having wings like theirs. He would come home for dinner and his dear mother would greet him with a firm hug of boundless tenderness. The older sisters, always ready to play with their long-awaited little miracle, the apple of the family's eye, would spoil him during dinner, showering him with the best morsels.

They were all gone; normally he would not even remember that they had ever existed.

Shaking himself out of a trance, he looked around. The Ha'ami sat transfixed as he did, listening to the strange tune played by the girl in green.

Ha'akon could not take his eyes off Eli. Her small fingers moved gently over the strings of the *kithára*, and the music that came from the instrument penetrated him with the force of the tide. His mind flashed back to the happy years he had spent with Layla. When he had been forced to move to the Upper Castle, he had promised her, with the naive certainty of a ten-year-old, that he would do his best to become a full-fledged warrior as soon as possible and return to her. He would sneak out in the evenings just to spend a moment with his beloved. How many punishments he had served for this...

The melancholy melody flowed and he followed it, listening to his memories. Eli sat with her eyes down, concentrating only on her instrument. At one point she began to hum unintelligible words in a soft, beautiful foreign language.

Then, amidst the silence, a terrible shriek rang out. Everyone awoke as one and turned in that direction. The Eldest leapt from her seat and, with an animal roar, lunged at *Ta'uma* with her hands raised like claws ready to attack. Eli froze in her seat, clearly stunned. Before anyone had time to react, the woman was at her side. She reached for her face; the girl shielded herself with the instrument, clearly not wanting to hurt the matriarch who kept shrieking.

'How dare you defile our thresholds with your vile speech! Die, you foreign scum! To me, warriors! Slay the elven hag!'

She failed to reach Eli with her claws, so she started spitting and kicking. Ha'akon awoke from his stupefaction, sprang from his seat and started running towards them.

He wasn't the only one. Several other Ha'ami did the same, including Temina. His sister was already in the middle of the action, grabbing the Eldest from behind and trying to pull her away, but the woman fought back with such ferocity that it took three men to finally bring her out.

With terror in her eyes, Sig asked them to handle her as gently as possible. Joined by Perin, she directed them to the healing room to give the matriarch something to calm her down and make her sleep.

Stunned, Eli stood alone with her broken *kithára*. Temina put her arm around her.

'Are you all right?' she asked. At least she was able to find some words. Ha'akon was still baffled.

'I'm sorry,' Eli said without looking anyone in the eye. 'Temina... the performances are over, can I go now? Will it offend anyone?'

'No,' the woman replied softly.

'I need to change.' Eli whispered.

'Of course. Your clothes are at my house, we'll go there right away. I'll tell the servants to bring us some warm coats. Wait here.'

Turning, she gave Ha'akon a meaningful look. He knew he had been given the task of looking after Eli until his sister's return. But he still didn't know how to act, what to say and felt like a completely clueless dimwit. He looked around the room. Some of the guests were whispering and giggling. Others were still sitting with confused faces. The servants began to shuffle around in silence. Ha'teng pretended not to be there, and a fully drunken Ha'min collapsed on the floor. Out of the corner of his eye, Ha'akon noticed his mother barking orders and Keera already herding the next performers.

'I've ruined your evening and this instrument. I'm sorry.' Eli turned to him unexpectedly, helplessly holding out the broken *kithára*.

'I'm sure they have a bunch of them,' he finally managed to blurt out and took what was left of the device.

His sister returned and wrapped a cloak around the girl.

'*Neru –*' he started, but she just waved her hand.

'Tomorrow,' she cut him off and walked towards the door.

The Governor slowly returned to his seat. The wine and the singing would soon lift the spirits of all the revellers and the incident would become the talk of the City of Sisters and the rest of the Fortress, that's for sure. Hopefully, that would be the only consequence of Ha'teng's coarse joke.

'Are you all right now?' Temina asked as she wrapped Eli in a woollen blanket. They sat on the floor, facing the fireplace and gazing into the flames. They were alone, the herbalist had sent all the servants away.

'Would you like a drink?' she asked, but the girl refused. She felt empty inside. The day with all the conversations, the questioning, the new people and on top of that the crazy attack of the old woman had exhausted her.

'Your song,' Temina asked hesitantly. 'What was it about?'

Eli looked thoughtfully into the fire.

'About longing for those we love,' she replied. 'This is the story of Ethiel, a daring sailor who ventured across distant seas. Hostile winds blew her ship off course, onto the reefs and into the sea. Ethiel and her crew settled on a deserted island and set about building a new ship that would carry them back home... This is a song about a brave but torn heart that longs from afar for all that it loves, knowing that this is the price to be paid for satisfying its thirst for adventure... In Ha'ami these words would sound like this:

In the night, amidst the tempest

Amidst the restless storms

Amidst the blowing winds

Amidst the roaring waves

I think of you, my lost forest

Your peace is my strength

Your light is my beacon in the darkness.'

She paused as tears filled her eyes and her voice trailed off in the middle of a word.

'When you sang,' Temina crooned, exuding her comforting warmth, 'childhood memories flooded my mind. Me, Ha'akon and Layla... We planned to run away together to the mountains and live on our own. No one would tell us what to do. We would spend our days catching frogs in the stream and eating forest fruits and honey...' Her voice was full of longing too. 'Those were my happiest moments...'

Eli looked into her eyes, in which that strange melancholy had set in again, ill-suited to her cheerful, energetic friend.

'Tell me more,' she asked. 'Tell me about your childhood.'

Temina hugged her knees and began to spin tales of her youth. It was wonderful to listen to the carefree memories that Eli herself did not have.

Chapter IX
Dead reptile talk

LINA CAREFULLY ADJUSTED THE BLANKET on the sleeping old woman.

'You can go now,' she whispered to Sig. 'I will watch over her and take care of her as best I can.'

The First Sister just looked at her with determination and shook her head.

The young healer sighed to herself. So much trouble for the Eldest. That's why it's best to leave honourably. Otherwise, the burden would be unbearable for the whole tribe. They should show respect for their matriarch and let her leave this world. She was tormenting not only herself, but also those around her. One cup of the right herbs and she would fall asleep in peace forever. Sig objected vehemently whenever such a suggestion was made. One more piece of evidence to confirm the rumours that the Guardian of the Temple herself was out of her mind.

Lina brought a jug of water and a blanket, but the priestess did not even look at her. The healer heard her muttering to herself.

Cursed be she... cursed... cursed... my brother is right... we should not allow this scum at our doorstep... she has sullied your good name... I will avenge you, Mother... I swear...

Her head is burnt out with weed, Lina thought. She knew that there were no more relatives of Sig among the living. She suspected that she was talking to the ancestors again, something she was known for.

The healer moved towards the other patients who were still in her care. At least there she could do something practical.

'Time for me to go,' Ha'akon said to his mother. The feast was drawing to a close. Some of the guests retired to their private chambers. Others had less patience and gave vent to their passions under the tables and in the corners and corridors of the Assembly Hall. Many of the women who had not yet been taken cast increasingly lascivious, dazed glances at him. But the one that occupied his mind was no longer in the room.

His slightly dazed mind kept contemplating the slender waist outlined beneath the provocative malachite dress that exposed her back. The petite figure with the *kithára* and the magical melody that stirred his memories. Green eyes, usually flashing with determination, but now filled with a strange sadness.

A ride on a cool night will do me good, he thought, pushing away desires that had no chance of being satisfied. At least for now.

Akona held out her hand in farewell. He kissed it and left.

Eli walked distractedly through the empty streets of the City of Sisters. The events of the day and the evening swirled in her mind... she let them flow uninterruptedly. So many new experiences! Her thoughts wandered freely, as did her feet, and at one point she realised she didn't know where she was. But before she could think how to get back, she heard that voice again. It was speaking directly to her soul. The girl felt it with all her being. In her head, in her guts, in her heart. It urged and lured her.

She looked around and saw that she had unknowingly wandered near the Temple of the Ancestors. The dark building with its smooth, pulsating walls beckoned her inside. Eli knew where to go. As if under a spell, she turned towards the stairs. With each step, the tingling in her body increased and her will weakened. A hissing tone took over her. As if she was a puppet, it led her inside.

The building was empty and dark, the faint light of the olive lamps fading. The tread of elven boots, however, made no sound on the smooth floor. In silence, she moved forward involuntarily, watched only by the grim statues of Ha'ami's legendary ancestors.

The entrance to the underground was shrouded in darkness, but that was no problem for her. Her feet found their own way. Her senses dulled. The only thing that reached her was a whisper in her soul.

What do you want? she repeated over and over, but received no answer.

The bones of the dead crunched beneath her feet and she heard the snakes parting as she approached. The girl turned to the dragon's skull, the only clear object in the crypt. It glowed with a pale emerald light and looked as if it might come to life and speak at any moment.

Somehow Eli knew what she had to do. Or rather, some guiding force was definitely pushing her into action. Clinging to the remains of dead animals, she climbed to the top of the pyramid of bones and stood before the huge skull.

Touch it, the wheezing voice in her mind commanded. She reached out and placed her hands on the body of the dead monster.

Suddenly she found herself in the middle of a memory. In a dragon's lair, years ago. She saw the world through the eyes of a primordial creature. She was it. Felt his pain, knew his thoughts, his consciousness, his emotions....

He knew he was dying. His fate was sealed. With his left eye, the only one that was still intact after the warrior had knocked out the right one, the dragon watched the dark silhouette climb up his body, his exposed chest, where the scales were soft, where the path to his heart was straight. He knew the young man would soon finish his job.

Spark (as the mortals called him, for his real name would fill many a book) could still muster one last burning breath, similar to the one that had scorched the young man's face in his belated defence. This time he would not miss his target. He had it right in front of him. A single swipe of his powerful paw would be enough to knock the man down like a flea, break his neck and end his life. They would both have died, buried forever in the cave.

But the dragon didn't do that.

Spark was one of the first to observe the beginnings of the world. He was also one who had an eternal, childlike joy for life. His tricks with light and colour, his aerial acrobatics and his retellings of classic stories were a constant source of amusement to his fellow tribesmen. In the thousands of years of his existence, he has never met a creature he wished to harm and has only used his powers in self-defence.

This young warrior sneaked into his cave while Spark slept and attacked him by surprise. The lad planned his attack well. First, he brought down a huge boulder, pinning the dragon's massive neck to the ground, not only maiming it but effectively immobilising its upper body. Then the warrior began to deliver precise, well-considered blows to every weak spot. Spark tried to defend himself, but quickly realised he was defeated.

The blood gushing from his open wounds mixed with his attacker's. Their minds met for a moment. The dragon felt the desperation and hatred of his conqueror.

The day before, he had witnessed the painful farewell of the young man and the injured girl whom the dragons had found unconscious in a valley after her cruel tormentors had thrown her off a rock when they had finished abusing her. The inherently good creatures took her in and kept her alive, though some injuries are incurable even to their ancient magic.

Then this lad came searching for her. For many days he begged the girl to return with him to their home. In vain. She could not live with the wounds that had been inflicted upon her. She decided to stay in the valley. No tears or pleas could move her petrified heart. The warrior left with a growing hatred for those she had chosen to live with.

Out of despair the warrior decided to go back and take revenge on the dragons. On those who had saved her, who had become her new tribe.

Now Spark felt his wounded love, sincere and simple, as strong as if it pulsed through his own veins. He felt the young man's sorrow, born of powerlessness. The burning rage directed at himself for failing to protect the one he loved most. The desire for revenge, the hatred for her tormentors, for the dragons, for the world, for himself, took control of his mind, his will and his emotions.

With madness in his eyes, the man stood on the dragon's chest and raised his sword with a cry of pain. Their eyes locked for the final moment.

Eli's head exploded with light.

Ha'akon did not urge his mount. He had much to think about. The night air helped to clear his head, especially after all the liquor he had drunk at the feast. He rode into the square by the Temple of the Ancestors when, to his surprise, he saw *Ta'uma* climbing the steps. Leaving his horse at the bottom, he followed her. Once inside, however, he saw no sign of her. He guessed that she must have gone into the crypt. Worried, he quickened his pace.

A greenish glow shone from the entrance to the underground. Ha'akon drew his sword and ran down the stairs. The girl stood atop the pile of bones, her hands resting on the dragon's skull, which glowed like an emerald in the rays of the rising sun.

'Eli!' he shouted.

She didn't answer. She stood with her eyes closed, shrouded in a magical glow. He sheathed his sword and began to climb towards her, led by pure instinct. All he thought about was how to separate her from the source of the light, how to break this curse, this spell, whatever it was. When he found himself beside her, dazed, he tried to push her out of the way. To no avail. She remained immobilised by some unknown force. He grabbed her in the middle and pulled her backwards with all his might. Again, to no avail. Breathing heavily, he tried to push the huge skull, to knock it off the bony mound. It did not budge. Angry at his helplessness, he grabbed the girl by the waist again, clasping his legs as far as the surface would allow. He pulled. It finally let go.

The light went out and they rolled down. He held her tightly in his arms as they hit the debris-strewn ground.

'Eli?'

She didn't say a word. He sat up in the total darkness and cradled her limp body.

'Eli!' He shook her gently. She opened her eyelids and his first instinct was to push her away. Her eyes glowed with the same radiance as the dragon's skull had before. Emerald light washed over them.

She looked reptilian.

'Ha'akon.' Her lips uttered a wheezing whisper that sounded unfamiliar. It was not her voice. 'I want to show you.'

She raised her hand to his face and he had no time to react.

'I want to set you free.'

A green glow pierced his consciousness.

Again, he stood on the dragon's chest in its lair.

Again, he raised his sword to strike.

Just as he had seen it a thousand times in his dreams. Again, he stared into its huge eyes, a moment before the last breath left the giant chest of the primordial lizard.

Once again, he saw the infinite wisdom of this magical creature, drawn from its connection with every living thing.

He saw the boundless goodness and nobility of the oldest tribe to inhabit the world.

He realised that what he had just done was an incredible crime against Mother Nature, against Ami herself.

He had attacked out of pure hatred. Without justification. With no honour. In its sleep.

The dying gaze of the dragon's eyes touched the deepest recesses of his soul. There was no anger in it, only forgiveness. That feeling, like a mother's forbearance towards her child, soothed his grief and shame.

And the dying monster took pity on the pain of his murderer. With his last breath, he tried to cast a spell, not to destroy him, but to heal him.

He could not finish. Ha'akon drove his sword through his heart.

Then the dragon dissolved into an emerald-green, luminous flood, the primordial energy of creation.

When Ha'akon opened his eyes, he was in the crypt, plunged into total darkness.

He heard movement to his right.

'Eli?' he whispered.

''Who's here?' she said, this time in her own voice.

'Ha'akon.'

Silence.

'Where...?' she asked finally.

'In the crypt.'

A sound came to him. The girl drew in air slowly, then let it out with a swish.

'Do you know how you got here?'

Silence again.

'Yes,' she replied finally. 'How do we get out?'

'I know this place by heart,' he assured her. 'Take my hand, I'll lead us out.' He heard a faint crunch that signalled movement. He reached out his hand in that direction, met her fingertips. She gripped onto him tightly. Slowly they rose to their feet.

They moved in the dark, stumbling over snakes and bones lying everywhere. Finally, they reached the stairs. He drew her closer, embraced her and helped her up. Once inside the Temple, illuminated by the diffused light of the lamps, they stopped and looked at each other. The girl looked slightly confused.

'Why have you come here?' he asked without reproach.

'Spark...' she stammered, 'I mean... the dragon called me.'

She was still clinging to his hand.

'Why? And why you?'

'I don't... know... why me... I don't understand his choice.' Eli breathed heavily, as if it was causing her pain. 'I only know he wanted to give you a message... I was only the bearer.'

She looked pale, but her body seemed inflamed.

'Let's go outside.' He suggested. 'We both need some fresh air.'

Eli nodded. He took her in his arms again and led her towards the exit. Once they were outside, she shivered slightly.

'I feel sick, I need to sit down,' she said.

He helped her to rest on the steps, her back against the pillar. He sat down beside her. Breathing still seemed to be giving her trouble.

'I will take you to Temina,' He offered. 'You need help.'

'No.' She shook her head. 'Just give me a moment... I'll be better soon.'

He felt the weight of her body on his shoulder. They both closed their eyes and tried to regain their balance.

Eli tried to even out her breathing and gather her thoughts, to take in the sensations and feelings that Spark had conveyed to her. She couldn't help but think of the dragon as an old friend. For a moment she was one with it and it seemed as if she knew every corner of its consciousness. What a magnificent creature it was... She had never felt such power and such love for all of existence at the same time. The good that was in it surpassed her most naive dreams.

Eli didn't know why it had chosen her. She didn't feel worthy of interacting with such a wonderful, timeless being.

She sighed, letting herself sink into the memory.

The girl realised her head was resting on Ha'akon's shoulder. The scent of his body was strangely soothing. Eli thought about what she had learned about him that evening. Straightening up, she clasped his hand with her fingers.

'I'm sorry...' she stammered. 'About Layla... I'm sorry this happened to her... to both of you.'

She felt the muscles in his arm contract slightly.

'Honour... strength... brotherhood...' he whispered, a little to her, and a little as if to himself. 'Ha'ami do not care about feelings. They do not value long lasting sentiments. The only bonds that count are those of family, of tribe, of brothers in arms. And yet, when I met her, I knew from the first moment that what was between us was stronger than all the laws of my people, stronger than all the rules and traditions, stronger than death...'

'Elves believe in such eternal love,' Eli said sympathetically. 'Even if they live hundreds of years, they choose to spend that time with the one chosen person to whom they give themselves infinitely.'

Though she meant it to sound reassuring, she felt she had given vent to the bitterness that was welling up inside her.

'Did you meet someone like that there?' He looked at her thoughtfully.

The girl just smiled, dispirited, and looked away. It took her a moment to find the right words.

'The elves see us, short-lived creatures, as a passing moment. They know that after a while we will disappear from their lives. That's why they don't bond with humans, they don't give us a place in their hearts, we don't ignite passions in them. Elves are incapable of loving humans...'

'The elves are not,' he said.

She felt the penetrating gaze of the ruler and shook herself out of her melancholy.

'Enough about elves... tonight is about dragons,' said Eli, looking directly at him, full of inner peace brought on by the memory of a wonderful experience. 'And about forgiveness.'

Ha'akon replied with a sad smile.

'Spark...' He whispered the dragon's name. 'What an extraordinary creature.'

She nodded eagerly.

'I have never felt such instinctive, unconditional love... for anything that lives,' the girl marvelled.

'I realised too late what I had done.' Ha'akon's jaw clenched as he struggled to find the words. 'I was blinded by my own despair, eager for murder, eager for revenge: the way I was raised. I committed a true and undignified act of bestiality by ending this existence.' He gazed into the distance.

'This act, which is the source of my greatest shame, is also the one of which I must constantly hear songs. It is the one for which my people admire me. It is one whose stigma I carry on my shoulder... I deserve this punishment. What I did was a crime against nature. Against Ami. This dragon... this creature was no beast.'

The warrior rubbed his forehead with the palm of his hand.

'You are right,' Eli replied calmly, squeezing his hand tighter. 'Spark was no beast and did not deserve to die... But is this murder really any different from any other murder? Does any cruelty, any taking of life, make sense?' she asked quietly.

He considered.

'It doesn't. But I didn't know that at the time.' There was weariness in his voice now. 'I threw myself into the fight to forget both my pain and the memory of the carnage I had wrought in that cave.'

'The Dragon Fury... I've heard the stories...'

Ha'akon shook his head at the sound of the nickname.

'I was a fool... as if a new act of evil could tarnish the previous one. One day, standing in the blood of unknown people I had slaughtered, I realised that what my tribe celebrates is a great mistake,' he said simply.

The girl was beyond surprised.

'You really... you really think so?' she gasped.

He pointed to the sleeping city.

'This is my world, Eli. Like all of us, I am but a small part of the reality around us. We don't choose the laws that govern us. I must obey them, I must interact with them. We're all bound by rules we didn't invent. All we can do is make the best use of the little influence we have.'

'Not that little.' She nudged him lightly with her shoulder.

He grinned wider, tilting his head to watch her with a gleam in his eye. He looked a little like he had been caught in a prank, but he quickly turned serious.

'Power has only one meaning to me. To correct past mistakes. To prevent the ones to come. Unfortunately, I keep making them myself. One after another. I'm not a very good learner. Only on the battlefield do I feel in control. Years of training... I know how to deliver the precise, necessary blows. I know how to defeat an opponent without taking a life. Politics... well, it's not my forte. Day after day, I lose because of my impulsiveness. Therefore, the score remains against me. I am far from fulfilling the hopes the dragon placed in me by giving me the chance to live.'

'One thing is certain, Ha'akon,' she said. 'You are your own worst judge.'

He nodded.

'You've hit the mark again. How do you do it?'

She felt herself blush under his gaze.

'I'm a rather poor oracle. Apparently, it's because I too often assume good intentions... which makes it easy to deceive me...' she murmured for no apparent reason.

'I do not deceive you.' He lifted her hand to his burned cheek and kissed it respectfully.

Eli knew she was already quite red.

'I'm a bit cold,' she said, changing the subject. To her relief, he gave a nod.

'We should go back,' he confirmed, standing up and pulling her to her feet. 'Eli,' he said, his tone playful this time. 'You have already managed to insult the entire Ha'ami company at the feast today, to break into our holy place and almost destroy a relic, to extract the most embarrassing confession from the lord of the fortress... will you dare to commit another outrageous thing tonight?'

'Which Ha'ami rule should I break this time?' she laughed.

'Not Ha'ami,' he replied cheerfully. 'Your own. It's late, we've both been through enough today. Will you ride with me to the Upper Castle? My word of honour, I'll treat you better than a sack of oats.'

'Much better?' she teased.

'A little better.'

She looked towards the hill and sighed heavily.

'That would probably be my wisest decision of this day and evening...'

'I completely agree with you,' he admitted.

With a slow step they began to descend towards his waiting mount.

Ha'akon felt more drunk than when he left the feast. He still didn't know what to make of everything that had just happened; it would take him days to put it all together in his head. He had no idea who this extraordinary girl was, what powers she had, why he had managed to open up to her. One thing was certain: for the first time in a long while, his heart was light. Unencumbered by memories. He felt as if someone had removed the cast-iron armour he had worn for years. For the first time in his life, he was able to put into words the feelings he carried deep within his soul.

'What is its name?' asked Eli, stroking the mount's nostrils. The animal gave a friendly snort.

Ha'akon leapt to his saddle.

'Razor.'

'Because it runs so smooth?'

'Because it can act quite blunt,' he corrected.

She laughed out loud.

'I did not suspect you of such a sense of humour.'

'Indeed, of the two of us, I am the more surprising one,' he retorted, holding out his hand to her.

'Well... if I had to judge after tonight, it seems to me that we are equals in that respect,' She replied, pulling herself up deftly and sitting on the front of the flat saddle.

'Let it be so.' He put one arm around her and held the reins with the other. He urged the horse and they set off. He felt her slender but strong and resilient body moving freely to the rhythm of the mount's steps.

'Can we go faster?' she asked suddenly. 'It's been so long since I galloped.'

In response, he merely touched Razor's flanks. The horse immediately leapt into canter.

'Wonderful,' he heard her sigh and couldn't help but think the same.

He felt he could gallop with this strange girl forever.

Chapter X
The game of appearances

THE GROOM RUBBED HIS EYES, but it didn't help much. He still couldn't see anything. There was darkness all around. Yet he could feel someone poking at his feet.

'What?' he muttered. Suddenly the light of a torch flashed in front of his face.

'Get up and saddle the lord Ha'akon's horse!' the order sounded.

Immediately he jumped to his feet, pulled up his breeches and slapped his own face to make sure he was fully awake.

'I've just unsaddled it,' he croaked to the guardsman standing over him. The answer was silence. He trudged towards the stables, wondering if he had dreamed earlier that the Governor had returned from the City of Sisters with this foreigner, and then they had walked together towards the castle. It must have been only a few moments ago, for he had just finished grooming the horse and laid his own head down on the hay.

Semi-conscious, he led a very disgruntled Razor out of the stall, the horse whinnying slightly to express its disapproval of night rides.

'It's not me you should be complaining to, brother...' He patted the horse's side and tightened the girth. After a while everything was ready and he led the animal outside. It was freezing cold. Lord Ha'akon was already waiting, impatiently slapping the leather gloves in his hand against his thigh. When he saw his mount, he quickly pulled them on, leapt into the saddle, squeezed Razor's flanks and set off at a gallop.

The stableman wondered if he would now have a chance to sleep, at least until sunrise.

Since returning from the feast, Ha'akon had not been able to sleep.

The Council, the search for solutions for the salt supply, the plans for the next war expeditions, the feast, the memories, Layla, the dragon and finally her, green eyes and a slender waist that almost fit in his hand... Justice, righteousness, integrity, loyalty and finally feelings... the impossible choices that lay before him. He cursed his weakness, his impulsiveness. For so many years he had managed to suppress all his passions. For so many years he had managed to forget, to exist only for his service. For duty, for tribe, for family. Until she came along and rekindled in him a zeal that had long since been extinguished.

His thoughts tumbled in an impossible tangle. He would follow one and lose track, then return to another. The fresh air of the winter night was just what he needed.

He galloped out of the Stone Nest, straight into the embrace of the night. Just him and Razor. He could feel the taut muscles of his horse working in a steady rhythm. Warmth evaporated from the mount's skin, rising in a light mist as it met the icy wind. The chill tore into Ha'akon's lungs, spreading brutally through his cells. The scalding cold penetrated his face, his eyes, his exposed neck.

Inhale. Stinging pain. Exhale. Inhale. Forget it. Exhale. Inhale. Pain. Exhale. Inhale. Emptiness. Exhale. Inhale. Let it out. Exhale.

Just him and his mount. Merged into one in the darkness of the night. Melted together in a mad rush.

The sound of hooves pounding snow from the ground. The crunch of his leather armour rubbing against his body. Darkness entering his eyes, taking the place of the swirling images before.

Inhale. Exhale.

After returning from the feast, Eli collapsed on the bed and fell asleep instantly. Ha'akon offered to see her back to her chamber, but she thanked him and quickly left on her own. That day and night had drained her of all emotions. Although she awoke to the sound of a horn calling for exercise, she immediately closed her eyes again.

It was not until the sun was high in the sky that she managed to get out of bed. She was astonished to discover that, in addition to her breakfast, they had brought into the chamber her travelling bags, which had been confiscated during her arrest. The only thing that had not been returned were her weapons. The rest of her possessions, everything she had ever owned in her life, now lay at her feet. She sipped goat's milk and looked through her belongings with excitement, feeling like a small child presented with toys, greeting each item as if it were an old friend, each with its own story, each bringing back memories.

A knock at the door interrupted her sentimental journey.

Opening it, she saw a guard announce that she was summoned to Ha'akon's chambers. The order immediately brought her back to reality. She asked for a moment to change and finish her morning routine. She needed to put her thoughts in order.

All the experiences of the previous day were jumbled in her head. She knew she had to focus on the facts, not the premonitions that had so often led her astray.

First, she discovered that while the laws of Ha'ami were harsh, many members of the tribe had learned to circumvent them rather than obey them. Temina, the girls she met, Peri, Ha'min, even Ha'akon himself. Almost everyone she met along the way suppressed their needs and feelings to fit in with the reality around them. Only bastards like Ha'teng seemed to be content and growing stronger in this brutal world. But perhaps that was just an appearance. Maybe he was just better at disguising himself. However, she was confident that as far as she and Tallen were concerned, the Guardian of Defence would use every means at his disposal to prove that he had the upper hand.

Secondly, the Ha'ami considered themselves the chosen people; they felt they were the highest race of all. Other tribes could only serve them. They had a great dislike for non-humans and an open hatred for elves. These prejudices were deeply rooted, as she learned the hard way. There was no way she could count on any member of the tribe, not even Ha'akon, to treat Tallen fairly. She decided that she must continue to study the code. Knowledge is the strongest weapon. That is what she had been taught.

Third. Amazing, but true... A dragon spoke to her. One of the wisest creatures in the world. Spark saw in Ha'akon something worth saving. He believed in him and wanted to communicate this to both the lord of the castle and, for some unknown reason, to Eli. The question was whether the dragon's hopes for the ruler should be translated into trust on her part.

And one last piece of news. She was naive, but not to the extent that would stop her from understanding that the Governor felt some attraction to her, and that his own mother was presenting Eli to him as if she were a commodity at a bazaar. Though she didn't understand Akona's intentions, perhaps it had something to do with something the girls had mentioned – that *Ta'uma* was usually placed in the "care" of a warrior, whatever that meant. She assumed the lord was genuinely interested in her himself, hence the courtesy he'd shown her yesterday, or today's kind gesture of returning the travelling bags. What he expected in return was another matter entirely.

She sighed. It was hard to assume anyone's good intentions in this place.

The vision she'd had the night before had filled her with an unexpected kindness for the distraught, wounded young man, whom even a wise dragon saw as someone special... but she'd also seen what Ha'akon was capable of. He himself admitted that he had grown accustomed to operating in a world of harsh rules by which he had to abide. But, as he said, he was aware of his own violent nature, and his intense emotions had led him to terrible crimes in the past.

She didn't know if she was ready to see him again... especially since she didn't know the reason for the call.

But she pushed those thoughts away and focused on what her goal was: to free Tallen. She would do whatever she had to do, that was all that mattered now. She took a deep breath, washed her face, tied her hair into a loose knot and followed the guard with a slight trepidation but also a strong determination to bring up the subject of the elf.

Unexpectedly, it was Ha'sani who greeted her in the Governor's office.

'Only you?' she asked.

'Yes. Disappointed?' He smiled without malice.

'Surprised.' She breathed a sigh of relief.

'Everyone else is out in the field training. Archery... and I needed a discreet place for our conversation in the meantime,' he explained, motioning her to a seat.

She sat down, curious as to what the man in charge of the fortress' supplies could possibly want from her that needed to be kept secret. She remembered their strange encounter in the stables.

'First of all, let it be clear that Ha'akon knows of everything I'm going to offer you today and is a guarantor of any agreement we may reach.' He took the chair opposite. He was serious, but his face and posture signalled openness.

'I see.' She nodded, growing curious.

'Your elf friend is awaiting trial.' He stated the fact without emotion. He did not speak with Ha'teng's sarcasm or Ha'min's warmth. He was the epitome of concreteness.

'As far as I know, yes,' she confirmed.

'Do you know what he is in danger of? I hear you've been reading up on our penal code.'

You can't sneeze in this fortress, lest everyone find out, she thought, and answered aloud:

'I'm afraid I haven't been able to get that information yet.'

'At stake are years in the dungeon, corporal punishment, death or a mixture of all of the above,' he enumerated dryly, and at these words Eli felt a cool shiver run through her body. It must have shown on her face, but Ha'sani did not make it clear that he had noticed anything. He continued in the same matter-of-fact tone.

'Perhaps you are aware, however, of how sentences are pronounced?'

She moistened her lips nodding in confirmation.

'Judgements must be unanimously approved by the First Brothers,' she replied.

'Exactly. And here's one last important detail relevant to today's... arrangements. According to Ha'ami law, a dungeon sentence can be converted into a ransom. And that brings us to the main issue.' He leaned slightly towards her. 'I understand you have... friends who would be willing to drop coin...' He looked intently at her wrist, where she wore a dwarf bracelet.

'Zak?' She suddenly understood and quickly tried to gather her thoughts. 'What are your expectations?'

'You see, Eli, I am currently trying to establish a business relationship with the dwarven trading post run by the aforementioned gentleman. Unfortunately, I'm afraid I've encountered serious obstacles, both internal and external. These problems are of an emotional nature, if I may say so, and that is never conducive to business,' he explained.

'Ha'ami despise trade with non-humans, and the dwarves will send you to where the trolls winter,' she guessed.

'Unfortunately, I have to admit that both tribes do indeed lack pragmatism...' He spread his hands helplessly. 'I thought, however, that a letter of recommendation from a trusted friend of Zak's would certainly help to break down the barriers of suspicion on at least one side. And favourable terms of trade would convince even the most sceptical of my people.'

'What is your offer?' She decided to switch to an equally practical tone.

'I like the way you think.' He smiled. 'My proposal is this: I can guarantee that the elf will not be put to death. I will do my best to see that he receives a punishment that can be exchanged for ransom. I expect at least ten carts of salt. That would be a start. I also hope to begin broader trade negotiations, so I hope Zak will agree to accept Ha'akon's personal invitation to Stone Nest. We will, of course, guarantee him and his companions safe passage through Ha'ami lands.'

Eli thought for a moment. She had no idea how Zak and his company had fared after their paths had parted years ago. From what she understood of Ha'sani's words, the dwarves' search in the Dragon Mountains must have been successful and they had found the wealth they had dreamed of. She was glad, for she remembered how hopeful they were setting out for those parts. True, Zak was her close friend, she treated him and his loved ones as her own family. He also owed her a debt of gratitude, which he vowed to repay one day... But to send him a ransom demand of unbelievable magnitude and asking him to undertake a personal, risky expedition to the land of Ha'ami... Such a request would have damaged many a friendship. On top of that, she would have to take the word of a man sitting in front of her whom she did not trust.

'What do you know of the dwarves, Ha'sani?' she asked, buying herself some time to think and analyse his intentions.

'Nothing except the quality of their work,' he admitted with disarming honesty.

'Then you would be surprised to find that they have much in common with your tribe,' she continued, studying his reaction carefully. 'For a start, they are very proud and loyal to their friends. I spent a lot of time in Zak's company and was always impressed by the brotherhood that binds them. However, they are as vengeful as they are loyal. If not more so.'

'As if I was looking in a mirror.' He smiled without resentment.

'It will not surprise you, therefore,' she continued, 'that it will be difficult to persuade them to trust Ha'ami. you have rightly pointed out that you are unlikely to succeed without... outside help.'

'For which we are prepared to show great gratitude,' he agreed, slightly inclining his head towards her.

She weighed the words in her mind.

'The mutual friendship and respect that binds me to Zak–' she pointed to the bracelet, '–are built on sincerity and purity of intent. There is no one I know with as open a heart as he. You ask a lot of me, Ha'sani. I am to risk the trust of one friend for the safety of another...'

She hesitated.

'Our agreement will be guaranteed by Ha'akon. You have our word of honour.' He repeated without resentment, but with emphasis.

'I cannot make this decision alone. I must speak to the elf. He is directly affected by this.'

He did not flinch, but looked at her for a moment in silence.

'All right,' he said finally. 'But know that this should absolutely stay between us. Ha'teng must not find out.'

'It will be difficult for me to keep a secret from my most trusted friend in this castle, but I will try,' she replied without blinking.

'I know, I know.' He waved his hand. 'But I prefer to make things clear.'

'That always helps.' She admitted.

'Meet me at the stables. I need to change,' he added. 'I don't want anyone to recognise me.'

She tried not to show that her heart was filled with hope. She wondered if this was really Ha'sani's idea, as he had eagerly presented it, or if Ha'akon was trying to win her affection in this fashion. Either way, she was glad that any possibility, even the faintest, of an improvement in Tallen's fortunes had arisen. She ran to her chamber, wondering what contents of the returned travel bags might be the best consolation for an elf in distress.

All the flames of the olive lamps went out at once, as if from an imperceptible gust of wind. The soft sound of a flute rang out in the darkness of the crypt.

I was wondering when you'd show up. Spark laughed as the blurred silhouette of the player formed in the air.

Shaped out of a fine mist, the figure was shrouded in a heavy cloak with a hood so that his face was invisible. Apart from his hands, which moved efficiently around the instrument, the only visible part of his body were his feet, clad in winged boots.

Is this show really necessary? The dragon yawned theatrically. He knew he had to wait for the tune to end. That was the ritual.

Welcome, Primordial One, the newcomer finally spoke as the last note died away.

For hundreds of years, dragons had argued about whether the creature that now appeared in the crypt of the Ancestral Temple of Stone Nest had a gender. Spark had no interest in the debate. Vain deliberations. They really knew nothing about the messenger of the Almighty Ones. They had to give him a name themselves, for he had never introduced himself to them.

They called him Whisperer in the Common Speech. Spark, however, preferred a name from one of the long-forgotten languages. It reminded him of the warning sound of a flute that announced the appearance of this strange creature.

Ulula - he greeted the newcomer. - *Did you miss me?*

You have broken the law of neutrality, Primordial One, the hooded being said in an indifferent voice.

Me? I am but a dead prisoner in this barbarian city, the dragon replied innocently.

The Girl with No Name must find her destiny on her own.

That is true. However, there is a small inconsistency in your plan... She won't find anything if she dies, will she?

Perhaps.

Perhaps she won't find it, or perhaps she'll die? Spark teased. He was playing for time. He knew what was about to happen. *Maybe you should just admit that you're comfortable with this. You're afraid of her.*

You broke the Law of Neutrality, the newcomer repeated.

Yes, you mentioned it. I would do it again. You had better do your duty now, Ulula. Unless you want to put me to sleep with your talk.

The messenger of the Almighty Ones made no reply. He raised his flute to his lips again and began to cast the spell.

The dragon's soul felt the magical bonds tighten one by one, slowly cutting him off from all consciousness.

As in his physical death, he thought now that he would have to trust what he felt in the young warrior's soul. May he be able to make the right choice. To save the Girl Without a Name.

As for her, now that she knows what lies inside this man, perhaps he will be able to trust him.

Two unique strands of destiny.

Perhaps they will come together.

Perhaps she will survive and fulfil her destiny.

Her power, once unleashed, will change the world.

For the better.

If so...

It was worth it.

Spark fell asleep.

Overjoyed, Eli followed a few steps behind Ha'sani, who was dressed in the simple uniform of a sentry with a leather helmet covering his face. In her hands she clutched a small pouch containing a few handfuls of dried fruits from the Green Kingdom and some elven bread she had found among the returned bundles. The bread was badly crumbled, but it retained its aroma; she hoped it would give Tallen a pleasant surprise. Unexpectedly, she stopped.

'What happened?' an anxious Guardian of Keys asked.

'Can you hear... the sound of a flute?'

'A flute? I think your ears are still ringing from last night's feast,' he joked.

She dismissed the strange thought. Perhaps she was indeed hallucinating. Quickly, and in complete silence, they continued through the stinking corridors beneath the fortress.

When they arrived, Ha'sani whispered something to the guards in the dungeon, then pressed a few coins into their hands. Without a word, they handed him a set of keys. Soon they were standing in front of a familiar door. It opened with a loud creak.

Eli stepped into the musty interior, holding an olive lamp in front of her, giving off a faint light.

'Tallen?' she whispered uncertainly.

No one answered. She took a few steps forward but saw no movement. Instead, she heard a strange scratching and squeaking of rodents from the corner of the room.

'Tallen?' She repeated louder, raising her light in that direction. She saw the silhouette lying on the ground.

The girl ran to him immediately, speechless with shock.

The elf was unconscious. His emaciated body was almost naked, and his injuries were much worse than the last time. His sides and legs bore burn marks, his skin was badly smeared, his open wounds oozing pus. Horrified, she began to kick away the rats that were nibbling at his toes. The aggressive creatures turned towards her, but when they saw the speed with which Eli was dealing the blows, they retreated into the darkness. At least for the time being.

She set the lamp on the floor and knelt beside the wounded elf, resting Tallen's head in her lap. She repeated his name like mad, unscrewed the canteen she had brought and gently poured the cool liquid over his face, wiping away the dust and blood with the sleeve of her blouse. To her relief, she could hear him breathing.

'Wake up, please, Tallen,' she whispered over and over in the elven tongue, like an incantation, and her warm tears trickled down his sunken cheeks.

He opened his eyes slowly.

'By all the demons, what have they done to you?' she sighed and swallowed a sob.

'Eli, my little one... what are you doing here?'

'I brought you water... fruit from the Green Kingdom.' She spoke with difficulty.

Unable to get another word out, she carefully helped him to a sitting position. She put the bottle to his lips, lifted it and let him drink slowly.

'Don't cry, child.' When he had finished, he wiped the wetness from her face with a dirty, mutilated hand. 'It doesn't hurt me.'

'How could he–' she breathed out.

'Little one, you have to get out of here,' he whispered.

'I won't abandon you... I... I'll make a deal with them to let you go,' she assured him desperately.

'You can't trust them, Eli. Leave me and go.' He spoke indistinctly, and a strange wheezing sound escaped his lungs with each word.

'Hurry up!' Ha'sani's urgent voice reached her. She couldn't move. She couldn't just close the door and leave her friend alone again in this darkness.

'Please try to eat... at least a little.' She placed the leaf-wrapped food in front of him. 'Tallen... I'll get you out of here today. I swear it.' Painfully, she planted a kiss on his mutilated hands.

'No... Get away from here, please... You're in danger–' he started, but she put a finger to his lips.

'I swear,' she repeated. 'I'll come back for you in no time.'

The girl struggled to her feet and made her way shakily towards the exit. She felt an intense hatred and disgust for Ha'teng, Ha'ami and all that surrounded her. Filthy degenerates.

Both she and Ha'sani were silent on the way back.

Eli was determined. She would not give up, she would not rest until she had the elf out of this foul place.

It seemed to Jor that he could hear her voice from his cell, carrying down the narrow corridor. He must have been hallucinating. Besides, what could his princess be doing here?

All the while, he had been waiting for the announced interrogation. He felt no fear. He was impatient. He wanted to show his resistance to the oppressors of his people as soon as possible.

If they killed him, he wanted to die with her name on his lips.

She was the only one who could give them all back their freedom.

Ha'sani was not sure if he had done the right thing by taking her to the dungeon. He had not checked the prisoner's condition beforehand. Ha'teng was not known for his delicacy during interrogations, and after yesterday he must have been extremely angry as too many things had not gone his way. Admittedly, he had not had much time in the morning, as they were going on a field exercise, but it looked like he had managed to make the most of even that brief moment. The girl seemed shaken. Ha'sani did not know if this would help his own cause or the opposite.

'Have you considered my proposal?' He asked in a low voice once they were out in the fresh air again. She looked at him for a long moment with piercing eyes.

'I will agree if you stop torturing my friend. Immediately,' she stated.

He hesitated before answering.

'I can't promise that.' He shook his head. 'Ha'teng must not know of our agreement. He will never accept it. The only thing I can guarantee is that the elf will not die. In what condition he will be released after the ransom is paid... I cannot take responsibility for that.'

He saw *Ta'uma* clench her fists, her body stiffening in readiness like that of a predator about to attack.

'What would you do if you were me, Ha'sani?' she asked finally. 'If your brother or sister were in captivity? If you saw treated this way?' She spoke each syllable in a voice full of pain but controlled.

Was this a test? Was this how she was going to decide if he was worth trusting? He decided to risk honesty.

'I would negotiate everything in my power.' He held her intense gaze.

'What do you think Ha'akon would have done?'

He smiled inwardly at the image.

'Ha'akon would have cut through his enemies or died in battle.'

'That's what I thought,' she concluded, turning on her heel. 'Have the servants bring the writing utensils to my chamber. You will have your letter. Tomorrow.' She tossed it over her shoulder as she walked away.

He breathed a sigh of relief and satisfaction at a task well completed.

She hadn't changed out of her blood-stained, filthy dungeon clothes. This memory was to spur her on, to give her confidence in the success of her plan. Slowly, she stretched her muscles and began to train.

Since her arrival in the Stone Nest, she had watched the Ha'ami warriors train every day. She knew they were much stronger than her, but also slower, as her duel with Ha'teng had proved. Specialised in spear and sword fighting, they were rather immobile and their footwork left much to be corrected. It was relatively easy to throw them off balance. At the same time, she was well aware that one well-aimed punch to the head would knock her unconscious. She had to do everything she could to stay out of range. She also had to be prepared for an unknown number of opponents.

She rehearsed different versions of familiar sequences, imagining herself surrounded.

Inhale. Swing. Exhale. Inhale. Dodge. Exhale. Inhale. Half turn. Kick. Exhale. Inhale. Strike. Exhale. Breathe in. Turn. Exhale. Inhale. Jump. Exhale...

She practised relentlessly until the sun sank behind the horizon and the horn called the warriors to their evening training.

The time had come.

Chapter XI
Do not judge a lizard by its size

THE WARRIOR'S HALL WAS FILLED with men, hungry after a long day, sitting on benches at long tables. Eli took a moment to study the scene, but it didn't look as if there were any formal rules about eating. The First Brothers ate surrounded by common guards, the young warriors sat with the old... Smoking cauldrons of food stood against the wall. Each man scooped up a bowl of the thick soup and sat down.

Undeterred by anyone, she walked over to the large cauldron, took a bowl and filled it with soup. Earlier she had spotted the table where Ha'min was sitting. Fortunately for her, it wasn't too crowded. She sat down and began to eat as if nothing had happened. She didn't need to raise her head to know what astonishment she had caused. It grew quiet around her, she heard the diners putting down their cutlery. It did not take long for murmurs and whispers to reach her. Then she felt a hand on her shoulder.

'Ta'uma.' She looked sideways at the owner of the large hand. The heavyset man towered over her, measuring her with an unfriendly gaze.

'What is it, Ha'stranger?' she replied calmly.

'This place is for warriors only,' he growled.

'Yes, I know,' she confirmed. 'Enjoy your meal.'

She turned back to her soup.

'Are you deaf or dumb?' a second voice asked. 'Get out of here!'

She swallowed a bite.

'Or what?' she asked. Without lifting her eyes, she took another spoonful of food. She sensed a slight consternation among the assembled. As she had predicted, Ha'min appeared.

'Calm down, all of you,' he announced as he pushed his way through the group that had managed to gather around them. 'Just a misunderstanding.'

He leaned over her. 'Eli, what are you doing? We're leaving right now, you don't want this trouble.'

'Don't I?' She looked up at him with a cheeky smile.

Unhurriedly, she rose from her seat, licking the spoon in her hand. She stood with her feet on the bench, making her the same height as the guardsman who had first approached her. She pointed the cutlery at him.

'All is as it should be,' she proclaimed. 'I am a warrior capable of defeating you or anyone else in this hall.'

Ha'min's jaw dropped.

The bully looked at her in surprise, then laughed out loud. Most of the heads at the tables were already turning in her direction.

'Want to duel, flea?'

He clasped his powerful hands on his chest, his biceps straining under his dark caftan.

'With you and anyone else who ventures it,' she replied, shoving the spoon back into her mouth. 'Granted, this disgusting soup is totally not worth it, but you could use a lesson.'

'How dare you insult me?' His face turned as red as a crayfish.

'Insult you? Are you the one who cooked this goo? I didn't know a comment about its taste would hurt your feelings.'

He swung his right fist at her head and she dodged, the momentum sending him across the table, right into her bowl.

'Oh, I see you like it. Have some more!'

She jumped onto the table and kicked another bowl and all its contents at him. The hot liquid splashed over him, he roared in anger and lunged at her. Ha'min grabbed his shoulder and yanked him back hard.

'Not here!' he shouted forcefully and, looking hard at Eli, added, 'Outside. Both of you to the square, the dining hall is no place for a duel.'

'Great!' Looking around to make sure she had the attention of the entire Warrior Hall, she leapt backwards, doing a somersault and landed softly on the other side of the table.

'Shall we go?' she asked, undeterred by the hatred boiling in the soup-soaked man's eyes, the intimidating whispers of the crowd, or Ha'min's judgmental look.

She continued her performance as planned.

The training ground was packed with onlookers, ready for a spectacle. Everyone, including the servants, wanted to see the cheeky girl get the whupping. Ha'min cursed under his breath as he drew a circle on the ground for the duel. What was she thinking? How could she do such a thing? First those stunts in the City of Sisters, and now this. She was really asking to be torn apart by spears. He met the questioning gaze of Ha'akon, now standing among the other First Brothers in the cloister, and could only shake his head in silent reply. *Ta'uma* had made such a public spectacle of herself that it was impossible to cover it up and leave it at that. She had knowingly broken the rules and insulted the honour of a warrior who had the right to demand satisfaction in a duel.

Ha'min turned to face the duellists. The guardsman stripped off his shirt and cracked his knuckles with a grim expression. The girl crouched in the middle of the circle, humming under her breath, braiding her hair carelessly and looking at no one.

'Duelling only within the boundaries of the circle!' announced the commander. 'To the point of knockout!'

He retreated into the crowd.

'Honour and strength!' Ha'min cried as a sign to begin.

The enraged man moved towards *Ta'uma*. She leapt from her crouch with incredible speed, uttering a battle cry in an unknown language, spun around and, before the man could reach her, delivered a powerful kick straight to his head. He stopped in mid-step, frozen. She spun in the opposite direction and smacked him again with her left foot in a mirrored motion. He lowered his arms and she nailed him again with a leap. He fell to his knees. She walked over to him and snapped her fingers at his nose. He fell to the ground.

Ha'min wondered if he was delusional.

The square fell silent.

Eli stood at the centre of the circle. She looked defiantly around. *This was the first one. How many more?* she thought. A good start, she just had to stay focused... one mistake could cost her everything.

'Will there be another Ha'ami man who dares to face me?' she exclaimed. Immediately, two toughs stepped out of the crowd. 'You'll do well!' She nodded in satisfaction.

They began to circle her, and she crouched down again, humming the elven battle song; she warmed up for the fight, feeling her blood begin to bubble and her mind enter a trance-like state. With soft, reptilian movements, she kept low to the ground, tracking the manoeuvres of her opponents.

The circle of warriors surrounding them now stood in silence.

Eli attacked first. With her left hand on the ground for support, she spun around and undercut the larger warrior's legs. He instantly lost his balance and collapsed with a thud. The other tried to grab her from behind, but she rolled to the side and immediately leapt into an offensive position. Wasting no time, she spun towards him and landed a kick to his face. Blood spurted to the ground from the guardsman's shattered nose. Meanwhile, the first warrior had managed to get up and grabbed her arm, aiming a sidewinder at her. Eli turned and kicked him in the groin. He just moaned and fell to his knees, letting go of her hand. She heard footsteps behind her and reflexively ducked. A fist flew over her head. She jumped up with a spring in her step. Standing close, she managed to grab the man's hair and yank him down. His face was impaled on her knee.

He flailed his arms helplessly. She added two more kicks for good measure, dropped him to the ground and immediately ran to the other warrior who was still clutching his sore manhood, leapt at his neck and wrapped her thighs around it, cutting off his air supply. At the same time, she drove her fingers into his eyes. He would have screamed in pain if he had been able to breathe, but he only gasped. She held him down until he fell and then pushed the unconscious body away.

In light leaps, Eli began to dance around the circle, amidst the stares of her stunned audience.

'Is this all the great Ha'ami can muster?' she exclaimed loudly. She pointed at more warriors. 'You, you, you, you and you! How about five of you trying to get me?'

The men looked at each other.

'Attack! Honour and strength!'

She laughed out loud and kept humming the familiar battle song. Victory had given her courage.

She must succeed. Full concentration. Every moment counted.

The five men moved to attack.

Ha'akon watched as the girl, a chant on her lips, deftly dodged the blows of the five warriors, slipping out of the siege and striking quickly and precisely when they least expected it. She made ruthless use of every missed swing, every dropped guard, every mistake. With the agility of a reptile and the swiftness of a whip, she struck until she was the only one left standing on the battlefield.

She saluted the defeated.

'Honour and strength!' she cried out.

There was thunderous applause and shouts of praise from the crowd gathered in the square.

Lizard! Lizard! cried dozens of throats.

The assembled Ha'ami, especially the *namio*, gave her well-deserved praise for her skill. In a few moments, she had won their sincere respect. Ha'akon saw one of the youths, Perin's son, run up to Eli, lift her up and place her on his shoulders, carrying her through the crowd as the warriors around held out their hands to congratulate on her victory.

'Does anyone else have any doubts about who this girl is?' he asked his companions. The answer was silence.

'I take it we'll accept her proposal?' he turned to Ha'teng. The latter nodded.

'Everyone to my chambers,' the governor ordered, turning his back on the square. 'Bring Ha'min and *Ta'uma* there,' he ordered his guards.

The First Brothers followed him down the corridor of the fortress.

'Did you notice that those lying on the ground are all members of your personal guard?' Ha'sani murmured at last.

'They were.' Ha'akon corrected him.

A familiar figure made his way through the crowd and put an arm around her.

'That was just great, *neru-to!*' Ha'perin shouted directly into her ear. 'You're even more amazing than I thought!'

He hugged her tightly and lifted her into the air.

'That was your advice. You yourself told me to give someone a public beating next time.'

She laughed as he hoisted her onto his shoulders and carried her off to the cheers of the assembled warriors. They moved back to the hall with the enthusiastic army of Ha'ami warriors. As they entered, she was seated at a table and a bowl of food appeared before her. The young men peppered her with questions, analysing parts of the duels, congratulating her.

Suddenly, the din subsided and the group gathered around them dispersed. Eight of Ha'akon's personal guards marched through the crowd.

'*Ta'uma*,' the leader addressed her. She thought she recognised him as one of the guards in her chamber. 'You are summoned to the First Brothers!'

Then, he looked around. 'And you, what, have you nothing to do? Disperse!' He shouted in a harsh tone.

Peri hugged her goodbye.

'Whatever you wanted to achieve with this show,' he whispered in her ear, 'good luck!'

'Come in,' Ha'akon commanded in response to a knock at the door.

'She is here,' the guard reported.

'Enter!'

He looked outside, through a window from which a slight chill radiated. Anxiety nagged at him. He did not feel in full control of his own emotions, so he delegated the interrogation to the others. A door slammed, then he heard soft footsteps.

'You wanted to see me,' her voice said. He turned. She was standing in the doorway, still flushed from recent exertion, her breath noticeably quickened, her green eyes sparkling with fresh triumph. It was the kind of euphoria caused by victory in the field that he knew well, that he had seen a thousand times. Never in a woman.

All he wanted now was to be alone with her. She attracted him. He wanted to feel her hot, springy body. Her warm lips. To lose himself in her touch, her scent, her heartbeat...

His train of frantic thought was interrupted by the applause that echoed through the chamber. He looked in the direction from which it had come. It was Ha'teng who had decided to express his ironic approval of what they had just witnessed.

'A magnificent display, *Ta'uma!*' he exclaimed. 'Thank you for providing our evening entertainment.'

'I just wanted to eat,' she replied calmly. 'Unfortunately, it turned out to be more complicated than I expected.'

Ha'akon took in the room with his eyes. The other First Brothers were seated, except for the Guardian of Defence, who was standing, leaning on his hip against the desk. His hands were clasped on his chest and he measured the girl with his penetrating gaze.

'Eli... right?' he asked with clear sarcasm in his voice.

'Have you forgotten my name?' she replied, slightly surprised. 'Or haven't you sobered up yet after last night's feast?'

'Oh, I'm fine, thank you for your concern,' he countered with the same tone. 'I'm curious though, is that the only name you use?'

They measured each other with their eyes for a moment.

'Yes.' She finally gave a curt answer.

'Do you have any witnesses who can confirm this?' Ha'teng probed.

'You are personally torturing the only witness in the dungeon,' she replied calmly. 'And I have repeatedly warned you that this is not a person who is prepared to cooperate with the Ha'ami.'

'Here you are wrong.' The commander caught her gaze, held it with his eyes. 'We found someone else who recognised you.'

'I don't understand what you're talking about.' The girl shrugged, though her fear was already palpable.

Ha'teng clapped his hands, the door opened and the guards dragged in a thin man with frizzy hair and tawny skin.

'Jor?' This time, her confusion must have been obvious to all gathered. The servant suddenly broke free of the guards and threw himself at her feet, shouting unintelligible words in his own language. She answered him in the same language, though the tone of her voice was reassuring. As the guards regained control of the man, *Ta'uma* turned to Ha'teng.

'What is the meaning of this? What do you want with this poor man? He has nothing to do with me,' she declared emphatically.

'On the contrary,' he replied, smiling with grim satisfaction. 'He claims to know your name and your background.'

'My name?'

Her surprise seemed genuine. Clearly, she was playing her learned role well....

'Yes, your name. Berennike, Princess of the Azzgoths.' Ha'teng announced without changing his tone. 'Do you deny that you are her?'

She understood nothing of the whole spectacle. First, out of nowhere, the guards dragged Jor into the chamber. When the unfortunate man saw her, he fell to his knees and began to beg forgiveness, though she had no idea what for. And then Ha'teng called her by a name she'd never heard before in her life, calling her princess. She looked around at the assembled people. Everyone, including Ha'akon, was staring at her in anticipation. She guessed they considered it a formality, that she would confirm the servant's words. They had already recognised her as someone she was not.

This is some kind of mistake, she wanted to say. *I don't know this man. I don't know what he's talking about.*

But she expected them not to believe her. Besides, she had her purpose. To save Tallen. No matter what the cost. She had to make a decision in the blink of an eye.

'As promised, I will answer all your questions. But only after the elf's freedom is guaranteed,' she announced in the firmest, loudest voice she could muster.

'The elf will get a fair trial,' Ha'aki almost interrupted her with his dispassionate, cold tone.

'According to your law, which is not particularly kind to strangers, especially non-humans,' she remarked.

'However, the information you provide us with may serve as mitigating circumstances...' Ha'sani interjected. He stepped into his role as negotiator with ease. 'How can we show our goodwill, apart from releasing the elf immediately, which is unfortunately not an option?'

She debated with herself for a moment. Once again, she had to make a decision at an impossibly fast pace.

'Here are my terms,' she began to dictate in a commanding tone. 'All interrogation of the elf will cease immediately. He will be taken to a dry, clean and warm place. He will not be shackled. His injuries will be treated. By Temina. He will be given proper food. I will be allowed to see him at any time. You will return to me everything we both had with us at the time of his arrest.' She looked only at Ha'akon as he turned back to the window. She hoped she had not forgotten anything.

'You will have my full cooperation as long as you guarantee that my friend will be treated with dignity.' Ha'teng snorted derisively at these words. It did not discourage her.

'One more thing. This poor man will not be punished for anything else.' She jerked her head at Jor. 'You will have him released from the dungeon.'

She waited for the ruler's reaction. For a moment there was a tense silence in the chamber. Then Ha'akon moved. Everyone in the room straightened and watched as he walked towards her. He drew a dagger from behind his belt, took her hand and made a cut in her palm. Eli did not step back, watching motionless as a trickle of her blood ran down to her wrist.

'By honour, I accept your terms,' he said, handing her the blade. She understood what she had to do. She took his hand and repeated the gesture he had made earlier.

'By honour,' she declared, looking him straight in the eye. They shook hands and their blood mingled, sealing the bargain. Ha'akon called the guard.

'Bring a bandage for *Ta'uma*,' he said, pointing to her hand. 'Also send a message to the dungeon. The elven prisoner shall be taken to the tower in a dignified manner. Summon Temina to give him the necessary assistance. *Ta'uma* will appear in person to oversee this. Understood?'

The guard nodded and left. The ruler turned to her again.

'So?' he asked, raising his dark eyebrows. 'It is time for you to reveal your identity to us.'

She didn't want her first words after taking the oath to be a lie, but she knew she had to say what was expected of her.

'You're right.' She slumped back in her chair and covered her face a little too dramatically, hoping to hide the lie she was about to tell. 'I am her. I am Berennike.'

Jor, whom everyone seemed to have forgotten, uttered an undefinable cry. He was immediately escorted out. The First Brothers looked at her with a strange mixture of surprise, relief and respect. She did not know who the person they recognised her as was. It didn't matter. Tallen was safe. At least for now.

Jor could hardly believe what he was seeing. Behold, the destiny of his people was about to change. She had returned. It was her. He had sensed it ever since he had met her, but now to hear the confirmation from her own lips made him euphoric.

He wished he had been more careful before. He shouldn't have spread the news so openly... someone had reported it. The message had reached the Ha'ami. He would have to ask for her forgiveness.

All he wanted was to serve her with his life and, if necessary, with his death. He believed she had come to free them. To throw off the yoke of the invaders. To restore to her people the dignity and freedom they so loved.

It was time for them to organise. In total secrecy. They must be ready to fight on her signal.

His heart was pounding. At last, he had hope.

They began by washing the elf's wounds with clean water. Temina then treated the burns and abrasions with a fragrant ointment before applying bandages. Eli watched her carefully as she squeezed Tallen's hand. He had not said a word since the herbalist had entered his cell.

'I leave you with this ointment and fresh bandages,' the lord's sister said in the vernacular. 'It should be applied at least five or six times a day. Instruct the servants to wash the bandages in hot water after each use.'

Eli nodded.

'I'll do it myself.'

Temina looked at her with a cheerful smile.

'I thought you were busy with politics, Princess Berennike.'

Eli blushed in embarrassment.

'I just want him to be free,' she stammered, lowering her eyes. 'I'm not going to get involved in any intrigues. Do you know what they'll do to me now?'

'I think they'll have a lot of questions to start with,' the herbalist replied. 'Your fame reaches every corner of the Ha'ami lands, not to mention the legends that circulate among the Azzgoth servants. The beating you gave the guards today has only added fuel to that fire of curiosity... I would like to hear your stories myself. Or at least see you tear those guys to pieces.'

She finished bandaging Tallen's legs, then set about setting his broken arm.

'Your hand isn't as bad as it looks,' she said. 'You've got four cracked ribs too, but they'll heal as long as you don't move too much.'

'As far as I know, he's not going anywhere anytime soon,' Eli joked when she saw the elf's grim look.

Temina also kept a cheerful face.

'No, I don't think so,' she nodded. 'Hey you, I need a cauldron of hot water!' she called in Ha'ami to the guards standing at the door. 'You two will have a lot of running to do down from here, but thank Ha'teng for that.'

They were at the top of the highest tower in the castle. The cell was spacious and clean and even had a small toilet. There was also a mattress for sleeping and a bowl of water for washing. Eli told the servants to bring a clean, warm blanket, a jug of water, cheese, bread and olives.

The room had two tiny windows, too small even for a child to squeeze through, but at least they let in fresh air and light.

When the guard returned with hot water, Temina dissolved her herbs in it.

'This will help the wounds to heal more quickly,' she said, handing the cup to Tallen. 'I'll leave you a pouch,' she added to Eli.

'Dose it carefully, as much as you have seen. Too much can lead to some very strange visions.'

She stretched and yawned. 'That's all for today. Meet me tomorrow, I hope to spend some more time with you... though I have no doubt that our brave warriors will pay you more attention now. I'd love to hear first-hand tales of today's hammering.'

She gave Eli a warm hug.

'Thank you, Temina,' the young woman replied. 'For everything you've done for me so far.'

'Come on, come on...' the herbalist laughed. 'You're welcome, what are friends for.' She turned back to the elf. 'Take care of yourself. This stubborn creature has worked more than a few miracles and taken great risks to get you out of this pit. I hope you know how much you owe her.'

'It is none of Ha'ami's business how much we owe each other. The likes of you are incapable of understanding things.'

Tallen spoke for the first time. But he did not honour the healer with the slightest glance.

Eli felt ashamed at the ingratitude he had shown the herbalist after she had bandaged his wounds with such care. Temina just smiled in response.

'Perhaps not... and perhaps even the bloodthirsty Ha'ami can still surprise you. At least some of them,' she replied, heading for the door.

'You didn't have to scold her like that.' Eli switched to Elven when they were left with only the sentries. 'She helped us.'

She handed him the fresh clothes she'd taken from his saddlebags after she'd spoken to the First Brothers and helped him pull them over his aching, emaciated body.

'I can manage,' he groaned. 'I didn't think you had friends here.'

She handed him his shoes, which were thankfully returned to her along with their bundles.

'That's a big word,' she agreed. 'But Temina helped me understand the place and showed me kindness. Ha'akon came to her when I was injured after a fight with Ha'teng.'

'Ha'teng is the smooth-talking villain. And Ha'akon?'

'The ruler of this fortress. And Temina's brother,' she explained.

'So, you are officially one of the cream of society here, Princess Berennike,' he joked.

'Very funny,' she grinned.

'Very silly,' he corrected her.

'I know.' She lowered her eyes like a small child caught red-handed. 'But I had no choice. They wouldn't believe me if I denied it. They even brought in a man who claimed to recognise me.'

'Have you thought about what they will do to you when the real Berennike appears on the horizon?' he asked, sipping slowly at his herbs.

'Maybe we can get out of here by then...' she muttered.

'Another insane plan.' He shook his head. 'My little one, I told you to stay away from court intrigues. These people are unpredictable.'

'Well... I did manage to get you out of the dungeon, didn't I?' she replied, slightly offended.

'I know and I thank you.' He stroked her hair. 'You are truly remarkable, my little friend.' She blushed at these words. 'I don't want you to put yourself at further risk, that's all. Don't trust anyone in this place, no matter how helpful they may seem.'

She nodded. She sat next to him in silence, supported herself carefully on his shoulder and listened to his calm breathing, like in the old days.

He kissed her forehead.

'Who knows maybe you really are Berennike... after all, they call her the Wild Princess. The description fits.'

He laughed.

'Sure... and you have simply not recognised my royalty all these years. It took Ha'ami to discover that,' she chuckled in reply. 'Do you know anything about her?' She became suddenly serious, realising that from tomorrow, people would start asking her questions she would not know the answers to.

'Her fame reached even our area. but I didn't pay much attention to those stories. They were just the tales of merchants infused with liquor.'

He shrugged.

'Tell me everything you remember,' she asked.

'It was a good decision, Ha'akon.'

Temina handed him a goblet of wine. They sat by the fireplace in his private chambers.

'You will gain more here by quiet conversation than by force.'

He took a sip thoughtfully.

'How do you see him?' he asked.

'Apart from the obvious exhaustion caused by your best friend's extraordinary hospitality, I must admit that the elf is impressive. There is an undeniable, otherworldly beauty about him, a pride, a nobility...' She ruffled her hair, which was now a mess. She was visibly tired. 'You know I don't like big words like that.'

'Yes, I do.'

That's not what he wanted to hear.

'Anyway, Eli treats him like the wonder of wonders.' She gave a long yawn. 'Oh, sorry, I should have said Berennike. So, it was confirmed after all?'

He nodded.

'Is it true that she beat ten of your guards?' she asked.

'Eight,' he corrected.

'By tomorrow, in the stories that will spread around the keep, it will be twenty,' she laughed.

He did not echo her. He was still lost in thought.

'What happened?' his sister asked him, suddenly serious, studying his face intently.

'Long day...' he just sighed. 'And I have to choose eight new guards tomorrow,' he added jokingly and sipped his drink.

'Maybe Eli will take the job?' She winked at him. 'Then you'll only need one.'

'Yes, that's right,' he replied with a hint of a smile. 'With her I will need only one.'

Chapter XII
Under the watchful eye of friends and foes

THAT MORNING, WINTER GAVE WAY to thaw. Instead of snow, a drizzle fell from the sky and a curtain of grey descended on the Stone Nest. The kitchen hand cursed under his breath as he shuffled through the slush-covered streets. He was sure he would lose his balance at any moment and fall on his face, it was so slippery. He had no idea how he had managed to reach the dining hall. Scolded at the entrance for being late, he hastily wiped his feet on the straw laid out by the door and began to drag the cauldrons of food into the dining hall. To his surprise, it was quieter than usual.

While a few tables were busy eating, the other half of the room was empty. Warriors, mostly the younger ones, were gathered at the front door, impatient, clearly waiting for something. Seeing this, the cook breathed a sigh of relief and calmly placed one of the cauldrons on the table. There was no need for him to be in such a hurry for fear of the hungry young men. He wiped the sweat from his brow.

Suddenly there was noise, applause and cheers from the gathered crowd. 'Lizard! Lizard!' shouted the warriors. Curiously, he craned his neck to look for the girl who had earned that nickname. Apparently, she had given fifteen Ha'ami a good thrashing yesterday. She must have been a giantess.

Suddenly he felt a blow to the back of his head.

'What's this, sleeping on duty, you swine?' the overseer rumbled in his ear. 'Get another cauldron! Do you think it will grow legs and trot over here on its own?'

Willy-nilly he rushed into the kitchen, shielding his head from further blows.

Eli had not expected such a welcome. When she arrived for breakfast, Ha'perin and the other *namios* were waiting for her. In fact, they almost carried her into the dining room. She didn't have to worry about the food; the bowl appeared in front of her as soon as she sat down, or rather as soon as she was seated at the table.

'You're lucky to have your first meal in the Hall,' Peri laughed. 'You're tasting the Queen of the Winds herself today!'

'Queen of the Winds?' She looked into a bowl filled with a brownish-green, thick liquid.

'A wonderful soup of peas, broad beans, beans and chickpeas. A real assault on your insides!' he explained.

'Sounds very nutritious!' she replied amusedly, picking up the spoon. She didn't get to eat much though, as the *namios* bombarded her with questions about the previous day's fight. She tried to answer simply, not wanting to boast or raise herself above the defeated warriors. She knew she had made at least eight new enemies in the fortress, and she did not want to make any more. The youths insisted that she demonstrate the blows they had witnessed yesterday. In particular, the three kicks she had used to subdue the first tough had caused a great deal of excitement. Tired of their insistence, she agreed, and when they made room for her between the tables, she repeated the sequence she had used the day before.

'I see breakfast is finished and you are all ready to go about your duties, right?' Ha'min stepped between them with a stern expression that didn't quite match his face. He stood like that, hands clasped over his chest, until the *namios* had dispersed through the dining hall.

'I have duty in the stables today,' Ha'perin whispered to her.

'Let's go then,' Eli said, licking the remains from her bowl. She grabbed an overbaked flatbread on the way out and they headed for the door.

'Are you sure?' asked Eli, standing up to her ankles in the mud in the middle of the square by the stables. 'I have a feeling we're both going to come out of this badly.'

'Are you scared?' Peri asked with a mischievous look on his face.

'I'm just warning you,' she replied, suppressing a laugh at the sight.

'To battle!' he shouted. 'Honour and strength!'

She struck the first blow, aiming from above in a slight leap, but he blocked it and the two sticks collided with a deafening sound, the echo of which was carried under the courtyard. He attacked immediately. One. She blocked it. Two. Blocked. Three. It was a powerful blow, brushing her shoulder and forcing her to get down on one knee, which soaked her trousers through.

'Are you all right?' He leaned over her in dismay. In a flash she swung her stick and tripped him. With a soft thud, he fell into the mud.

'I'll manage somehow...' She walked over to him and reached out to help him up. He grabbed her hand, but instead of pulling himself up, he pulled her hard towards him, and as soon as she fell, he pinned her down with his weight, trying to block and immobilise her.

'Good thinking,' she laughed.

She tried to wriggle out of his grasp like a fish caught in a net. Dirty water rushed into her eyes and ears, but fortunately she was lying on her back and could draw breath, despite the human mass crushing her. Unable to slip out, she concentrated on immobilising him. She put her arms around Ha'perin's muscular neck and intertwined her legs on his right shoulder. This allowed her to push off the ground and her back blocked his left arm. Although she lay beneath him, he could not move and his air supply was cut off.

'Tell me when you've had enough,' she giggled. 'Just don't attack me with the Queen of the Winds. That would be really dishonourable!'

'You little demon...' he whined, all red in the face. 'All right' he wheezed out after a while. 'Let's start again. I demand a rematch.'

'What do you think?' Ha'akon turned away from the window.

Ta'uma and the young warrior, covered in mud from head to toe, were duelling again, amidst a constant barrage of laughter and jokes.

'I think she is a very clever girl,' Ha'min replied. He did not take his eyes off the two youngsters in the square. 'For one thing, she's very good at taking advantage of her opponent's weaknesses and overconfidence.'

He paused for a moment, waiting for the next skirmish to be decided.

'And the second?' Ha'akon pressed him.

'She is aware of her shortcomings and covers them up with technique. Her training is deadly...' he muttered as the girl knocked the *namio* to the ground once more. He tutted in admiration.

'This boy is Perin's son, isn't he?' the ruler asked.

Eli and the warrior chatted for a while, then hugged each other goodbye. She went to the stables, and he headed for the castle.

'Yes... would you like to have a closer look at these martial arts *Ta'uma* uses?' Ha'min replied.

'If she can single-handedly take out eight men, just think what an equally or better trained army of elves can do,' Ha'akon muttered.

'You're making the same mistake as your guardsmen,' the older warrior smiled. 'You judge her by her physique. She doesn't win because of her muscles. She is fast and accurate, that is true. But above all, she uses her brains.'

The ruler groaned at this comment.

'I want you to organise individual training for these two every day,' he ordered. 'I think we should take a closer look at her tactics.'

'Of course.' Ha'min nodded in understanding. 'Will you take part?'

'When I find the time.' Ha'akon replied.

Seeing a trail of her muddy footprints being left behind, she wondered if she should enter Simronil's stall. She wanted very much to tell him everything that had happened the previous day, so she stopped for a moment on the straw in front of the entrance hoping it would absorb some of the moisture and only then moved inside. He whinnied softly when he saw her.

What happened to Eli? she heard him ask in her mind.

Oh, nothing, I was playing with Peri...

She waved her hand.

Elf?

Moved to the tower, the plan worked.

Suddenly she heard a small cough behind her. She turned around. Deep down the corridor, she saw a stick figure of a man.

'Jor?' she asked in surprise.

'My Lady...' He bowed low, removing the mask from his face. He spoke in his native tongue.

'What brings you here?' she asked, wringing her ponytail that was dripping with water. He stared at her as if petrified.

'Is something wrong?' she said to encourage him. He licked his lips nervously.

'I came... I came to thank you for standing up for me and... to congratulate you on your victory in the duel. He spoke quickly, barely breathing, as if he wanted to get all the words out at once. Lady, you defeated twenty Ha'ami alone, single-handedly... you are astounding!' he declared pompously.

'Eight,' she corrected him.

'That was incredible!' he went on as if he hadn't heard her. 'And now again... you won with such ease against another warrior!'

'Oh that? It was just a child's play.' She waved her hand.

He blinked, as if he didn't understand what she meant.

'My Lady...' He dropped to his knees again. 'I know... I know I'm a nobody... but I've come to offer my services... if you ever... ... if you need anything... I'll do anything... for you... I swear...' he stammered, almost out of breath.

Eli did not know what to make of this poor man. He seemed to be a very lost soul. She wanted to lift him from his knees, but realised she was all muddy. When she tried to wipe her hands on her trouser legs, she got even muddier. She looked around in embarrassment, grabbed a wisp of straw and dried her hands with it and approached the servant.

'Thank you, Jor.' She patted him lightly on the shoulder. 'I appreciate your... friendship. If I am in need, I will certainly think of you.'

He lifted his head and looked at her with the green, bright eyes of a faithful dog. They glowed as if he had a fever. He took her hand and pressed it to his lips. Eli stepped back quickly.

'My Lady!' He mumbled emotionally. 'I know it's unforgivable... it's because of me that they found out who you are... I promise I will be worthy of your trust!'

'Ah, that! Don't you worry. What's done is done, I suppose it had to come out eventually. Never mind.' She was at a loss for words. 'As for my hand... I'm just all dirty, I need to get clean.'

'Let me escort you to the baths!' he offered with the ever-present pathos in his voice.

'You really don't have to bother...' she started, but when she saw the glassy look of the eyes in his emaciated face, she changed her mind. 'Alright, go ahead,' she agreed. 'By the way, tell me what you've heard about me so far. I'm curious to know what news has reached you in the last few years.'

Eli waved goodbye to Simronil. She wondered if she had acted wisely.

My Dearest Papa,

As a brat spoiled to the marrow of my bones, I disobeyed your advice. The winding paths of fate have brought me to the Stone Nest in the land of Ha'ami.

The harsh laws of this place do not allow me to leave at present. My only hope lies in friendship with you.

Ha'akon, known as the Dragon Slayer, the Governor of this stronghold and the surrounding lands, is a just and honourable man. Whatever agreement he proposes, he will keep his word. Sealing the deal between the two of you is a matter of to be or not to be for me.

Forgive me if I ask you to make a difficult decision. You know that I wouldn't ask for your help if things weren't extreme.

I hope to see you soon, as well as my dear Kaz, and the rest of the company, although the road here is neither the shortest nor the easiest.

Oh, and the local food is very much to your liking. So much for the good news...

Yours always in devotion and love.

Eli

Ha'akon read the letter, then handed it back to Ha'sani.

'Are you going to send it?'

'Yes, at once,' the Guardian replied enthusiastically. 'Along with an invitation to the Stone Nest. When they arrive here, we will present our terms for the elf's release.'

'Provided he lives long enough,' the leader corrected him. 'We don't know what punishment Ha'aki will propose, and we need unanimity.'

'Well...' Ha'sani shrugged mischievously. 'Even if the prisoner comes out of this a bit battered, we will make a deal.'

'A bit battered?' Ha'akon raised an eyebrow.

'It wouldn't be the first time we sent a prisoner away on a stretcher,' the man answered lightly.

'What exactly did you promise *Ta'uma?*'

'Only that the elf would avoid a death sentence. I also described all possible scenarios, such as corporal punishment or years in the dungeon.'

As usual, Ha'sani's tone was concrete, as if he were making an offer to buy clay pots. 'I have said that I will only do as much for her as I am able... The most important thing now is for Zak to get here as soon as possible. I hope this message will be enough to convince him.'

Ha'akon knew how much the young Guardian of the Keys underestimated the importance of emotions. This plan could all come tumbling down like a house of cards in an instant.

'I have received word that the roof of the armoury in the eastern part of the castle has collapsed under the weight of the snow,' he said, to change the subject. 'With the thaw beginning today, repairs can finally begin, but I wanted to see the extent of the damage for myself first. I will leave immediately.'

'Yes, I heard about it. I will come with you,' Ha'sani suggested. 'I'll take my men, you'll need to have the depot moved elsewhere in case the weapons we stored there need cleaning and drying.'

They rose and moved towards the stables. Ha'akon was relieved to return to his daily duties.

Eli took in the atmosphere of her surroundings as she made her way through the streets of the City of Sisters. Immediately after bathing and visiting Tallen, she had fled the Upper Castle to avoid being called in for interrogation; she preferred to flip through the pages of the legal codes rather than answer Ha'teng's questions. After spending many hours in the Archives, she finally discovered something that intrigued her. An ancient Ha'ami tradition called *Koroi Karn*. Anneke couldn't explain it in detail, but from the description it seemed to allow a pardon for a prisoner. She wondered who could help her understand this better. The archivist recommended talking to Ha'aki, but Eli shuddered at the thought of meeting the fierce Guardian of Tradition.

She decided to clear her head and take a walk around the area. On the lower levels of the fortress, merchants and craftsmen were setting up stalls, servants were moving in various directions in a constant rush. All the bustle reflected the confusion in her mind. She still believed that she would find a way to save the elf from the ordeal. Although she had accepted Ha'sani's offer, she was not at all sure that she could trust him or that Zak would come. As she wandered through the busy crowd, she noticed how many people were giving her curious looks, pointing at her and whispering to each other. She decided to find a quieter place and turned towards the Temple. Once inside, she was disappointed to find that she could not feel the tingling sensation she had felt before. Spark was no longer calling her. Still, she felt like being close to the dragon again and remembering that wonderful experience of the presence of the magnificent being.

Several women bustled about, changing the oil in the lamps and cleaning the ancestral statues. They looked at her unkindly, but she decided to ignore them and marched towards the entrance to the crypt. When she finally reached the vaults, she took a deep breath relishing the solitude and silence. She sat down on the last step of the stairs, not wanting to disturb the atmosphere with the crunch of bones under her shoes. Resting her head on her hands, she allowed herself to reflect on the events of the past few days.

Ah, Spark, she thought. *If only I had an ounce of your wisdom...*

Unexpectedly, she felt a hand on her shoulder.

'Hello, *Ta'uma.*' She heard Sig's soft, melancholy voice. 'Don't get up.'

The priestess held her down with a gesture and sat beside her.

'Hello.' Eli replied politely. They hadn't seen each other since the fateful evening of the festival... she wondered if she should ask about the Eldest Woman's health or if it would be better to avoid the subject.

'It's a fascinating place, isn't it?' said the First Sister. As usual, she had a slightly vacant look in her eyes, her presence creating a strangely unsettling atmosphere. 'I myself like to come here to meditate... to draw strength and wisdom from our ancestors.'

'Yes.' Eli replied briefly. 'You can get away from the hustle and bustle here.'

'What brought you to the City of Sisters today?' Sig asked.

'I was in the Archives, I wanted to read about your traditions,' explained Eli. It occurred to her that the priestess might have answered her questions. 'I read about one of your customs today, but even Anneke didn't know what it was.'

'Yes?' the First Sister wondered.

'Its name was–' Eli frowned, trying to pronounce the words correctly. '–*Koroi Karn*. Brotherhood of Blood.'

285

'*Koroi Karn!*' breathed Sig. 'It's a very old tradition, not many people remember it.'

'Will you tell me about it?' asked Eli, although the priestess' misty eyes made her feel uncomfortable.

'Fine.' The woman there whispered, looking around absently. 'I will'.

Sig rushed to the crypt as soon as it was reported that *Ta'uma* had come to the Temple. That she had the audacity to come here after all she had done at the feast. And on top of that, it was revealed that she really was the princess of those savages from the East. At first, the priestess was about to ask her out, but as she walked agitatedly like this, she remembered her brother's recommendations. He had commanded her to be sensible and cautious. He asked her to gather information that could be useful. With a heavy heart, she pledged to feign friendship to this cursed Stranger.

Sig now had to focus all the power of her will to restrain her agitation and fulfil the promise she had made to her brother. Slowly, she descended the stairs and forced herself to speak politely to *Ta'uma*. Suddenly, the girl asked her about *Koroi Karn*. Sig had not expected to hear a question about such an ancient tradition from the Stranger. It took her a moment to organise her thoughts. Finally, she decided to explain this forgotten custom.

'The Brotherhood of Blood is one of the oldest Ha'ami traditions, deeply rooted in our values... by invoking it, a person agrees to take over the fate of his or her brother or sister.'

'Take over the fate?' the girl asked in surprise.

Sig slowly nodded her head. She wondered how much to go into the details of this archaic practice that truly reflected the spirit of her tribe. She limited herself to giving a few examples.

'It could mean taking on the duty of a duel, making a covenant in the name of another, or even serving a punishment in their stead.'

She doubted *Ta'uma* understood the full, deep, spiritual meaning of this tradition.

They sat in silence for a while. The priestess' thoughts, as was her wont, began to wander into strange realms. She had almost forgotten where she was and what she was doing here, when suddenly the Stranger broke the silence.

'Can anyone invoke *Koroi Karn*?' she asked.

The priestess forced herself to concentrate on formulating an answer.

'No. It is only allowed for related people. But our law also accepts tribal ties.'

'So, any Ha'ami can declare *Koroi Karn* for another Ha'ami or, say, Azzgoth for Azzgoth?' the girl inquired.

'Azzgoth for Azzgoth?' Sig's surprised eyes bulged. 'I don't think anyone but the Ha'ami would have the honour...'

She had to take a break. She was finding it difficult to control her reluctance any longer. She turned away and took a deep breath.

'However, in principle, yes, it is possible.' she confirmed at the end.

All she wanted to do now was to return to the temple and rest before the Eternal Fire, to smudge herself with the herbs that had always brought her solace.

Fortunately, *Ta'uma* seemed satisfied with this answer and rose from her seat.

'Thank you for the explanation,' she said. 'I'll be going now... I still have to visit Temina in the Healing Hall.'

The Healing Hall. The Eldest Woman. A cold sweat broke out on the priestess' back. Her fingers stiffened. She would have liked to close them around the girl's neck.

It's not time yet... she thought. *The Brother will take care of everything.*

'I hope to see you again soon,' she only said in a voice that was not her own.

The Healing Hall was a beautiful, tall building, one of the largest in the entire City of Sisters. When Eli stepped inside, she realised that it was a veritable maze, and she had virtually no idea how to find Temina.

She stood there, confused, until she heard a familiar voice.

'Welcome to our doorstep.'

She was relieved to see Perin appear before her like a stately goddess in a blue robe that flowed softly to the floor. Her friend's mother looked like the epitome of serenity. She embraced Eli in greeting.

'What brings you here, Berennike?'

Eli realised that from now on everyone would call her by that name.

'So nice to see you!' she exclaimed warmly. 'I'm looking for Temina... I didn't realise the Healing Hall was so big!'

'The Herbarium is in the left wing,' Perin explained to her. 'Come, I'll take you there.'

They walked between the columns along a wide corridor with bright walls without decoration. After a few turns they reached the place. The Herbarium was filled with light, coming from windows set at an angle on a high wall. Rows of shelves stretched as far as the eye could see, filled with small and large pots containing plants of many colours. Once inside, Eli was struck by the smell of the place. It wafted into her nose with a whole cacophony of different scents, mixing and changing with every step.

'There she is.' Perin pointed to a figure standing on a ladder by one of the shelves.

Temina was busy pruning the leaves. As usual, she was wearing dark hooded blouse and baggy trousers.

'Eli!' She greeted the newcomer by her own name. What a relief! She leapt to the ground and hugged Eli tightly. Perin politely bid her goodbye and left.

'Let's go to my place!' Eli's friend took her hand and led her back into the corridor and then up the stairs to the first floor. The room they found themselves in was relatively small, filled with shelves holding vials of various sizes and colours. Most of the shelves had doors with visible keyhole locks. In the centre was a table with laboratory utensils and a multitude of manuscripts scattered about. Dried herbs hung in bunches from the ceiling.

'A picture-perfect herbalist's workshop.' Eli looked around curiously at her surroundings.

'So it is,' Temina confirmed, knocking a stack of papers off her chair onto the floor, to make room for her friend. 'Would you like a warming drink, or are you hungry?'

'I'd love a warm herbal drink,' Eli admitted. 'But honestly, I can still smell a hearty breakfast.'

'What did you eat today?'

'Only soup in the Warriors' Hall.'

'What?! Where?'

Temina almost dropped the teapot she was holding in her hands.

'You sound like I shared raw meat with a bear in its cave,' laughed Eli.

'Close to it. I can see that your skills have impressed them.'

'Apparently. Although, to be honest, I don't understand all the fuss about the soup. It wasn't even that tasty, and it pretty much blew my guts out.'

'The pride of Ha'ami warriors often comes down to important things like soup and riding, don't forget that,' Temina said jokingly, filling a kettle with boiling water from a small hearth.

'Yes, I noticed,' Eli muttered.

'How is your friend?' the herbalist continued. She placed a small cup in front of her. She sat down in the chair beside her, not even bothering to remove a book from the table.

'Better,' she admitted. 'But his injuries are serious.'

'I've seen worse,' replied her friend lightly. 'He looks strong. He'll be left with scars, but other than that he should recover almost fully... well, except maybe his right hand. That will be a problem,' she admitted. 'Some of the bones are quite crushed.'

Eli grimaced. Seeing this, Temina poured a brew into her cup.

'You've done all you can,' she comforted her. 'In Ha'ami we say "*a hard law, but a law*". What you managed to bargain with the First Brothers is almost a miracle. I've never seen them agree to let go of a prisoner like that before.' She put her hand on Eli's knee, sought her gaze. 'Really, he should be grateful to you.'

'Grateful?' Eli murmured, not raising her eyes. 'It's all my fault. I don't know what's going to happen to him now.' She was on the verge of tears. 'His trial is the day after tomorrow. I can't stop thinking about it, I can't sleep.' She rubbed her forehead nervously and sipped her hot drink slowly, trying to regain her balance.

Temina looked at her worriedly.

'Maybe you want something to help you sleep?' she suggested.

'You have a herb for every worry,' Eli smiled sadly. 'Thank you, I prefer to keep my mind awake. But can you tell me about this concoction that makes you lie still like a corpse, even for a few days?'

Temina walked over to a dark wooden cabinet in the corner of the chamber. With a key hanging in a bundle at her belt, she opened the brass lock, took something out, returned to Eli and showed him a small vial containing a small root.

'The common name is deadwort. Any contact with the skin causes muscle stiffness and even temporary paralysis. The oil made from it, when rubbed under the nose, makes you lose consciousness immediately. An infusion in small quantities will put you into a state of hibernation, allowing you to sleep through the night... or a whole week, depending on the dose.'

'Deadwort.' Eli looked at the inconspicuous looking plant. 'Who would have thought that something so small could be so powerful...'

'Look who's talking!' The herbalist winked at her. 'There are many stories circulating among the Ha'ami of instances where the deadwort has been used to incapacitate opponents. There is also an amusing legend about king Ha'aliki. Well, he was once invited to a feast by his vassal, the prince of Karisia, a small country to the north. The occasion was the celebration of the coming of age of the prince's daughter, who had just reached her sixteenth year. King Ha'aliki, bored with the long, lazy winter months, decided to have some fun at his vassal's expense, and added an infusion of deadwort to the wine at the feast. All the nobles fell into a slumber, which he kept them in for a few months, while the king and his men hung around the castle, enjoying the immobilised guests as they pleased. Suffice it to say that when they finally left the castle, more than one lady was pregnant, including the sleeping princess... who was awakened only by the contractions of childbirth. Apparently, she had given birth to twins.'

Temina giggled.

'Even now, Karisia people are telling legends of the powerful sorcerer Ha'ami, who had cursed their ruler and the entire court, and of a sleeping beauty waiting to be rescued.'

Eli's mouth dropped open in astonishment.

'Is this true?'

Her friend shrugged.

'Who knows... So many stories end up becoming legends. At least this one is funny.'

'Not to the princess,' Eli remarked sourly. 'But I understand your paranoia about the possibility of being poisoned better now.'

'Yes,' Temina admitted. 'The deadwort infusion has no colour or taste. In fact, it cannot be detected in food or drink. If you like, I'll show you how to make it. It's a very interesting process.'

'Gladly.'

Eli guessed that her friend was trying to distract her from her dark thoughts.

'Great. Hang on, I'll find some gloves and masks or we'll both fall down here.'

Digging through the clutter on the table, Temina began to explain the process of distilling the brew.

The assassin followed *Ta'uma* as she walked briskly through the empty streets of the Stone Nest. The melting snow had almost completely disappeared, leaving only a thin layer of moisture on the cobblestones. It allowed him to move almost silently, though he still tried to keep his distance from the girl so as not to give himself away prematurely. The king's orders were clear. She was to die as soon as possible. No traces. No clues. He was proud to have been given this mission. He had waited a long time for the chance to prove himself.

The Moon was new, and low clouds covered the sky, making the night very dark. Berennike was alone. All he had to do was choose the moment when she would be in a place invisible to the guards posted on the walls. He followed her footsteps like a puma stalking its prey.

When they had finished making the sleeping concoction, Temina took her to her home for supper. Afterwards Eli refused to spend the night there, wanting to get back to the Upper Castle as soon as possible to see Tallen before going to sleep.

She was hurrying through the empty streets, barely able to see the road ahead in the dark of the night, when a tall silhouette suddenly appeared in front of her. The warrior, too, spotted her at the last moment and lunged at her.

'Watch where you're going, stamp crab,' he muttered. She smelled the sour smell of wine on him. He grabbed her by both shoulders and looked at her with slightly confused eyes.

'Well, what have we here? A princess in the flesh.'

She tried to pull away gently, but he held her with a surprisingly firm grip.

'Yes, right, the Princess,' she confirmed. 'I'm in a bit of a hurry, so...'

'You're in a hurry?' He blew his stinking breath in her face. 'Where to? What for? The night is young and I've just been looking for some nice company.'

He pulled her towards him.

'Great, good luck.' She felt his hands tighten on her shoulders. 'I'd make a rather dull date tonight.'

'And I think a woman like you, prancing around with elves, should try a real Ha'ami man!' He pushed her against the wall of the building and pinned her down with his heavy body.

Eli had lived near the port for a while and had to deal with the drunken, horny sailors who roamed the streets. It had taught her that there were two equally effective ways of getting out of a situation. The first was direct confrontation. The second was far more devastating in its consequences for the attacker. She assessed the situation and chose the more brutal solution.

The clearly aroused warrior had already managed to stick his tongue in her ear. He was much taller than her and lifted her up so that her legs dangled slightly off the ground.

'A true Ha'ami man, you say?' she asked, moving her hand to his crotch. She massaged his groin through his trousers. She felt it bulge. He looked into her eyes with a misty look. She smiled encouragingly. 'I'm curious to see what you can do.'

'Get ready to get the screw of your life.'

He set her down on the floor and began to feel her body impatiently. He slid his big paw under her blouse, his other hand still gripping her left shoulder. Her stomach rose to her throat in disgust, but she continued to rub his manhood, waiting for the warrior to relax completely. Finally, he made a strange whimpering sound, released her from his grasp and quickly pulled off his breeches. As he did so, she looked down, a look of utter disappointment on her face.

'Oh dear,' she sighed in disappointment. 'How tiny...'

'What, you wicked bitch!'

He went red in the face with anger. Furious, he tried to grab her again, but she recoiled. His lowered trousers restrained his movements.

'Elves have much bigger ones!' She called out and broke into a run.

She didn't expect him to be able to catch up with her. She looked around after a moment to find that he wasn't even trying. He stood still embarrassed, trying to pull up his breeches. Soon he was out of her sight. She quickened her stride even more, not wanting to bump into any more weary night hikers and breathed deeply to calm the nausea. She knew that if she stopped, she would immediately throw up.

The assassin cursed under his breath. The brainless fool had foiled his plans. The girl ran towards the Upper Castle. He would have to wait for his next opportunity.

No longer needing to hide in the shadows, he stepped out into the street. As he passed the drunk, the man looked at him with dull eyes, recognising him immediately despite his stupor. He stopped trying to buckle his trousers and straightened up, wobbling slightly.

'Brother... I just...' He began to stammer, but did not finish.

With a quick movement, the assassin drew a dagger and plunged it into his throat. He drove it all the way through, pulled out the blade, wiped it on the injured man's sleeve, and then pushed the warrior deeper into the alley. The man staggered and fell onto his back, wheezing.

Chapter XIII
To err (and pay for it) is human

LIKE A DRAUGHT ANIMAL, WITA pushed a cart loaded with barrels of wine to the Upper Castle. Sweat dripped from his forehead, forcing him to bend his head and walk blindly. As he made his way slowly up the cobbled street, he almost stepped on a Ha'ami warrior lying on the ground.

He carefully put down the two-wheeler he was pulling, first made sure it did not roll away, then leaned over the man. The man did not move. Wita assumed he was drunk after a night of partying, so he turned him around to help him sit up. Then he saw the man's face horribly contorted and the blood drying on his neck and chest.

'Hey there!' He heard a voice behind him. He looked round. Two guardsmen were standing at the mouth of the street.

'What's going on over there?'

They hurried towards him.

Wita stood with his head bowed.

'I found him wounded...' he murmured quietly.

They looked at him coldly. Then they swept their eyes over the body lying on the pavement.

'Wounded!'

Wita immediately felt the hard blow of the blunt end of the spear on the back of his head.

'On your knees, dog, you are under arrest!'

'I... didn't... I'm just bringing the wine,' he said, bursting into tears and obediently falling to the ground as commanded.

'You will pull this wagon and then we'll take you to Ha'teng for a talk,' the warrior shouted. 'You will remember this day for the rest of your short, mangy life!'

A wave of cold terror swept over the burly servant. Nevertheless, he meekly rose to his feet and began to trudge along again with his burden, this time accompanied by one of the Ha'ami. The other guard remained by the body. Although Wita was many times stronger than the man who accompanied him, it did not even cross his mind to resist. In a feverish whisper he repeated prayers to his gods. Perhaps they would have mercy on him after all...

Eli was not greeted with applause in the warriors' hall that morning, but as she poured herself a bowl of soup, she was immediately invited to join various tables. She eagerly sat down with a group of *namios* she knew and spent the meal teasing them about their techniques for using kitchen utensils in duels. As another round of laughter erupted, she felt a hand on her shoulder.

'Hello, *neru-to*!' She heard Ha'perin's voice. 'I hope you've recovered from rolling around in the snow yesterday.'

'Our skirmish didn't require much effort, so it didn't tire me out,' she replied, supported by the general merriment around the table. Peri, as always eager for a joke, joined in the banter.

'That remains to be seen. We have a summons to the training ground. Wolf wants to teach you a lesson in person... and I have been given the honourable role of training dummy,' he declared, crossing his arms proudly over his chest and cocking his head.

'A lesson?' She was surprised. 'Well, I suppose I'll find the time in my extremely busy day to give you another thrashing.'

'The pleasure will be all mine.' He ruffled her hair, which she had so carefully braided earlier.

'Oi!' She waved her hand at him like an annoying mosquito. 'Do you want to start now?'

'As far as I'm concerned, we could dance here, but I'm afraid we'll get another penalty and I'm in no hurry to clean the outhouses,' he replied cheerfully.

'Lead the way then.'

She bade the *namios* goodbye and they made their way through the dark corridors deeper into the fortress.

'I suppose you're missing some fascinating agenda for the day?' she asked him on the way.

'Indeed. Today we are practising digging trenches. That's why Ha'min has time for us. Especially in winter, it is the most eagerly awaited pastime of all warriors,' he replied.

'Digging trenches?' She stopped mid-step. 'Is that some kind of punishment? Don't you have helpers?'

'No and no,' he laughed. 'We do it at least once every few days, to improve skill, speed and endurance in this key combat activity.'

'I don't understand... what has that got to do with fighting?'

'Trench warfare is the simplest tactic in both open battle and siege. He explained with a twinkle in his eye. Good trenching has helped us win more skirmishes than the best trained army.'

'Interesting...' she sighed thoughtfully. 'Indeed, today you will miss out on wallowing in the mud in this thaw. You must be very sorry,' she added finally.

'Of the two evils, I choose you.' He ruffled her hair again. This time she did the same, and so they marched on down the corridor, giggling like children.

Over breakfast, Ha'akon spoke to the First Brothers about the trial plan for tomorrow, but out of the corner of his eye he followed events in the hall, where the commotion was concentrated around the table where Eli had taken her seat. Her presence enlivened the scene once again.

Their discussion was interrupted by a guardsman who approached them with a grim expression.

'Yes?' Ha'teng raised an eyebrow.

'We found a dead Ha'ami,' the man reported to the surprise of those gathered.

'Whose?' the Guardian of Defence asked curtly. The warrior turned to Ha'aki and nodded.

'Throat slit,' he explained, and the First Brother's face took on an angry expression. 'We have already caught the murderer. Servant,' the warrior added immediately, anticipating the outburst.

Ha'teng rose from his seat, followed by Ha'aki.

'Lead the way!' he ordered, and then they moved towards the door.

'I'll go too,' Ha'min said after a moment. 'Training with *Ta'uma.*'

'Good luck taming the little beast,' Ha'sani commented. 'Let me know if you need any help.'

'I can manage,' the trainer murmured.

'I'll gladly come by later to check it out', retorted the youngest of the First Brothers. When the older warrior was gone, he turned to Ha'akon. 'As for the collapsed roof of the armoury, I've calculated the cost of rebuilding it...'

The ruler listened without much interest. His thoughts were elsewhere.

'These are the private training rooms of the First Brothers,' Ha'perin whispered in her ear as they stood in front of the huge iron doors. 'Only they and their bodyguards are allowed in here.'

'Honour has struck us like a donkey kicking its driver in the gob,' she muttered. 'So, shall we go in?'

'Let's wait for Ha'min' the *namio* hesitated.

'Maybe he's already there?' she asked, pushing the door open.

The hall was empty. It was a spacious room, clearly designed for the practice of one-on-one duels. The walls were lined with equipment of all kinds: shields, spears, short and long blades, axes...

Eli broke into a run at the sight of her and Tallen's saddlebags lying there. She would have recognised them anywhere. With a cry of excitement, she grabbed the hilt of her favourite elven sword. One by one she showed Ha'perin her collection of weapons, which she had finally retrieved, when they heard the door creak.

'Patience is not one of your virtues,' Ha'min remarked as he walked towards them.

'I never said it was.'

She swung the blade skilfully. It had been made especially for her and fit her hand perfectly. It always seemed more like an extension of her arm than a foreign object.

'Today we do not want to kill each other,' the trainer scolded her. 'Put the iron down, I know you missed it, you'll play later.'

'Yes, sir Wolf!' She saluted with her sword and sheathed it. 'At your command!'

'We'll begin with wrestling... To the centre, both of you,' he snapped.

Eli exchanged amused glances with Ha'perin.

'Well, it's a good thing we didn't have your beloved Queen for breakfast this morning, Peri.'

Ha'min ordered them into position for the attack.

'What now, do you have a moment to entertain yourself?' Ha'sani asked as he finished the estimate. The ruler looked at him as if he had just woken up. 'Shall we go and see how our old man handles the princess?' the Guardian of Keys added.

Ha'akon nodded without a word and together they made their way to the training room. When they arrived, the girl and Ha'perin were rolling around on the floor, re-enacting the wrestling holds the Brothers had seen earlier in the square outside the stables.

The boy was definitely doing better than before. But this kind of fighting was actually to the girl's favour, as it evened out the advantage of height and strength, giving a chance to whoever had the better technique. After another defeat of the *namio*, Ha'sani couldn't contain himself and began to applaud.

'Nice leverage,' he complimented. 'You must have had a great teacher.'

She brushed unruly hair from her forehead as she got to her feet.

'Yes.' She confirmed, adjusting the knot in which her long curls were tied. 'Wrestling is the dwarves' favourite form of combat... they taught me everything.'

'Really?' He was excited as usual when the subject came up.

'Of course.' She caught her breath. A blush rose to her cheeks. 'Because of their size and the fact that they tend to fight in confined spaces. The tunnels and chambers underground are not very large.'

'It makes sense,' he nodded. 'In portraits, in stories, they're usually depicted with hammers or axes...'

She laughed out loud.

'I know. They're mostly ceremonial weapons. Try swinging an axe in a narrow corridor... not recommended!'

'What about the elves?' Ha'akon interjected suddenly. 'I've seen your weapons. Are those the kind of swords they use?'

Eli reached for her blade and pulled it from its sheath.

'Very narrow,' Ha'amin remarked.

'But it has a unique fuller.' She pointed to the blade of her weapon. 'Look at the shape. It makes the sword extremely strong and rigid.' Everyone regarded the design of the weapon with curiosity. 'Would you like to try it?' she suggested, looking at Ha'perin.

'I don't know if that's a good idea, you're both tired already. Maybe we're done for today,' Ha'min began, but then they heard the sound of a blade being pulled from its sheath. They turned in that direction.

'Why not?' the Governor asked curtly with a serious look on his face.

Ha'akon was troubled by an undefined unease both in her presence and when she was not around. Now that he was next to her, he was completely at a loss as to what to say. This was a new experience.

He cursed himself mentally for agreeing to the duel. He had no idea what had made him do it. Maybe a puppyish need to show off in front of a girl. It was too late now. They faced each other in concentration, swords crossed. He with his heavy, one and a half-handed blade, she with her narrow elven sword. He did not want to harm her.

They both raised their weapons almost simultaneously. He slashed from above, Eli swung up and deflected his sword so that the blade spun to the side and she slid under it.

He attacked with more determination, but her style was to dodge and evade. As always, she tried to capitalise on her opponent's fatigue. Ha'akon, however, was neither a *namio* nor a guardsman. He was the best fighter in the Stone Nest, and perhaps in all of

Ha'ami Land. He closed the distance quickly, leaving her no choice but to defend herself.

They crossed blades several times. He knew he had the advantage and did not use all his strength. She noticed. She shot him a crooked smile, went down in a flash and smacked him in the calves with the hilt of her sword. He jumped back. She immediately lunged for his stomach, but he managed to parry the blow.

They twirled in a battle dance for a long time in the silent presence of the others, who made not a sound.

At one point, he grabbed her left wrist, turned her around, and tried to pull her towards him to end the duel, but her scent, her proximity, completely distracted him. This gave her time to twist her right hand and strike him in the face with the hilt of her sword. He felt she didn't use all her strength, but it was enough to knock him off balance. He let go of her hand.

Ha'perin let out a short cry. Eli glanced hesitantly around the room, darting his eyes from Ha'akon to the others and back again.

She attacked with a series of short slashes, but he countered with powerful blows that pushed her back against the pillar that held up the ceiling. Eli retreated under the pressure of his blows until her back was against it. Now he had her. She still had time to dodge, but then he knocked her sword from her hand and aimed his blade at her. She raised her hands in a gesture of surrender.

They both breathed heavily, Ha'akon more from anger than fatigue. He knew full well that she had given him the victory, and in a way that no one else would have noticed.

And yet he could not take his eyes off her sparkling green eyes as she looked at him apologetically.

'Well done for your first time, littlun, hardly anyone can keep up with this daredevil... and you were doing so well for so long. He gave you a bit of a head start today.' Ha'min walked over to Eli and patted her on the shoulder. 'Well, that's enough skirmishing for this morning. It's time for us to see how our diggers have fared.'

Ha'akon sheathed his sword.

'This elven blade is indeed not the worst,' he muttered. 'Let's go then.'

He turned to the door, without looking at her. A ride outside the fortress would actually do him good, he thought.

Wita knelt in the middle of the square opposite the stables, surrounded by a circle of Ha'ami guards. He passively accepted the blows they gave him. His face must have been a bloody mess by now. He did not know by what miracle he was still on his feet. His body was much tougher than his mind and it would not give up, even if he wanted it to. He would have rather lost consciousness than endure the pain they were inflicting on him. Worst of all was the grim commander. Apparently, the dead warrior was one of his troops. This master wore iron-studded knuckles instead of gauntlets, and he lunged furiously at Wita wherever he could. On the head, chest, hands, crotch...

At first the servant begged for mercy, explaining that it wasn't him, that he'd only found a dead guard. No one listened to him... The commanders immediately agreed with the patrol's report. And they began a merciless torture with no end in sight. One by one, the warriors approached the man and beat him until they were exhausted. One was replaced by another. And the next. And the next...

Wita felt even his strong thighs begin to wobble, and a pool of blood surrounded his knees on the cobbles. In his mind he prayed to all his gods for a quick death.

Suddenly he heard a cry and the beating stopped. The sounds of a quarrel reached him. Finally, small hands touched his face and he felt a wet cloth rub his blood-soaked cheeks. He struggled to lift his swollen eyelids to see the face of the same noblewoman he had seen a few days earlier when she refused to take her place in the sedan. The bright green eyes looked at him with a gentleness and pity he had never experienced before in his life.

'Poor man...' she whispered, and the coolness of her hand soothed the pain in his tortured face.

'You should wait until after the judgement.' He heard a deep male voice above him.

'This is just a warm-up, Ha'min,' the icy hiss of a master with knuckles sounded. 'And compared to what's in store for this rogue, it's child's play.'

The woman crouching beside him rose to her feet.

'Ha'aki, aren't you the one responsible for upholding the law?' She asked emphatically. 'Then you know he deserves a fair trial.'

There was a tense silence. Wita could barely see the feet of the people around him.

'Do not interfere in Ha'ami affairs, *Ta'uma*,' the same commander whispered threateningly. 'You have no say here.'

'That is enough.' The voice of the lord of the castle cut through the air. 'Tomorrow is Judgment Day. Take this man to the dungeon. Until the sentence is passed, no one is to approach him. The prisoner must be able to stand up for his own trial. That is our law.'

Wita felt the noblewoman press a damp cloth into his hand before two guards pulled him to his feet and dragged him towards the dungeons. He knew that the cruel lord was right. A miserable end awaited him.

'These are terrible people, Tallen...'

Again they sat shoulder to shoulder, leaning against the wall of his cell, chewing the dried fruit she had brought.

'They've beaten this poor man to a pulp. And he doesn't look like the sort of person who would hurt a spider.'

'An ant. You say, *He wouldn't hurt an ant,*' Tallen corrected her, quoting the elven proverb.

'No one has any reason to hurt ants,' she objected. 'Ants are harmless and look friendly. Spiders, on the other hand, are an abomination. There are a thousand reasons to squash them as soon as you see them.'

He smiled to himself. He knew how much she hated the creatures and it was a constant source of jokes for him. This time he held back, but she still noticed his grimace.

'You're making fun of me again!' She pointed at him accusingly. 'While I'm telling you, I don't know what would have happened to him if we hadn't just come back from training! They would have bludgeoned him to death!'

'Maybe it would have been better for him...' he muttered. 'You don't know what they'll sentence him to in their supposedly just judgement. Maybe that death would have been easier than the suffering he's still going through.'

'Do you mean to say that I have done wrong?'

She looked at him with those big innocent eyes.

'I want you to understand, little one, that you can't defend all the oppressed in this world, no matter how hard you try.' He hugged her comfortingly. 'You didn't do anything wrong, you acted on a heart reflex, but that's not always good advice... especially when confronted with these people.'

'You're probably right,' she sighed. She rubbed her forehead with her hand, brushing back her tangled curls.

'Do you remember Zak?' She changed the subject, clearly wanting to talk about something else.

'How could I forget? Only once in my life has a dwarf knocked me out with a headbutt.'

They both laughed lightly.

'It was Kaz who hit you. His twin brother,' she corrected. 'And you deserved it.'

'Oh... what about them?' Tallen muttered.

The boisterous family could stage a brawl whenever they thought the elves weren't being careful enough with Eli. The actual fight broke out only once, when she lost control while learning one of her Gifts. As luck would have it, the dwarves happened to knock on the door and found him treating her for a serious haemorrhage she had suffered as a result of misdirecting her power. They rushed at him like a pack of wild boars.

'They have found the treasure they were looking for,' she announced with a cheerful expression on her face. 'They're rich, they've set up a trading post and even the Ha'ami want to do business with them.'

'You see, the key is to have simple dreams...' he replied without contempt.

'And, as in their case, to work very hard for them.'

As always, she was a little oversensitive about her foster father.

'It would have been useless if it hadn't been for a stroke of luck and a certain talented person who helped them a lot...'

She blushed, as usual, when someone paid her a compliment.

'Oh, nothing really,' she murmured.

'Why did you suddenly remember them?' he asked, getting the impression that she had brought up the dwarves for some reason.

'Oh yes... I heard rumours at the castle.' She looked away. He knew there was something she was not telling him.

'Rumours? Anything specific? Will they show up here?' He made a blind guess, since they were talking about trade.

'No,' she denied it. 'Just so...' she sighed heavily. 'I still can't think of a way to prevent your judgement.' She abruptly changed the subject. 'And that's tomorrow... I don't know what else I can offer them.'

He put a firm hand on her shoulder and looked at her seriously.

'Eli. Don't do anything more. You have no friends here. They all have their own reasons for talking to you or caring about you... more or less obvious. But they are all selfish.'

'I was thinking...' she began uncertainly. 'Maybe if I tell Ha'akon the truth about myself... about our expedition... maybe he will understand, maybe he will let us go.'

He gave her a moment to consider her own words.

'Do you really think that will convince him?' he asked finally.

She bit her lip nervously.

'No,' she confirmed quietly. He let her go and leaned back against the wall.

'Besides, from what you've told me, one man doesn't mean much in this country,' he added, 'Not even a ruler.'

She did not seem entirely dissuaded from her idea. So, he continued.

'What do you really know about him, Eli? You've only known him a few days. The only thing he did for you was to graciously return your property and let you heal when his executioner beat you.'

'Yes, but Spark –'

'This story should make you think all the more. The revenge, the violence, the cruelty... yes, he regretted it. And what did that change?'

She gave up, hung her head.

'You're right,' she sulked.

'Eli... I just want to protect you.'

'–from my naivety and stupidity. As usual.'

She got up and turned towards the door.

'I'll think of something, Tallen, I'd like you to trust that I can take care of us for a change,' she said, still irritated.

He stood up, not wanting them to part in anger.

'I know you won't give up.' He pulled her close, hugging her. Eli nodded sadly.

Then she turned and walked away.

Tallen sighed heavily. He didn't know if they would ever stop having the same fight. It didn't look like it, at least not any time soon.

His little mouse crawled onto his battered palm, sniffing the food. He handed it pieces of fruit with his left hand, lost in thought. He knew now that the voice he had heard earlier belonged to the dragon Spark, the name he had revealed to Eli. He was still haunted by the thought of the danger the beast had mentioned during their conversation. What did he know? What had he warned of?

Tallen was sure he was right about Ha'ami. He didn't believe in the selfless intentions of a single person in that fortress. He also feared that the whole story of the princess would drag Eli into a new complex web of intrigue and conspiracy, creating enemies who had previously remained indifferent. Though the consequences would be even more difficult to predict than if she revealed the truth... In vain, he urged her to flee. She would not leave him.

Either way, the events of tomorrow would gain momentum. At least they will find out what final torture these barbarians will choose for him.

She really needed that bath today. No day here had been easier than the last. She was completely exhausted.

Feeling the warm water relaxing her muscles and clearing her thoughts, she plunged into the hot depths up to her head, surrendering to the glorious weightlessness.

All Eli dreamed about now was the bed. When she had finished the soothing ritual, she quickly wiped off the moisture and pulled on a light tunic with the intention of going straight to sleep. She shuffled silently through the corridors of the castle to her chamber, meeting no one. Water dripped from her wet hair onto the floor, causing the robe on her back to stick to her body.

I'll dry off by the fireplace, she thought, knowing that once she was in the warm room, she would fall lifeless on the bed. She closed the door behind her with a sigh of relief.

'Be greeted.'

She turned abruptly at the words.

Ha'akon was sitting in an armchair by the fireplace. She was suddenly aware of how little she was wearing.

'Be greeted.' she replied.

She watched him hesitantly and at the same time began to shuffle along the wall towards the wardrobe, trying to find something to wear.

'What brings you here?'

He stood up and began to walk towards her. She tried to look indifferent, but felt her muscles tense reflexively.

'I've come to... talk to you,' he replied, his eyes sweeping over her face and body. 'About our duel.'

She really didn't want a showdown with the lord of the castle. Not now. Not after all this time. She thought feverishly about how to get out of this situation peacefully. Ha'akon was an honourable man, so she had to find a way out that wouldn't offend his pride. He was standing right in front of her.

'Talk about a duel?' She continued to move towards the chest, but he blocked her path. 'You defeated me.'

'You allowed me to win,' he corrected her.

'You also faked blows. You were clearly distracted, it wasn't a good time to fight,' she replied.

'Do you know what distracted me?'

She could smell his masculine scent, the warmth of his breath on her neck. The hair on the back of her neck stood up.

'I'm very tired, can we postpone this conversation until tomorrow?' she tried to save herself in a last-ditch effort.

'I'm afraid it can't wait until tomorrow.'

Saying this, he hugged her tightly and kissed her. She put her hands on his chest, trying to push him away, but he held her tighter and continued to caress her. His hands went under her tunic, down her still damp back and buttocks.

She pushed her head back as far as she could without hitting the wall.

'Ha'akon... no...' she breathed.

He looked at her in surprise. Eli guessed he wasn't used to being refused. She slipped nimbly from his embrace.

'I can't.' She raised her hands in an apologetic gesture. 'I am not Ha'ami. If we...' She hesitated, choosing her words carefully. 'That would make me no more and no less than a kept person.' She slowly retreated deeper into the chamber. 'I will never be anyone's kept woman, Ha'akon... never. Not even yours.'

He looked at her with fevered eyes. A grimace of rage suddenly crossed his face.

'Is that the only reason?' he asked, clearly suppressing his anger.

'Yes, the only one.' She tried to strike a conciliatory tone. 'But good enough. You know well how difficult it is to earn the respect of your people. Please don't put me in a position that makes it impossible.'

He breathed heavily, opened his mouth to speak, but immediately stopped. He lowered his gaze.

'Ha'akon?' She asked uncertainly.

He did not look in her direction again, leaving the chamber without a word.

As soon as the door slammed behind him, she let out a loud sigh of nervousness. Her legs went limp and she crouched down on the bed to calm herself.

How am I going to get out of this... Her mind whirled.

Anni hid in the shadows of the corridor. She froze in her tracks when she saw the Lord of the Stone Nest leave *Ta'uma's* chamber shortly after she returned from the bath. He looked very distraught. She did not want him to notice her.

She was so frightened by his angry face that she sat motionless for a long time after he had gone. She finally decided it was too late to go to master Ha'teng. Even his appetite for news had its limits. It would be better if she told him everything in the morning. She curled up in a corner, intending to wait out the night.

Anni had always been a vigilant sleeper.

Unexpectedly, she was awakened by a loud noise. She shuddered in shock, then became still again as *Ta'uma's* bedroom door swung open violently. A dark silhouette emerged from inside in a tremendous rush.

Anni did not move. Fear pierced her like a blade of ice. For a moment she wondered if she was dreaming. The shadow that ran out of the chamber resembled a ghostly apparition... there was something deadly about it.

She froze as it spotted her and turned towards her. She recognised the sure, sweeping gait of the mysterious figure. She knew him very well. That made her even more paralysed.

'Lord, I don't–' she stammered as strong black-gloved hands cupped her head. She felt a tug and then there was nothing.

Anni fell senseless to the floor. She didn't even have time to think that this was the end of her.

Long after Ha'akon had left her chamber, Eli turned in bed, pondering the implications of recent events. What did his silence mean? Had she offended him? If so, how long would he hold a grudge? In the end, she concluded that she was probably exaggerating the whole thing out of weariness. After all, the lord of the castle had girls in bunches. So what if one of them refused his urges? Surely, she would soon find comfort in the arms of another.

The memory of his touch and kiss, however, haunted her late into the night. Her thoughts turned to alternative versions of events. What if she had not gotten used to suppressing any sentimentality over the years? It was safer that way, but she was still losing something that could have brought her, if not happiness, then at least some joy.

In the end, she managed to push those sad thoughts away as well. She had to concentrate on one thing. Getting them all out of this place. That was all that mattered now.

Finally, she fell into a restless sleep where she fought a bunch of horrible enemies... there were too many. They crushed her with their hideous mass. She ran out of breath...

Suddenly she realised it wasn't a dream, something was covering her head and cutting off her air supply. Some kind of weight was crushing her form. In a panic, she put her hands up to her face and felt strong hands pressing a pillow into her, preventing her from breathing. She struggled against them for a moment in vain and then, in a reflex of desperation, she pulled from under the bedclothes the elven dagger she now held at her side and began to strike blindly. The attacker released his grip. She drew in a breath. He was clearly trying to grab her wrist to keep her from retaliating. Seizing the moment, she impetuously threw him over the edge of the bed. Unfortunately, he managed to knock her weapon away from her, and it fell to the floor with a clatter. It wouldn't be easy to find it in the dark. Eli didn't even try. She sprang to her feet and, with a leap, landed a kick in the face of the assassin, who managed to get to his feet. With impressive agility, he sidestepped her blow, grabbed her ankle in mid-flight and knocked her off balance. She tumbled face down onto the bed and rolled to the other side, expecting an immediate blow. She was not wrong. His elbow landed where she had just fallen.

They stood facing each other now, between the pillars that supported the canopy. She could hear his breathing. She knew that she had been struck at least once by a dagger in the soft tissue, though most of the blows had slipped under her ribs. It was clear that her attacker was quickly analysing the situation.

Unexpectedly, he turned and ran for the door. He opened it and disappeared into the dark corridor. Eli cautiously approached the fireplace and grabbed a chair, pulling it to block the handle.

Then she curled up into a ball on the floor by the fireplace, wondering who was hunting her. Or Berennike.

The furious killer dragged the dead fat woman into a privy deep in the corridor. At first, he thought of throwing her through the opening, but she was too big, even with the boards tilted back.

Then he just put her in, pulled her pants down and slammed the door. Let them think she had died of indigestion or some other disease that fat scums die of. No one would bother with a dead maid.

This was the second time he had failed. But he couldn't complete the task without making more noise, which would attract the guards.

Surely the girl would be more careful now. If they were to continue to act in secret, a different kind of action would be needed. He knew his commander had a plan in reserve. This herb-drugged priestess had proven surprisingly useful.

He felt a sting in his side and rubbed at the moisture that was seeping into his uniform. The wound wasn't deep, but it was annoying. And he would have to explain it somehow if anyone noticed.

Another failed hunt. The king will grow impatient. They must close this case as soon as possible.

Chapter XIV
Justice versus law

HA'RIM HAD ANOTHER STROKE OF bad luck on his watch. This time, during his morning rounds, he discovered a dead servant girl in the privy. He was sure the night watch had noticed her, but they preferred to have the morning watch deal with her. He cursed them wordlessly with all his might.

He'd seen this Ha'teng rat in this part of the castle many times, so he guessed she had been sent to spy on *Ta'uma*. And now she met the end that all such wretched creatures deserve. She had shat herself to death.

He hurried to report to First Brother, leaving his partner Ha'toru by the lifeless body.

Ha'teng wanted to see the corpse for himself. When they led him to it, he merely cast an indifferent glance at the naked, fat body.

'As if it didn't stink here enough already,' he muttered, twisting his face in disgust.

'At first we thought she had died of poisoning,' Ha'toru explained dispassionately. 'But it looks like she messed with someone, because he broke her neck.' He pointed to the unnaturally hanging head.

'Maybe he got carried away with the hanky-panky,' Ha'rim ventured.

The Commander just gave him a grim look.

'Demons know how these rats fornicate. Maybe even the latrine is a good place for them.' The guardsman shrugged.

'It is of no consequence. I suppose nobody noticed anything? Both guards shook their heads. 'I have more important things to do than hunt down a human garbage killer.' Ha'teng turned away with an indifferent expression. 'Have this abomination removed and burned.'

Ha'rim acknowledged the command. He watched the commander walk down the corridor.

Ha'ami rarely cared for slaves, but the guard knew that this particular rat was one of Tiger's most loyal informants. Still, the guard expected her demise to at least anger him. But apparently any attachment to servants was completely alien to Ha'teng. As were other human emotions.

The Day of Judgement dragged on as usual. Neighbourhood disputes, petty thefts, fights... Ha'akon thought that all these cases should be decided by the commanders of the individual wards or localities, but Ha'aki always insisted that, according to tradition, only the First Brothers had the right to do so. Punishment also had to be decided unanimously. These two circumstances meant that for most of the minor offences they would simply agree to Ha'aki's proposal, allowing them to deal with as many culprits as possible in one day. When it came to more serious matters, Ha'akon preferred to spend more time on them, and usually felt that the others were treating them a little too lightly. The decision to cut off someone's arm should not be taken lightly.

They were seated in intricately carved and very uncomfortable chairs, lined up in a row on the platform, looking down on the accused from above. There was also a small table with a jug of water and wine for each of the First Brothers, which some of them had been eagerly using since the morning.

They began with the alleged murder of a guardsman found in an alley. The accused servant was of immense stature, taller and heavier than any man Ha'akon had ever seen in his life. At the same time, after a few sentences it became clear that he was a complete imbecile. Retarded in his development. A heavy thinker. A moron. There were many expressions to describe people like him. People like him were sent by the Ha'ami to die alone in the forest to return Mother Nature's mistakes to her.

Ha'aki formulated the accusation in a few blunt sentences as the giant sobbed like a child, tears dripping from his swollen eyes. He stammered vaguely that he had only found a corpse. For Ha'ami, the sight of a man crying so publicly was unbearable.

'How did he kill him?' Ha'akon pressed them.

Ha'teng nodded at the guard, who placed a short dagger on the table in front of them.

'With a weapon he took in battle,' the First Brother explained. 'The slain man had his trousers unbuttoned and was probably pissing in the alley when this scum decided to attack him.'

'What reason did he have?' the ruler continued, annoyed by the sound of sobbing.

'Do such brainless bastards have to have a reason?' Ha'aki growled angrily. 'If they had the chance, they'd slaughter us all.'

Ha'akon frowned. This one didn't look like he knew how to use a weapon. Besides, if he wanted to, he could crush a human skull with a single blow of his fist. Why would he bother with a dagger? And then there was the precision of the blow to the throat... He turned to Ha'teng.

'Are you absolutely sure, *koru*?'

The man nodded impatiently. He seemed offended by the question.

'I have no doubt,' he affirmed.

'Very well then...' Ha'akon decided that the fate of the imbecile is not worth arguing about. 'What punishment do you suggest, Ha'aki?'

'Death by dismemberment,' the commander declared in a voice as sharp as a knife of ice.

All present confirmed their agreement and the prisoner was ordered to be escorted to the dungeon amidst his incessant wailing.

'If he howls like this in court, imagine what he will do at the execution!' Ha'sani sighed as more defendants were allowed into the room.

After the events of the previous night, Eli had no desire to leave the chamber. Besides, it was Judgment Day and she was not allowed to see Tallen.

She didn't know if she should tell anyone about the overnight visitor. She was becoming convinced that her friend was probably right, and that she couldn't trust anyone in the fortress.

To her surprise, breakfast was brought to her by an unfamiliar servant, this time with a small dragon tattooed on her arm. She wondered why Ha'teng had dismissed Anni.

The strange circumstances kept piling up. Her anxiety grew.

By the time Eli had finished eating, the irritation had not left her. She paced the room like a wild animal in a cage. She looked out the window. The sun was already high in the sky.

She threw the elven cloak over her tattered clothes and headed for the stables. With a somewhat naive hope in her heart, she took the longer path that led not far from the Hall of Justice. She hoped that at least she would be able to see something through the window.

She moved around the fortress with much more confidence than she had at the beginning. She hardly ever got lost. Especially when she went outside.

For a while she wandered around the courtyard where the First Brothers had gathered, until she saw Tallen being led by the guards to the trial. She became angry at the sight of the chains that bound him again. Heavy shackles encircled his wrists, ankles and even his neck. She rushed over to him.

'Is this really necessary?' she snapped at the guards, pointing angrily at the iron dragging on the ground. 'We are in a fortress filled with thousands of Ha'ami warriors, surely no prisoner can be strong enough to get out of here on his own.'

'Ha'teng's orders.' the guard replied indifferently.

'How else,' she muttered to herself. 'How are you?' she turned to Tallen in Elven.

'Happy as a dancing calf,' he joked.

'Move!' The guard interrupted her curtly. She glared at him, then embraced her friend's neck and hugged him tightly, whispering a few words of encouragement.

The guard grabbed her collar in a decisive move and pulled her back violently.

'Everything shall pass,' Tallen murmured, smiling reassuringly.

They were finishing a short recess while waiting for the next defendant. Ha'akon listened to Ha'sani's report. It seemed that the collapsed armoury had, by some unfortunate coincidence, caused a landslide and damaged the water supply below. They would have to call in Keera and her army of engineers to repair the damage and restore the flow.

They were talking by the window when he saw the guards leading the elf in. It was the first time Ha'akon had seen him in daylight. The prisoner was as tall as the warriors who accompanied him, had a strong but slender figure, and held himself upright despite the shackles on his arms and legs, the heavy chains trailing behind him, and the days spent in the dungeon and under Ha'teng's interrogation. The injuries he had sustained were clear and consistent with the description Temina had given him. His right hand looked quite crushed and he doubted the prisoner would ever be able to use it again.

Ha'akon could not help but think that if this elf had trained the girl in such a way, he must have been a deadly effective fighter himself. This made him curious. He thought he would like to see a demonstration of the prisoner's combat skills. Well, it didn't look like it would happen in the near future. Or ever...

Unexpectedly, Eli appeared on the square. She exchanged a few words with the guards and then threw herself around the elf's neck. The warriors immediately pulled her away. She did not seem moved. She stood and followed them with her eyes until they disappeared into the doorway of the building. Her gaze as she looked at him... Ha'akon felt a tightening in his chest.

Last night had been a huge disappointment. The thought of the girl gave him no peace. The non-human whose fate now lay in his hands seemed to be the most important person in the world to her. She had said many times that she treated him like a brother. Ha'akon did not believe it. His wounded pride told him that he had a rival in the elf.

'Here we go again.' Ha'sani yawned and stretched. 'Not even halfway through...'

They returned to their places.

The non-human was brought in.

Ha'akon remembered that Temina had called the elf beautiful and noble. The ruler of the Stone Nest didn't consider himself an aesthete like Ha'teng, but he understood why his sister was fascinated by the foreigner. There was something otherworldly about him. He seemed immaculate, despite his condition. A dignity radiated from him. He looked at them with bright blue eyes, without a shadow of fear or humility. His gaze moved slowly from one judge to the next. Finally, it rested on Ha'akon.

The ruler took this as a challenge.

'Elf *Thairác*,' Ha'aki read out. 'Charged with violating the laws of the Ha'ami lands by trespassing without permission.' He lifted his eyes from the parchment. 'Do you plead guilty?'

The prisoner did not speak.

'If I had not heard him speak to *Ta'uma* with my own ears, I would have been convinced he was a mute,' Ha'teng sneered. 'I wouldn't count on him to answer us.'

The elf paid him no attention. He still challenged Ha'akon with his gaze.

'Do you have anything to justify yourself?' Ha'aki repeated.

Silence.

'Good. Noted. The accused pleads not guilty and has presented no extenuating circumstances. Sentence proposed: death by disembowelment. Agreed?'

'Agreed,' Ha'teng replied immediately with a satisfied smile.

'I disagree,' Ha'sani said almost simultaneously. Ha'aki raised his head with a questioning look on his face.

'We know the circumstances of the border crossing from *Ta'uma's* testimony, don't we?' the youngest of the First Brothers explained. 'We know that the elf on trial entered our territory to escort a noble-born woman. We should consider this a mitigating circumstance.'

'*Ta'uma's* nobility has not been officially recognised by the Council, therefore by law,' Ha'aki remarked sourly, but Ha'sani interjected.

'Are you saying that the lack of paper makes Berennike not Berennike?' he replied gruffly.

'Ha'sani is right,' Ha'min interjected. 'We'll approve this at the next council meeting, it's just a formality. The elf acted honourably in escorting the Azzgoth princess, even though he knew he was risking his life. I do not agree with the death penalty,' he finished, looking questioningly at Ha'akon, who was still silent.

The ruler listened to their debate with one ear, wondering which course of action was right. A severe punishment is expected by the entire community, for most Ha'ami have sucked the hatred of elves from their mother's milk. Too light a punishment will cause unnecessary ferment within the ranks... However, Ha'akon gave his word that the prisoner would not be deprived of his life. This agreement between Ha'sani and Eli would be of great benefit to them, but for practical reasons it had to remain a secret for the time being.

And finally... Eli. Berennike.

The way today's matter would be resolved would also affect his future relationship with the girl... if he could have any hope of that.

Who knew, perhaps the non-human standing before him was the main obstacle in his path.

He was torn from his musings by Ha'sani's loud tone.

'The principles of Ha'ami honour demand that this prisoner not suffer death. Therefore, I request that the sentence be commuted to life imprisonment.'

'Do you know how long elves live?' Ha'teng snorted. 'Our great-grandchildren will endure his mangy presence within these walls.'

'Imprisonment is too mild a punishment for a non-human for this offence,' Ha'aki objected in a firm tone. 'Ten years in the dungeon and fifty lashes.'

'You might as well gut him,' Ha'sani grumbled. 'That's what fifty lashes will do to him. All that will be left is to scrape his guts off the platform.'

'That's true,' supported him Ha'min. 'I agree to corporal punishment, but not death.'

'*Koru*, what do you think?' Ha'teng finally decided to speak directly to Ha'akon, interrupting his gaze duel with the elf. The latter kept a stony face the whole time.

The ruler rubbed his brow.

'How many lashes did the girl we tried before get?' he asked, trying to remain indifferent.

'The servant girl who secretly bore a child with Ha'ami?' Ha'aki made sure. 'Twenty.'

'All agree to ten years in the dungeon and twenty lashes?' Ha'sani concluded in a flash.

'Not all,' Ha'aki objected. 'For this offence he should get at least thirty.'

'Are we going to haggle like bargainers in a bazaar?' the youngest of the First Brothers taunted him.

'I am not the one to be guided by the opinion of a woman in this matter,' his opponent sneered in exasperation. He straightened up, his defiant gaze fixed on the Governor.

Ha'akon was not easily provoked.

'Do you have something specific to say?' he asked firmly.

'Non-humans do not deserve our favours. First you had ideas about the dwarves, now we take pity on the elves... this is not how Ha'ami act. Ha'ami show strength,' explained the other.

'Strength and vengeance are two different concepts,' Ha'akon corrected him. 'Honour dictates the consideration of a just judgement.'

'A just judgement?' he hissed. 'Are you really going to pretend that's what you are after?'

'Pull yourself together, man,' Ha'sani sighed. 'It would be better if you ordered a break and went to cool off.'

But no one seemed to pay any attention to his words. The rest of the congregation stiffened in anticipation of developments.

'Talk straight.' The ruler was still in control of himself, but he could sense that Ha'aki was definitely pushing for a confrontation.

'The Azzgoth wench may rule in your breeches, but not in this hall,' the Guardian of Tradition taunted.

Ha'akon rose from his seat.

'Bring the prisoner out,' he ordered the guards dryly. 'All but the First Brothers will leave the courtroom. This debate will continue behind closed doors.'

Simronil greeted Eli with a happy whinny. She fed him, watered him and began to comb his beautiful fur in their regular ritual.

Elf court? he asked her thoughtfully.

Yes, she sighed. *I hope they stick to their agreement...*

Eli... he nudged her with his nose. *Eli brave.*

'I heard you were hanging around.' Ha'perin's round head appeared in the stall door. 'I thought you could use some company today. And I see I was right, you're ready to start talking to yourself,' he added, smiling uncertainly.

'It's a long-lost cause...' she turned in his direction. 'After all, I'm the most engaging company I know.'

A horse's head nudged her side.

'Right after my dearest friend here, of course,' she added.

Ha'perin laughed out loud.

'Sometimes I feel he really understands us.'

'Me too.' She confirmed eagerly.

'Would you like to see the city?' he asked, pointing in the direction of his secret passage. She accepted, and the two of them sneaked down the alley to the roof. They spent the afternoon there, her friend doing his best to distract her from her dark thoughts. Eventually, the sky began to turn grey and they heard the call for evening exercise.

'Come, you'll laugh at me, and then we'll go to the Warrior's Hall together. That's where they announce the... you know... judgments.' He looked at her uncertainly.

'Sure, let's go, she agreed.

Ha'min was not in the square today. The First Brothers were to dine together at Ha'aki's chambers after the Judgement Day. Eli could barely see what was going on around her, her mind was on one thing. Her stomach seemed to be pulled against her spine. She was plagued by an irresistible feeling that things had not gone her way, despite her agreement with Ha'sani.

Whatever happens, you must remain calm, she repeated to herself. *And look for a solution.*

In the Warriors' Hall, Peri tried to force food down her throat, but she refused. The meal dragged on and on. Finally, Ha'aki's adjutant stepped into the middle and began to read out the sentences in a loud voice.

Her heart stopped.

And then she heard it.

Ten years in the dungeon and twenty-five lashes.

He did not receive the death penalty. It seemed that Ha'sani had fulfilled his part of the bargain. But then joyous whistles and applause rang out around them, and Ha'perin's face turned white as parchment.

'I bet five dinars that the elf will fall after fifteen!' one of the *namio* at their table shouted.

'I'll throw in ten dinars!' replied another.

'No way, did you see how Ha'teng managed to wear him down already? Skin and bones alone, even twelve lashes will be too much for him!'

They began to place bets amidst the general merriment.

'Eli...' muttered Ha'perin. 'Let's get out of here.'

'*Fall*? What do they mean, Peri?'

'Flogging is not a light punishment, *neru-to*,' he explained, weighing his words. 'The whip that is used is a real instrument of torture woven from a rope nailed with sharp iron. Besides, the condemned are not bandaged afterwards. If they don't die immediately, they usually bleed to death...'

She felt she couldn't move.

'How many...' she choked out finally. 'How many lashes can one survive?'

He lowered his eyes, did not answer.

She turned to *namio* who was sitting on the other side, and grabbed his arm.

'How many lashes can one survive?!' The young man looked at her with slight consternation.

'The greatest feat I know is twenty-one,' he replied with hesitation.

These words began to bounce around in her head like a rubber ball. Their echo disturbed all other thoughts.

Lina carefully held the mirror to the Eldest Woman's lips. It fogged slightly, evidence of life still smouldering inside her.

'There's not much of it left,' she said softly to Sig, who was sitting by the ancient woman's bedside, her fingers clenched tightly over her withered hand. 'She will be in the Fields of Glory by morning.'

The priestess nodded.

'I want to say goodbye to her,' she whispered. The healer left the chamber.

Sig rose and placed a soft, respectful kiss on the sleeping woman's forehead. She knew that others would see her attachment to the matriarch as an unwise sentiment and a sign of weakness. But she could not accept losing her. It had to happen sooner or later, but she wanted to care for her as long as possible and make sure she died with dignity.

They were not related, but the Eldest Woman meant more to her than anyone else in the world. Sig was the only one who knew her real name. Alikia. She had met her as a little girl, hiding in the temple from her mother's wrath. Her main offence was that she was not a boy, which earned her a frequent beating for some reason. Not quick enough. Not clever enough. Not agile enough... She was simply not enough. But she was no exception. Her mother treated all her daughters the same way. That is, those who managed to survive, for many of them died at birth or were taken into the forest, deemed too weak to become Ha'ami.

Their mother let them all know what a disappointment they were to her. She would whack them with whatever she had at hand when she was at home. Fortunately, she spent most of her time with the warriors, unsuccessfully trying to have the son she wanted. Eventually she gave birth to a boy, but he was stillborn. Devastated by the loss, she died soon after.

Sig's four sisters were given to different households in the City of Sisters. Sig remained in the Temple, which she had long considered her home. Alikia, then High Priestess, introduced her to the secrets of the Ha'ami rituals. She was the noblest woman under the sun, respected by all in the Stone Nest, her wisdom and knowledge seeming infinite. For this reason, she was chosen to hold the position of Eldest Woman. Unfortunately, as she grew older, her mind became weaker and there were rumours that it was time to banish her to the forest.

Sig strongly objected to this. Instead, she took the matriarch into her home, hiding her from the world and surrounding her with loving care. She was determined that Alikia should retain her dignity until the last years of her life.

And she would have succeeded had it not been for the Azzgoth witch who, in the course of a single evening, managed to make Alikia the laughing stock of the entire city, even undermining the sound reasoning of Sig herself, who had previously vouched for the Eldest Woman. After the incident, Alikia was beyond saving. Perin and Akona insisted that it was time. Finally, today, she received the infusion that would end her life.

'Goodbye, Mother,' the priestess whispered tenderly into the dying woman's ear, waiting for her to draw her last breath.

The evening meal was tense; the First Brothers were tired after spending all day in the courtroom and had lost all appetite for socialising, and Ha'akon was still digesting the earlier argument. Never before had anyone challenged his authority so openly.

The solemn silence was broken by a guard. He whispered something to Ha'aki, who merely waved his hand.

'Send her to all the demons!' he added impatiently.

'Is it nice to treat your own mother in such a way?' joked Ha'teng, who had been in a bad mood all day.

No one laughed. The host just gave him an angry look. The guard left and the same silence returned. The servants distributed the dishes, but none of the guests were tempted to start a conversation. Ha'akon preferred it that way.

Unexpectedly, the guard returned. Ha'aki stopped him with his eyes in the doorway. He rose from his seat.

'I'll take care of her myself, if you are such yellow-bellies,' he snarled at his subordinate.

'What is it?' the lord of the castle asked. The last thing they needed today was a scandal at the end of a long day.

'Ta'uma...' the guardsman began, but the host cut him off.

'I said I would deal with it myself,' he said and took a quick step towards the door.

'Just a moment.' Ha'akon stopped him and stood up. 'What about her?'

The guard looked uncertainly at his commander. The latter gave a brief nod.

'She is here. She wants to see you,' he explained to the lord of the castle. 'It is urgent,' he added.

Ha'akon had expected this confrontation, but had hoped it would happen tomorrow.

'I was on my way anyway', he announced.

'Me too.' Ha'teng rose in his wake.

'And me.' Ha'min followed.

'Give me a moment, this won't take long,' Ha'akon stopped them as he headed for the corridor.

'I told you, it's no use, they won't let you in.' Ha'perin tried again to persuade her to leave.

'Listen to the clever *namio*, princess. Get out of here before the commander loses patience with you,' a guard standing outside the entrance warned her dryly. 'Believe me, you don't want Ha'aki to come here to explain why you won't come in.'

'If you won't let me in, I'll wait here until they're finished. Either way, I'll see Ha'akon!' she replied firmly.

'I am here.' They heard the voice of the Governor appearing in the corridor. As at the previous First Brothers dinner, he was dressed in black trousers and a cobalt sleeveless robe. He did not appear to be carrying any weapons.

'What do you want to talk about so urgently?' he asked dryly.

The sentry retreated inside, but left the door open.

Ha'perin discreetly took a few steps back.

Eli looked into Ha'akon's face, which at the moment resembled a harsh mask. She had not expected kindness. But she hoped it would at least inspire compassion in him. After all, she knew that somewhere, deep down, the lord of the castle considered himself a just man.

'Ha'akon,' she began, trying with all her might to hold back her emotions. 'I have heard of the punishment you have decided for the elf... for my friend. It is... a very severe punishment. I... do not understand...'

'The punishment is in accordance with Ha'ami law,' he answered in an official tone.

'But... he will die!' The words sucked the air out of her lungs.

'Perhaps,' he confirmed.

'You mustn't let that happen!' she heard herself say.

'I mustn't?' he repeated with emphasis, his voice sounding frigid.

Desperate, she stepped closer and took his hand in hers.

'I beg you.' She felt she had no choice. 'Save him. You can still pardon him... I have read your laws, I know it is possible if you convince the Council. They will listen to you.'

He did not answer.

'I'll do anything you want, but please don't let him die!'

His features hardened even more.

'Anything I want?' he repeated in a strange metallic voice. He looked as if she had insulted him.

She fixed him with a tense stare and merely nodded in reply.

He tore his eyes away from her. He looked down the corridor where the other First Brothers had emerged, and they both began to walk towards the men.

'Ha'akon!' she repeated insistently.

He let go of her hand and took a step back.

'The elf has been sentenced according to Ha'ami law, unanimously by the court of the First Brothers,' he said icily. 'If I had disagreed with the verdict, I would have expressed it on the spot.'

She felt the ground slip from beneath her feet. She wobbled slightly.

'Ha'perin,' the ruler spoke louder, nodding to the *namio*. 'Take *Ta'uma* back to her chamber.'

Eli couldn't believe what she heard. She had been wrong. Tallen had been right. She had been so naive...

'Layla...' she whispered so that only Ha'akon could hear her. She stared into the floor, trying with all her might to hold back her tears.

It was as if he woke up at the sound of that name.

'Layla was right not to go back with you... you would never protect her. All you care about is appearances,' she finished quietly. 'You are unworthy of any affection.'

His mask had fallen. He looked as if she had plunged a dagger into his guts.

'Greetings, Berennike,' Ha'teng's insolent voice rang out. She looked at him angrily. 'Have you come for a guest performance? I am afraid we are not in the mood for your singing.'

'Let's go, *neru-to*.' She felt Ha'perin's hand on her shoulder.

She gathered herself, straightened her back and raised her head proudly.

'I have come to tell you that you are liars,' she declared forcefully, looking at them in defiance. 'Murderers. Cruel men. Real non-humans. That is what the Ha'ami are. There is no honour in you.'

She felt a powerful blow to her jaw, staggered backwards and fell into Ha'perin. Her ears rang, and only after a moment did she realise that it was Ha'aki who had struck her.

'We have put up with your impertinence long enough,' he hissed angrily.

At the same moment, Ha'akon delivered a powerful fist to his solar plexus, knocking the commander back against the corridor wall.

'Enough of this!' he shouted, sweeping in for another blow.

'*Namio*, out!' Ha'min shoved Ha'perin and she felt her friend pull her as far away as possible from the angry warriors the others were now trying to separate.

As they emerged into the courtyard, she finally let out a single, muffled sob.

'*Neru-to...*' Peri whispered.

'Let me go,' Eli croaked. He loosened his grip and she broke free, almost falling to the ground. He reached out to catch her but she pushed him away. 'Leave me alone,' she said and ran off into the night, not wanting to say anything to him in anger that she might regret later.

She stormed into her chamber, slammed the door and sat on the floor by the fireplace, trying to calm herself. She breathed heavily and slowly, understanding almost nothing of what had just happened.

After dinner with the First Brothers, he was content to sit by the fire with a cup of wine. At last, fate had smiled upon him. The elf had been sentenced to a punishment that would surely slaughter him. It will all happen independently of him, in the full light of Ha'ami law. He will not have to get his hands dirty.

As for Berennike... until now he could count on the protection of the Ha'akon, but today the ruler himself has painted himself into a corner. There is no place among the Ha'ami to display weakness. If you show it, you can be sure that others will take advantage of it. This is what happened...

The execution of the elf should be a turning point.

The king will be satisfied with the completion of the first part of the task. The despair-stricken Berennike will certainly be an easier target... they will wait a few days to lull the girl's vigilance, and then strike again. Admittedly, he hasn't come up with a plan yet, he'll probably have to figure it out himself, as so far his subordinate has only brought him disappointment.

Besides, the princess might still do something stupid. With her behaviour so far, she has proven herself to be unpredictable, but she also fails to see the wider consequences of her actions, as she understands little of the reality around her.

Knowledge is the most powerful weapon, after all.

He smiled with satisfaction, pleased that he would soon be able to fulfil the task entrusted to him and gain further favours from the king.

As if through a heavy curtain, Eli heard banging on the door. She wasn't sure where she was. She opened her eyes to find herself lying on the floor by the fireplace. She couldn't quite feel her body as she slowly pulled herself up on her arms. The thumping increased.

'What's going on in there?' She heard a voice from outside.

With difficulty she crawled in that direction, pushing back the chair that was blocking the door handle. A sentry stood in the corridor with a drawn sword in one hand and a torch in the other.

'What is it?' Eli asked in an unconscious voice.

'You were screaming,' he explained.

'No, I was not.' She tried to remember what had happened.

'You were calling for help.' He was relentless, trying to get past her and into the chamber.

'I must have been dreaming,' she mumbled embarrassed.

The man looked at her impassively.

'It is my duty to check the room', he announced dryly.

Eli stepped back. He hurried inside and made his rounds while she walked over to the table and poured herself some water.

'Why did you block the door?' he pointed to a chair.

'I don't like draughts,' she replied, swallowing the cool liquid. Her senses began to return. The guard eyed her with suspicion.

'Is there something wrong with you? Shall I send for a healer?'

'There's no need.' She shook her head. 'I'm sorry for the inconvenience. You don't need to notify anyone... It was just a nightmare.'

'I have a duty to report it to the commander.' He straightened his shoulders.

'As you wish.' She walked over to the fireplace and threw in the wood. 'Good night,' she sent him away curtly.

The sentry stood there for a moment, measuring her with his eyes, but finally, as Eli sat down heavily in her chair, he turned on his heel and left. She waited a moment for his footsteps to die down in the corridor, then got up and blocked the entrance with the same chair.

She sat down and tried to comprehend what had happened.

She was Seeing again.

A place full of screaming people.

Tallen in chains.

The whipping.

The death.

Was this the future?

Jor hid in the shadows as usual. He was getting better at it, especially since the night he had been whipped. He doubled his vigilance. He tried his best to silence the footsteps of his bare feet, the breathing of his frail chest. He devoted every spare moment to the same activity. He just had to know where she was, what she was up to.

Berennike. His beloved Princess Berennike. Brave. Invincible. He had been the first to recognise her, and his tribesmen had laughed at him when he had mentioned the name. Now their giggles had died away, replaced by excited whispers. The Azzgoths in the keep watched her movements, waiting for a signal. They discussed what her plan might be... slowly they all rallied around the Princess. For the first time in a long while, they had *hope*.

A trusted stable boy woke him in the middle of the night to tell him that she had arrived unexpectedly. Now, together, they watched from afar as she strode across the square with her magnificent mount. She was sad. Jor was not surprised. He'd heard that her companion had been sentenced to harsh torture.

Jor knew little of elves and was rather indifferent towards them, but the very fact that a non-human had accompanied his beloved Berennike to the lands of Ha'ami, risking his life for her, commanded his respect. It was whispered that it was the elves who had sheltered her for all those years. Who knows, she may even have formed a strategic alliance with them.

When he offered her his services, he meant it, but in reality, he had no idea what he could do to help her. He thought that perhaps at least a conversation in his mother tongue would be some comfort that night. Finally, he plucked up the courage to walk across the square to her.

She smiled melancholically at the sight of him.

'It's good to see you when you're not sneaking around, Jor,' she greeted him in Azzgoth. 'What are you doing here at this late hour?'

He came as close as he thought appropriate, not wanting to offend her.

'My lady...' he bowed low. 'It's hard to sleep on Judgment Day... it's usually full of bad news.'

'For you too?' She stroked her steed thoughtfully.

'Many of us will be severely punished for minor transgressions,' He explained. 'One Azzgoth girl as gravely as your friend.' He lowered his head to pay his respects to the elf.

'Yes? Who is she? What has she done?' Her green eyes had a somewhat distant expression.

'Hilde... a servant who bore a Ha'ami child,' he replied.

'Purity of blood,' she guessed.

'Yes,' he confirmed. 'She is to receive twenty lashes. She will probably pass away after ten as she is a girl of small stature...'

'It's interesting how everyone in this place can count their lives in lashes,' she remarked sadly.

Jor didn't quite know what she meant. He didn't care about the fate of any Azzgoth who fraternised with the enemy, but he was appalled that any of his tribesmen could be subjected to such torture by Ha'ami.

'What about the baby?' She became interested. The question puzzled him. No one else cared about it.

'The baby? They took it into the forest after it was born.'

That was how all infants unworthy of becoming full-fledged Ha'ami were treated. Berennike did not seem surprised. She lowered her eyes and returned to stroking the horse's neck.

'So then, the day after tomorrow this girl and my friend will appear for torture as accidental companions in misery,' she said thoughtfully. 'Fate can be cruel... and unpredictable.'

'My Lady...' He took a step forward, but her mount shook its head in displeasure. He hesitated. The princess whispered a few words of reassurance in a foreign tongue. Jor took courage. 'Even if your companion dies, know that you are not alone here. We... we are with you.'

'We?' His words seemed to puzzle her.

'All the Azzgoths in the fortress,' he declared exultantly. 'We are only waiting for your sign. We know that you are here to lead us to liberation. Together we will return to our homeland!'

She raised her beautiful, almond-shaped green eyes to him. They radiated sincerity and gentleness. They seemed to penetrate his soul.

'I have not come to free you, Jor,' she replied calmly, and he shuddered at the words. 'Each of us holds his freedom in his own hands. Believe me, the best leader is of no use if his people are enslaved themselves. Just like Ha'ami...'

He did not understand what she meant.

'Ha'ami are enslaved?' he repeated dully.

'Their bonds are less apparent than yours, yet they exist... in the end, each of us has two choices. To accept what binds us or to rise up,' she explained.

'Throw off the yoke,' he nodded.

'It's not that easy.' The shadow of a sad smile appeared on her face. 'Disobedience to oppression can have all sorts of consequences, it doesn't always have a happy ending. Yet it doesn't change the fact that you have to take care of your own freedom, Jor. All of us have to. I cannot give it to you. Each of us must take it with our own hands,' she finished.

He nodded, already understanding what she was urging him to do.

'Yes, my lady. I will pass on your words to our tribesmen.' he confirmed.

'If you think it will help them...' Her gaze drifted off again, somewhere far away. 'Now, if you'll excuse me, I'd like to be left alone.'

'As you wish, my lady. But if you need anything–' he offered again.

'Yes, I know, you and your companion will be there in the shadows,' she said quietly. 'It will be warmer for you in the stable.'

He bowed again and walked towards the buildings. He couldn't wait to bring the news to his brothers.

Ha'akon was furious with himself. If he could go back in time... everything he had done today had shattered his fragile hopes.

She hated him. Not only that. She called him dishonourable. Unworthy.

Was she right?

Once again, he was caught in the maze of duty, law and feelings... both noble and very basic.... He could tell himself as much as his heart desired that he had acted in accordance with Ha'ami law, and that the elf had a chance of surviving this flogging.

He presented himself to Eli as a righteous and honourable ruler who would root out injustice among his fellow tribesmen. But today, the difference between who he pretended to be and who he really was, was revealed once again. No, he was not worthy of her affections.

On his evening rounds, he happened to meet a guard who told him that the girl had woken up screaming during the night and that he had been unable to enter her chamber because the door was blocked from the inside.

Had she barricaded herself in because of him? Was she afraid that he would come in the night to force her into submission? Had he lost her respect to that extent?

He was ashamed.

He now stood like a fool on the walls, watching her from a distance as she walked with her mount and then had a brief conversation with a servant. A slave could count on a better word from her than the lord of the castle.

He clenched his fists against the cold stone in helpless rage.

The first person he had cared for in years feared him, hated him, had nightmares because of him....

It would be better if he started to stay away from her... his concern for her had become too obvious and made them both easy targets.

These are the rules of Ha'ami. Don't show your feelings. Duty is all that matters.

Chapter XV
The torture of waiting for the torture

THE BEEKEPER'S SETTLEMENT, DEEP IN the forest, was enveloped in fog. Even the murmur of the nearby river was silenced by the milky blanket that covered the surroundings. A bony man sat alone in front of his hut, sipping chai: hot herbs flavoured with milk and butter. The brew was meant to give him strength for the day ahead. Suddenly, like a stray soul, a rider on a black horse emerged from the damp clouds. As he approached the buildings, he spotted the only villager who was already awake.

'Ishan?' he asked in a harsh accent.

A Ha'ami. This was indeed unprecedented. Warriors had never ventured this far. Though the village supplied the fortress with honey, servants were always sent here.

The villager shook his head.

'Na'avi.' He answered briefly and gave his name. 'Ishan there.'

He pointed to a hut in the depths, occupied by a couple of newcomers from the north, along with a dozen other people.

Everyone here had come from somewhere. Not young or strong enough for the Ha'ami to take them in, they found refuge in the thin, mountain forest. They lived mainly off the gifts of nature. What they had in excess, they traded. Especially honey, which was hard to come by but in high demand.

Na'avi was young, though a hard life had aged him prematurely. He was born here, in this wilderness, and he would probably die here.

A warrior wearing a helmet that hid his face pulled a coin from under his cloak and threw it in his direction.

'Call him,' he ordered. It was clear that he was used to being served.

The local grasped the piece of metal greedily. He didn't know what he could do with it here, but it was rumoured to be valuable. Usually, their trade was to barter for what they lacked. Coins were said to be worth much more. Now he had the chance to find out.

He finished his chai, stretched his skinny legs and crawled awkwardly towards the hut built on stilts. The people here had no tools for building sturdy structures. They hastily assembled them from whatever they could find in the forest. There were usually no windows, just a single hole in the roof for the smoke to escape. They cooked on a hearth in the middle of the house. The heat came from the crowded human mass.

Na'avi pushed aside a sheet hanging in the doorway and wandered among the sleeping bodies. When he found the man, he kicked him without mercy.

'Ishan!' He grunted in a low voice in the common language, spiced with the dialect of the Forest People. 'A Ha'ami is asking for you.'

'What?' the old man mumbled in surprise, not quite awake yet.

'I don't know, go and see.'

The man rubbed his eyes and slipped out of his wife's embrace. She squeezed his shoulder in her sleep.

'Ishan,' she mumbled. 'It's not time yet.'

'Apparently there's some Ha'ami,' he answered.

She sat up abruptly as if someone had poured a bucket of cold water over her.

'Ha'ami? Where?'

'Outside. He's asking for you,' Na'avi repeated irritably.

The two old people looked at each other with obvious concern, then got to their feet and followed him outside. Their places on the floor were immediately claimed by the sleeping bodies next to them. Every bit of empty ground was priceless.

The rider was still waiting outside the hut. He did not bother to dismount.

'Ishan?' he asked again when he saw him.

'Yes,' replied the old man. 'And this is my wife, Aya.'

The masked warrior did not answer. He picked up a pouch attached to his saddle and threw it at their feet.

'What's this?' the beekeeper wondered.

'Your daughter is dead. I know she shared what she could with you. She was my servant. This is the reward for her loyalty.'

Na'avi knew that all the children of the old people found work in the fortress, but only one cared for them. She often sent them various goods... especially meat, which the whole village enjoyed.

'Anni!' cried the old woman, hiding her face in the dirty apron she always wore.

The old man was more awake and fell to his knees.

'Thank you, lord, for the news and the consolation in our grief. It is a terrible loss. How... how did our girl die?'

The warrior only measured them with a contemptuous glance of icy blue eyes, turned his horse around and rode away, and the echoing sound of hooves plunging down the muddy path soon drowned in the fog.

Eli spent a sleepless night in the stables. She lay staring blankly at the ceiling, but her mind refused to rest. She heard footsteps in the corridor and looked indifferently towards the stall entrance.

'I have heard the news.' Temina looked at her sympathetically and cautiously opened the door. She sat down beside her on the hay and held her hands in a caring gesture.

'I'm sorry... although I did tell you that we have strict laws. Therefore, this punishment does not surprise me. I know you don't want to hear it, but many Ha'ami were pleased when the sentence was announced. You know how much they hate elves.'

'Quite pointlessly!' exploded Eli. 'You know very well that this battle is a big lie!'

Temina moved away at this outburst.

'I'm sorry...' Eli stammered. She regretted the impulse.

The vision of last night was still clearly in her mind.

The herbalist gave her a moment to calm down.

'The only thing we can hope for now is that your friend will have enough strength to survive the flogging,' she said, meeting her gaze.

'Even if he survives, his wounds must not be bandaged. He will bleed to death,' she replied, her eyes fixed on the floor.

'I'm sure we can convince Ha'akon to let me take care of him,' Temina said softly.

'Ha'akon could have pardoned him,' Eli snapped, suppressing another burst of anger. 'He did nothing to help him. Your brother is...' She bit her tongue. 'Really, you don't want to know what I think of him right now.'

A long silence fell between them. It was broken again by the herbalist.

'I know you feel disappointed and offended by what has happened.' She spoke slowly and with concern. 'You are entitled to that, as I understand it, Ha'sani made you a promise, guaranteed by Ha'akon. And while they have kept it, for the elf has not been sentenced to death, the sentence that has been passed carries such a risk.'

She squeezed Eli's hand harder. 'I am sorry for your friend, I have seen how... how attached you are to him. But I want you to know that if it was you, my brother would have done anything to prevent it... That is why he worked so hard to recognise your nobility.'

Eli was too tired to listen to the praise of Ha'akon's generous character.

'Ha'akon would never let anything happen to you,' her friend repeated emphatically. 'You can be absolutely sure of that.'

Unexpectedly, a new thought appeared in Eli's mind. She tried desperately to grasp it. Temina seemed to study her face intently.

'Will you accept an invitation to dinner at my house? You shouldn't be alone.'

'Yes... I would like to... I would like to go to the City of Sisters right now. To see the site of tomorrow's execution.'

'Yes, of course. I can take you there in my sedan.'

'Let's go.' Eli grabbed her arm with her trembling hands. 'But on foot. A walk... I need a walk.'

'Fine,' her friend agreed with a strange look on her face. 'If that's what you want. The roads are full of mud today. It won't be the nicest walk.'

'That's okay,' Eli laughed, not knowing why. 'I didn't have a bath anyway.'

'Let's be on our way then, you slob.' Temina tried to maintain a playful tone, though her gaze expressed concern.

Eli got to her feet and went to the door resolutely, trying to keep brave. She knew the execution would take place in the square in front of the Temple. The important thing now was to get inside that building. The conversation with the herbalist had inspired her with a plan to save Tallen.

The priestess had just finished smudging herself with the soothing herbal smoke that always brought her comfort when she was told that *Ta'uma* wanted to see her.

This was the last person she wanted to see, but she remembered the mission her brother had given her. She decided to be strong.

For Alikia.

She made her way to the main aisle of the temple, where Berennike was waiting for her, clearly upset. Her clothes were crumpled and dirty, she looked pale, her hair dishevelled, as if she hadn't washed for days. Sig rejoiced in her misery, but had to hide it.

She greeted *Ta'uma* as politely as she could.

'I'm sorry to bother you so unexpectedly,' stammered the girl. 'I wanted to talk to you about tomorrow's execution... as far as I know, you're in charge of it.'

The priestess nodded.

'We are just beginning the preparations. It's going to be a very exciting day!' she burst out excitedly. Sig loved every official event that made the Temple the centre of attention in the Stone Nest.

The girl seemed put off by her enthusiasm.

She fell silent for a moment, as if considering something. The priestess stood somewhat helplessly, waiting for further developments. Finally, Berennike seemed to make a decision.

'I have come with an official request,' she declared firmly. 'Before you answer whether you agree, I would like you to hear me out.'

Surprised, Sig focused all her attention on *Ta'uma*. The longer the girl explained her plan, the more the First Sister could not believe her luck. Her Brother had been trying for days to find a discreet way to exterminate Berennike. And now she herself was coming to the Sig with an idea that, if completed properly, would lead to just that.

Thank you for your support, Ancestors! the priestess thought. *Alikia will be avenged!*

'Do you agree to my proposal?' *Ta'uma* raised her blackened eyes.

Sig did not answer right away. She didn't want to look too happy.

'Why... why do you want to do this?' she stammered.

'It's my duty. It's how I feel,' the girl replied.

'I understand.' The Guardian of the Temple nodded. 'But few will. It's better if we don't tell anyone about this.'

'That's what I was hoping for.' Berennike squeezed Sig's hands in gratitude.

'I will help you,' the priestess promised, suppressing her excitement

The First Brothers and Sisters gathered in the main square to discuss the execution plan. Sig, who was in charge of the ritual, and Ha'teng, who was responsible for security, showed them the details of how the platform and audience would be set up, while the workmen erected the makeshift wooden stage on which the condemned would suffer their punishment.

'The Council will sit here, on ceremonial chairs, at the top of the stairs' the priestess pointed.

'You can take these three,' Ha'sani remarked. 'Keera and Ha'akon and I have something else to do.

'You're not coming?' Akona looked at her son in confusion.

'We have a serious problem with the water supply in the Upper Castle,' he replied sourly. 'We've been trying to fix it since yesterday, we need to give it our full attention or we risk flooding the city.'

'And all three of you are indispensable there?' Ha'teng asked in an equally sour tone.

'I was the one who asked them both to be here,' the First Sister hastened to explain. 'We'll be there all day as well. The situation is really chaotic, decisions have to be made on the spot, I can't count on sending messengers back and forth.' She clasped her hands in a firm gesture, ready to pick a fight with anyone who doubted her suggestion.

But no one did. Akona considered for a moment whether she should at least press for Ha'akon's presence in the square tomorrow, but seeing the expression on her son's face, she gave up.

She had heard of the events of the past few days. The whole city had been buzzing with rumours of the trouble *Ta'uma* had caused. Perhaps when it was all over, the lonely girl would be easier to handle than she was now, so focused on her single purpose. If not, there was always the option of sending her to the king to gain his favour and smooth relations between the capital and the Stone's Nest.

Either way, tomorrow will change everything, whether Ha'akon is here or not. Perhaps distancing himself from the problems surrounding Berennike will do him some good.

'I have made you some herbs, they will help you calm down,' Temina said, handing her a mug of hot liquid. Eli sat at the window and stared dully into the falling dusk. She had arrived at the herbalist's house immediately after her conversation with Sig. Everything was set. Her final plan to save Tallen. It must work.

'Thank you.' She accepted the cup from her friend's hands.

'Are you sure you don't want anything to help you sleep? You look really ghastly, despite the bath.'

'No, I mustn't sleep, I can't stop thinking about tomorrow.'

Temina said nothing, sat down next to her and put her arm around her.

'So many people doomed to suffer,' continued Eli, resting his head against her shoulder. 'This girl... Hilde, I think that's her name.'

'What girl?' The herbalist was puzzled.

'The one who is also to be given twenty lashes,' Eli explained with sadness in her voice. 'Nine months she had carried her life inside her... only to have it forcibly torn from her, and then thrown out into the cold, to die. But it wasn't enough. Not enough, no... it is still necessary to subject her to unbearable pain and public humiliation... and finally to death. And for what? Because she fancied a wrong man. Is this really an adequate punishment?'

She thought of an infant wailing in the cold, frozen or devoured. A single tear rolled down her cheek.

'It's our law, Eli... It's our world.' Temina whispered to her friend.

'Yes, it's your world...' she replied and turned to the window again, sipping from her mug. 'Temina?'

'Yes?'

'It's a sleeping potion, isn't it?'

'Forgive me,' replied the herbalist. 'You need your rest.'

'I must be there by dawn.'

'You will be. I will wake you. Now lie down, please.'

He couldn't believe his ears when he heard Sig's news, and then Ha'akon himself decided not to come to the execution. Everything went unexpectedly well....

It's called slaughtering two deer with one arrow, he thought. Literally!

He couldn't wait until tomorrow.

Chapter XVI

Execution

WITA DESPERATELY CLUTCHED IN HIS hands a piece of cloth handed to him by the good woman. He did not know why, but he clung to it like a talisman. He was not used to such gestures. From time immemorial, his stature had commanded respect, but when people realised what a gentle nature he had, how incapable of aggression he was, they always did the same thing. Mocking and bullying. And all he wanted was to go through life in peace, earning his bread and a roof over his head through honest work. He stopped dreaming of friends and family, because his own people despised him anyway. He did whatever was asked of him, he endured hardship patiently.

He did not know why the gods had decided to end his life in such a cruel way.

He cried desperately all night, until he heard the iron lock on the door.

He was afraid of pain, afraid of death.

The guard jerked the chain hard.

Wita rose to his feet and trudged resignedly towards his fate.

Temina kept her promise and woke her before dawn. Eli hastily washed her face, put on the warm, dark Ha'ami clothes her friend had prepared and wrapped herself in her elf cloak, ready to leave. She refused breakfast. A large, thorny lump was in her throat; even water was hard to swallow.

In the darkness, they walked together to the square in front of the Temple of the Ancestors, where the execution would take place. The platform where the punishments were administered rose grimly. Workers were hovering there, busy arranging the tools the executioners would use that day. Sig was directing them.

Temina waved to her. The priestess approached hastily.

'Glory to this day!' Her expression was surprisingly sober. 'What are you doing here so early?'

Eli noticed that the Temple Guardian was looking at her nervously, as if she expected her to change her mind and cancel the plan, they had made the day before.

'We came to get good seats,' the herbalist explained.

'Ah yes, I see.' Sig resumed her slightly distracted tone. 'We're getting ready to put on a great show. There is a section reserved for the Ha'ami.' She waved her hand. 'The closest to the dais!'

'Thank you.' Temina replied hastily and turned in the direction indicated. She noticed the look of disgust on Eli's face.

'Apologies,' The priestess huffed. 'But I can't talk to you here any longer, although I'd love to tell you about today's programme. It's our first public punishment this winter, but those cursed workers, nothing's ready!'

She turned on her heel and walked towards the platform.

'A *show*? A *programme*?' Eli spat angrily.

'Yes, I know... Those are not very apt terms for the situation,' confirmed her friend. 'She lives in her own world, my dear. You won't change her.'

They took their places on the benches at the front. Behind the platform were the stairs to the Temple and ten chairs. For the Council of First Sisters and Brothers, Eli guessed. Just before dawn, the guardsmen led by Ha'teng marched into the square. His men lined up around the dais and also along the passage left for the convicts.

As the gloomy day dawned and the sky brightened, the area filled with onlookers. The atmosphere was festive, the crowd excited, as if they had come to see a juggler's show. Young children impatiently asked their mothers when the spectacle would begin... As she watched the instruments of torture, Eli was glad she had not had breakfast today. It was beyond her comprehension that people could invent so many ways to inflict pain and treat it as entertainment.

She heard a group of people sitting behind them excitedly discussing Tallen: Is the elf's blood red too? After how many lashes will he lose consciousness? Will he beg for mercy? Will he scream? If so, in what language?

Anger gripped her, and she was about to turn and scold them when she felt a hand on her shoulder.

'I have found you at last!' a familiar voice sounded. Ha'perin squeezed onto the bench next to her, much to the displeasure of her neighbours.

'I brought wine!' He pulled a bottle from behind his chest. 'In case you need to warm up.'

'It's morning.' She said with a wince.

'It's cold!' he replied. 'And gloomy, and wine cures both these ills.'

Eli was not convinced. She fidgeted impatiently, staring at Sig... who finally gave her the agreed sign.

'Temina, I feel sick, I need to get away,' she said to her friend.

'I'll come with you,' the herbalist declared.

'No... please, that's not necessary. Keep an eye on my place. I'll be right back,' She requested. Her friend stayed where she was and did not seem to be pleased.

The herald announced the beginning of the execution and the arrival of the Council of First Sisters and Brothers. As the crowd erupted in cheers and applause, Eli shuffled between the cheering onlookers and approached the priestess, who grabbed her hand and pulled her under the dais. No one seemed to notice as they slipped between the guards in the general commotion.

'Sit here until I call you!' Sig instructed her, then returned to the square.

The girl huddled on the ground and wrapped herself in her elven cloak, glad she would not have to watch the executions. As the Temple Guardian had told her, they began with minor offences. Cutting off hands for stealing, pulling out tongues for cheating, burning marks for disobeying masters... She covered her ears so as not to hear the cries of the prisoners.

It went on for an eternity, until finally the flogging was announced. Her heart beat faster. This was the moment. They led Tallen in.

The guards pushed them through the exuberant crowd. It was winter, so the onlookers lacked the usual rotten fruit and vegetables to throw at the convicts. The bloodthirsty mob had to resort to spitting and throwing slush, a much more boring pastime.

Tallen cared little for what was going on around him. He didn't look at the angry, animal-like faces. He paid no attention to the blows of the guards or the shouts of the crowd. The only time he had to slow down was for the girl walking in front of him. Short, petite, tawny like Eli, in tattered robes, her head shaved, almost naked, she kept stumbling and sobbing loudly about her child. She kept falling on the cobbles, so that at one point the guards began to drag her along, her shackles clanking on the stones. Finally, they reached the platform and climbed the stairs. Standing there was the same dimwit who had interrogated him earlier, with a silly grin on his face as usual. He must have felt particularly important that day.

The herald read the sentence. Tallen did not listen. He concentrated on withdrawing into himself, cutting himself off from the coming pain. When he saw the whips being prepared, he had no doubt that he would not survive. But he intended to die without giving them any satisfaction. They led him to a large stake and chained him with shackles, his arms stretched out. Someone tore his shirt from his back. They dragged the girl to the second stake.

Elves never practised public executions. The custom itself was the height of barbarism. Tallen now stood with his back to the chattering crowd and his face to this Council of theirs. Some members were missing. A proud elite of Ha'ami, upholding traditions not practised by the wildest of beasts. Tallen felt boundless contempt for them. The girl next to him sobbed in disbelief as they read her sentence. He could smell urine. She must have wet herself with fear at the sight of powerful, masked, black-clad torturers with whips.

Suddenly he heard some kind of scream, then everything around him went quiet. It lasted for a moment, time seemed to stand still. He turned his head, as far as he could, and saw the mad priestess who had ordered the execution, standing and jubilantly explaining something to the man with the tiger tattoo. The commander, with an indifferent face, nodded to his guards. Two of them moved to where she was pointing, and one hurried off in another direction. Meanwhile, the two slowly climbed the stairs to the Council of Sisters and Brothers. When they arrived, the priestess was explaining something to the others. They were clearly beginning to argue. The tall, short-haired woman could not hide her agitation, while the oldest man with grey hair was furious. He gesticulated vigorously to protest something. To no avail. Finally, it seemed, he had to give up and slumped back in his chair in frustration, covering his face with his hands. However, he picked himself up and rushed downstairs. He passed the elf, and shot him an incomprehensible glance. Tallen could hear his raised voice from behind, but the words were muffled by the howling of the crowd, which was clearly growing in discontent. After a while, the old warrior returned to the door of the temple, resigned.

The priestess and the executioner returned to the platform. The loud voice of the herald, speaking in the common language, rang out. This time Tallen listened.

'We are witnessing a unique event. This woman has stepped forward to enforce the ancient law of the Brotherhood of the Blood and has offered to take the place of the convicted servant, Hilde, by virtue of tribal kinship, and she shall take over her fate!'

The crowd made an indefinable noise. Of surprise. Of disbelief. Of shock.

Probably the mother, Tallen thought, *or the sister...*

'Hilde,' Guardian of the Temple turned to the sobbing girl. 'Do you accept the sacrifice? If so, you may go free and your blood sister will take your place. If not, you will stay here and suffer the punishment.'

The girl did not seem to understand what was going on, only blinking her eyes and gasping for air in silence. When Sig repeated the question, she only managed a single word.

'Yes!'

The servant girl was unshackled from the stake and dragged away by the guards, still sobbing and stammering something unintelligible in her language. After a while, the guards led the new person in. Tallen turned his head to look at her.

'You thought I was going to let you have all the fun to yourself?' she said to him in elven dialect.

'Eli...' He looked at her in disbelief.

The guard closed the shackles on her wrists and, with a quick flick of his dagger, tore open the blouse on her back.

Ha'min was unable to see what was happening. From a distance, he only noticed Sig stop the execution and lead a hooded figure, who had appeared from nowhere, to the platform. She debated with Ha'teng for a moment, then they walked together towards the other council members. Ha'min could tell from the way they moved that this was not going to be good news. He shifted uneasily in his chair.

Sig's eyes lit up with excitement.

'Something special has happened,' she explained. 'This is the first time in my time that someone has invoked the *Koroi Karn* and agreed to take the place of a convict.'

Ha'min felt a growing uneasiness in his stomach. From the expression on Ha'teng's face, he knew who this volunteer was.

'It is *Ta'uma*,' the commander of the security squads confirmed in a solemn tone.

Akona was the quickest to respond.

'I thought only family or tribe members could request *Koroi Karn*. She is not related to an elf. Besides, he would have to agree to it.'

'It's not about the elf,' Ha'teng explained reluctantly. 'She wants to trade places with this servant girl. She claims that since they are both Azzgoths, she has the right to do so.'

'We must send for Ha'akon,' the ruler's mother said matter-of-factly.

'I have already done so,' the Guardian of Defence replied.

Perin was outraged. 'Berennike cannot take the punishment of the commoners. She is of noble blood.'

'We have not yet acknowledged her nobility...' Ha'aki interjected.

'There you go again,' growled Ha'min.

'Again, because nothing has changed,' Ha'aki replied. 'There is no decree. She should be punished, like a servant, if she wants to take the punishment upon herself.'

The older warrior lost his patience and grabbed Sig's shoulders.

'Why is she doing this?' he asked, shaking the priestess. 'She must have given a reason!'

The priestess harrumphed, not knowing what to say.

Ha'teng pulled him back.

'Calm down, old man,' he said in a cold voice. 'This misguided adventuress is asking for a pardon for herself and the elf. If we don't agree, she's willing to take the punishment.' In a hushed tone, so that only Ha'min could hear him, he added, 'I have tried to reason with her. She doesn't listen.'

'The decision to pardon her must be made unanimously by the Council,' Ha'aki went on in his firm tone, undaunted by the anger of the Guardian of the Youth. Not everyone is here, and besides, I know for a fact that I will not vote to pardon a non-human.'

Ha'min looked around at the faces of the First Sisters and Brothers. If only Ha'akon were here... but there's no way he'll make it before she's killed.

He slumped back helplessly in his chair.

'Can't we wait until the other members of the council arrive?' asked the ruler's mother, her face pale.

'Do you have an artistic programme in store?' Ha'teng asked ironically. Akona glared at him. He realised he had gone too far and straightened up. 'Their arrival won't change anything. As far as I can see, we will not get the unanimity we need to pardon them both. And *Ta'uma* is determined.'

'I will speak to her,' the older warrior sprang from his seat and ran down the path. He couldn't leave things like this.

Eli waited calmly for the situation to develop. She did not expect Ha'akon to be absent from the execution. Her plan was to finally awaken the ruler's conscience and obtain a pardon for Tallen. She did not tell Sig this. She only told her that she wanted to summon *Koroi Karn* for the sake of her countryman. Only in Ha'teng's presence did she make her request. She knew from reading their laws that in the worst case, if they did not agree, as a noble she would not face the same punishment as the servants and they would have to commute her sentence to a lesser one.

This was her convoluted plan. Yesterday, for some reason, it had seemed very clever. Now that she was surrounded by grim guards, and even the Beautiful Demon was trying to talk her out of it, she was no longer so sure of her brilliant intentions.

She saw Ha'min coming towards her. She had hoped for good news, but there was no sign of it on his face.

'Eli,' he wheezed when he was finally beside her.

'Wolf.' She turned to him.

'Don't do this, littlun. These henchmen will smite you.' He grabbed her arm.

'Your henchmen. You can pardon us.' She looked at him calmly, without anger or fear.

'We can't,' He corrected. 'We don't have the whole Council. This is the law.'

'You have the law. I have free will,' she retorted.

'Child, wake up, what are you hoping for?' He grabbed her arm. 'Ha'akon's not here, those scoundrels won't agree to wait, they'll have you chained to that post in a minute and whip you to death before he gets here.'

'And you, Akona... have no say in this?' She said reproachfully.

He was at a loss for words. He just stared at her. She realised that no one could help her. She was alone and had to make a decision.

Such a short life... she thought. She looked around the square, the faces of those gathered blending into one. The sun must have been high by now, but it was hidden behind winter clouds. Tallen stood with his back to her, chained to the stake. She was glad that at least he would feel no pain. Who knew, he might even survive. Maybe he's strong enough...

The dream of the night before came back to her. A shiver ran down her spine. She knew the pain that awaited her.

But it was not what she feared. There was only one thought that filled her with fear.

She could not live without him. Ever since she had opened her eyes in the Green Kingdom and seen his face, she had not wanted to spend a single day without his presence. He was everything to her, even though she knew he would never return her affection. It didn't matter. Without him there was nothing. And she couldn't let him go alone.

'Well, Ha'min... I think I'd rather die on my own terms than live a miserable life as your puppet. Tell them to watch carefully, for you could use a lesson in strength, honour and brotherhood.' She gently pushed his hands away and unbuttoned her cloak. 'May I ask you to keep it, Wolf? I don't want it in my way. I'll come to you for it afterwards.'

Ha'min returned upstairs with a bundle in his hands.

'She will not agree to step aside from *Koroi Karn.* She says honour demands it.' He glanced hopefully at Akona, hoping that she had convinced the others to find another solution. Unfortunately, she only said in a resigned voice:

'Then do your duty.'

Sig and Ha'teng nodded. As they walked away, the old warrior grabbed the commander's arm.

'When it is over, you will let Temina in at once.'

The man just measured him with an icy stare. The Guardian of the Young held him tighter.

'Do you understand?'

Wordlessly, the man jerked away, turned and walked towards the execution site. Ha'min watched as the guards led Eli onto the platform and the herald announced the replacement. The gathered crowd was silent at first in disbelief, but soon murmurs of displeasure began to ring out. The girl had gained quite a reputation among the young warriors, as well as in the City of Sisters. The fact that she was being given away to be tortured like a servant was not easy for this part of Ha'ami to accept.

The veteran warrior, angry as never before at his own powerlessness, returned to his chair to watch the embarrassing spectacle from there.

'Have you lost your mind?' Tallen couldn't believe his eyes.

'That's a fascinating topic for discussion, but perhaps for another time. Right now, we have twenty lashes to count for me and twenty-five for you,' she said calmly, almost cheerfully.

'Eli, what have you done...' he groaned.

'My plan didn't work. You were right. Too high a threshold for Eli's feet, all that court intrigue...' she explained. 'Looks like I've been had.'

'What were you hoping for? What was the plan that involved such risks?'

'The plan was that they would pardon us.'

'It doesn't look like it,' he remarked.

Two massive executioners were unfurling long, thick whips, studded with iron nails.

'Yes, I realise that now...' She sighed heavily.

'Do you have another plan?'

'Not to bleed to death. Oh. And not to shit myself with pain.'

'You're standing in the girl's piss...'

'I sniffed it out.' She wrinkled her nose.

The drums began to beat loudly and the executioners took their places.

'I've actually dreamed of torture so many times that this whole situation is very familiar...'

'It's not a dream. Eli, listen to me. Focus, please, I can help you to disconnect from the feeling... remember, we have practised this... look at me!'

They heard a swish and the first lash of the whip fell on their backs. It made no impression on Tallen, but he saw a grimace of pain cross Eli's face. She gritted her teeth.

'Breathe... focus!'

'It wasn't that bad,' she mouthed. 'Nineteen more... as long as these dimwits can count.'

Swish again.

'Eighteen.' She exhaled.

'Eli.' He turned to her and saw the huge wounds on her back. Streams of blood began to run down the exposed skin. 'Look into my eyes. This is only a passing moment, remember? Retreat into the depths!'

'It's no use, Tallen. I'm hopeless at this...' She smiled resignedly. 'For so many years you have not taught me, now it's too late.'

If only he could have touched her, he would have had the chance to embrace her with his Gift. But she was too far away.

'Seventeen.' she hissed, limping more and more visibly. 'Sixteen... fifteen... you should have left me in the bushes or thrown me in the river when you had the chance...' she laughed quietly.

'And lead a quiet life? Never!' He tried to hold her gaze.

'It would have been longer... fourteen...'

'It's more interesting with you.' He watched in horror as her body turned to bloody pulp.

'That's how you should have named me when you found me. More Interesting...' she croaked. 'Thirteen...'

More blows fell again and again, cutting deeper and deeper. He felt the warm blood rush to his ankles. Her face grew tighter and paler.

'Twelve...'

'We have finally managed to close the gap,' Keera reported with satisfaction. She came out to meet Ha'akon. Her dark clothes were caked with mud. On her shaved head she wore a leather helmet for protection underground. The ruler had always held this Sister in high esteem. She was precise, quick to act and did not beat about the bush. The girls trained under her tutelage became masters of their craft, allowing the city to develop and introduce upgrades not found anywhere else.

'I need two more workers to put up a makeshift roof. We won't be able to finish it in this weather, it will have to wait until spring.'

'Are you sure the water from this well is safe to drink?' Ha'sani asked.

They were standing by a large hole in the ground, between the wall and the armoury.

'I would wait a day or two until the natural flow of the stream has flushed out any sludge that might have got in there,' she confirmed. 'And I'd recommend that no one takes a piss into that pit,' she finished with a wince.

'Do you think we're that dull?' Ha'sani laughed.

'I'm just saying.' She patted him on the shoulder.

'Thanks for your help, Keera.' Ha'akon turned to her. 'You and your engineers... I don't know what we'd do without you.'

'You'd be walking around dirty, drinking water melted from the snow.' She grinned, showing her teeth.

'A fair vision,' he affirmed. 'I instructed my men to close the baths in that part of the castle and post guards there. I also ordered water to be brought from the other wing to the houses and other facilities.'

'Other facilities?' Irony blossomed on her face. 'Well, yes... I suppose unwashed whores are not to your taste? But perhaps you can survive two days without screwing, can't you?'

'I don't mind the slight smell, but to each his own...' Ha'sani winked at her.

'Since you have your basic needs met,' Keera declared. 'I will return to the trench. I want to take a closer look at the situation around the bend–'

She didn't finish. Her gaze was fixed on something behind Ha'akon's back. The ruler turned abruptly. A rider galloped towards them as if on fire. Ha'teng's guard. Ha'akon immediately felt an unpleasant pang in his stomach. Something was wrong.

The warrior reined in his horse right in front of them. He didn't even jump down, but hurriedly gave his message, barely catching his breath.

'Ta'uma... They're whipping *Ta'uma!*'

Ha'akon did not wait for an explanation.

'To me!' He shouted as he ran towards where he had left the Razor. 'Everyone to me! Mount!'

He leapt into the saddle and squeezed the flanks of his steed into a gallop. He did not look back. He didn't know how many people had left in his wake. He raced on, oblivious to everything and everyone around him.

The narrow streets of the city were deserted as most people had gone to the execution.

The guard's words echoed in his head... how... why... what had happened there.

He knew he had to get there before it was too late.

Finally, he emerged onto the main, wide road that led to the heart of the action.

He rode down the hill so that he could see the square in front of the temple, the platform where the convicts were being punished, the stakes to which the whipped figures were chained: one tall, male, fair-haired. And another, small, brown. She was weak on her feet from the impact of the blows.

Ha'akon could not remember the last time he was scared. He was not afraid of death, not afraid of pain, not afraid of danger.

But now he was frozen with fear.

He squeezed the sides of Razor even tighter.

He couldn't lose her.

Not again.

Not again.

Tallen watched as Eli's body went limp with pain. Despite this, she continued to speak to him in a cheerful tone.

'Eleven...' She slipped in a pool of her blood.

The crowd gasped in horror.

It reached him now that he could not hear the howling and cheering that had gone on during the earlier torture. There was a surprising silence around them.

'On your feet, little one,' he encouraged her. 'Just a little more. You can do it.'

'Yes, I know... I fell asleep.' She pulled herself up with her shackles, stood up shakily. 'What a boring game... ten...'

She staggered again.

'Spread your feet wide, it's easier to keep your balance.'

'It's a bit slippery in here', she breathed. 'At least you're not standing in anyone's piss... nine.'

He looked down at the planks beneath her, the wood soaked with the rust-coloured sweat that dripped from her shoulders and trickled down her calves.

'You haven't put on the shoes I made you,' he chuckled.

'I thought they were too good for the occasion. These rags will be impossible to clean... eight.'

'Eli?'

'Yes?'

'Hold on a little longer. It'll be over in no time.'

The only thing he felt was the weakening of his limbs. He knew he was bleeding to death. But that knowledge was nothing compared to the agony he felt as he watched the whip turn her body to a bloody pulp. Seven. She shrank under the repeated blows. He tried to speak to her, to keep her conscious, but he could see the life fleeing from her with each blow. 'Six.'

'Five...' She spat blood. And laughed.

'What happened?'

'I think they've already gone through to the other side.'

Her head wobbled between her arms.

'Not yet. But they've got a few strokes left.'

'Tallen... I'm glad... it's with you... Four.'

She fell to her knees.

'A little longer, my little one. I'm happy too. If I'm going to die, I don't want to be with anyone else but you.'

She gripped the stake tightly and straightened up.

'Three...' she breathed out. 'It's not just death. Living with you wasn't the worst either... Thank you... for everything.'

'You are the best thing that has ever happened to me.'

The words came with difficulty. He could feel his breathing getting shallower and shallower. It wouldn't be long now.

'You too... just don't tell Simronil. Two,' she croaked and gave him a long look as she leaned her chest against the stake. 'One... you will achieve a historic feat... you will survive more lashes than anyone.'

Blood trickled in a small stream from the corner of her mouth.

'A little more and we'll both be legends,' he said, but she just coughed, her legs wobbling again and she collapsed numb.

'Eli!' he shouted, and the gathered crowd let out a deep sigh.

Suddenly he realised it was no longer quiet and the blows had stopped. Shouts could be heard, faint at first, but growing louder by the moment. The chorus of voices merged into one great uproar.

'Berennike! Berennike!' rang out across the square.

Tallen heard the clank of weapons being drawn.

Someone unshackled him from the post, his knees buckled beneath him and he collapsed into a pool of his own blood. He crawled to her with what strength he had left.

'Eli... My little one...' he whispered over the din. He touched her face and gave her the last of his magic. Suddenly there was someone else with them. A healer. He could not remember her name.

Eli opened her eyes.

'Tallen... is it over?'

'Yes, you were great.'

'Temina...' she whispered. 'Help him... please... promise.'

'I promise.' The woman confirmed, putting on a mask and pressing something against their faces.

'No...' he said, but at the same moment his thoughts were shrouded in darkness.

Chapter XVII
In the name of the Wild Princess

JOR ARRIVED AT THE EXECUTION site relatively late, even though the servants had been given leave to watch the spectacle. He had no desire to be there; he wasn't thrilled by the torture of his brothers. All he hoped for was to see Berennike again, even if only from a distance.

The square was filled to capacity. Of course, the servants stood at the back, separated from the Ha'ami by a line of guards, but Jor didn't mind. The less gory details he saw, the better for him. He found a group of familiar Azzgoths in the crowd and struck up a conversation with them, paying no attention to the events on the platform.

'Look, they're bringing Hilde,' someone said, standing on tiptoe to peer over the heads of the crowd. From a distance they could see the silhouette of the Azzgoth girl as the guards dragged her on shaky legs to the platform. The elf was escorted in after her. For those gathered in the square, this was the first elf they had ever seen, so all eyes and tongues were on him. Even Jor looked at him with curiosity. The stranger was taller than he had expected, and although his build was slimmer than Ha'ami's, he looked like a strong warrior.

'I bet a copper that the elf will survive,' someone from the crowd shouted.

'Twenty-five lashes? Not a chance! I accept the wager!' answered another voice.

The people began to place their bets when suddenly there was a commotion at the temple. The Ha'ami ran back and forth, conferring among themselves. Out of nowhere, another figure appeared at the execution site, one that Jor would recognise anywhere.

'Berennike!' He sighed loudly and the others looked at him in disbelief.

'Berennike! It can't be!' whispers spread.

'What's she doing there?'

'Shhh! Be quiet, so we can hear!'

The herald shouted the announcement. The crowd passed his words from mouth to mouth, and it took a moment for them to reach Jor and his companions.

Berennike is taking over Hilde's punishment!

This is unheard of!

Is it possible?!

What now!?

What are they going to do with her?!

They did not have to wait long for an answer. The young servant girl was unshackled from the stake, and the black-robed woman replaced her. She had exchanged a few words with the elf.

'This cannot be!' cried Jor. 'They're killing her! They will kill Berennike!'

Everyone around him looked at each other in fear. Cries of dismay and horror rang out.

The executioners raised their mighty whips. Thick ropes swished through the air.

Jor's throat went dry and the air left his lungs with a groan as the first blow fell on the back of his beloved princess. And then another. And another. The square fell silent. Even the Ha'ami watched in disbelief. Suddenly, Berennike slipped and sank to one knee. The crowd let out a murmur. The elf shouted something to her. She rose to her feet, laughing. His princess. Brave even in the face of torture. Willing to suffer for her people. Jor saw successive lashes of the whip batter her body.

What had she said to him?

...You have to take care of your own freedom, Jor. All of us have to. I cannot give it to you. Each of us must take it with our own hands...

'They're killing her!' he cried again in despair. 'They will kill our Berennike!'

This was picked up by other voices in the crowd.

'Murderers!'

'Berennike! Berennike!'

The tension in the crowd grew with each lash of the whip. The Ha'ami guards tightened their ranks and pushed back the advancing people. The shouts in Azzgoth grew louder. Someone groaned when a spear struck him in the face. Another received a blow to the stomach. Suddenly Jor, along with everyone else, let out a loud sigh.

The tortured girl slumped to the ground beside the stake, obviously unconscious. Perhaps dead.

The crowd went into hysteria.

Ha'teng watched the situation in the square carefully. The stillness did not please him at all. It was not normal for an execution to take place in such silence that the crack of the whip could be heard in the air. He signalled to his squad leaders to tighten their ranks and be on guard.

He looked for Ha'akon out of the corner of his eye. He knew that if his friend had been here, he would not have accepted the Council's decision so easily. Perhaps he would still come.

He let Temina walk to the platform. He watched the flogging, but there was nothing unusual about it. He knew that eventually both punished would lose consciousness and the show would be over.

Suddenly, shouts began to ring out from the far end of the square, and soon grew in strength.

The mob chanted Berennike's name and a few other words in an unintelligible language. The shouts grew louder with each passing moment, echoing across the square. Soon the crowd was pushing dangerously close to the line of armed men that separated the Ha'ami from the servants. Ha'teng gestured for one of his commanders to call out the cavalry.

Then the situation spiralled out of control. A mob of slaves ran amok, attacking their masters. The guards were joined by other Ha'ami and *namio* warriors from the crowd, who stood with their backs to the Temple, instinctively forming a battle formation in accordance with their training. Ha'teng gave hasty orders. In a flash, he saw Temina rush towards the unconscious girl. With his other eye, he noticed the First Brothers running towards him down the steps of the Temple of the Ancestors.

He surveyed the square. Fortunately, there were riders coming directly from the main road. He blinked. They were led by Ha'akon, galloping like mad. Their eyes met. The ruler pointed his spear at the platform where the wounded *Ta'uma* lay, then at him again. Ha'teng knew what to do.

The First Brothers were already at his side.

'Ha'min, we need to get all the sisters and children into the temple, make sure they are protected.'

He laid a hand on the elder warrior's shoulder. The man just nodded and ran ahead, calling for men to secure the passage.

'Ha'aki, take command, block this mob,' he turned to the other commander. The warrior looked at him in surprise. 'I must escort Temina and *Ta'uma* to the Healing Hall. I will be back shortly.'

'We should all be here,' Ha'aki objected. 'Every Ha'ami is needed here now.'

'I'll only get one *namio*.' He turned away. 'Ha'perin! To me!'

'Can you make it among these savages with the wounded woman?' Ha'aki raised his eyebrows in surprise.

Ha'teng drew his sword.

'When we're finished with them, there won't be any savages left.'

He ran to the platform without looking back.

Hysteria swept over the place where Jor stood. Servants rushed at the guards with fists, the ranks of the Ha'ami collapsing under the pressure of the human mass.

Jor snatched a spear from a fallen guard and, with the battle cry of the Azzgoths, aimed it at the warrior's chest. The blade slipped from the breastplate, but he swung again, stabbing the guard in the shoulder. The Ha'ami screamed in pain and tried to grasp the weapon with his other hand, but just then another man from the crowd grabbed a cobblestone and smashed it on the guard's head. He beat him with it until his helmet was smashed into the centre of his skull, his brain spewed to the ground and his body stopped moving.

Jor raised his spear and gave a cry of victory. Pushing back the line of warriors, the crowd of servants turned to face the Ha'ami people.

When Ha'akon stormed into the square, it was utter chaos. The crowd chanting Berennike's name rushed the Ha'ami warriors who had separated them from the dais. There was no way the ruler could make it through the rough human sea to the Temple. He communicated with Ha'teng and saw him running towards the bodies lying under the stakes. He also noticed Temina kneeling beside them to help.

'By the ancestors, what is going on here?' exclaimed Ha'sani, who had stopped at his side.

'How many men do we have?' cried Ha'akon, looking back for the first time.

'Thirty, maybe forty!'

'Formation!' the ruler gave an immediate order. 'Spears! Shields! Drive them back! Block the road! Don't let them surround us!'

He saw a line of warriors already forming at the temple to protect the sisters and children as they made their way inside. Similarly, groups of guardsmen were holding off the mob's attack with learned discipline, slowly advancing. He realised that they needed to swiftly surround the square and close the circle. That would be the quickest way to regain control. He looked around and saw more troops of cavalry coming towards them. He signalled for them to join the formation.

He acted in a learned routine, but at the same time watched what was happening on the platform.

If she was dead...

He saw Ha'teng and the other warrior lifting the bodies. Temina looked in his direction and motioned to him with an open hand.

He breathed a sigh of relief.

'Is she breathing?' asked Ha'teng as he saw Temina remove her mask after administering the sleeping potion on a cloth.

'Both are!' she exclaimed. 'But barely!'

'To the Healing Hall!' he ordered. 'Ha'perin, take the girl on your shoulder, I'll cover you!'

'We are taking the elf too!' Temina announced. 'I gave her my word!'

He looked at her incredulously. She had a determined look on her face.

'May the dragon burn you, damned women!' he shouted in anger. Looking across the square where absolute anarchy reigned, he handed his sword to Temina.

'Do you know how to use it?'

She nodded.

He threw the limp non-human over his back, and Ha'perin did the same to *Ta'uma*. Almost the same. The *namio* was definitely gentler.

'Let's go!' Ha'teng ordered, and amid the din of battle they marched around the Temple, shielded by a line of warriors, until they turned into the side street that led to the Healing Hall. The noise of battle had died down considerably.

It was not the first time he had carried a wounded man on his back. But it was the first time it had been an enemy, not his brother. He could feel his uniform soaking up the elf's blood. A few more steps. He looked back at the others. Ha'perin was right behind him, Temina at the end of the group. Suddenly her eyes widened.

'Bewa–!'

She didn't have time to finish before he felt a pain in his side. The weight of the body he was carrying crushed him to the ground and he had to get down on one knee. He looked ahead. Standing in front of him was a thin, scruffy man, wielding a spear that he had probably wrenched from a Ha'ami warrior earlier, and now plunged into his right side. Too shallow. Too clumsy.

'How dare you, dog!'

Ha'teng grabbed the shaft of the weapon, jerked it away from his body, twisted it and yanked it from the servant's skinny hands. He struggled to his feet. At least ten new ruffians emerged from the side streets. They wielded sticks and stones picked up from the road. One of them had a sword.

'Berennike!' called one of them pointing at the girl on Ha'perin's shoulder.

'Get out of the way, trash!' Ha'teng thundered.

'Give us Berennike!' They blocked the small group's path, raising their makeshift weapons.

Ha'teng bent his knees and lowered the elf's body to the ground.

'Please try to take her from us. I wish it so much.' He raised the spear in a defensive stance.

The rebelling servants were undeterred and rushed at him all at once. Seeing this, Ha'perin slowly lowered the unconscious *Ta'uma* to the pavement. Ha'teng looked over at the *namio*.

'It's time to practice, boy!'

The laughter froze in his throat as he saw a huge silhouette emerge from the other side of the street. Trudging towards them was a giant. The same one they had sentenced to death for killing a guard.

'Temina! Behind you!'

He had no time to do more, his opponents were upon him with all the fury they had accumulated in their years of service in the Ha'ami stronghold.

Wita had already bid farewell to life. He stood on a cart, surrounded by Ha'ami warriors, shackled, clutching a pathetic piece of cloth in his hands... He waited his turn. He was the last.

'So that the executioners can have their fun with you without haste,' the squad leader who guarded him sneered with a grim snicker.

He just wanted it to be over as soon as possible, although he knew his strong body well and did not expect a quick parting from the world. He would surely suffer for a long time... and he was so afraid of pain. The guards knew this well and chatted merrily about the order in which they would like to see his limbs cut off and quartered. Wita trembled with fear at the thought of what awaited him.

Before his time came, a strange thing happened. The noblewoman who had taken pity on him and wiped his face, who had stopped the warriors from beating him in the square, dared to replace another prisoner. Wita had never heard of such a thing. He did not understand why this girl had decided to do such a thing. But he remembered the look on her face as she recognised his pain. He had never met anyone with such kind eyes.

'What a pity,' he thought.

From his seat he could see them tormenting her as she fell lifeless on the wooden planks. Immediately, however, the entire square rose in her defence. Servants rushed at the guards. They snatched their weapons from them, attacked them in a frenzy, and shouted one name.

Berennike.

It seemed to him that they had called her something else before. He was probably wrong.

The squad that had been guarding him turned to face the charging mob. They had all forgotten him. Wita just cowered in the corner of the wagon until the noise of the battle died down around him. He opened his eyes to see a shadow standing over him.

'You are free!' laughed a thin boy with dark skin and curly hair, showing him a set of keys in his hand. He unlocked his shackles. 'We are all free! For Berennike!' shouted his saviour, jumped off the cart and ran forward, brandishing his captured sword.

Wita looked around. He saw several Ha'ami guards lying on the ground. Many servants as well.

He got to his feet uncertainly. He didn't know what to do, where to go. There was still a fierce battle going on in the square. He decided to seek shelter. He walked slowly around the Temple, dipping into one of the side streets. Unexpectedly, he came upon another battle. He saw two Ha'ami warriors fighting a group of servants, and a short-haired woman kneeling on the ground beside two bodies. Wita was about to retreat in the other direction when he recognised the wounded. It was the same merciful noblewoman and the elf condemned to be whipped.

'Keep away!'

The Ha'ami woman swung her sword in a defensive gesture. Wita raised his hands.

'My Lady...' he stammered. 'Let me help. Where... where shall I carry her?'

She looked at him suspiciously.

'Why should you help us?'

'She... is a good maiden...' he murmured slowly.

A look of surprise crossed her face, but she nodded and lowered her sword.

'Can you manage to take them both?' she asked.

He merely gave a nod, then carefully threw the elf over one shoulder and Berennike over the other.

'Hey, there!' The woman called to her companions, who were engaged in battle. 'Let's go! Cover us!'

She turned back to Wita.

'Come!' She snapped and turned to the right.

He followed her, as did the younger Ha'ami. After a few turns, they reached the door of the Healing Hall, where she immediately ordered him to put the wounded on a stretcher.

'Thank you.' She measured him with an attentive gaze. 'Stay here. You can make yourself useful. There will be much to do today.'

He nodded and moved aside, waiting to be assigned some tasks. Soon the orders started pouring in and he fell into the usual rhythm of completing them. He moved furniture, held the wounded, carried corpses. As if he had been doing this all his life.

Ha'teng dealt blows with the fury and precision of a beast of prey. He could not believe that these louts dared to raise a hand against their masters. When he had slaughtered all those who stood in his way, he ran to the Healing Hall to see if Ha'perin, Temina and the big man had managed to get *Ta'uma* and the elf there. The *namio* stood at the door of the building, guarding the entrance.

'Inside?' Ha'teng asked briefly.

'Yes.'

'Stay here. I will send you reinforcements.'

Ha'perin nodded. With a quick step, the commander moved to the back of the building where the horses were kept. He jumped onto the back of the first one at hand and, spear at the ready, set off at a gallop back to the square.

There, the mob was still advancing with the fury of a sea storm. He saw that the entrance to the temple was barred and guarded by Ha'min and his troops.

Ha'akon joined the arriving cavalry and with a clever manoeuvre, they worked to push the crowd directly into the spears of the Ha'ami led by Ha'aki. Ha'teng, quickly assessing the situation, urged his mount and started up the Temple steps.

'Send some men to guard the Healing Hall, the Archives and the School!' he yelled to Ha'min. 'The side streets are full of armed marauders!'

'I don't have that many to spare!' exclaimed the old warrior.

'In that case, let go of the Archives. There's nothing of value there anyway!' replied Ha'teng and rode off towards the fighting horsemen.

With joy coursing through his veins, he dealt deadly blows to the mangy riffraff who stood in his way. At last, he reached Ha'akon.

'They are in the Healing Hall!' he called, answering the question in his brother's eyes. The relief was obvious.

Ha'teng didn't add that the elf and the girl would surely bleed to death. He had done his friend's will, and that was all that mattered. Now he could only hope that fate would smile on them all.

'What now, *koru*?' He smiled predatorily. 'Time to unleash the Dragon Fury?'

This nickname brought a strange expression to the ruler's face. They raised their swords and gave each other a war salute. They always became brothers in battle. Always the two of them. Always together. Always victorious.

The world was put back in its place.

Epilogue

ZAK LOOKED DOWN FROM THE hill at the Stone Nest in the distance.

'It will be another two days' journey,' he muttered to his twin brother Kaz. 'Maybe our asses won't freeze off.'

Kaz gave a sign in reply.

'Yeah...' Zak nodded. 'Warm springs... Surely they will invite us there to heal our old bones, the sons of the wolfs they are.'

He turned to the guards that the lord of the fortress had sent to accompany the group. The six men were warming themselves by the fire, away from the dwarves they were travelling with.

'Hello, boy!' One of them looked in his direction. It was the one who had opened his mouth to him more often since they had left.

His name was Ha'roli. 'Rumour has it that the Ha'ami have built solid roads in their land. I don't see any trace of them!'

The warrior rose reluctantly and walked to the edge of the ridge where the dwarves looked down.

'All good roads lead east.' He pointed with a leather-gloved hand. 'Roads to the mountains are for peasants and shepherds only.'

'Then we will keep up our dizzying pace,' Zak muttered from under his moustache.

'The day after tomorrow we will be at the gates,' Ha'roli affirmed.

'And the girl... you say she was in good health the last time you saw her?'

He asked this at least twice a day, always examining the tone of the guardsman's voice to see if he was lying.

'Yes,' confirmed the guard, already used to the dwarf's abrupt nagging. 'Two arms, two legs and a sharp tongue. Does that fit the picture?'

Zak just grunted.

'Do you usually feed the birds in winter?' He nodded towards the fortress, a dark cloud hovering over it.

The warrior blinked.

'There was probably a feast and they threw away the leftovers.' He shrugged, turned and walked back to the campfire, ending the conversation.

'Sure, a feast, you son of a goblin,' Zak growled. His brother gestured once more. 'You're right. I know of only one food that attracts such a wake of scavengers. A dead carcass. He'd better be telling the truth. One scratch to my little girl, and as sure as my name is Zak, they'll know the wrath of the dwarves.'

THE END OF PART I

How to say...

There are two things in life that one apparently cannot buy, no matter how wealthy they are: health and time.

Therefore, whenever someone grants me the gift of their time, I feel they share with me something the most precious they have.

Ewelina, you have been the most dedicated reader and the most skilled critique who rather asks questions than imposes her opinion. Thank you for the calls at odd hours, messages at night and day and day and night and endless energy that you shared with me.

Magda and Iza, my professional β-readers – thank you for the most frequent message starting from 'I finished, when is the next chapter coming?' It was your level of enthusiasm that kept me going!

My parents and sisters, who are probably the only ones in full understanding of the sentiment I have towards writing and towards this book. Since they knew it came from the stories I wrote as a kid. I know, mum, you told me you'd only read my book if there will be dwarves in it. I am sorry I made you wait for them until the last pages. Hope it was worth it.

Racim, who I never met in person, but who possesses magic powers of translating my words into visuals despite very vague descriptions I was ready to share... you are a true wizard of a brush!

Vidya, who agreed to arrange the weirdest photo shoots in the history just to try to convince me to have also some normal-looking pictures of myself. Thanks to you I had some I could put in this book!

The translators – Kasia and Agata, who also became my sparring partners and the word champions, doing everything to bring Ha'ami world to life, working with tight timelines and unmatchable dedication.

Miss Ewelina Szyszkowska, my first and only contact with a truly professional editor. Thank you for valuable sparring, precious advice and coaching. Even though I did not always look like I am listening, your every word was sinking into the sponge of my brain (eventually).

To all my friends, co-workers, people of good will some of whom I have never met but they still sent me messages of encouragement along the way: just listing your names would take another book... a phone book to be exact, and those are extinct by now, therefore I will send you my gratitude individually instead of printing it here. But you know who you are and each good word added a little push for me on my publishing journey.

But the most of all...

To the two people that mean the most to me in the world.

My husband, who not only sparred with me when it comes to kicks and grips, and chokes and wounds, but also showed the most patience with my writing in the weird morning hours or night hours or weekends or holidays... edited Spanish version of the book, is my chief operations officer, chief confidence building officer and chief energy booster. When people ask me how did I manage to write a book when having full time job and family... he is the secret to it. Thank you for helping me to make the dream come true!

My daughter, who had to bear with me dedicating quite some time to her older sister Eli. My greatest inspiration. The embodiment of strength and kindness and the biggest fan of lizards that there is.

To all of you, who put your faith and support in me, I hope the book that came out of it was worth to bear with the annoying author.

The Author:
Ula Gudel

This is my first book in the series and there is more coming soon!

If you ever feel like reaching out, sharing your thoughts, reviews, ideas, questions, learn about coming books, get access to some Lizard stories and content... you can find me at:

ulagudel.com

IG: ula_gudel_author

Ula Gudel Author Pages on FB, Linked In, Amazon.

Made in the USA
Middletown, DE
20 August 2023

36711784R00221